Nadinium Sky

R.A. George

ISBN: 978-1-9160723-1-2

Acknowledgments

I remember my kids first day at school. The bittersweet feeling of releasing them into the big wide world for the first time. How would they fare? Would they be safe? I needn't have worried but that didn't stop me worrying in the first place. To a lesser extent the same is true of this book, but it's out now and here it is in your hands ready to read. Be gentle with it, however it won't be gentle with you. We all have to make allowances.

As with everything important in life there are those who help you along the way (both directly and indirectly) and I'd like to express my appreciation of all of you.

First and foremost, my beautiful wife (and sanity reader) Dina. She's believed in me from day one and has always been a source of encouragement and inspiration. On top of that, having to read each scene (in a completely random order to add to the confusion) was a labour of love and I'm eternally grateful for spotting the numerous howlers that the reader has mercifully been spared. I hope you enjoy reading it properly darling...

To the editor Nick Herrmann, the first outsider to read it and the first one who made me truly believe in the book. His constructive (yet gentle) advice has guided me along the path from writer to published author. He has also been a goldmine of suggestions in terms of character, plot and language which has improved this book beyond recognition from its first draft. Also a big thank you to Sarah and Helen of Cornerstones for putting me touch with Nick.

To Rick my copyeditor and proof-reader. Thank you for adding some grease to my book. Your input, comment and advice have been priceless.

Next my test readers, Colin Lacy, Kim Acres, Louise Cimelli, Pete

Johnston, John Hammersley and Jonathan Daniels. Thank you for your patience, time and ideas. The signed copy is in the post!

To Bethany for lending an old luddite her social media expertise on Twitface.

Then there's others who've not been directly involved but have helped the book along the way. My lifelong friends John and Gary who sat patiently while I bored them to death, generally and in particular about the struggles of writing. Mikey my cousin who also had to listen for hours instead of talking about football. To Sue, my 'big sis' from your 'little bro'. Costas for our 'Tactical' meetings. To Selma, Rosie, Wendy, Sameena, James, Deepak and Phil at work. All my friends at LAS. Kieran for repairing my PC when all seemed lost. Finally, even though I've never met you, Imran Iqbal. My eternal gratitude goes out to all of you.

Next there's the people who are most important for me in life. Dina (again) Thomas, William, Mum, Dad, Bobby, Jan, Ray and Val.

If I've missed anyone off the list, please accept my apologies.

Finally, a big thank to you dear reader for buying (or borrowing) this book and giving me a chance. I hope it repays your leap of faith...

2nd November 2019

Contents

Prologue

'Failed!'

Eleanor Buckley stood stone still. Mind racing, disbelieving, hand trembling. She didn't notice the almost audible gasp that went around the room. All eyes focused on her.

It was final results for Settlement Protection Corps elite officer training. Four months of unrelenting pressure, being pushed to the very limit of your capabilities. Out of an original intake of over a hundred, only twenty-one remained.

The harsh lighting and sparse surroundings of the gym did not reflect the enormity of the occasion. Captain Sinclair standing at the front, Sergeant Bruno next to him with lights reflecting off his bald, almost polished head, like a billiard ball Eleanor often thought, with the clipboard containing their futures in his hands, reading out the results. No second chances. Once you failed that's it. No coming back. Returning to the day job of infantry gruntery if you were lucky. The surviving cadets were seated on two rows of cheap plastic chairs. Each name was called out. The owner of that name stood to hear their fate then sat back down again. The voice repeated louder this time with a force that almost knocked her down by itself. 'Buckley. Failed! Sit down.'

There it was again. That word. 'Failed'. The confirmation. Her knees gave way and she fell back down on to the chair with a noise that belied her small stature. The impassable cliff face of failure loomed in front of her, towering above. Eleanor was trying to take in the shocking finality of the news. It reminded her of the time she had been in a car crash. The serene progression, then the violent unexpected jolt to one side. The new reality kicked in. The remainder of the names and their results passed almost unheard. Then somewhere in the distance, Eleanor heard;

'Champion recruit. Cadet Mann.' Naomi Mann' 'Naomi fuckin Mann' she thought 'This can't be happening. Naomi 'just about scraped through every module 'Mann. Naomi who had to be dragged back from the brink of failure more times than she could count.

The ripple of applause jolted Eleanor out of her double state of shock. There had to be some mistake, but watching a smiling Naomi walking forward to accept her award, the one that should have been hers, was almost too much to take. Watching her shaking the hand of Captain Sinclair and Sergeant Bruno only served to multiply the sense of injustice and rage burning inside Eleanor. She

1

noticed Bruno flinch with pain as Naomi shook his hand. Through the befuddled mess of her mind the spark of an idea kindled, connecting two separate thoughts that started to crystallise into a single idea. Eleanor tried to push it to one side but it continued to grow unabated.

Naomi returned to her seat, clutching the trophy close to her chest and smiling. The laser-like gaze of Eleanor following her every inch of the way. Bruno called the group to attention and Captain Sinclair stepped forward.

'Ok at ease. I'd like to say a few words. First of all, well done to Recruit Mann. I'm sure she'll make a splendid officer in the Corps, as will you all.' There was a cheer from the recruits. 'What you've come through is no common training. You stand before me now as elite officers of Settlement Protection Corps, and as such you will be expected to be able to handle whatever is thrown at you in the course of your duties. I'm not going to lie to you. Not all of you will survive. You knew that when you joined, but the training you've undergone will stand you in good stead. You'll be given your assignments over the coming days and the best of luck to you all.' More cheers from the recruits. 'One last thing. To those who didn't quite make the final cut. I'd like to extend my sympathies.' He looked over at Eleanor and the other two recruits who had failed. 'You came close but if we're going to send you out to face the perils of the universe there is no room for error.' There was a round of applause for the failures. Eleanor stood still as death, making no eye contact with the Captain. The class was dismissed. As the ceremony ended the scraping of chairs and the hubbub of conversation interspersed with laughter filled the room. Recruits embracing, some were crying, others stood silent, lost in their own thoughts. Naomi was talking excitedly to the Captain, sharing a joke and laughing.

Eleanor heard a voice next to her. It was one of the other cadets. Velásquez. 'I can't believe it, I'm in a state of complete shock', he said. Velásquez put his arm around her but she didn't respond. Her stare was fixed on Bruno. 'If I could have put my life on somebody passing it would have been you Eleanor. Top of every module, a natural leader. I don't understand. It must be a mistake.' Velasquez told her.

She turned to him. 'Congratulations on passing. You deserve it.' The words barely came out. It felt like trying to talk underwater. Managing to force a smile as Velásquez continued to speak to her, the burning in the pit of her stomach and the ringing in her ears were all Eleanor was aware of.

Bruno was talking to Captain Sinclair and Naomi when he looked across at her. Eleanor glared straight back at him. His eyes narrowed and the merest hint of a smile played across his mouth. It wasn't the smile of friendship or sympathy. It said everything Eleanor needed to know. It conveyed more information than ten pages of text, or an hour's talking could ever do. The train of thought that had started with Bruno's flinch smashed its way through all other explanations as it fully came into focus. Her legs shaking and unsteady, almost dragging her feet, she moved towards Bruno with her focus fixed on him. The smile played no more, but the eyes were still narrowed as she closed on him, her legs finding extra strength with each step.

'Is this what you meant by extra fuckin tuition?' Eleanor thought she had hissed it, but it came out as a strangled squawk. Half noticing the open mouthed shock of Captain Sinclair, Eleanor gathered speed. I'm going to rip Bruno's filthy lying tongue out and shove it down his throat. I'm going to eat his intestines! It didn't matter anymore. All that mattered was getting to Bruno, who by now was adopting an expression of feigned innocence. As if to say 'What, who, me?' Another few steps and he was hers. Except her legs were suddenly no longer moving as she crashed to the floor, hitting her head. For a moment thousands of shimmering wriggling tadpoles swam before her vision then vanished as quickly as they appeared. Shaking her head, Eleanor could feel her arms being restrained and forced behind her back.

She could hear a voice. 'Eleanor, what the hell are you doing?' She instinctively jerked her head back and felt the crunch of a breaking nose. The voice let out a surprised yelp and the grip loosened, only to be replaced by several others. Looking round to see Velásquez sitting on the floor groaning, holding his nose, blood pouring out between his fingers, Eleanor was dragged to her feet by rough hands as she managed to lash out with her free leg at Bruno, who moved out of the way with contemptuous ease.

Bruno turned to Captain Sinclair. His eyebrows raised and mouth open. 'Sir......' he said, 'I told you she was crazy. We've always got to be careful with these prison recruits.' He turned to her curling his lip with contempt. 'Buckley you didn't just fail. You're disqualified! Caught cheating and taking drugs! No return to unit for you my lovely. Dishonourable discharge, jail and good riddance as well.'

'Sergeant Bruno!' shouted Captain Sinclair. Bruno stopped immediately as the Captain continued. 'There has to be a disciplinary hearing before that.' The words hit Eleanor like a million-volt electric shock, as she thrashed violently against those restraining her. Someone whipped her feet away from her so she was held horizontally. Eleanor had one last weapon at her disposal, and spat with all the remaining energy into the face of Bruno. A feeling of triumph surged through Eleanor as she noticed the momentary shock wipe the sneer from his face. The mixture of spit and blood ran from his eye, down his cheek and the expression was one of disgust and anger. Now he was the one who had lost control and his

3

six foot four, seventeen stone frame put everything into his fist as it hurtled towards Eleanor's face. She'd had her moment. Knowing what was coming Eleanor didn't care and the only thing she sensed was a white flash then blackness.

♦

Two days earlier

Eleanor was looking down at the face of Naomi; even in the pale moonlight she could see it was lined with exhaustion.

'I can't. There's nothing left!' Naomi managed to gasp. Propped up against a tree. Her voice pleading, her eyes begging for it to end.

Eleanor was fighting the urge to scream at Naomi as well as her own fatigue. 'Look, I'm not letting you give up after all we've been through. Remember, we pass and fail together.' She leant forward and despite her limbs feeling like rubber, grabbed Naomi's jacket and dragged her to her feet. Surprised at her own strength Eleanor looked into Naomi's tear stained face and she softened her voice. Wiping away the watery snot that was running into her mouth. 'We've come so far together, we're nearly there. You can't give up now, we're on the home straight of the final lap.' She encouraged Naomi as much as herself.

It was the end of an overnight eighteen-mile march in full kit. They had navigated their squad to the point ready for a dawn attack on the enemy position. Naomi had collapsed, was sick and had refused to move for the last five minutes. Eleanor felt her impatience with Naomi rise as out of the corner of her eye she caught the amused sidelong glances and eye rolling of the squad of veterans they were leading. She could feel their gaze upon her, knowing they were assessing her and Naomi with the considered judgement of experts in their field. Eleanor and Naomi were the final two. All the others had completed their forced march and attack over the previous couple of days.

'We can leave her here Miss and pick her up after.' It was Sergeant Consten. 'It's getting light in about an hour and we need to be in place ready for the assault.'

'Give us a couple of minutes.' Eleanor told him

'Ok Miss, but we can't delay any longer than that.'

Eleanor took Naomi's water bottle and shook it. Empty. 'I drank the last of it nearly two hours ago.' admitted Naomi sheepishly.

'So you just forgot all the stuff about water conservation.' Eleanor opened her water bottle and handed it to Naomi. 'Take it.' she snapped, 'I won't be needing it anymore.' she lied. Naomi gratefully snatched the bottle and gulped down the last of Eleanor's water. 'Better?' Eleanor asked, then noticed the life returning to

4

her companion's features, then told her. 'You've got a choice to make. You can get back down there and have a nice rest against the tree and wait to be picked up, and then you can have another rest. It's called the rest of your life regretting about how at the very edge of succeeding you decided to put your feet up knowing that when it came down to it you bottled it and didn't have what it takes.' Naomi's eyes flickered up at Eleanor, hardly daring to look at her. 'Or you have another choice', Eleanor continued... 'You can drag yourself along with me. You can actually become something of worth instead of a snivelling miserable failure. You can succeed where nearly everyone else fails. Do you want to go through the rest of your life thinking you succeeded 99%, but ultimately failed? This is the wrong place to get tired. Now's the time to make that choice. Don't fuck me about!' Naomi flinched at the last words, closed her eyes, gently nodded, letting out a sigh. 'I'll take that as a "Yes" then...' Eleanor said, then turned to Sergeant Consten and said. 'Ok, we're ready to go.'

♦

'Can you see the dip in the ground to the right of the compound.' Eleanor handed the viewscope to Naomi. They were overlooking the objective in a clearing surrounded by woodland. Studying it through the scope, she'd noticed that the right flank of the position wasn't covered. Eleanor glanced at her watch. Thirty minutes to start the attack. Looking over at Naomi, she told her, 'Wait until I've worked my way around under cover. I want you to start a frontal assault. Pin them down and keep them busy. I'll click you on Comms to let you know when I'm in position. Eight of you should lay down enough fire to occupy them. I'll take the rest.'

'I see where you mean.' Naomi responded. There was a resolve in her voice that told Eleanor her little pep talk had hit the spot.

Eleanor put her hand on Naomi's shoulder. 'Good. You can finish this; I'll do the risky part. You need to keep your fire concentrated to the front so we don't get any blue on blue casualties. Make sure you don't pin them down so that they can't fire back. Remember we want you to occupy them, so I can outflank then take them from behind, the more they are looking at you the better chance we've got.'

They returned to the squad and divided it up. Naomi went back to the ridge with her group while Eleanor set off with the remainder towards their starting position. The enemy in the compound were Bots. They acted like (not very clever) humans and fired back. They used smart ammo which distinguished between human and other targets. Although it hurt like hell if hit, their ammo was only to

5

mark the attackers. Depending where they were hit they would be counted either dead or wounded. On the other hand, the attackers' ammo was live. It made them nervous but watching one of the Bots head fly off when hit made up for it. Its intensity was like nothing else in training.

Eleanor crept into position with her squad. She took one last look through the viewscope at the enemy. They reminded her of the second hand action figures with the square jaws and buzzcuts she'd played with as a child, handed down to her from her older brothers. It was still dark but the first glimmerings of pre-dawn were caressing the horizon. The forest was dead still and the only sound she could hear was the breathing of the squad. The smell of damp grass filled the air as the thin morning mist wafted lazily around them. Eleanor took a moment to drink in the beauty of her surroundings. The calm before the storm. Pity to spoil the peace, she thought as she turned to Consten. 'Ready?'

'Ready to go Miss.'

She clicked her Comms to notify Naomi. The silence continued for a few more moments, before the scene erupted into a kaleidoscope of colour and noise. The concentrated fire poured into the front of the enemy position sending debris flying in all directions. The sentries were attempting to return fire. A few were quickly taken out, sprawled in strange complicated positions. The remainder of the Bots were quickly emerging from the barracks. Eleanor looked through the scope and saw a sentry checking the tree line above them with his radar scanner. After a few moments, satisfied nothing was there he moved away. Eleanor searched for any other sentries and finding none quickly led her squad across the open ground to the base of the compound wall. Consten gave her the thumbs up. Eleanor took a deep breath of cold morning air and despite the adrenaline and cacophony filling her ears, she was aware of her heartbeat, steady and calm, and knew the moment had arrived.

'Ok, let's go.' After one final check Consten lobbed the grapple up to the top of the wall. Twenty yards along another squad member did the same. Both latched first time and he gave Eleanor a smile. 'Smart bastards.' she muttered and hauled herself up. At the top she poked her head gingerly over the top. Out of the corner of her vision she saw a shape and a flash at the same moment. The top of the wall next to her burst into sparks. 'Fuck, they're using live ammo!!' She waited for the second shot to hit. There was a pop as the Bot collapsed back over the parapet and crashed to the ground. One of the other members of her squad had taken him out from behind. Straddling over the wall, she attached the rope ladder to the top and dropped it down.

Some of the Bots rushing out of the barracks were now aware of her and started to engage. Kneeling down behind cover, Eleanor calmly picked them off one by one while the rest of her squad came over the wall. The main body of the Bots were still occupied by the assault on the front of the compound. They dropped down from the parapet and headed for the barracks entrance. Consten led the way in followed by two of his team. A few pops and some shouts sounded from inside. Consten emerged a few seconds later, same smile. 'All clear! he said

'Ok Consten lets line 'em up. Take your team around the right flank and I'll take mine on the other side. Get within thirty yards and on my signal we open fire.'

He nodded and was gone. Eleanor led her team silently along the side of the barracks. As she approached the edge of the building a Bot came flying around the corner looking over its shoulder. It exploded as several bullets slammed into it. Then the flash of tracer from several Bots that were following crashed into the ground in front of Eleanor. It's blank expression unchanged despite the maelstrom unleashed upon it. Unclipping a grenade, she lobbed it over the top of the barracks to where the fire was coming from. After a couple of seconds there was a muffled thud and the firing stopped.

Eleanor took a deep breath and charged around the corner. Several Bots were lying in various states. Some were trying to get up, some moving on the ground. She opened up on them and none were left moving. On the other side of the compound she saw Consten and his team in position and ready to go.

The majority of the Bots were returning fire to Naomi's squad up on the slope. Eleanor got her team in position, raised her arm then bought it down. Both teams opened fire. Eleanor emptied an entire magazine into a group on the extreme left of the wall. Bot heads and limbs spiralled through the air in different directions. One managed to turn and wildly fired in their direction. The hiss of the rounds passed within a few inches of her face, striking the wall behind her. Taking careful aim she popped a round into the centre of the Bots chest. It slammed into the wall and lay motionless. Within twenty seconds all the Bots were down. Their destruction total. She clicked the Comms and a few seconds later the firing stopped. Smoke filled the compound. The silence was deafening as the sun was rising over the top of the trees, bathing the scene in a gentle orange hue.

'Ok secure the compound, check for enemy survivors.' Eleanor barked then called Naomi down via the Comms and set about checking the compound was secure. Naomi staggered through the smoke, accompanied by her team. Helmet by her side and hair matted with sweat, they formally saluted each other.

'Objective completed.' Eleanor managed to say before embracing Naomi with each thumping the other on the back. 'We did it, we did it, we did it!' Eleanor repeated, her head was down, and tears were welling up. She looked up to see

Captain Sinclair approaching and alongside him Sergeant Bruno. 'Here they are.' Naomi turned to see them and they both stood to attention and saluted.

'Compound taken and secured, enemy destroyed, no casualties to report Sir.' Eleanor reported.

'So I see Cadet Buckley' the Captain responded 'very impressive.' He adopted a grave expression and turned to Bruno. 'Shall you tell them or shall I?'

Eleanor and Naomi shot each other a glance. What had gone wrong? What had they missed? To fail now after all they had done would be a killer. Bruno mirrored the mood.

'Best the bad news comes from you sir.'

Eleanor's heart sank. Oh shit! What now.

'Well the bad news ladies is that you've smashed the previous high score held by Sergeant Bruno. Fastest time and no casualties! What have you got to say Sergeant?'

'Completely devastated sir. I'll never get over it.' replied Bruno in a monotone voice.

Eleanor turned to Naomi. The light of relief and joy shone in Naomi's eyes as a smile broke out across her exhausted features. In that moment Eleanor knew they'd done it. The ordeal was over and they passed with flying colours. A loud cheer came from behind them and Eleanor and Naomi were mobbed by their squad members.

'Very impressive Miss.' said a still smiling Consten to Eleanor..... 'especially the way you dragged Cadet Mann back from the brink. *Very* impressive. We all really thought she was finished. I've seen experienced soldiers less fucked than that and not come back from it. You'll make a fine officer Miss, if I may so. I'll include that in my assessment to the Captain.'

Eleanor was overcome by euphoria and despite feeling more tired than she had ever been, she felt like she could have done it all over again carrying Consten on her shoulders.

'Thank you Sergeant, Cadet Mann is quite a tough girl under the soft exterior but what really got her moving was when I told her that the drinks were on you in the mess this evening, if she got through the exercise!'

'Only after you've bought the squad a few drinks each!!' They both roared with laughter. Through the laughter Eleanor noticed Bruno furtively watching her. His stare was running up and down her body, lips pursed in approval and gently nodding to himself. There was an empty coldness in his eyes and despite the steam of heat rising from her head in the icy morning air it sent a chill of fear up her spine. She had experienced that kind of look before.

◆

'Come on Eleanor, Bruno isn't *that* bad!'

'Well he definitely gives me the creeps. There's an emptiness there. You watch him the next time he speaks' Eleanor responded. There was the hubbub of numerous conversations over the sounds of laughter and glasses clinking in the Mess hall that evening. Eleanor and Naomi were alone, on a table, deep in conversation away from the loud chattering.

'Maybe it's your odd coloured eyes. I mean one blue and the other brown is pretty weird....' Naomi said and continued; 'but seriously he's been helpful to me and given me some words of encouragement and advice, so maybe you're being a bit harsh.' There was a defensive tone in her voice that Eleanor found puzzling.

'I can't do much about the eyes' Eleanor was earnest. 'Perhaps he just doesn't like my face! I dunno, he gave me a look after the overnight march like he was either undressing me or cutting my throat.'

Eleanor watched the festivities while Naomi looked into her glass in deep thought. Eleanor's body ached but she felt good.

'To be honest, I'm amazed I haven't been thrown off the course' Naomi confessed with tears welling up in her eyes, as if wanting to relieve herself of a heavy burden while admitting; 'I've just about scraped through on every module, and we both know I would have failed the last one if it wasn't for you virtually dragging me through by my hair. I don't even know how I've managed it.'

Eleanor saw that the tears in Naomi's eyes were ready to spill down her cheeks and thought Please not again. How does this girl get through life? She hasn't been through one percent of the shit I've endured. Had a privileged upbringing and she was constantly whining? What the hell had she really got to complain about? Eleanor had to be honest. She felt a measure of irritation towards Naomi, and the self-doubt that always got in her way, holding her back. If she'd been with someone else she wouldn't have cared, but there was a closeness that had grown between them and she felt responsible for her at the same time. It was a confusing mixture of emotions.

'Hey cheer up Naomi. Only a couple of days left then we get our results. We've done the hard work, nothing more to do but unwind.' Eleanor reached across and put her hand on Naomi's arm. 'I'm sorry if I was harsh on you earlier', she continued. 'It's just that I couldn't see you fail after all we've been through together. So many scrapes and close shaves but we got through it all. Now it's just what kind of assignment we get. Assuming we pass that is!' Eleanor laughed but Naomi continued to look down.

'I wanted to thank you for today.' Naomi said slowly raising her gaze to meet Eleanor's. 'I never thought I'd make it all through this and I'd never have done it without you. All I've ever wanted to do is become an officer like my Dad and his Dad before him going back generations. To make my family proud of me and I've never really questioned it. But now I'm so near my life's aim, I'm wondering if it's what I really want. Sometimes I wish I'd failed.'

'Well it's a bit late now...' Eleanor told her 'You should have thought of that at the start. You're committed now.' Naomi flinched at the harshness in Eleanor's voice and she looked down again. Eleanor immediately regretted it and softened her tone. 'Look if you're not sure you can always resign your commission after a year.'

'Really!' Now it was Naomi's turn to be harsh. Raising her voice 'Try telling that to my fuckin Dad. I'm sure he'll take it really well. No sons to fulfil his ambitions, just me and my sister. She's training to be a Doctor, so it's good old Naomi to carry the family flag forward. Don't think I'll forget the comments about me being a snivelling failure. Half of it was because you didn't want me dragging you down and having to get yourself a new buddy to boss around!'

Eleanor flinched at the words, realising she had sometimes pushed Naomi too hard, but it was for her own good. Eleanor would have passed regardless but Naomi wouldn't have without her. Her own actions were held up to her and Eleanor didn't like what she saw. Sometimes people do things which they think are right at the time, but look bad afterwards she told herself.

Their stare was now locked and Eleanor was leaning forward, gripping the edge of the table hard. For the first time in her life she consciously decided to back down and was the first to break the gaze. Letting out a deep sigh, she sat back. Naomi's eyes were still narrowed and her face was flushed.

'I'm sorry...' The words didn't come easily to Eleanor, as if they possessed a physical quality. It was like trying to regurgitate a pool ball. 'I didn't realise until now. I was so focused, not just on getting through but getting you through as well. Maybe I need someone to tell me what I'm like.' It felt strange having the tables turned. 'Sometimes I can be a total arsehole...'

At that moment the tall figure of Velásquez appeared at the side of the table followed by several other drunken Cadets.

'Ladies, ladies. You would have thought you'd failed, sitting there with faces like a pair of smacked arses!' There was a loud raucous roar from behind him. 'Let's Dance!' He took Naomi by the hand and they headed off to a waiting group in the corner.

'C'mon Eleanor!' called Naomi as Velásquez led her off. At the last moment she looked back at Eleanor and gave her a puckered smile and gently nodded at her. Eleanor returned it just before Naomi disappeared into the crowd.

♦

Eleanor slipped unnoticed out of the hall and was still thinking about Naomi's outburst as she walked through the grounds of the academy back towards her quarters. It had been a long shattering two days and she needed to sleep. To be honest she felt uncomfortable in social situations and still couldn't bring herself to overcome her natural caution in trusting people or letting them get too close. She'd been hurt and betrayed too often to drop her guard but she couldn't deny that Naomi's words had hurt her no matter how much she tried to shrug them off. The kitten had sharp little claws and had inflicted a painful scratch on a sensitive area. Maybe she had drawn that out of her before catching herself mid-thought. 'Stop being arrogant Ellie. You can't claim credit all the time', she told herself.

The evening was cool and the stars glittered overhead as Eleanor looked up at them wondering which one she would be assigned to. Ever since The Tube had been discovered humanity had found a way to the stars, undreamt of just a few decades earlier. No one knew who built it and The Tube wasn't the real name of course but that's what the people of earth had christened it. It was less of a mouthful than the official one. "The Interstellar Superhighway" they called it. What a load of shite. Still, since its discovery a network of wormholes had opened up the Galaxy and humans had become a star faring species way beyond their intellectual capabilities. Still war, greed and injustice ruled Earth and these led to vast tracts of the planet being uninhabitable. At least there was the possibility of new worlds to colonise and of course devastate in entirely new ways.

She heard voices up ahead around the corner. One of them she recognised immediately and before she could disappear Sergeant Bruno and another of the Academy Sergeants were approaching. Bruno turned to his colleague and said a couple of words. The other Sergeant briefly glanced at Eleanor and headed off towards the Staff Quarters. That left Bruno between Eleanor and the Cadet Accommodation block. Her steps momentarily faltered but she decided to press on, forcing her legs to obey. Maybe after a brief salute, she would pass and be safe. Make eye contact as short as possible. Bruno was still heading along the path towards her. In the dim light of the pathway she could see he was walking unsteadily. Oh shit, he's drunk. Again there was the strange smirk on his face. She was fighting the urge to run in the opposite direction. Stay brave Ellie, stay brave. Nothing's going to happen. You've been through worse. Looking up briefly, almost furtively, Eleanor saluted, holding his look for as long as she dared, before lowering her eyes and hand. Bruno returned the salute in a half surprised fashion and she was past him. Smelling the alcohol on him, the urge to run returned but she caught herself and tried to put as much distance between herself and him as fast as possible. 'I'm nearly away', she thought.

'Cadet Buckley!' The slightly slurred voice hit her between the shoulder blades like a punch. Fuck! Run Ellie run, she tried to tell herself, before turning to face him. Heart racing. Blood roaring in her ears. Mouth dry. Try not to look scared Ellie.

'Sergeant Bruno.' she said, trying to keep her voice steady.

'Not joining in with your fellow cadets? Thought you'd need a drink after this morning's efforts.' His voice although slurred had lost its usual harsh quality. It was a side of Bruno that surprised her. Perhaps Naomi did have a point. Eleanor relaxed a little.

'No Sir, It's been a long day and I wanted to turn in early and be ready for tomorrow.'

Bruno let out a guffaw. Eleanor was surprised to see an actual smile pass across his face before the fixed smile quickly returned. 'That's you all over Buckley. Girly swot to the end.' He stood slightly more upright and took a deep breath as though he had come to a decision. 'I was very impressed with your performance this morning. I didn't think my record would ever be broken.'

'I'm sorry it had to be your record I broke Sir.'

'Well, we're doing our final assessments over the next couple of days and I'm seriously thinking of putting your name forward for the Champion Recruit. What do you think of that?'

Eleanor let her guard drop for a moment and let out a gasp. 'Thank you Sir. That would be an incredible honour. I'm thrilled you're even considering me.'

Bruno took a step towards her. Eleanor felt his eyes peering into her heart and could see the unease that lurked there. He lowered his voice. 'I'm pleased it means so much to you, Buckley. It's between you and one other candidate. So I'm going to need some... assistance in coming to my final decision. Shall we say some "Extra Tuition."' She gasped for breath as his frame loomed large over her. She was back on high alert.

'Wha.... what do you mean Sir? I.... I don't understand...' she stammered.

'I think you know exactly what I mean Eleanor.' Using her first name felt more like a weapon than anything she had faced either in combat or on the course. 'Don't think I haven't noticed how you've looked at me over the past few weeks. That's understandable. I get it all the time. I know what you want and I can make sure you get it and more.' He boasted and the smirk returned. The smirk of

12

someone who had used and abused his position to get exactly what he wanted, when he wanted it. 'You'll enjoy it. I promise....'

Eleanor was almost too shocked to move and was struggling to keep her composure.

'Sir, I think you are very much mistaken. I didn't give you any such look. Why would I? I can get through this on my own merits. I'd rather not win the Champion Recruit if that's what it means.' She almost spat the last few words.

Bruno stepped forward and, moving with a speed that belied his size and inebriation, grabbed Eleanor's arm so tight it felt like it was in the jaws of a large ferocious beast. His voice took on a quivering growling quality. The smell of alcohol so strong she began to gag. Her hand began to go numb.

'I don't think you understand Cadet Buckley how things work around here.' Bruno's teeth gritted and flecks of spit hit Eleanor in the face. She noticed the white foam in the corners of his mouth. 'I ask and you fuckin give. Do you understand! That's just the way it is. Don't even think of telling anyone. It'll turn out very bad for you.' he warned her.

Eleanor's memory flashed back to her childhood and Uncle Steve, one of her mother's many 'Boyfriends' The same tone, the same voice, the same look. She knew what to do and adopted a conciliatory, fearful voice. 'Ok Sir, please don't hurt me. I know what you mean. I was just too nervous. Just don't hurt me. Please...' The plaintiff tone of the last word had the desired effect. His breathing slowed and expression relaxed a little.

The leer returned to Bruno's face. 'I knew you'd come round to my way of thinking. You have a bright future ahead of you Eleanor.' His grip loosened slightly. The circulation was returning to her hand. Smiling up at him, his face moved closer towards hers, filling her vision. At the last moment she threw her head forward. Bruno managed to evade her attempted head-butt, but his grip loosened just enough for Eleanor to twist her arm out of it. In the same movement she caught hold of Bruno's wrist and bent his hand back in. Stepping to one side, she kicked with all her force into the side of his knee so he collapsed to the ground. Eleanor still kept hold of his wrist and managed to lock his elbow.

'Fuckin little bitch!' he looked at her. 'You're gonna die for this!' Although Eleanor was quivering with fear she still had enough strength to maintain her grip on him. As if by instinct she kicked him in the ribs as hard as she could. It drove the air out of his lungs in a big 'WOOOOOOOOOOOOOFFFF.' as he sank forward gasping for breath. His eyes rolled back, his mouth soundlessly opening and closing like a landed fish. With her attention fixed on Bruno all the time she released her grip and took a few steps back...

13

'This is the way things work with me you big lump of shit.' She was almost screaming. 'If I had a gun, I'd shoot you in the head a hundred times, If I had a knife, I'd cut your bollocks off and make you eat them.' She moved back towards him. 'You may have got away with it before but not anymore. Not with me. I wouldn't let a predatory scumbag like you anywhere near me. You make me feel sick, you make my flesh crawl. If you ever come near me again, I'll rip your throat out. Do you understand me?'

He stopped gasping and smiled as he looked at her. Eleanor's white hot anger was once again replaced by fear. 'Looks like we taught you a bit too well.' Bruno said and climbed slowly to his feet, still breathing heavily and holding his side. Bending forward he looked at her and started to laugh. In the distance she could hear a group approaching, talking excitedly. 'Ooooo. Here they come to my rescue.' he said in a mocking voice 'To save poor little me from the big bad Buckley.' Eleanor turned and started to run. 'Bang goes Champion Recruit for you Eleanor.' He called after her. She didn't look back and didn't stop until she got to the Accommodation Block. When she got there Eleanor stopped trembling and, looking down noticed she had wet herself.

♦

In the court for the disciplinary hearing

Eleanor pleaded guilty to the assault charge on Velásquez; she felt really bad about that. Also, she pleaded guilty to spitting in the face of Bruno, which she didn't feel bad about at all. She was under the impression that once the court had heard her story of his attempted assault she would put some context on it and maybe mitigate any punishment. Naturally she pleaded 'Not Guilty' to the charges of taking a banned stimulant and cheating exams.

She sensed Naomi had been avoiding her in the past couple days before the final results were announced, but surely she couldn't have been in on it as well. Why would she speak up for a brute like Bruno? She had stood up for him when they spoke but Eleanor had thought that was just her usual weakness shining through. Perhaps Naomi had accepted his kind offer of extra-curricular activities she herself had so politely declined.

Within an hour Eleanor knew she was toast and had no chance. The prosecution council was an experienced captain and former Lawyer. Hers was a junior Lieutenant barely out of the academy himself. He did his best but was outclassed, outfought and outthought at every turn. Everything was set up perfectly against her. The blood tests, fixed. The assault accusations against Bruno. He had an alibi with two other sergeants. Captain Sinclair told the hearing Bruno was one of the

14

finest soldiers he had the honour to serve with. Eleanor nearly threw up when she heard that. Her past of petty crime and time in a youth offenders institute were bought up.

The only one who stood up for her was Consten when questioned by Eleanor's council. 'I've seen people on stimulants before sir. They couldn't have made the considered decisions that Buckley did. I said before and I'll say it again, I thought she was exceptional and so did the lads.'

'What have you got to say about the allegations against Sergeant Bruno?', the prosecutor asked.

'There's no denying that he's a brave soldier sir, but there have been stories circulating. I didn't give much credence and put them down to petty jealousies. He does inspire quite a following and sometimes it's not wise to say anything.', Consten replied

'Objection sir!' The prosecuting officer protested. 'It's Cadet Buckley who is on trial here, not Sergeant Bruno.'

'Upheld.' boomed the Colonel presiding over the hearing. 'Everything I've heard about Sergeant Bruno tells me he maintains the finest values of the Corps and I won't tolerate his reputation being besmirched in this manner.'

Consten looked over at Eleanor, pursed his lips and shook his head. Game over, thought Eleanor.

'Call the next witness!'

Into the room stepped a trembling Naomi. Eleanor's heart leapt. Finally, she's decided where her loyalties lie. Naomi's through the course. They can't take it away from her now. The prosecuting council stepped forward.

'Cadet Mann. Tell the hearing what you saw two weeks ago.' Naomi looked down. Her chest rising and falling in short breaths. Her hand was shaking. 'Cadet Mann, if you please?' Eleanor's heart sank, and she fully expected what was coming.

'I was looking for some notes I had taken from one of the courses.' Naomi closed her eyes and took a deep breath. 'I looked across on Cadet Buckley's desk to see if I had left them on there.' She hesitated.

'Continue please…'

'I noticed what appeared to be some old exam papers and written answers were on her desk. I picked them up to examine them, when Cadet Buckley came in. She immediately became angry, snatched them from me and started shouting at me about respecting private property.' All the time her head was lowered and her voice barely audible.

The prosecutor flourished the papers in front of Naomi. 'Are these the papers you saw?' Silence… 'Cadet Mann. Are these the papers?'

15

'Yes.' Naomi let out a loud sob.

Eleanor sat listening to the exchange in disbelief. A sickening, desperate anger burned at her insides like lava rising up through a volcano, burning its way into her chest. 'You lying, snivelling, backstabbing piece of shit!', Eleanor shouted.

Naomi put her face in her hands and sobbed uncontrollably.

Eleanor couldn't help herself, 'How could you! After everything I did for you and you stand up for that lying scumbag!', she shouted. Her hand shot out pointing a finger across the room where Bruno sat impassively.

The Colonel repeatedly hammered the Gavel. 'The accused will be silent! Or I will have you removed and the hearing will continue without you!'

'For Christ's sake Eleanor!', hissed her counsel. 'You've just lost yourself the case. Now for just once in your life sit down and shut up!'

She slumped in the chair and stared vacantly at the floor. The hearing continued until its inevitable conclusion. Eleanor was oblivious to the remainder of proceedings. Declining to be cross examined she sat in total silence. Mind empty.

♦

'Guilty!'

This time the verdict made little impression on Eleanor. It was as sure as night followed day. She turned to face the Colonel who addressed her.

'Buckley. You have shown beyond any doubt your unsuitability to become an officer in this or any other corps. Your reckless uncontrolled aggressive and overbearing manner is a danger to those around you. You have systematically lied and will stop at nothing to achieve your aims. I commend the bravery of Cadet Mann in exposing your lies. Even taking into account your exceptional record as a soldier I also have to take into account the previous record as a felon. Therefore, you will be detained for three months and dishonourably discharged. Dismissed!'

As she was being led away Eleanor looked around the room for Naomi, but she was nowhere to be seen. The only face she noticed was Bruno slowly shaking his head. There was nothing to say. It was over.

♦

The sound of the guard rapping on the door shocked Eleanor out of her sleep. There was no clue as to what time it was, if it was dark or light outside as there was no window in the underground holding cell. She was due to be transferred to the main detention centre to serve her sentence later that day. Considering her entire life's aim had been completely ruined, she had slept surprisingly well.

Eleanor was used to incarceration but the military had saved her from that, instilling a sense of purpose and meaning to life, teaching her something she was good at, something to be proud of and people looked up to her for. Now she was back in the same old situation.

Now she was awake, it hadn't all been a bad dream, the reality of it took hold. Sometimes bad shit happens Ellie, and you were in the way this time. She dismissed the thought. Perhaps it was life's way of paying her back for being too much of a hothead. Watching and waiting for her to trip up and now she had, it was sitting there arms folded, rocking gently back and forth laughing at her.

Hyuk hyuk hyuk, look at you now. Thought you knew it all didn't you and you really knew fuck all. Not so big after all are ya. No! No I didn't deserve this. I may have done some things I regret but I'm not bad and I've tried to be a better person, *Ahh stop feeling sorry for yourself. Poor little Ellie. Nasty old world been rotten to you then. Ahh diddums.* The prickling around her eyes told her that tears were not far off. *Go on then have a little cry. Boo hoo hoo* the voice mocked her. *Lie down, die and let it happen just like it always does.* It's not going to happen to me this time. I'm going to get back and clear my name and take back what should be mine Eleanor vowed. *Oh yeah! How you gonna do that then?* I haven't quite worked that part out yet...

A burst of laughter from outside shook Eleanor out of her thoughts. The door swung slowly open and a familiar hulking figure stood in the doorway.

'Thought I'd come and wish you luck Eleanor before your little trip.'

Eleanor sat up on the bed, mouth agape, frozen in shock and fear. Bruno's bulk made the room seem like a small cupboard. He seemed to fill every corner with his malign presence. There was the smell of drink on his breath, and she knew what he'd come for. This time there was no escape apart from death.

'Why you looking at me like that.' he continued in his 'what, who me?' voice. 'Nothing to say to poor old uncle Valerio?'

To her amazement Eleanor found herself laughing and the puzzled look on Bruno's face didn't help matters.

'Valerio. Fuckin Valerio... What kind of name is that?' She clenched her fist to stop the trembling of her hand, digging her nails into her palm, drawing blood that dripped on the bed sheets. 'I'll tell you what kind of name it is. It's the name of a bully and coward. A small man. A nothing man.'

Bruno's face flushed. She knew she had struck home and expected the blow to fall. But it didn't. Not yet. Perhaps he's drawing it out. Eleanor looked at his claw-like hands and the long dirty nails.

Then in a flash he was on her. She didn't even have time to raise her hands. His salivary mouth covered hers in a slobbering slurping embrace that choked her.

17

The stench of his breath, stale sweat and tobacco were as cruel and painful as anything his fists could inflict. The weight and smell pressed down on her and she was helpless. A big lumpen mass of evil was consuming her. Sucking her down into its dark world.

He moved back, his brutal mouth filling her vision. 'Small man am I?' His nails dug into her cheeks, breaking the skin into the flesh underneath. 'Gonna gob in my face now are ya?' His tongue slowly came out of his mouth. A big pink prehistoric monster of a thing as he ran it up the side of her face. She tried to bite his hand but the granite grip firmly clamped her jaw shut. 'Should have cooperated Eleanor. It's all your own fault.' She tried to scream but only a muffled groan came out. The tongue continued its journey up the side of her face. Her eyes were popping out in terror. The monster reached its destination and he jabbed it in her eye, then laughed. Pain and revulsion filled Eleanor. She was suffocating and starting to lose consciousness as her vision started to grey. The hand released itself from her mouth and before she could regain her senses she was on her front whooping in big breaths, before her face was thrust back into the pillow. This time just one nostril was clear. 'Now, now. Don't fall asleep on me Eleanor. I want you to find out what you were missing.' She could feel his free hand pulling her trousers down and she renewed her struggle. Bruno pressed her face harder into the pillow with every movement from her and she had to give up or suffocate. She could now feel him inside as his ravenous weight moved backwards and forwards on her. His grunting in her ear growing in speed and ferocity. The pain overtook every sense as she started to scream. The snarling grew louder and faster, increasing in violence and force as the beast consumed her. Her innards felt like they were being ripped out. The whole cell seemed to be shaking in a rhythmic earthquake of violence as Eleanor desperately hung on, helpless in its path. The burning agony growing with every violent thrust as her world was reduced into a diminishing tunnel, sounds muffled, light disappearing into the distance, drawing her down into the depths of despair, agony and terror. Then he stopped.

She lay still, nothing left, nothing to give. Nothing.

'There. That wasn't too bad now was it.' he whispered tenderly in her ear. Her head was released from the pillow and she drew in rasping breaths as he got up from her. Turning around to face him, Eleanor drew the covers up over her exposed lower half. Bruno stood over her, covered in sweat and still breathing heavily as he adjusted his trousers. Trying to speak, only a wheezing whisper came out. Blood slowly trickling from one nostril. 'Sorry? Want to thank me for giving you a good time?' Bruno said. She leant forward and weakly beckoned him. 'No no no. Not falling for that one again. You'll have to speak up I'm afraid.'

18

Eleanor leant forward again. This time she had enough breath. 'Is that all you've got, small man...' she managed to croak. The look of shock on Bruno's face was quickly replaced by hate and anger then fear. He moved toward her and was stopped when the voice of one of the guards called through the door.

'Hey Bruno! Times up! They'll be here in a minute.' He looked over his shoulder. 'Like now! You've had your fun.'

He turned and looked at Eleanor and opened his mouth as if to say something. She stared back. Then he left as quickly as he arrived and the cell door clanged shut behind him leaving Eleanor on her own and more alone than any time in her life.

1

Darkness. Sounds. Confinement… Then there was the pain that came in waves, roaring up and down his body, crashing on his nerves with a ferocious regularity until eventually they began to subside.

Light. Blinding white light searing into his brain. He was unable to resist his eye being forced open. The light was taken away and he could perceive vague shapes moving around. There were noises coming from the shapes. Thick growling and moaning sounds alongside squealings that hurt his head. One of the shapes breaks off from the other and grew larger. It has a face and is holding something out to him. It's shiny, round with a thin line coming out of the top. He can feel the round object being put on top of his head. A sudden dizziness and disorientation engulfed him, tumbling end over end. Not knowing up or down. Quickly followed by a rushing sensation, a falling towards something, a sense of direction. Things are coming into focus. THHHWWWWIPPP! The world snaps into sharp vision. He remembers everything. The face smiled at him.

'There you are little fella. Wakey wakey' The kind one said. 'I fixed it on him; we should be getting readings. Ok this is subject 021161R, or as I prefer to call him. Billy'

'Well I can't see anything yet and I've told you to stop treating them like your pets!' A second voice came from behind the kind one. It struck fear into him. Billy remembered everything now. The pain, the cruelty. There was only hate when he was around. When he had first become aware, the sounds were just echoes in his mind, until the last time he had been awake. Suddenly from a meaningless jumble they had carried meaning. The meaning he had been aware of from very early on was the vindictiveness of the second voice. Even his face conveyed it. The way he looked at him had a feeling of spite that could only be sated by inflicting pain and fear.

Billy heard another voice, softer this time.

'I'm picking him up OK Dr Walker. It must be your equipment not working properly.' This new voice belonged to a female, taller and darker skinned than the other two. She was wearing a shiny object on her head like the one that had been placed on his. He was aware of a gentle soothing feeling.

'Hey there...' Panic spread through him. What was that? A voice from nowhere. It didn't come from his ears but inside his head.

'Ahh... That's better.' said the cruel voice. 'I'm getting a reading. Ok proceed please Ava.'

Billy waited for the pain he associated with the voice to arrive, but it didn't.

'Don't be frightened.' It was the voice inside his head. 'You're going to feel a lot better in a moment.' He could sense the kindness. A feeling of euphoria out of nowhere overwhelmed Billy. Every pathway of every neurone zingled with indescribable beauty. Colours, iridescent shimmered across his mind's eye, orange tinged with gold, greens overlaid with flecks of sporadic yellow flew past, brushing against him. Lightning flashed pleasure through his every nerve ending in a pyrotechnic display of joy. Hundreds of voices singing a beautiful soothing harmony were carried as sound became colours, colours became feelings, and feelings became sound again, each superimposing itself over the others. Then just as quickly as they appeared the sensations diminished shrinking into a little white light moving into the distance that vanished in a gentle puff. Why couldn't it last forever, pathways in his brain opened up and feelings he'd been unaware of were laid before him in a panoply. The first one that he got was excitement immediately followed by yearning. 'How was that? Feeling better now?'

'I think that hit the spot.' said the kind one. There was laughter as he continued, 'but we don't want him chasing the man now do we Ava, so better ease off a little.'

'I sensed his pleasure. It certainly reassured him after I communicated with him. I think we uploaded successfully. I'll check the readings.' This time the voice came through his ears.

'Hey! We're training him to kill. Not to fall in love with you Ava! It's not a person; it's not one of your so called psychofriends. It's only a Gargoyle, and a fuckin ugly one at that!' Dr Walker reminded her.

'Well Dr Walker, your method of liberally inflicting pain at the first opportunity didn't exactly work out well did it? It's taken weeks to move forward just a little. We've made more progress in the last couple of sessions, than all yours combined. Every single measure is up apart from fear and hate. Also it's "Psychic" not "Psycho"'.

'I said "psychic", anyhow if I wanted him to fuck his adversaries to death then I'd stick with the hearts and flowers approach. But we don't, do we.'

The contempt dripped off every word and landed on Billy, burning holes through him like acid. He struggled against his restraints and hissed at the cruel one.

'Who you hissing at! Have some of this!'

Billy was immediately paralysed by a pain so intense, he believed his body was submerged in flames, his limbs were being ripped backwards and his eyes

21

were going to pop out and land skittering at the feet of the hated one who'd casually crushed them underfoot. The pain switched off and a terrified Billy slammed back out of his paralysis.

'Anymore? Thought not. Well at least we know he can understand us.'

Ava was outraged; 'Firstly your cruelty towards a sentient being is sickening. Second, I should remind you that killing is a subordinate function of the Gargoyles, and it's for defensive purposes only. We capture them, clone them to accept mind control and send them out, where they lead us straight to the Nadinium. You know, the whole purpose of the Mag program and the trip to Magdur. They're not your playthings to exercise your sadistic tendencies upon for your own warped pleasure. Finally *Doctor* Walker, I'd appreciate it if you would moderate your language which has no place in a professional environment.'

'Well your concerns are duly noted and duly fuckin' dismissed. These things have no rights and since their capture, are purely property of the company. They are not your personal pets Dr Felton and they are not your patients Miss Matthews. I'm the one with his neck on the block if this doesn't work out, not you two. I'm the one under pressure from Dr Khan to complete this phase and we are way behind schedule. We can do what we like, when we like with them, like this.'

He saw the cruel one reach over for a switch and turned him off….

♦

'He's an idiot! ' Ava looked across at Harry Felton who was placing Billy the Gargoyle back in his pen. His was the fourth in the row. The other pens contained variations of the Gargoyles. Some slept all day and came out only when the lights were turned down in the evening when the whole pen area was lit in an eerie dull red. One, 191065N or 'Horace' as Harry called him sat quietly watching the comings and goings throughout the day. His orange tinged eyes observing everything and giving away nothing. Sometimes they changed colour almost imperceptibly to yellow. Ava found him the hardest subject. There was an occasional glimpse of the inside of his mind but too brief to make any sense. Nobody saw him eating, just feed left in the bowl that was gone by the morning, but he'd not been observed to move all night. The only time they had taken him out to be uploaded was just over a week ago. They had tranquilised him, triggering the other Gargoyles to go berserk in their cages. Harry was on the verge of calling in Blue security team when they instantaneously became silent again. An invisible mute button had been pressed and they reverted to their normal behaviour patterns.

22

Billy was about the same size as a dog but infinitely more dangerous than the most ferocious Rottweiler. He lay completely inert and didn't respond when the restraints were removed. Harry shut the pen and Billy stirred, slowly lifting his head and looking around. He rose unsteadily, his almost ape like form tottering in a slightly drunken fashion, before he moved to the front of the pen where Harry placed his hand through the feeding slot and stroked the back of his grey fleshy head. His tenderness contradicted by his mouth full of razor sharp teeth. Sometimes a hint of violet or turquoise would shimmer across his skin. Perhaps it was a form of communication or a reflection of his internal state of mind. But only Horace had the orangey yellow eyes. His head reminded Ava of a film she'd once seen of the long extinct piranha fish except there was something oddly human about the eyes. A hint of sensitivity and longing were contained within them. His body, though it appeared puny was a coiled spring of lithe strength that could snap into action in a nanosecond. As he stretched out his arm Ava felt that he was studiously examining his slowly unclenching fist as one by one the pearl white claws unfurled, each possessing a gentle pure incandescence that was starkly at odds with their ultimately lethal purpose.

'There there, Billy me little fella. Back home now.' Harry turned to Ava. 'Who's an idiot? Dr Walkabout?'

'Why do you call him that, and do you have to give everyone a nickname?' Ava was smiling and felt at ease with Harry's laid back Australian charm, although she knew a fierce passion and burning intelligence lay not far beneath the calm exterior. 'What's mine?', she asked.

'Dr Matthews of course!' He replied, eyebrows raised with feigned innocence.

'Well that's a problem as I'm not a doctor. Psychic Consultant is my official title.' Ava looked quizzically at Harry and a smile flickered across her lips to break the spell of mock indignation.

'Well Psychic Consultant Matthews' replied Harry in an official sounding voice. He looked up at Ava while still stroking Billy. 'I don't think he's an idiot. More overworked and under pressure. He applied his own preconceived methods early on, with no success and has grown increasingly frustrated. He should have called you in earlier, but you know what pride and stubbornness can do. He's not interested in listening to our ideas, when he does and they work he claims them as his own. It doesn't matter though as long as we get there in the end.'

'It seems to me that he's more concerned with turning them into killing machines, fighting off their former buddies, the indigenous Magdurian creatures, than prospecting for Nadinium.' Ava tried to keep the concern from her voice although she wasn't entirely sure she had.

23

'I'm not happy with that either, every time I've raised it with him he just seems to get angry. I suggested that they need some kind of intelligence instead of being unthinking killers, but....' A sadness became apparent on Harry's normally cheery features. Harry's voice quivered as he looked back down at Billy and stroked him on the back of the neck. Turquoise waves gently glistened across Billy's back and side.

'But what?' Ava gently prompted him. She could sense the conflicted emotions arising from his mind. Don't probe Ava, let him give it voluntarily, she thought. 'Harry?' There was a silence between them. The pure white light gave the labs a feel like an operating room, pulsing away, causing a dull ache in the back of their eyes.

Harry looked back up at Ava. 'When I graduated I had dreams of synthetic life being at the forefront of science. This was before the Great Heat and of course before The Bagama incident in Northern Australia.' This time the doubt and uncertainty were gone from Harrys voice as he took a deep breath and drew his shoulders back. 'Bagama wasn't the fault of the synthetics.....' Harry continued; 'The team had used unauthorised methods, this was in the days when single nucleotide DNA changes were applied and the results were not understood properly. Things are different nowadays in the Mag program.'

Ava knew that wasn't entirely the case. There were successors to the synthetics, but people were not easily fooled by a rebrand and they remained deeply controversial, unpopular programs. Riots and attacks on scientists were proof of that. Although large corporations supported by their client governments saw that the research program continued away in secret from prying eyes.

This was where the Mags came into the story. They had first been observed when the primary reconnaissance teams had landed shortly after the purchase of Magdur. Initial scans had suggested larger than normal deposits of a particularly pure form of Nadinium, and a team of scientists were bought in to investigate and gather samples. Although the exact locations were hard to pin down, they seemed to coincide with the gatherings of the small Magdurian creatures, the Gargs. Although they had seemed placid and docile, due to no natural predators, they became agitated when samples of Nadinium where taken. There were deposits on the surface that were easily collected. They discovered the tunnels, excavated by the Gargs, that had led to a sparkling treasure trove of the purest Nadinium seen anywhere. This was when things went very wrong, very fast.

The traumatised survivors told a terrifying tale of the gentle creatures suddenly transforming into a frenzied slashing horde. The claws that had been used for digging where transformed into razor sharp weapons that effortlessly slashed through the toughened protective suits and into the flesh of the unsuspecting scientists, who promptly bled out. Others had their oxygen supplies severed, leaving them to choke out their final seconds on the toxic atmosphere in an agonising death.

Then came the giant Mag. Only snatched descriptions of a creature of unnatural strength and violence, at least triple the height of a human, made it back with the survivors. No hint of its existence had been suspected until the Nadinium had been disturbed. Towering over all around them, the apparition of death had quickly transformed the those not touched by the Gargs into splattered puddles that bore no resemblance to their former, living state.

The single remaining EVA shuttle had limped back to the main base three days later. Some had died of their injuries on the return journey, others, relatively unharmed seemed to have lost the will to live and died of shock. The three remaining survivors told a tale of remorseless pursuit that had seen other vehicles picked up like toys, ripped open and the occupants plucked out and devoured like a box of chocolates. The chase had only ended when they managed to hide inside the titanium shell of the air lock of the last remaining vehicle, while the creatures spent the last of their energy trying to fight their way through. After an endless night, the assault ceased, and the creatures melted back into the landscape allowing the stunned survivors to nurse the shuttle home. At first there was incredulity at the tales of death, but this was soon replaced by a sense of panic that the Mags would follow them back and reap similar havoc upon their last remaining habitat, so the base was abandoned, and all staff were evacuated. Through the jumble of confused, contradictory accounts, the story of a systematic and coordinated assault became apparent. However, there was one thing the final three were adamant on. The purple, that filled their minds to bursting point and the piercing whistling that had deafened them, accompanied by a feeling that something too huge to contemplate was observing them and was probing their inner being. An ocean of consciousness trying to squeeze itself into their thimble sized minds. None of them survived the trip home to Earth.

And yet the lure of Nadinium called out across the stars. The following year they came back prepared. A full scientific expedition backed up by the considerable military resources of Ateus Industries. Atmospheric processing plants better known as APP's were set up across Magdur. Roving Terraformers were sent out to seed the landscape. A permanent base was established, and the forces swept out in search of their quarry, the Mags, which were to be captured and studied, except they only seemed to have existed as a ghost in memories of the dead. There was the occasional sudden movement in the distance, but all that remained were a few scratches in the parched Magdurian dust. The tunnels excavated by the Gargs had disappeared. Only a few sparse traces of Nadinium remained, scattered across the surface. Any sign of the previous year's expedition had vanished. It was as if the whole surface of Magdur had been scrubbed clean of all traces. This led to rumours that the whole thing had been a hoax, to cover up a manmade disaster.

It was pure luck that they eventually stumbled across the lone straggler who led them to a small group of Gargs, caught out in the open of the early light of the Magdurian Dawn. They didn't stand a chance, most tried to flee and were quickly killed, but four were captured alive. As they were being trussed and stored for transportation, it appeared. The giant of the previous expedition's nightmares. They were not exaggerating about the size or ferocity, but they were prepared as the creature was killed by a well-aimed depleted uranium round to the head, that ended its assault with a sudden kinetic finality. The mutilated corpse of the giant was taken back to the base for further study, along with the terrified Gargs.

Still there was no sign of the Nadinium, despite the repeated scans, only a few surface traces were found. After a whole fruitless year, the base was being wound down. In a final desperate throw of the dice, one of the Gargs was sent out wearing a tracker, and that's when they hit the jackpot...

Ava was shaken from her thoughts by Harry's gentle yet insistent tones. 'But over a hundred innocent people were killed. Not just killed but ripped to shreds.' Harry stopped stroking Billy and removed his hand from the pen, closing the feeding hatch. 'I knew some of them....', he went on; 'The impact was devastating. I've never really gotten over it.' He looked at Billy and the smile reappeared. Billy stayed near the hatch waiting for Harry to come back. 'The thing is Dr Ava.....' She liked Harry's honest easy charm and appreciated his candour. '.....is that these beings should be trumpeted to the whole universe, not hidden away like a dirty secret.'

'You know that's not possible at the moment. Their mission is secret and you signed the classification papers to that effect.' Although Ava felt sympathy, she was now adopting her official voice. 'The location of the Nadinium is their primary objective, you know that.'

'That's another thing. I don't think this Nadinium stuff is all it's cracked up to be. "The answer to all our energy needs forever" my arse!' Harry sneered. '"A miracle cure to heal the environment." Total rubbish!'

Ava was surprised at Harry's sudden change of tone again, but she decided to let him continue and blow his own anger out. It's good to get it off your chest.

'The same people who destroyed the environment are telling us they've now got the answer? I don't think so....' Harry continued; 'Not since the Great Heat started.' He took a deep breath. 'Sorry to get on my high horse again, but making vast tracts of my homeland uninhabitable is too much to take, and Australia was lucky it could cope. The other areas that were poorer couldn't. All those mass migrations and wars. No wonder people don't trust The Company anymore.' Walking across from the pen he put his hand on Ava's shoulder. 'I named him after my pet dog, when I was a child.' Ava was thrown momentarily.

'What?', she asked

'Billy....', Harry said; 'He's named after my dog. He disappeared one day. My parents told me he'd run off but my older brother told me he'd been stolen for food. I didn't believe him then, but that was before I found out about the Wandering People.'

'You'll be wandering around looking for a new job very soon if you don't get the next subject ready for tests!' They snapped around to see Leighton Walker standing by the entrance of the pen area looking at his tablet. The atmosphere in the room immediately became tense. 'I'd like another crack at 191065N, or "Horace" as you've affectionately christened him, so get him ready please Dr Felton.' The patronising tone grated on both Ava and Harry. Walker had a manner about him that even if he had confirmed their deepest closely held beliefs, it would still raise the hackles. The Gargoyles sensed the change in the room. 'And another thing, Dr Felton.' This time Walker looked straight at Harry. 'I don't want you putting your hand in the pen with a Gargoyle that is not sedated. I don't care if you have your head ripped off, but I do care about having to terminate one of our hard won subjects and starting again. Do you understand?'

'Yes Dr Walkab...Walker', replied Harry in a low voice. His face was red with embarrassment and anger.

'Good, as long as we understand each other we'll get along fine.' Walker turned to Ava. 'If I could have a moment Miss Matthews. Alone if you please.'

◆

Walker ushered Ava into his office and they sat facing each other across Walker's desk. No sign of pictures of family members or any personal mementoes on his desk. Only necessary, functional items. Ava wasn't surprised by the sparseness of the room as he sat back in his chair and placed his hands together.

'First of all Ava, I wanted you to be one of the first to receive the good news...' There was an uneasy emphasis on the last two words that loaded them with an ominous significance. Ava sat in silence; eyebrows slightly raised as Walker continued. 'We going to be playing host to some... guests.'

'Guests? Who?' Ava was incredulous.

Walker sighed and smiled the empty smile of one about to drop a rather large bombshell. 'Over a thousand of them, to be precise...'

Her mouth fell open as the shock of the news sank in. 'More than a thousand, you gotta be kidding me…'

The look on Walker's face showed that this was indeed not the case. 'I'm afraid not Ava. This has come from on high. Apparently, the decision was made when we weren't finding any Nadinium deposits here. It was deemed that the profit motive had shifted from prospecting to settlement. As you well know, these planets cost a lot of money Ava and the Company wants a quick return on their investment.'

'I assume they know about the recent discovery of the Nadinium deposits, so why would they be sending settlers? It's plain crazy!'

'For once I agree Ava. I asked if we could send them back, but that was given short shrift. Even when I told them the planet's atmosphere wasn't breathable and wouldn't be for at least 6 months, they ignored me. So, we've got to put them up, in the lap of luxury may I add. The living quarters of the base are being expanded and they've even thought of some nice shops, restaurants and entertainment to pass the time of their incarceration. All the comforts of home, here in Pangea base, Magdur.'

'So, what about the Mags. Especially the Gorthon. These things are potentially dangerous. They may be genetically modified and enhanced but the anomalies remain.'

'Well that's where you come in. I want you to prepare for the separation of the lab facilities from the civilian habitat. The settlers must have no inkling of what we are doing here. We've got a few weeks to prepare. It's just an old research facility that has temporarily been converted to accommodate them before their eventual home is ready.'

'Eventual home? What the hell! They'll choke to death out there, that's if they don't get devoured by the wild Gorthons that seem to pop out of nowhere.'

'Well it seems that the company have anticipated the Gorthons at least. They've got their own company of SPC accompanying them.'

'SPC? You mean the butt of all the Security team's foul-mouthed jokes. That SPC?'

'The very same.' Walker let out a long breath and shook his head. 'On top of this the mobile Terraformers keep being found mangled at the bottom of precipices, despite the Autonav showing no sign of a fault, and now I've learnt that another one of the Atmospheric processing plants themselves has gone offline. A previously unblemished record has gone to fuckin shit.' Ava drew a sharp intake of breath at Walkers language, but he continued unperturbed. 'This is a real clusterfuck Ava and we're right in the middle of it, all of which brings

28

me onto my next point.' This time Walkers smile was less sinister, but still Ava was cautious,

'Which is…'

'Well Ava, I'd like to thank you for your assistance earlier today. I think you played a significant role in uploading the emotion software into our subject. It's moved us substantially forward in our research. Dr Khan will be most appreciative.' Now he leant forward in his chair. Ava could sense what was coming next. 'However, what I didn't appreciate was your attempt to undermine me in front of my…subordinates.' He let the last word hang before continuing. 'It's crucial that I maintain discipline, and your intervention was unacceptable. Just because you've been parachuted in by senior management to act as a consultant doesn't give you the right to question me in a disrespectful and condescending manner. You've been here five minutes and suddenly you're an expert!' His voice was rising and complexion reddened. Ava sensed he was struggling to maintain his composure. 'Do you realise the amount of work I've put into this.' The tensions of the past weeks evident in his voice.

Ava felt a degree of sympathy for Walker, but that was dwarfed by her contempt of his arrogant ham fisted hubris as she tried to maintain her calm exterior. '"You've" put into it? Only you?' Ava raised her eyebrows. She held Walker's gaze and his expression became more defensive. 'You mean you, with the significant help of your team who have put a tremendous amount of work into the Gargoyle Mag program.'

'What are you insinuating Miss Matthews?' Walker asked and continued; 'They've done the donkey work. I'm the brains and drive behind the team.' He raised his chin slightly to show his inflated self-regard. Even in conceding he still put himself first.

'I'm not *insinuating* anything Dr Walker....' Ava responded; 'So you view them as Donkeys do you? I'm sure they'll be very interested, but not entirely surprised to hear that.' Ava was trying to keep a lid on her emotions but they finally boiled to the surface. 'You seriously underestimate your staff Dr Walker. But I would say it's almost impossible to underestimate you?!' Walker flinched and his eyes were wide open. 'Perhaps if you showed them the respect they deserve and didn't treat them with the same casual cruelty you show your test subjects you might have shown more progress. A couple of day's work surpassing three months' work tells me everything I need to know Doctor.'

Walker rose to his full five foot six height. His quivering finger pointing at the door. 'You have over stepped the mark Miss Matthews. Get out. Now!'

'Don't worry, I've said all I needed to say.' Ava rose to leave. At the open door she turned to Walker. 'I'll be including your comments and above all your

methods in my report to Dr Khan. I'm sure he'll be very interested to read them.'
Walker strode around the desk towards Ava as she turned her back and left.

'Out!' He screamed and slammed the door behind her.

Everyone outside suddenly returned to what they were doing before the shouts had started, pretending they hadn't heard a thing. As Ava left the office with a broad grin spread across her face.

'That put the jumped-up little jerk in his place' she whispered to herself as she left the lab area. Despite the burden that had been placed on her, it felt good to get things off her chest to that little creep, really good…

2

The black circular shape moved smoothly against the background of stars. The only clue to any observer that it existed was the light that played around its periphery in a constantly shifting kaleidoscope of distorted shapes and colours. It travelled steadily in its path as it had done so for aeons, occupying the point where the gravity of the host star and the planet balanced perfectly in the eternal dance of orbital mechanics. The deep perpetual blackness of the wormholes' mouth reflected the endless destinations that connected it to the cosmos. Light years covered in days, solar systems in minutes, billions of miles in a heartbeat, through the higher dimensions of space where time and distance took on a different meaning. In the totality of the blackness, a silver jewel of light emerged. Microscopic against the vastness of the exit of the everlasting tunnel. Moving swiftly away from its home for the past six months, the Arion had entered the final stage of its odyssey across the stars, as it turned towards the blue and white marble of Magdur.

Filaments of incandescent matter whipped off the host star in great arcs. The result of the tormented magnetic forces that battled with the huge dent in spacetime made by the mass of Ereus. Snapping with powers beyond human comprehension, hurling trillions of tons of ionised matter out into space. One of them sped towards Magdur where the skewed magnetic field would funnel them towards the poles, that stood at right angles to the planets' orientation before they crashed into the upper atmosphere, exploding in an array of pink and green aurorae. The ethereal curtains almost reaching down to the surface.

Celina Novak stood at the bridge window watching the planet coming into view. Magdur could be mistaken for Earth from a distance, but as it grew and details started to emerge, she could make out the outlines of the continents. The terraforming had started to lay down the first grasslands and forests were starting to form. There were still the red and brown of the desert areas, but these would succumb to the march of the mobile terraformers. Remembering from the maps, Celina saw the outlines of the coasts and the areas where the Nadinium deposits were predicted in the highest abundance.

'We're go for orbital insertion.' came the announcement over the Comms. Celina looked across at the Arion's captain, Elvira Marcelo, whose attention was fixed on the screen in front of her.

'Proceed'. Myra responded. Such a small word that contained huge significance. Five hundred light years from Earth, they had arrived home.

31

There was an awed hush as the beautiful fragile globe of Magdur hove into view. There were murmurs, gasps and even an occasional sob as the hint of a tear played at the corner of Celina's eye. Looking down at the white streaks of cloud, the sun was glistening off the vast ocean. Small island archipelagos stretched in a turquoise sea. Patches of green stood out on the wide expanse of water. The snow-capped mountains looked only a few inches high, some jutting above the wisps of cloud cover, as the star's waning light briefly reflected off a ribbon of river, before it quickly disappeared behind the curve of the planet, in a riot of deep reds and purples as they entered the night side.

Flashes of lightning separated by thousands of miles danced to each other's tune in a coordinated display of pyrotechnics, illuminating the cloud tops. A river of orange lava from an erupting volcano wound its way across the landscape, while ghostlike sprites leapt hundreds of miles into space, seemingly to beckon the new visitors down to the surface, before the new star that would become their sun, reappeared in a blaze of triumph over the horizon. The long drawn out shadows of the pink cloud tops spread their fingers across the landscape in a spectacular vista. The dazzling rays of Ereus quickly washed out the purple and red hues of the horizon, bringing the landscape once again to life.

Celina watched the scene unfold as her mind raced. As Settlement Administrator the responsibility laid heavily upon her throughout the six-month journey through the tube from earth. 54 years of life had taught her a lot, but nothing could prepare her for this. The news had reached her about the true state of affairs on Magdur, causing at first a void of despair to open up within her, but that was quickly replaced by the steely resolve, and clear thinking that had served her throughout her career, to overcome the problems before her. Over a thousand passengers would have to be relocated until the atmosphere was readied and the settlement complete, but a research facility? What the hell are they thinking, containing those…things. So close to the civilian population. "There is no need to concern yourself about the Mags, Ms Novak. They've been neutralised and we are "repurposing" them.", they had told her at her briefing. So, when she opened her final instructions after leaving Earth, the full extent had become apparent. The 'anomalies' as they were euphemistically called, had dogged the project from early on and weren't showing any sign of improvement. The first meeting with the base director was going to be a very interesting conversation. She sighed to herself, then turned towards Captain Marcelo.

'I've got a meeting to attend Captain, please inform me when we are ready for passenger disembarkation.' Elvira Marcelo responded with a curt nod, as Celina turned and left the bridge, with the weight of a new world upon her slim shoulders.

To: Michelle J. Farrington @ electron.com
From: robert.nash@ galactic_vistas.com
Subject: Re: Are we there yet? Yes we are!
Hey Michelle

Here we are at Magdur already! The past six months have just flown by (literally) and the excitement is at fever pitch. Sorry I didn't get in touch sooner but as you know email while in the tube is impossible (supposedly). Still we're here now and thank goodness for the entangled electron email protocol. It's almost as good as live text. Instant communication across the Galaxy. Who would have thought it?

Before I start, I must tell you one thing. The ship is INCREDIBLE!! The scale of it is overwhelming. During the approach in the orbital transfer vehicle I could see the Arion in the distance, parked amongst all the other vessels. It grew in size and kept on growing, dwarfing everything else around it, shining like a silvery white mountain floating in space. It was so big they had to use EVA vehicles to get from one end of it to the other. Even from a mile or so out it filled my entire field of vision. I looked over at little Ollie and his eyes were nearly popping out of his head. He's become obsessed and hasn't stopped talking about it since.

When we got aboard it's actually quite homely. The quarters are like an exclusive apartment in one of the gated districts in the cities. No shortage of things to do. Shopping, leisure, restaurants and of course auto cinemas. There's an eco-dome that even has a blue sky with a moving sun above if we get homesick, which is good because Amy and Sam are struggling if I'm honest. I think Amy is worried about her parents who had the opportunity to join us, but you know what the oldies are like. Sam is attending school, but I don't think his mind is really on it. We've been getting the 'Are we there yet?' from Ollie over the past couple of weeks, so it shows he's getting a bit impatient for the next exciting event. Kids nowadays. Instant gratification or nothing. No patience.

Still thank goodness for Galactic Vistas. When we saw the video of Tim J. Kiefer reporting back from Satses 3 I knew we had to go for it. I always thought that it was only for the likes of the Milky Way's richest man to migrate to another planet, but now it's been brought to the masses. I still can't get over the fact that we've got this far. Through the application, then selection and finally the lucky draw. I don't mind the job as a PA to offset the cost of passage and in a way it gives me something to keep my mind occupied. I've already made a friend; a guy call Kyle Heath and I've even got some spare credits at the end of each month to spend when we all travel to the mall. Amy is helping out at the pre-school where Ollie's play group is.

We've been told that we are first going to be taken to a holding area as a temporary measure as the settlements are not complete yet, plus the atmosphere is still not quite ready for us air breathing earthlings, but it shouldn't be too long. It's got all the luxuries of G.V.S. Arion, so I can't envisage being too unhappy. Some people are upset about it, but I say what's a few weeks when we're got the rest of our lives to look forward to.

One last thing. I spoke about Ollie looking out at the Arion. I felt a bit sad in a way because I wanted him to look back on mother Earth for one last time, even if its beauty has faded. The equatorial deserts are really quite prominent from high up. I expected that but what I didn't expect were the ugly black scars littering the surface, the almost florescent yellow rivers and worst of all the small remaining patches of green. Do you remember when Mum and Dad took us up to the space hotel for the day? Clutching our atlas and looking down upon the scene below? The lush grassland and forest? The little islands glistening like a string of pearls in the vastness of the turquoise ocean. Well not anymore. There were no little islands to be seen and even the mainland had changed noticeably. It reminded me of Dad's last days before he passed away. The weakness of someone who once seemed indestructible as the illness ate away at him. That was what I saw looking down. A planet in its final days. A jaundiced shadow of its former self fading away. Whatever awaits us on Magdur it surely can't be as bad as what we left behind. Anyway, why would they send us 500 light years when they could just as easily make us ill and miserable back on earth?

Hope you are all well. You need to get yourselves on the 2nd wave so you can join us. I've been hearing rumours of conflict flaring in the water regions again. News is scarce here, so I look forward to hearing from you for further details.

Say 'Hi' to Charles for me.

Love to all,

Rob, Amy, Ben and Ollie.

To: robert.nash@ galactic_vistas.com
From: Michelle J. Farrington @ electron.com
Subject: Re: Are we there yet? Yes we are!
Rob!

At last. We were beginning to worry you'd been sucked into a black hole! Funny you should mention the space hotel. I was only telling Charles about it a couple of days ago. It's the kind of thing that stays with you for life. I hope to get the opportunity to do it again one day when I board the Arion (or one of its sister ships) ready to set sail to Magdur.

A few weeks ago I travelled back to England to see Mum. She's much better after her fall, but I don't think she's ever gotten over dad's death. The medication that gave us such hope only hastened his end. I tried to persuade her to come with us but she wasn't having any of it. I think she's still angry with you, as she didn't mention you by name once and I only got a sullen silence when I spoke about you. I took a trip down to Hayling Island or more appropriately what's left of Hayling Island. Do you remember the holidays there and the rollercoaster? Me hanging onto you as it slowly clanked its way to the top, before plummeting off the edge and into the tunnel at the bottom. I was crying and laughing at the same time. Mum was waving to us from the ground (she always was a coward when it came to that kind of thing) and Dad looked green with fright. You were the only one not scared! Well that's now about a mile out to sea. Just the rusting top of the rollercoaster poking out of the water. To think we were at the top of that not so long ago. At least it didn't rain so I suppose that's an improvement. In fact, I've forgotten what it feels like to have the patter of rain on my face.

Out here rain isn't an issue as the desalination plants give us all the fresh water we need (as long as you can pay that is). We did have a shooting a while ago when someone found some guys trying to syphon off his water supply. They killed him for water. What is the world coming to!!

Talking of which. The rumours are true. Ateus Industries sent its forces out to Europe once again. Apparently, there were incursions by the Grod Corporation as well as Badakar Services, but there's been stories circulating that it was staged so that Ateus could use it as an excuse to crack down on those pesky governments of Spain and Greece who refuse to pay the water fees. They shut the desalination plants down for a week and there were riots in the streets (fuelled by the usual suspects may I add). Eventually the governments collapsed, more riots, massacres and the closure of several 'Insurrectionist' channels and news sites. Ateus shares are up by over 10%.

Charles is well, and I've noticed he's losing his hair (HA!) He's very busy at work, but that keeps his mind off things and Daniel is starting high school next week.

I'll keep you updated of any developments and I'll continue to work on Mum all the way from sunny California. I'm sure she'll see common sense in the end.

Your loving sister
Michelle xxx

◆

Confidential
To: Brandon.Schofield@Ateus_Industries.co.uk
From: Celina.Novak@galactic_vistas.com
Subject: Re: Arrival

Mr Schofield

We have completed the transfer of the settlers from the Arion down to Pangea base. For the most part they seem to have accepted the delay with equanimity. I suppose that they are still dazzled by the thought of being on another world, but I suspect that this will start to wear off pretty quickly unless we keep them occupied. This is going to be a challenge as I've been told by the base leadership team that the terraforming is at least 6 months behind schedule and the construction of the settlement areas is also delayed. There have been issues surrounding the mobile Terraformers and unbelievably the Atmospheric processing plants are starting to exhibit problems. As soon as the atmosphere is cleaned this should kill off the remaining Mags allowing our modified versions free reign to sniff out the Nadinium without the worry of being attacked. From what I've heard (although I've yet to have an extended meeting with Dr Khan) progress has been (yet again) behind schedule. The Gargoyles have only just succumbed to psychic control. The Gorthon is being readied for its excavation role, but as we've only based our new variation on a dead specimen it's hard to evaluate. The same applies to the Bornix and we aim to use its aerial capabilities to increase the Nadinium prospecting. Again, there are issues with these in terms of both control and stability. Dr Khan has assured me that all possible measures are being taken to ensure a swift start before we move on to the next phase of our project.

36

Talking of which the settlers are being isolated from the main Lab area where the Mags are being developed. All efforts are being made to avoid a breach, although a carefully selected few are to be allowed for some limited contact with the settlers, to add a veneer of plausibility. I suggest a few low-level staff who are easily cowed.

Finally, one of the Janitors for the labs, a Mr Eric Herzog, met with an unfortunate accident when he got too familiar with a Gorthon and met a sticky end. We've managed to contain the situation and the protocols were swiftly implemented. Not even Dr Khan knows yet. The other Janitors are too scared to work near the Gorthon now. I suggest we draw a recruit from the Arion staff. Suitable financial incentives will be made available.

I didn't anticipate such a workload so soon after arrival, but I assure you that I shall not sleep peacefully until the issues are bought under our control.

Yours
Celina Novak
Chief Colonisation Administrator

Confidential
To: Celina.Novak@galactic_vistas.com
From: Brandon.Schofield@Ateus_Industries.co.uk
Subject: Re: Arrival

Ms Novak
First of all, let me congratulate you on completing the transfer of the settlers down to the planet surface. I have the greatest confidence that you shall address the issues with both the speed and energy that is your hallmark, and I shall be expecting positive news shortly, I have no doubt of that.

To the first issue of the Terraformers and the APP's, please use whatever resources you have at your disposal to resolve this unforeseen setback and make this your top priority.

Next the settlers must be kept malleable and compliant, therefore make sure that the leisure resources are kept to the highest standards possible. Also the ships counsellor, Mr Burgman is to be used to reassure and comfort the settlers before they are dispatched to their final destination.

I agree with your plan to integrate a select few of the lab staff with the settlers, however I would also recommend a couple of more senior members to oversee their activities. I will leave you to select the most suitable candidates.

Finally, while I'm concerned and disappointed that a member of staff was killed by one of our subjects, the blame does not lay at your feet and I trust you to take the necessary measures to rectify the situation satisfactorily.

I look forward to your next progress report.

Yours,
Brandon Schofield
Ateus CEO

4

Sophia Whittaker cried for the Nth time that afternoon. 'I DON'T WANT TO GO!' She screamed at her parents.

Her mother's face displayed a look of vexation. 'But Luke and Madeleine are expecting you. Isabelle will be very disappointed not to see you. Again, may I add.' Danielle Whittaker turned to her husband. 'What do we do now? I'm getting sick of this. Sophia's done nothing but cry and act up since we left earth. All over that stupid boy. Chris, tell her please. I'm not getting through to her.'

'I heard that! He's not a stupid boy and stop talking about me like I'm not here.' Sophia snapped and returned to her crying only after quickly checking to see if she had caused enough exasperation to her parents.

'Sophia. Darling… 'Chris began, using a ruse when he wanted to be good cop and the voice of reason. '.....Look, you know why we decided to leave earth. It wasn't an easy decision. Do you think I wanted to leave your grandparents back on earth? No, they wanted to stay. Same for mum as well. But we couldn't stay any longer. It's to give you and Jasmine a better future.'

Sophia had a furtive peek between her fingers before covering her face again.

'Another five years and where we live will be under the sea. At least Magdur won't be the hellhole that mother Earth has become. I doubt anyone or anything will be living there in a hundred years' time', her father said.

'We could have moved.' Sophia responded. She knew the answer before she even said it, but it didn't stop her.

'Where to?' Danielle cut in. Striding towards her errant daughter, hands out and palms upward. 'Come Miss know it all. Where? Our home was worthless. Nobody wants to live in a house that is shortly going to be under water, unless they're interested in marine research. There's hardly any safe space to live anymore. How many more times do we have to tell you, WE HAVE NO CHOICE!'

Sophia looked back up and noticed her mother's tears of frustration. Danielle tried to soften her voice and seem more reasonable although she was near the end of her patience. 'You will meet another Alex darling. In this base there are dozens of young lads who would make a much nicer boyfriend for you.'

'But I don't want them. I want him!' Sophia knew her parents didn't approve of Alex. He was a couple of years older, different and had a whiff of danger about

39

him. Not one of the chinless wonders that come from her parent's friends circle with their expensive clothes, nice hair and obsession with looks and fame. He had shown her the grittier side of life, smoking, drinking, and snogging. There was something else on the menu as well he wanted to show her but so far her fine upbringing hadn't let her, but it wasn't far off. Then one day without warning he disappeared, along with his family. They moved away and a devastated Sophia swore to find him. A few days later her parents told her of their decision. Life hadn't quite been the same since. 'You never liked him. If you loved me you wouldn't have left, for my sake', she pleaded.

'How dare you!', her mother challenged her. Sophia knew she had overreached this time. Danielle's voice was quivering with anger and the attempt at reasonableness quickly evaporated, as she took Sophia by both arms and sat her up straight moving aside the long dark hair that had fallen across her face. Sophia looked down shamefully before meeting her mother's piercing gaze. 'Listen to me....' Danielle continued; 'We love you more than you love yourself, even though you are a silly selfish little girl. We would *never* do anything that isn't in yours and Jasmine's best interests.' Sophia's younger sister looked on, sanctimoniously nodding as her mother went on; 'You might, but we won't. Fortunately, your younger sister has a maturity you've never possessed. At least Jasmine understands why and what we're doing.'

Sophia's tears of rage spilled down her cheeks. 'Yeah! Mummy and Daddy's little princess isn't she. Couldn't do any wrong. Always took her side, never mine.'

This time it was Sophia's father who spoke up. 'What is the matter with you? It's always your feelings that are the most important aren't they. Nobody else's matter do they. Does it never occur to you that there are actually more important things to worry about than your stupid ex-boyfriend!' His voice filled the room and Sophia was shocked to hear him shout like this. 'Alex Hyland was a gobshite tearaway and he had his hands in the knickers of half the girls in the neighbourhood.'

'That's not true.' screamed Sophia again. It was a shock even though she had sensed it, she didn't want to believe it.

'Chris, stop. We agreed we'd not say anything about that.' Danielle looked across at him.

'I knew that all along.' They all looked across at Jasmine. It broke the momentum of Chris's tirade. 'Everyone knew apart from you that is Sophia. You're not stupid. You knew but wouldn't admit it. Well now you do, so get over it.' The younger daughter intoned. The last words had a quality of disdain that carried more impact than the increasingly less reasoned words of her parents.

40

Sophia tried to feign surprise and hurt. 'And you never thought to tell me. Some sister you are.' She snatched a little vanity box she had received for her last birthday from her bedside table and threw it at Jasmine. It hit her on the arm and she let out a yowl of pain.

'I've had enough of this.' Chris was pointing his finger at Sophia, moving menacingly closer to her. 'Alex Hyland is hundreds of light years away and that's still not far enough as far as I'm concerned. Whatever happens, you're not going to set eyes on him ever again and thank god for that. Now get on with it and stop making our lives a bloody misery. How about maybe you think of someone else instead of yourself first for once in your pampered little life.' He turned to the others. 'Come on; let's leave her majesty to her own devices. She can sulk in her room until we eventually move out to the settlement as far as I'm concerned.'

'Good, because I am!' She shouted at them as they left her room and closed the door behind them. This time it was her hairbrush that was thrown at the door and it landed with a clatter on the floor as it broke in two. Sophia could hear the raised voices through the closed door of her room and thought; 'Good I'm glad they're arguing'. Her self-important anger quickly deflated when a few seconds later she heard laughter. Despair filled her and she cried even more, as she sensed the tension waning from the apartment. Sophia knew about Alex from Alex himself but chose to ignore it. It was the way he made her feel that she liked. It was… different but she couldn't put her finger on it. She knew what her parents, sister and everyone else were thinking as well. Their minds were an open page to Sophia. Sometimes even though no one was speaking it was like being in a crowded room where everyone shouted at each other.

Sophia had thought from an early age that everyone could read the thoughts of others as naturally as they could hear their voices, but as time passed she gradually came to realise it was only her. The special mark on her left forearm told her that. The bird in flight, its wings spread wide and the long graceful neck almost reaching her hand. Nobody had a beautiful swan on their arm like Sophia. Her mother used to tell her she'd pay a lot of money to have a tattoo like that and Sophia was born with it, that made her even more precious. She recalled the moment when she had realised the power she possessed back in the kitchen at home in West Sussex. The late summer sunlight was shining in shafts between the blinds. Looking up at her mum's adoring face.

'Ok sweetie, what am I thinking of now then?' Mum was looking down as she challenged her to read her mind.

'Jasmine's dinner!' she had excitedly squealed, jumping up and down on the spot. Her mother laughed while preparing the meal.

'Ok, OK. You got me there!'

Dad entered the room. Mum smiled and said to him. 'Hey Chris. Sophia is showing me how she reads our thoughts.' Sophia noticed the sly wink and smiled at her dad. 'So, what am I thinking of now?' she said still looking across at him. Some disturbing unfamiliar images crossed little Sophia's mind.

'….Sausages?' This time the shrieks of laughter came from her parents. Sophia felt her blushes and cried with the embarrassment of it all. Dad swept her up!

'Ok poppet! Let's go and play with Jasmine in the garden before tea', Dad said. 'Off you go, both of you.'

Still looking across at Mum who still had her eyes shut, tears of laughter running from them and her hand over her mouth, Sophia could still hear the giggles from the garden when she got out there. From that moment she resolved to keep her thoughts to herself and had grown adept at blanking them out for most of the time, although not completely. They remained a background noise, forever hissing and bubbling away. Occasionally a nuisance, more often than not, useful. She hadn't had a surprise in years.

When they had arrived at Pangea base, there had been a strange other presence she had noticed, as if someone was calling her name in a crowd or whispering in her ear. Sometimes probing as if trying to read her thoughts instead of the other way round. Other times her mind was filled with flickering, twinkling colours and a sense of movement as though sweeping across a mysterious impossible landscape, every so often there was a cry of pain in the darkness. Then there was the shadowy creatures with cruel bared teeth that sought her out. Moving closer with each heartbeat so that she could feel the hot breath on her face and hear the hiss of the frantic claws rushing past her ear. It felt so real that she started the first time it happened. But the strangest of all was the eerie purple glow that enveloped her in a fog, seemingly alive and listening to her thoughts.

♦

She checked her reflection in the mirror that lined the corridor of the lab area. Looking a bit tired she thought, noticing a few bags under her eyes. 'Must be the shifts catching up. Oh well only another three hours and I'll be finished for the day', she thought. 'It's amazing what you see as a cleaner sometimes. Not even the utility Droids can do this to the standard required'. She smiled at herself, which was a bit silly as she knew they were two way mirrors and the people inside would notice her grinning like an idiot. For now, she considered; I'm scheduled to shovel shit from those pens. I don't know what they keep in there, it must be the size of an elephant. And the smell! Once she had adjusted her breathing apparatus and taken a whiff. The tang of ammonia and a sort of strong cheesy fragrance singing over the top of it, with a hint of coffee. Weird. It made her eyes water. Once she'd heard or rather felt a low rumbling coming from one of the pens further along. She wasn't allowed that far along by the security team member.

'Sorry but you don't want to know what's in there and remember you've signed the confidentiality clause. You'd be better off without that knowledge inside your head I promise you…' Then he stopped himself. Whatever it was he had seen bothered him and made her even more inquisitive. It was better than in the vegetable lab. Nothing exciting ever happened here. Her reverie was interrupted by two familiar voices in conversation approaching.

'I'm telling you it was a roar of some kind. Are you deaf?' Said the higher pitched, slightly tinny voice.

'You know something Jonathan. I think the exciting nature of your job has given you an overactive imagination. All those genetically engineered broccolis must go to a man's heed after a while.' The dollop of irony was difficult to ignore even, with the Scots accent.

'Titter ye not Doctor Roe.' Replied Jonathan as he wagged a long bony reproving finger at his stouter colleague. 'It might be boring fluff to the sensational physicists such as your good self, but the preservation of food on Magdur will be a matter of life and death.'

'Oooo. *Doctor* Roe is it now.' The second voice went up even higher in tone, mimicking Johnathan's. 'Well the glorious science of Botany hasn't gotten us 500 light years across the Milky Way galaxy and the only life and death situation will be the people who commit suicide after nothing to eat but broccoli for the past six months.'

'Sooo sorry I'm not aux faux with Heisenberg's uncertain relatives but if the superstar scientists didn't have anything to eat there wouldn't be any special theories to….' There was a pause. A distant metallic like screech but with a throbbing undertone on the very limits of perception sounded from somewhere deep inside the base. 'There it was again! You must have heard it this time.'

'I'm afraid all I heard was a whining sound conflating two of the greatest ideas in the history of...' They both stopped and saw her standing there with her cleaning equipment. She smiled again. This time at the odd juxtaposition of appearances. The lanky gangling figure of Dr Gough, and the shorter squatter figure of Dr Roe or Dr *Low* as she privately referred to him.

'Don't worry about me Sir. I'm nearly finished here.' She said in a half apologetic manner.

Dr's Gough and Roe momentarily looked at each other. 'Ahh Miss.' Dr Gough said in his best patronising tone as he approached her. 'I'm wondering if you could adjudicate in a discussion between my good self and my esteemed colleague here,

43

Dr Roe.' The esteemed colleague gave Dr Gough a sidelong look that said more than the flowery language ever could.

'Well I couldn't help overhearing your conversations as you were approaching and no, I didn't hear a roar Dr Gough. Sorry.' She raised her eyebrow in mock apology. Dr Gough snorted in derision at the sudden answer. Not so flowery now.

'Ha! Told you it was your imagination.' A triumphant Dr Roe laughed. 'You're losing your marbles I'm afraid old chap.' The last part in a mock upper class accent drove the point home. Shaking his head Dr Gough looked across at his esteemed colleague once again.

Watching the standoff between the two friends, she spoke up again. 'I did hear something though. More like a mechanical noise. But I don't think it came from anything living. The cooling system perhaps? Keeps me awake at night.'

'See', Dr Gough said as he turned to Dr Roe. 'I told you I'm not going mad.' Dr Roe pursed his lips and shook his head. 'Thank you miss...'

'Wells. Eleanor Wells, sir...'

'Thank you Miss Wells.' He moved closer and peered over the top of his glasses. 'Very interesting eye colours Miss Wells. Brown and Blue. I've never seen that before.'

'Thanks to my brother sir. He hit me in it when we were kids. Only playing mind you, although my mum didn't quite see it that way. Still, it's given me a good ice breaker I suppose.'

'Well Miss Wells. It's been a pleasure.' Dr Gough offered his hand in a polite Victorian handshake. 'Keep up the good work, you never know where it can take you!'

Oh I do Ok, thought Eleanor. 'And I'm grateful to have the opportunity to meet two such fine gentlemen. Sir.' Eleanor noticed Dr Roe raised his eyes behind Dr Gough's back and they continued on their way. She liked Dr Gough. A clever man who was nice but naive. Dr Roe seemed the wiser of the pair. Watching them with a wry smile as their animated conversation continued until they exited the lab area at the far end of the corridor.

A soft but insistent female voice sounded over the speakers. 'Anti-Gravity Alert, Anti-Gravity Alert. Please secure all items. Unauthorised personnel must vacate the area immediately'

A less gentle voice followed the announcement. 'Oi! You should be finished and out of here by now. You know the rules.' Eleanor turned to see the man carrying a clipboard walking towards in blue overalls and a hard hat that looked about 4 sizes too big for his head. His short legs were almost a blur of movement, as he briskly approached her. Eleanor recalled her meeting earlier that morning, where she was told some heavy cooling equipment was being moved to the power plant and coming through her section. She never ceased to be amazed at the way a hugely heavy object could be made as light as a feather in the confined spaces of the base as they floated effortlessly through the corridors. It was important to remember though that the mass was still relevant and carried the same inertia. A fact seemingly forgotten by an unfortunate, if that's what somebody dying of stupidity can be called. Thinking that he could hold back a 3-ton fusion magnet moving at only walking pace was the last bad decision he made, just before it squashed him against the wall like a fly. They were taking no chances after that.

The man stopped just close enough to try and intimidate Eleanor without directly challenging her. She looked down at him and knew she could have him on his back and squealing for mercy in under 3 seconds. She smiled at the man.

'I'm sorry. I was just finishing up.'

'That's not good enough. You know the movement of these items is a closely controlled process. Any hold up can add hours to the transit time.'

'I'll move my equipment now.'

The man let out an impatient sigh and looked back down at his clipboard. 'Are you new here? I don't recognise you.'

Eleanor decided to keep the conciliatory tone for the moment. 'Yes I'm Herzog's replacement.'

He quickly looked up. 'Did you say Herzog? I heard he met with a nasty accident.'

'I wouldn't know that I'm afraid. Nobody tells me anything unless it's directly related to my work', Eleanor lied.

The man held his hand to his ear. 'Ok just clearing corridor 2E now.' He looked back at Eleanor. 'Right I'll give you a hand.'

'Thank you sir', Eleanor replied in her most grateful voice.

They placed the cleaning equipment in the storage cupboard and secured it, just as she could feel her feet lifting from the floor. She turned to see the man in the overalls floating like a little blue balloon, although weightlessness seemed to imbue him with a graceful nimbleness that belied the huffing effort he had expended in 1 G. She looked along the corridor to see the white wrapped cooling plant elegantly approaching with its attendant guides. Eleanor floated around the corner and out of its way, the weightlessness diminishing in the adjacent corridor as her feet gently came to rest on the ground. It reminded Eleanor of the slides in the park she loved so much as a child. The thrill of the slope and the soft landing. She turned to take a last look at the beast sliding towards its destination but was confronted with the little man once again.

'Ok you've had your fun. Off you go, I've got to work ahead to make sure there's no more miscreants like you in my way.'

This time Eleanor didn't say anything as she once again turned back. There were hushed voices coming from the opposite end of the corridor. The type of conversation conducted in shouted whispers. It was that horrible little creep Walker talking intently to one of his young lab assistants, the blond one who wore glasses, his hand on her upper arm. As usual Eleanor pretended not to notice while listening carefully.

The girl hissed. 'I told you. I won't!' Eleanor noticed that she appeared to be sobbing. They both turned and looked intently at her. Walker snapped his hand away. Eleanor walked past, seemingly oblivious. She could feel their eyes boring into her. The silence obvious. After a few moments she heard the conversation restart.

This time it was Walkers voice. 'We can speak later...' There was a softness in it that was totally at odds with his usual strident arrogance. 'In my room.'

'Ok...' There was a hint of trepidation in the girl's voice.

The dirty old goat, he's trying to take advantage of his position, Eleanor thought, having seen his type before and being all too aware of what they were capable of. What to do? Report him? To who? *Looks like Ellie is going to stick her boot right in the middle of where it's not wanted. You'll look an even bigger asshole than you already are.* That's not true, I'm only trying to help. *Help my ass. Being nosy that's all it is. Go ahead shoot yourself in the foot as usual.*

She glanced back over her shoulder. They were gone. Once again the corridor was silent.

◆

Eleanor thought back about her conversation with Dr's Gough and Roe. There *was* a noise Ellie. She had heard something like that before on the other side of the pens. But she wasn't going to tell anyone. Not yet. There were lots of secrets about the base she knew, that even some of the most senior staff members didn't. Being the Janitor opens all sorts of doors. Having worked as the Janitor in the labs for the past two months gave her a unique insight into the inner workings of Pangea and its occupants. How the civilian areas were kept separate from the labs? How most of the lab workers were kept separate from the settlers, except the select few, of which she was one.

She thought about the day she accepted the role of lab janitor and its strange requirement's. 'Remember Miss Wells, not a word. We are placing a great responsibility upon your shoulders and you come with the highest recommendation, and we know you won't ...disappoint us.' The final words carried an unstated yet definite sense of menace as to the consequences of a betrayal of that confidence. 'You see nothing and you say nothing…' Fate, for once, had played into her hands.

But in seeing nothing, Eleanor saw everything. All the secrecy regarding the creatures, the Mags, they called them. That there was more than one type of Mag. Even some of the people working on them didn't know that. Moving amongst the settlers, after all what would the Janitor know? She kept an eye out for her real subject of interest, always wearing her cap down over her eyes and being careful not to be noticed. Scanning the everyday life going on, silently watching. Being antisocial had its uses sometimes. She knew they were on there somewhere and it was only a matter of time before she found them.

What she didn't know was, now she had tracked down Bruno and, as a bonus Naomi, what to do about it. For months she had planned to kill the pair of them. The hunter stalking its prey. The sick fantasies running through her head day after day, each more sadistic and twisted than the previous one. Shoot them in the face while they begged for mercy and forgiveness. Tie Bruno up and cut Naomi's throat while he watched before castrating him and choking him on his own balls. Getting them in an airlock and slowly sucking the air out, smiling through the glass and seeing their faces as they gasped away their last agonised moments. All involved excruciating terror and torture before she gradually came to realise that she had become as twisted and sick as those she swore to destroy. Then there were the practicalities. A six foot four trained killer like Bruno and a SPC officer are just going to meekly acquiesce to her demands and offer no resistance? Really? She had no access to firearms. No matter how many scenarios played out through her head, she could see no realistic way of getting them into position, let alone actually killing them. Then what would make her? Even the voice was shocked. *Ellie the fuckin psycho on the rampage again. Twisted with hate because the world hates sick Ellie. Stupid bitch.* The violent daydreams had to stop. They were doing more harm to her than anyone else. But then what? Get them to confess all, take them back to earth and then kill them? How could she destroy them without destroying herself? Justice generally worked for those who had the money to pay for it. Not for nobodies like her. Driven by an undimmed rage for the past two years she hadn't thought beyond it. The set-up, the lies, the tongue in her eye, the violation of her body. The wanton, sadistic cruelty of it all. It had burned a big hole in her. Anger without direction to channel it is the most useless of emotions. Eleanor thought about all those who must have been stuck in the same trap as herself. Not looking beyond the sating of a visceral desire. All those mistakes and pitfalls they must have blundered into through anger, lust or greed. Eleanor thought she'd learn from them but she didn't need to. She would make enough new mistakes of her own that would more than compensate. Even the planning to

47

get to this stage, although detailed in itself, was only concerned with getting into position and striking. Not what to do afterwards. The move off the Arion down to Pangea base had been both a blessing and a curse. None of the other Janitors were interested. They were only concerned with returning to earth to collect their pay and wait for the next assignment. They looked at her like she was crazy when she stepped forward at the meeting, but the anger Ellie inside had made her, not for the first time, act before thinking. To pursue the vengeance that drew her in and yet repelled her.

She had seen death on more occasions than she cared to remember, and had taken lives in combat. They were distant targets, not human beings, not people with parents, brothers, sisters, children or lovers. A squeeze of the trigger, a little puff of smoke and they just dropped, dead before they even hit the ground. Like putting a sick animal out of its misery. Getting one back for the friends she'd lost, for the civilians they'd killed. Right was on her side and she had no qualms. That was before the ambush.

*

They'd been returning from patrol, early evening but it got dark very quickly in the south with the forest closing in on them. Progress was slow, they were lost. The musty smell filling their nostrils. Sounds were muffled, shadows played tricks on their minds. Senses straining at maximum to pick up any hint of danger. Then the explosion ahead. The gunfire, the shouts, the screams... The figure appeared from nowhere. One moment nothing, the next standing in front of her large as life, raising his gun. Finger on the trigger. Their eyes locked. Eleanor beat him to it by a millisecond, but that's all it took, the wafer thin divide between life and death as she pulled the trigger and the bullets ripped through him. He slumped to the ground with the minimum of fuss. No scream, no last look or clutching at the wound before sinking slowly to his knees uttering some final meaningful words. One moment he was alive, the next he wasn't. Eleanor didn't have time to contemplate it, there would be years to do that as she rolled to her left and took cover. The ambush was over in seconds as the enemy melted back into the thick forest. Silence reigned once again, the smoke wafting gently in the thick air. She became aware of the bedlam that had broken out around her. Up ahead three dead and twice that wounded. They'd have to carry them back to the compound, if they could find it. Eleanor looked down at the shaking hand that pulled the trigger, then over at the body who had been a living and breathing person a few seconds earlier. Wanting to walk away and let the forest reclaim him, something inside her somehow compelled her to go and stand over her victim. He couldn't have been more than fifteen years old, a kid, and could have been her little brother. There was a peaceful, almost serene expression on his face, no hint of the fear and pain he must have suffered in his final moments, his gaze fixed on Eleanor. She half expected him to speak to her. 'Next time Ellie, this will be you...' Was he there because he wanted to be, or was he forced? What caused him to hesitate, did he feel fear or pity? Nobody would ever know. Her face was reflected in his glassy eyes. People used to think that the face of the killer was fixed in the eyes of their victim for eternity. A cruel taunting voice sounded inside her head. '*Murderer...*' Every syllable drawn out to emphasise the reality of her action. It was her or him and he'd lost, but the cold sickening feeling of desolation inside told of a different sentiment.

A voice startled her out of the dark thoughts. 'Good work Private Buckley. You saved our lives. He won't be murdering our boys anymore.' She tore herself away from the dead gaze. The face speaking to her was familiar but she couldn't find the words or the name to respond. Eleanor swallowed and nodded as the tear trickled down her cheek.

*

Eleanor killed again a couple of days later and again after that, but the only face she saw in her dreams was the boy's. Eventually the fog of guilt and self-loathing that occupied her dissipated to be replaced by emptiness. She found that she'd been awarded a medal. 'For exceptional bravery in the face of the enemy.' but it was 'lost' at the first opportunity. She thought that killing Bruno and Naomi would be easy. They weren't some innocent kid caught up a war they didn't understand. They were her reason to exist. But when really it came down to it, the face of the boy appeared instead of the pleading faces of her enemies.

Another war, another continent. This time Eleanor was a sergeant, a veteran, a leader by the age of twenty-two.

*

Looking out across the canopy of trees from the open side of the hovercopter. The roar of the engines and the wind blocked out by the Comms chattering in her earpiece. The clearing with the settlement were up ahead. 'Thirty seconds.' The terse words of the pilot bringing her to life. She turned to her squad and signalled them to be ready. They'd done it hundreds of times before, exit the copter and form a defensive formation until it lifted back off, then move out. All in less than a minute. The column of black smoke told them where their target lay. As they circled over it she realised they'd been beaten to it. The burning huts and dead strewn in various direction told a story that words could not. Then she spotted the neat rows of bodies lying face down, even from above the bound hands could be seen. The huddled villagers surrounded by armed men were awaiting their fate in numbed, paralysed fear. As they came in to land, the red dust kicked up and obscured their vision. They exited the copter.

She turned to her Corporal. 'Set the men up on the edge of the village. I want you zeroed in on the big bastard with the blond hair.' She turned and pointed to the black clad figure staring over at them. There were only ten of them. Each armed to the teeth. 'On my signal take him out.' She turned and strode toward the blond figure.

'Seems you're too late. You've missed all the fun!' The white teeth flashed a smile but even behind the silvered sunglasses Eleanor could sense the anger in the eyes. 'Just finishing up here and getting the prisoners ready for shipping out. Sergeant…?'

'Buckley sir. And you are?'

'Captain Reukers, Fifth Special operations group.' He gave a perfunctory salute. 'Thank you Sergeant Buckley. As you can see they put up quite a fight', gesturing to the various bodies littering the ground. None of them were armed and no weapons could be seen.

'I can see Captain.' Eleanor took a deep breath. 'It's lucky they didn't have any weapons otherwise you would have been in real trouble.'

The confident smile disappeared from Reukers face. A large daggered tattoo adorned his right forearm. The sinews under it tightened as he gripped his automatic gun. 'We stockpiled them over behind those huts.' he responded before swiftly changing the subject. 'We weren't expecting any friendly forces in this area. Lucky there weren't a blue on blue contact.'

Eleanor raised her eyebrows and walked toward the bound crumpled bodies neatly lined up. The moaning and whimperings of the huddled villagers could be heard as she passed. 'And these?' she turned to Reukers. 'They were going to head-butt you to death I suppose.'

'Terrorists.' He responded as if he were describing a minor inconvenience. His face looking around before turning back to Eleanor. 'They need to be dealt with, quickly and severely. That's the only language these animals understand.'

A shout came from behind him and they turned to see the cause. A young boy, about the same age as the one in Eleanor's dreams, broke away from the huddled group, running towards the tree line about fifty yards away. Reukers casually called 'He's mine!' as he raised his gun and fired a single shot, dropping the boy just a few yards from the sanctuary of the forest. A wail of grief and terror rose up from the villagers. It was quickly silenced by some shots in the air from the soldiers surrounding them. Reukers turned slowly back to Eleanor. 'As I said, it's the only language they understand.' As the self-assured smile returned.

Eleanor stared back. 'I want you and your bunch of murdering scumbags to get the fuck out of here now.'

'I appreciate your concern for the welfare of these people Sergeant, but you're getting mixed up in things that don't concern you and heading for a whole world of shit, so why don't you take your little squad and get back to being the hero someplace else...' The casual tone chilling Eleanor's blood as he cocked his head quizzically to one side.

'Captain. There's thirty of us and ten of you. Each one of your men has a bullet pointed at their head and you have two pointed at yours. One click on my Comms and you'll be joining your victims in the dust, so I repeat, get the fuck out of here now.' Eleanor was surprised how calm she sounded as the message seemed to sink in.

The smile remained on Reukers face but his voice betrayed his anger. 'This won't be the last you hear of this Buckley.' Eleanor felt the final word blast from his mouth, landing on her with a force that felt like a physical blow. He turned to his men and motioned them to lower their arms as he walked toward them.

Controlling her fear Eleanor called after Reukers. 'The only reason I didn't click the Comms Captain is because I want to see you face the justice of a firing squad.' He hesitated momentarily, then without looking back continued towards the vehicles parked on the edge of the village.

When they were gone Eleanor beckoned her squad. The villagers were still terrified and refused to budge, but Eleanor put her gun down to one side and walked toward the group offering her water bottle. A small child looked up at her and held her hand out. Eleanor leant down and handed it to her. The child snatched it and eagerly gulped down the cool liquid. The pain Eleanor felt inside relented a little.

◆

When leaving the detention centre and out into the big wide world, the anger was a comfort blanket that she wore to protect and drive her at the same time. Only low paid menial jobs would take her. Overtime, double shifts. Living in shitty flats in run down tower blocks with mouldy damp on the walls, she had saved her money. There was no way she was going to live back at her mother's, even if she could track her down. Mother's messed up life on top of hers was something she could do without. She did visit her brother Nathan, serving life in prison for catching up with 'Uncle' Steve, after she had told him of the visits he had paid her.

'Don't make my mistake Ellie.' he told her. 'Look how I've ended up.' She cried harder than at any time in her life. The victim's irrational guilt still polluting her thoughts.

51

'I wish I'd never told you.' She said between heaving sobs. 'I'm so sorry'

'After what he did to you, my little sister, he deserved to die. I succumbed to my lust for revenge and look where I am now.' he replied 'My problem was our beloved brother, Leo telling the police in exchange for his cooperation. He was the one who put me up to it. I'm sure Steve was his dad. Killed two birds with one stone there, didn't he. Direct yourself to something positive Ellie. Aim for justice but don't let it dominate your life. You need to breathe. I know it's hard but you have to think of yourself first.'

She hugged him, left and completely disregarded his advice. He's never been through what I've suffered. The powerlessness, the pain, the defilement. All needed an object to focus on, and Bruno's grinning, mocking face was all she could see. His momentary flash of weakness and fear in the cell was all the fuel she required to sustain her. Through the long slogging hours, she accrued enough money to hire the private investigator. She discovered Bruno had left the academy shortly after to apply for the trip to Magdur on the G.V.S Arion. Why? And why he was taking Naomi she hadn't figured out yet. Using the remainder of her money to buy a false identity. She was keeping Eleanor. Fuck losing her first name, she thought. Having lost enough already, that was one step too far. To apply for the janitor's job, to land it (after she'd frightened off the other applicant identified by the investigator). Each step painstakingly planned, like an assault on a forest compound. No stone left unturned, every eventuality planned for. No possibility of failure. Now here she was, in a research base, on a planet orbiting a star five hundred light years from earth, or six months by The Tube. Naomi was Bruno's weak spot. Naomi was *anybody's* weak spot. Aim for her first. Eleanor smiled grimly to herself, relishing the thought of being alone with Naomi Mann once more. I wonder what she's got to say for herself. I'll scare the shit out of her…

5

'Anything?'

'Not yet. Give me time.'

'I've given you six months and you've shown me nothing.'

'Well, it's not that easy. I can't seem to find the right moment. I can't be too obvious.'

'Time is running out, and the perfect moment isn't going to arrive anytime soon. You need to force the issues and get moving. Perhaps you should try a less direct approach.'

'How about those around him? Maybe that could be a way in.'

'You need to do something and fast. All I need is to be in position then I'll work my magic. You've done so well and we can't let this opportunity pass otherwise all our plans will come to naught.'

'Someone's approaching. I've got to go.'

'Don't fail me.'

'I've never failed you and I never will.'

6

The moon's light reflected off the pitch black water, as smooth and still as obsidian. Behind her she could feel the creature moving slowly toward her, reaching out but not quite touching, the breathing silent but deafening, heavy yet soft. A reverberating presence just behind. Don't turn around; it'll know who you are, she told herself. She was frozen to the spot with terror. A paralysis so complete, she couldn't even breathe. As long as it was light she knew the creature couldn't touch her, but the moon was sinking. A figure appeared on the horizon, silhouetted against the moonlight. It was holding something. A rope, and it was formed in a lasso. The figure, tall with a hunched back and long spindly legs turned, the two dim orange lights of its eyes peered straight at her. She was unable to see but she felt the figure smiling at her, she knew what he was going to do next as he raised his arm and lazily twirled the lasso around before throwing it at the moon. 'No please don't', she thought. The rope hit the moon but didn't catch and slowly slid off and landed in the water with a gentle splash. The moon's reflection momentarily rippled before the waters once again stilled. A groan came from the creature behind her as the figure patiently and deliberately pulled the rope in and coiled it up. It looked and smiled again. He wasn't going to miss this time, the creature's breathing quickened in anticipation. The tips of her fingers began to tingle and became numb. The feeling spread to her legs and they started to turn to straw, unable to support her weight. The lasso flew upwards and this time it caught. The creature drew nearer, its face millimetres away from her ear. The mouth beginning to open, the breathing becoming louder. It was probing her mind, calling out to her with a silent voice. Searching her mind and digging into her memories, drawing them out into long delicate filaments, each one containing a thought, iridescent against the darkness, so slight but strong, quivering and resisting against the creatures pull. The figure began to disappear over the horizon towing the moon behind it. 'Please don't go, don't take it with you'. The moon sank lower. Turning to face the creature, the features barely visible in the disappearing moonlight as it reached, touching her face the moment the darkness enveloped them like velvet, taking on a distinctive physical quality. Something was building in her throat, fighting its way out starting with a low groan gradually building to a screaming crescendo.

Ava felt a blow to her head and wetness on her face. Her limbs were constricted as she opened her eyes and saw the light shining through the bathroom door that she'd left slightly ajar. She wiped the water from her face and looked up at her bedside cabinet, the cup still hanging over the edge emptying the last of its contents on her. Ava's breathing was still fast and shallow as she noticed the sweat soaked sheets entwined around her legs. A loud knock on the door sounded, startling her.

'Are you ok in there? I heard some shouts.' It was Elizabeth from next door.

Ava extracted herself from the bedsheets, went to the door and opened it peering furtively out at her neighbour, face burning with embarrassment. Elizabeth was one of the junior research assistants in the labs.

'I'm ok thanks, Liz.' Ava sighed. 'I was having a dream; I've probably been working too hard. I fell out of bed then the water spilt on me, but I think I'm safe from drowning.' She laughed nervously.

'Are you sure you're ok. Do you want me to stay?' the look of concern apparent on Elizabeth's face as she removed her glasses.

'No, I'm ok thanks. I'll clean up and get back to bed; I'm not due to get up for another few hours.'

'I've noticed how hard you've been working in the labs with Doctor Walker. I know it's not my place but you really should ease off a little.' Elizabeth offered.

'Well I wouldn't mind if we were achieving something. He doesn't exactly make it easy for us.' Ava immediately regretted her indiscretion to a junior member of staff. Elizabeth frowned and puckered her lips, which made Ava feel even more embarrassed.

'As long as you're ok.'

'I'm fine. See you at breakfast.' Ava escaped back into her room, shutting the door as fast as she dared, trying not to slam it in Elizabeth's face.

Ava replaced her soaked t-shirt and went into the bathroom, then looked at herself in the mirror. How can I start today when yesterday is still dragging me down? A stranger stared back at her from the other side of the mirror. The face of someone half recognisable in a crowded street, catching their eye, realising they weren't who she thought they were, then the embarrassed look away. In the prime of life and yet she looked tired. Ava had broken through each of the glass ceilings placed in her way. Despite the brilliant academic career, the intense training to become a consultant psychic, she was all too aware that even the youngest natural psychic had powers that far outstripped her and yet they all seemed so reluctant to pursue it professionally. She couldn't understand. The dark especially and the nightmares were taking their toll. They had stalked her throughout childhood into adolescence. Her mother used to leave the hallway light on, rather than having Ava waking up screaming and sweat soaked in the night, but that had only increased her dependency. Since college they had got less, sometimes with months between, but she still needed some light in the room. When alone that is.

The creature was a new element in the dreams as was the probing. Both had started since Ava had arrived at Pangea Base and commenced work on the MAGs. Doing to them, the same thing the dreams were doing to her. She never shared her doubts with anyone about the program. The potential dangers, the deception and ulterior motives troubled her increasingly deeply. And yet she was complicit, suffering from an inner shrinking and lacking some vital element of life.

"A unique opportunity to expand the frontiers of psychic research." the recruitment consultant had trumpeted. "You've been headhunted from an initial list of thousands." He flattered and massaged her ego and she allowed him to, even though it all seemed too good to be true, and indeed it was. Her first doubts had arisen as early as the second week. The creatures were living, breathing, thinking Magdurian beings. Walker's approach to them was a disgrace. He would argue that he has to maintain his impartiality, but there was more to it than that. It was the power over pain and pleasure, life and death and how it was exercised with such arbitrary spitefulness. She could sense the thrill of excitement when he turned up the pain meter on 'Billy'. The reckless pursuit of results, regardless of the methods was hard to take; including the routine boorishness he subjected his team to.

Harry was hard to read, even though he appeared an open book. The attention he lavished on the MAGs pushed the boundaries of objectivity, but it's good practice to care for your subjects. Other issues on the Gorthon program were beginning to surface in terms of downloading the software into their brains, and of course editing the DNA and updating that. Small changes had disproportionate increases in the anomalies, the modifications only pushing the issues further along the line as they chased their tails in ever decreasing circles. Already Titus the Gorthon had nearly broken loose twice. She was relieved that Dr Khan had accepted her recommendation, despite various protests, that a weak spot at the base of the Gorthon's and Hyperthon's skull had been included as a failsafe. Another episode and he'd have to be terminated and a new one regenerated. Then the frightened janitors had gone on strike after the death of their colleague before a new one was recruited from the Arion.

Even though Ava was tired to the bone, she knew she wasn't going to get any more sleep. Cupping her hands under the tap, she sloshed the cold water onto her face and returned to the room, then dug out the morning schedule for the Gargoyle tests, sat up in the bed and promptly fell asleep. This time there were no dreams, good or bad.

♦

As the moon disappeared over the horizon, the teeth and claws came snapping out of the darkness, tearing at her flesh and digging into it, holding her in place. A mouth appeared above her, gnashing and lunging towards her. There was no escape. Her head was inside the mouth as the fangs pressed against her neck and throat.

Alex Hyland was waiting for her, smiling. "About time, I've been waiting for you", he said. Inside was lit by hundreds of candles in a serene golden light. How beautiful she thought before her head began to separate from her body and blood began to fill up the space covering her mouth and nose, running in her ears, inside her head and filling her eyes from the inside, the candles floating but still burning as she could now see inside her own head, the tranquil light still shining…

'Sophia, are you ok?' It was Jasmine; 'I thought someone was in the room with us.'

'The light was beautiful.' Sophia was still half in the dream. 'I saw Alex.'

'You're awake now. We're on Magdur, in the base. Mum and Dad are in the other room. You're safe now.' She smiled and stroked Sophia's head.

Sophia was fully awake now and remembered the arguments with her parents and sister, but also the cascade of disturbing thoughts. Concentrating hard to block them out had made her seem increasingly distant, cutting herself off from her family. The previous evening things had come to a head at the evening meal. Sophia had sat at the table toying with her food.

'This is getting beyond a joke now Sophia.' said her father. 'Is there anything you want to tell us? Are you feeling ok?'

'Stop firing questions at me all the time! I'm fine. Don't keep on.'

'Well for someone who is fine you have a strange way of showing it.' This time it was her mother. 'Hardly eating. Staying in the room all evening. Your test results at school have crashed. We're concerned and we've booked an appointment with the doctor for tomorrow morning. We need to get to the bottom of this. 'She banged her hand down on the table and looked straight at Sophia demanding a response, which was the cue for her to resume the crying. 'I give up! You're coming tomorrow, even if I have to drag you by the hair, do you understand!' She pounded her hand even harder this time knocking a plate off the table. Chicken salad scattering on the floor. 'Look what you've made me do now. Get out of my sight!'

Sophia ran to her room where she remained until Jasmine woke her. Her sisters face was lit by the light shining through the open door. She had apologised to Jasmine about throwing the vanity box. Sophia loved Jasmine more than anyone in the world, and had instantly regretted hurting her, which is more than she could say for her parents at the moment. She had considered telling them about the strange goings on inside her head but they wouldn't understand, accusing her of making excuses for her abominable (their word not hers) recent behaviour. She welcomed the visit to the doctors in the morning. Perhaps he would give her some peace and block out the thoughts.

'Please don't be scared Sophia. I know what's wrong', Jasmine said

Sophia smiled 'You don't Jasmine. You think you do, but you don't'

Jasmine took a deep breath. 'I get the thoughts too you know but I block them out.' Sophia sat bolt upright in bed. 'I know you're special. I've always known. I'm the same.' Jasmine's gaze was fixed on Sophia's, who felt more naked than at any time in her life but at the same time a huge weight had been lifted from her shoulders. 'It's hard in this base. It wasn't like that at home, it feels more open, as if the top of my head has been taken off and the whole world is peering in.'

Sophia leant forward and hugged her younger sister harder than she'd ever hugged anyone in her fifteen years of life. There were tears again, but this time of joy and relief. 'I thought I was the only one. Why didn't you tell me earlier? I've felt like I'm going mad.'

'It was only recently that I realised.' Jasmine said and continued; 'I wasn't sure if you were first of all. I started noticing I knew what mum was thinking, then it started happening at school. There was another signal much stronger, distorted and hard to pinpoint and it's only been on here that I realised it was you. I'm not getting it as loud as you are, you must be more sensitive to it.'

'How come I couldn't pick you up then?'

Jasmine shrugged. 'I don't seem to be able to send the thoughts out like you're able to.'

'I didn't know I could. The noise here is deafening. Back home I can handle it but here I'm overwhelmed. It's like trying to drink the sea. I don't know how much longer I can deal with it.'

'I've read up on it online. Natural Psychics who can send out are very rare. It's estimated a few hundred out of a world population of about twelve billion. There are some who've trained themselves but hardly any of them are able to make any use of it. Nearly all of them keep it to themselves. Secrecy seems to be almost part of the natural state of being a Psychic and with good reason. There are rumours they've been kidnapped and experimented upon and all kind of horrible things happening to them, so keep it quiet. Don't tell anybody', Jasmine told her.

The enormity of her sister's words were sinking in. At least she wasn't going crazy, but at the same time she was in danger. Crazy sounded a whole lot better at that moment. 'I'll let the doctor think there's something wrong with me. Rather that than someone discovering.' Sophia said and smiled at Jasmine and put her hand on her younger sister's shoulder. 'I used to think it was my swan birthmark on my arm that made me special. No one else had one. It's funny what you think when you're little.' For the first time since she left earth Sophia laughed.

Their mother's voice sounded from outside. 'You two! This is no time for talking, go back to sleep. Now!'

'Yes mummy, sorry. Sophia was having a nightmare. She's ok. I'm going back to bed now', Jasmine responded.

The voice softened. 'Ok sweetie. Good girl.'

Jasmine turned back to Sophia. 'We need to talk about this when we're alone. I'm going to sleep.' She kissed Sophia on the head again before returning to her bed.

So I'm not alone. There is a light at the end of the tunnel. Sophia quietly exhaled as she looked across at the already sleeping figure of her beloved sister. The noise didn't bother Sophia as much as she drifted back off to the land of dreams. This time they were pleasant ones about Alex.

♦

Eleanor sat alone in the Cafeteria, looking down at the coffee she was drinking. The surface rippled as her hand shook almost imperceptibly, as she lifted the cup to her mouth and took a sip, the warm flavour tasting familiar and comforting. She tended to wear her cap in public places, but her eyes were on constant alert, flitting around the scene. She was still haunted by the fear in the voice of the young assistant talking to Walker and had learnt by bitter experience that some things are not as they appear, but still, why would a pretty young woman be attracted to a reptile like Walker? It wasn't as if he had the personality to compensate... She sighed to herself.

'I dunno...'

Squeals of laughter burst out from just behind her. Startled, Eleanor turned to see a dark haired man with piercing blue eyes speaking to a group of young children. His kindly smile seemed to radiate its warmth into the hearts of his audience. One of the children was sitting on his knee looking adoringly up at him as she pulled on his jet black beard. He jerked his legs up and shouted in mock pain. Some of the children weren't quite so sure this time and put their hands up to their mouths.

'Daniela, I don't remember giving you permission to tug my *beard*!!' The last word said in an ogre voice. There were a few stifled giggles as some of the older ones caught on.

Daniela looked up nervously. 'I'm sorry Counsellor Marcus, I was only trying to stroke it.' There was a hint of a tear in her eye and her bottom lip protruded.

59

'Well why didn't you *say* so. All you had to do was ask him.'

Done like a professional, thought Eleanor as she chuckled to herself. He placed his hand on his beard and whispered before looking back down at Daniela. 'He says you can stroke him as long as you don't frighten him this time.'

Daniela reached up and gingerly ran her hand over Marcus's beard. 'It tickles...'

'There there, that's better. The lord Ykdar will be pleased with you my dear.' A gasp of delight escaped Daniela. Marcus gently took her from his knee as one of his followers, picked her up and returned her to the group. The other children looked at her with a mixture of jealousy and awe.

Marcus looked at the group. 'Now let's see how much you can remember from our story earlier.' The children looked up in anticipation. 'Right, who can tell me where the lord Ykdar lives?' A group of hands shot up. Marcus pointed to one of the younger ones near the front. 'Cody?'

The boy's face was bright with certainty. He stood up from his chair. 'Uldir, Counsellor Marcus...'

A smile burst across the face of Marcus. 'Well done Cody, that's correct!' A spontaneous round of applause burst out. Cody sat back down again licking his lips, his little chest heaving with pride and excitement. This time Marcus raised an eyebrow. 'Now you are obviously all quite clever.' He looked towards the skinny man standing at the back with the blond hair. 'Even cleverer than some adults I know...' The skinny man opened his eyes wide, putting his hand on his chest.

'Surely you don't mean me Counsellor Marcus?' All the children looked around at the skinny man.

'What do you think children? Are you cleverer than Brother Aaron?' Marcus asked. Eleanor noticed there was a darker tone in Marcus's normally cheery voice.

'Yeeeahh!' they shouted.

'Oh no you're not!' replied Brother Aaron.

'Oh yes we are!' responded the children before they giggled amongst themselves.

'Well that's settled then', continued Marcus as they turned back to him. 'Right then. Who...' he let the last word hang for a moment before blurting out 'is the Mother of the lord Ykdar?'

There was silence amongst the children. Ha! Bitten of more than you can chew Counsellor Marcus Eleanor thought but as she looked at the sea of puzzled faces, a solitary hand slowly raised itself from the back.

'Please stand Priya...' Marcus encouraged. The young girl stood nervously from the chair. None of the certainty of Cody was in her face. 'Well...', Marcus asked.

'Ontris... Counsellor Marcus.'

Marcus looked sternly back at Priya, her face a mask of trepidation. Oops that didn't go too well did it. Poor lamb. Put her out of her misery Counsellor, Eleanor contemplated

'I'm very sorry Priya...' replied Marcus in a low voice. The girl's shoulders sagged before Marcus raised his head and smiled. 'You *are* indeed smarter than Brother Aaron. That is the correct answer!' Priya raised her arms in triumph and turned to Aaron who shook his fist in an 'aw shucks' fashion. 'And I have a special prize for my star pupil today.' Marcus produced a brightly coloured book, 'Tales of the Tadarida.' and presented it to Priya who hugged it close to her chest as her smile beamed across the room.

The children burst into song as Eleanor looked at their happy smiling faces with envy. She couldn't ever recall the safety and security those lucky kids felt. Only gnawing hunger and uncertainty.

*

She wasn't sure if the shivering in bed at night was because of the cold or the fear. The screaming every night from outside her bedroom seemed to come from another world and the door was her only protection from it. The passage light outside cast a dull glow with shadows dancing back and forth across it.

In the corner stood the old battered wardrobe and the creatures of the night that inhabited it. Scratching at the door, whispering, trying to reach out and draw her in. Sometimes they'd come out to play hovering over her, dark shifting shapes that just missed Eleanor's face so she felt their breeze, waiting for her to show any sign of weakness before they pounced. There was one girl, Gabrielle Kemp, who had dared to open her wardrobe and had disappeared without a trace. Until someone allegedly spotted her at a shopping mall a few weeks later.

Then there were the dreams, the huge rolling brown boulder that followed her relentlessly. Chasing her down, just behind, ready to crush her like an ant if she momentarily slowed down or stumbled. The roaring angry voices accompanying it directed at her, somehow blaming Eleanor for what, she didn't know, before waking up, bathed in her own sweat. Still too frightened to leave the sanctuary of her bedroom.

Eleanor badly needed to go to the bathroom. Ignore it Ellie, it'll soon go away. But it didn't, burning and pushing at her bladder, the pain growing relentlessly until she could endure it no longer. She peered over the covers. Outside it was quiet. The light was still on, but the dancing shadows were gone. The sound of the telescreen drifted in from the other room. The wardrobe stood in its silent vigil over her, waiting patiently to release the monsters contained within that would devour her. If only she could get to the light before it noticed. As she lifted the cover the wardrobe creaked loudly, daring her to take the risk. The pain was becoming unbearable as she could hold it no longer, until the warm wetness was spreading into her pyjamas. Eleanor screamed. 'Mummy, mummy!'

The thudding footsteps approached and shadows under the door resumed their infernal dance. Mummy's voice was slurred again. 'Facking kid. Wha'sit dis time!' as the door burst open the light from the passage streamed in.

Eleanor jumped out of the bed, safe from the wardrobe's attentions. 'I couldn't help it mummy.' Remembering the same sickly sweet smell on her mother's breath from the hiding she got the last time she had wet the bed, Eleanor knew what was going to happen. She trembled in anticipation. Rather that than the monsters.

'Look at der state of ya!', her mother said and moved forward, pulling the sheets back. The wet stain on the bed sent her into a frenzy of rage as she turned and struck Eleanor across the face. The burning sting of the blow was quickly replaced by another, then another. Her eyes red staring out from the deathly white face. The spit flying and the black stumps that were once her teeth bared as the blows continued to rain down. 'You fackin dirty little caah! Look at the piss everywhere.' Wheezing from the exertion, she raised her hand to strike again, the nicotine discoloured fingers ready to swoop down across Eleanor's face.

'Stop it mummy. Please don't hit me anymore...'

The hand resumed its journey down towards Eleanor's face striking home with even greater force. Don't cry Ellie, don't show any fear, she told herself.

'Ooo do you think you're talking to? Don't you give me any lip.'

Anger filled Eleanor as she stared back up into the eyes of her tormentor. Screwing her face up, she hissed, 'When I'm big I'm going to hit you back.' The vehemence of her voice surprised Eleanor as a look of fear flickered momentarily across her mother's face, before she raised her hand to strike again. Eleanor flinched in expectation of the next blow.

A shadow appeared at the bedroom door behind her mother and spoke. 'Leave her be.' The spectre of Uncle Steve appeared filling the doorframe. Eleanor couldn't quite make out his face with light behind dazzling her. 'You go clean yourself up Ellie. We'll sort this out won't we.' He moved forward blocking out the light and put his hand gently on her shoulder. His touch sent a wave of nausea through Eleanor as she involuntarily shrunk away. Steve laughed the hollow laugh she'd heard so many times. It was almost a spoken laugh, a sound more to reassure him rather than his victims.

Even the terror that was her mother seemed pacified by the solid bulk of Steve. Her mother turned to him and draped an arm around him, giving him a long sticky kiss on his cheek. 'My 'ero.' She turned to Eleanor. 'Lucky you've got someone who makes a fuss over ya.' All the time Eleanor could see his eyes fixed upon her, his expression unchanging. The same cold look as the last time he'd visited her.

She retrieved her only other pyjamas from the draw and made her way to the bathroom. 'Don't worry Ellie; I'll clean the bed for you', Uncle Steve offered. As she made her way past him Eleanor looked up into the eyes of her mother, seeing the fear and helplessness lingering there, clouded by alcohol. That one look told Eleanor her mother was all too aware the visits paid by Uncle Steve, and no help would be coming from that direction. Ever.

Eleanor reached the bathroom and turned the lock, relishing the protection it gave from the outside world as she thought about his last visit. She couldn't remember when they had started, but she knew she wanted them to stop. Ellie was his beautiful girl and he was her 'special' uncle. Remember she mustn't tell anyone otherwise she'd be in big, big trouble; the police would come for her and take her away to a nasty place where nobody loved her. No Special Uncle Steve to look after her. Imagine that…

She removed the wet pyjamas, throwing them in a pile in the corner, and turned on the hot water tap as the squeal of it filled the room. Don't use all our daily water allowance up Ellie, she thought as she watched the sink slowly fill halfway up. Even then the water was tepid and felt slightly gritty with a red tinge to it. She washed herself down, dried off then put the clean Pyjamas on. Looking back up at the door Eleanor could see through the frosted glass the shape of her mother returning to the lounge. Uncle Steve was alone in her room. Eleanor withdrew into the corner and sat down on the floor, drawing her knees up under her chin. A strange smell of bleach and Brussel sprouts mixed with urine lingered in the air as she sat in silence staring at the door. There was a creak of a floorboard as a shape appeared outside. The door handle slowly turned and there was a push on the door. It held. A large knuckle rapped on the glass and a half-whispered voice sounded.

'Ellie. Are you ok in there?'

Her mouth was dry as her words seemed to stick in her throat. 'Yeah I'm ok.'

'Ok don't be too long. I've cleaned your bed.'

'Thanks…' She heard his footsteps move away along the passage. The light switched off and she heard the lounge door click shut. The only sound Eleanor could hear was her breathing, as she strained to hear the slightest noise from the passage. A car passed outside, and she saw its lights crinkled on the windows. In the distance a siren sounded. Looking for bad girls like you Ellie, Steve often told her. She got up switched the light off and walked to the door. Turning the lock as slowly as she could Eleanor could hear the scrape of metal on metal as it gently clicked. Carefully opening the door, she looked along the passage, the light from the lounge door glowed gently under the door. Eleanor was still too small to make the floorboards creak as she made her way, silent as a cat towards her bedroom, wondering what or who was awaiting her within.

*

'YEAAAAH!'

The cheers of the children filled the Cafeteria. The thoughts of her childhood quickly evaporated as she lifted the coffee to her lips and took a sip. It was cold and she spat it back in disgust.

'Ok children! Same time tomorrow for more fun and games with Counsellor Marcus and his friends!' Their parents had returned. A few of them gathered around Marcus, the smiles and wide eyes of the mothers showed the esteem they held him in as the children, almost unnoticed clung on to a hand or hugged a leg. The remainder drifted away. Priya was still hugging her prize.

As she stood to leave, Eleanor spotted a familiar figure across the Cafeteria. Miss Matthews, the psychic, who was absorbed reading a device. Making notes and hardly noticing the untouched food beside her. She'd seen her around the labs a few times. The dark burnished sheen of her skin seemed to glow in the bright lights of the Cafeteria. To Eleanor, she projected a quiet dignity that in normal circumstances she would have found standoffish, but somehow she felt admiration for. She knows about the creatures in the pens and I'll find out from you Miss Matthews. Eleanor looked ahead and her mind returned to her cleaning tasks for the afternoon as she left the Cafeteria.

♦

To: Wilhelmus.schuiling@familyofykdar.com
From: marcus.burgman@galactic_vistas.com
Subject: Re: Early Days

Greetings Brother Wilhelmus

Please accept my apologies for not writing earlier but I've been consumed in the Lord Ykdar's work. I'm so excited, indeed blessed to be spreading his message amongst the pilgrims on this long odyssey across the stars to our new home. The scale of Zuzemis' creation is simply too much for mere mortals such as myself to envisage. I feel so insignificant against it all, but I'm sustained by the certainty that I'm doing the great one's work. We have a daunting task ahead of us in bringing truth to the souls upon this great adventure and I'm certain we can show them the love that the lord Ykdar brings us every day.

We have been held inside what seems to be a research facility, called Pangea that has been converted for our stay. What they research here I don't know, but I'm sure they wouldn't put us near anything harmful. We are told it is only a short-term situation, until the settlement is ready to receive us, however the main delay is caused by the conversion of the atmosphere to one suitable for humans. They seem to be carefully avoiding telling us any more than that, which does make me slightly anxious. Some of the settlers have confided in me about their own doubts but I've tried to project confidence that all shall be well. I've looked out of one of the few windows in this place and all I've seen is a rugged desolate landscape, although there are a few hardy scrubs scattered here and there. Also, there appears to be a slight purple tinge to the sky. I thought it was the glass of the window, but we were told it is indeed the natural colour of Magur's sky. Most curious indeed.

We held our first young disciples playgroup earlier today. It was a great success and oh how they loved it. The fellow believers you carefully selected who have children brought them along and encouraged their friends to join them. It warmed my heart to see the love contained in their eyes. I was amazed at how quickly they picked things up and I didn't even need the primed ones to answer the questions I put to them.

I still have my responsibilities as Pangea's welfare counsellor which I take very seriously of course, but it does limit my true calling as the lord Ykdar's servant, but my heart is steadfast and I'm certain I shall succeed in that aim.

I shall endeavour to keep you updated of our progress as before our final journey out the settlements that are being prepared for us.

Your friend and confidant
Marcus

To: marcus.burgman@galactic_vistas.com
From: Wilhelmus.schuiling@familyofykdar.com
Subject: Re: Early Days

Brother Marcus
I am so proud of you and all you have achieved since our paths first

crossed. That lost young man who became a leader and perpetuates the word of Ykdar, just as he did himself during the dark times as he gathered those around him to fight the followers of Xerdarr. Remind the followers that he too had doubts and it was only the strength of his belief in both himself and the greatness of Zuzemis that kept him going while others' nerves failed them. These are early days but from small acorns grow mighty oaks.

I'm heartened to see you have made a start with the young disciples. Children have the purest hearts and it's important to set them on the right path early and away from malign influences.

Remember it was Lord Ykdar himself who said that the way to truth is through helping others, so don't worry too much about the tasks that fate has bestowed upon you as you are still doing his work, even when you are not using the gift of oratory that you have been blessed with.

I look outside at what was once my beautiful garden that has now yellowed and withered in the baking sun. It thirsts for water that I cannot provide but you are the water of Ykdar and such a garden you will grow that future generations will speak of it in great reverence and hushed tones.

Blessings be upon you every day my dear boy.
Wilhelmus.

7

They had been travelling all night, as the first filaments of light broke the iron grip of darkness. He looked up at the opposite horizon where still high in the sky hung the glistening blue white light, silently winking and flickering, beckoning them back to their lair. They'd been grazing throughout the night. The day had become too dangerous since the white figures had appeared, with the strange breathing sounds like rocks scraping and tumbling down a slope, and coloured lights that seemed to emanate from the large shining eye that appeared to be their head. There were larger creatures with the strange round legs that the pale figures hatched out of. On one occasion they had almost seen him, but he managed to scrabble to safety just in time. He watched in silence, not daring to move or breathe as they carefully examined the markings he had left behind. Since then they had only ventured out in the dark.

He had become separated during the night from his companions and had searched around fruitlessly in the blackness, a growing feeling of fear and panic starting to shroud him. Not only of the white figures and their beastly queen, but also what would happen to him if he did find his companions. He'd seen the severed heads of those who strayed, leaving him in no doubt as to the consequences. He looked towards the blue white light in the sky hoping he would reach safety before the light would leave him cruelly exposed, but the gloom was ebbing away, and the life blood of colour was seeping back into the landscape around him.

He could see the figures in the distance, first of all as a cloud of dust but gradually individuals could be resolved, scrambling from cover to cover in an effort to avoid detection. He threw caution to the wind and scuttled across the broken landscape. His legs burned and his lungs were shrinking with every frantic breath as he let out a final desperate cry.

One of the figures stopped and turned, staring back at him, the early morning light reflecting in his orange eyes. He raised himself on his rear legs, seemingly beckoning. Then the figure turned and fled just as the flying creature roared over his head, trailing smoke, flames and sparks before it landed amongst the leaders of the fleeing herd, in a blinding, deafening wall of flame, sending parts of his companions spiralling in every direction. He looked around at the large creatures with the round legs bearing down upon him, at the same moment he was struck in the side, and the fizzling wave of agony swept up his torso as nothingness claimed him.

The memories still haunted Billy as he looked up at the orange light floating above him. It had been hanging there soundlessly for days. Each time he tried to move away it reappeared over him as soon as he stopped. Sometimes there was a gentleness emanating from it that soothed Billy as it coaxed his nervous mind to follow, other times it had shown him visions. Apparitions of hate, fire and something else less tangible as it tried to lead Billy towards the dark shape that patiently waited for them. A deep visceral dread acted as a barrier to Billy's curiosity, holding him back. At first he'd kept his distance, apprehensive yet compelled by the allure of the shape as the battle between curiosity and timidity raged within him, eventually conquering his initial reluctance as he ventured closer. He knew what it wanted. The space around gave substance to it. A shadow of nothingness suspended in space. Its absence betrayed its presence. A hole in the mindscape that Billy inhabited. The longer he ignored the calling the louder its siren voice sounded. The closer Billy ventured the more the burning tore at his flesh, consuming it with a voracious appetite, yet the greater the flames the stronger he became.

The invisible, clutching fingers of the shadow reached out to him, brushing against Billy, drawing him in, closing around him as he edged closer to the horizon, peering over the edge into the blackness below. The orange light drifted gently past him and down into the depths, inviting Billy to join it. A gentle hue of purple shone at the bottom as the invisible fingers closed around him, imperceptibly tightening their grip until it was almost irreversible, the force dragging him down approaching the limit of his strength to break free. The ringing reverberating, the burning searing and the clutch overwhelming. He could feel the point of no return rushing at him as he tried to recoil from the force that had lured him. The edges of his mind started to stretch and pull away from him. The purple hue became a steady glow as he felt the strands of his consciousness consumed by the shadow. His weakness against such a pitiless force fuelled his desperation before the inner strength that had been forged and tempered by the cruelties inflicted upon him started to resist. The grip of the dark fingers slipped, then relented as finally, exhausted he drew back to safety. A screech of anger and loss resounded from deep down inside the dark, reaching out with sound from beyond the horizon of his vision. The song of the predator robbed of his prey who wouldn't be denied a second time. Then another sound from the world outside the mindscape. A safe voice. Billy departed the mysterious world he sometimes occupied, diminished, numbed with shock and consumed with fear to see a kind familiar face smiling back at him from outside his pen.

◆

Tink, tink tink! The sharp metallic rap of Harry's keys on the side of the feeding bowl reverberated around the pens.

'Hey fellas rise and shine. Full English breakfast is being served. Chop chop!' He switched on the lights. Harry always enjoyed the morning shift, probably because it gave him the opportunity to also see what was happening in the afternoon shift as well. Night shift wasn't for him, he needed his beauty sleep, or so he said although he was aware there were several female colleagues (including Ava) who thought any upgrade on that front was completely unnecessary. All he really cared about was his beloved Gargoyles, especially his favourite. His focus was immediately on Billy.

'Morning little fella, what colour am I getting this morning? Green, blue or purple?' There was normally the frantic scuffling's of his Gargoyles when it came to feed time, except Horace of course, the miserable sulking little bastard. But this morning all that met him was silence. There was a different feel about the pen area this morning, but Harry couldn't quite put his finger on what it was. 'Hey guys! Wakey wakey.' Still nothing. Harry's normally cheery demeanour started to evaporate. He walked across to Billy's pen. Billy was sitting perfectly still at the back, silently staring at Harry.

Then Harry realised. He had grown so used to it over the past few months that he didn't even notice anymore, until it wasn't there. His head shot round to Horace' pen, who was nowhere to be seen. Harry's mouth became dry and his throat constricted as the tentacles of fear entwined around his insides. No silent brooding sentinel watching his every move with the orange eyes. Moving towards the pen, he got out his torch and shone it inside. Nothing. There was the hutch at the rear, pointing the torch towards it, what looked like the outline of a Gargoyle body. It wasn't moving and appeared lifeless. He rapped the torch on the wire mesh of the pen. 'Hey Horace ya lazy little bleeder! What's the matter, got a hangover?' Still there was no move from Horace. His instinct took over and he checked the other Gargoyles. Had they all been struck with a mystery virus? Have they gone on hunger strike?

Sometimes Harry could swear that the shimmering on their skin was coordinated amongst them through some form of communication, subtle and sophisticated. It was always too brief for him to notice, only catching the final flickers before they suddenly stopped. They were all like Billy. Sitting like ghosts at the back of their pens staring back at him. He could sense their fear. Without thinking, he unlocked Horace' pen and crouching in the gloom he approached the hutch. Horace wasn't even breathing.

'Shit, shit, shit. Don't worry Horace we'll save you!' He thought to summon the crash team to try and revive the stricken Gargoyle. How did this happen? What did I do wrong? I bet that Doctor Fuckin Walkabout drove him to this. Liberally dishing out the pain without a care in the world. I'd like to hook him up on the receiving end, see how he likes it, the puffed up little squirt.

Reaching forwards Harry saw a shimmer of red twinkle across Horace' back. He hesitated momentarily. A noise sounded behind Harry and he instinctively turned to look. At that moment a sickening pain exploded in his side as if he'd been kicked in the kidneys, knocking him onto his back. Gasping for breath, a shadow appeared over him as he looked up at Horace who was raised on his hind legs poised to strike. The Gargoyles eyes had taken on a blood red colour and were staring straight in to Harry's. His hands opened, exposing the vicious claws that were poised to strip flesh and sinew from bone. The sudden racket coming from the other Gargoyles filled his ears. Horace drew himself back to deal the fatal blow. Harry instinctively raised his arm to protect himself before it was knocked out of the way with a force he'd never experienced, numbing his entire arm and almost wrenching his shoulder out of its socket. Harry prepared to die. What a way to go, he thought, killed by one of my own creations. The irony of it all. It was almost funny. He knew this was it, and was surprised by his calmness as he prepared for death.

It didn't arrive. Looking up, just in time he saw the hind legs of Horace exiting the cage. Amazed to find himself still alive Harry scrambled out the cage in pursuit. 'HORACE, Horace! Get back in your cage now!' He was struck by the futility and stupidity of his words. Yes master, sorry. Only joking. I'll return to my cage immediately. Harry looked around for any sign of where Horace had gone. Broken glass and equipment were strewn around the floor. Raise the alarm first, he thought, worry about the consequences later.

The security alarm was on the wall next to the door. The team were always on thirty seconds readiness. Trained to perfection. Horace won't get far. The alarm was behind the glass. Just break it and get after him. Harry started to feel cold, giddy and his legs were shaking. Come on, man up. This is no time to shit your pants. Reaching for the alarm switch, he prepared to clench his fist of the arm that was still partially numb from the blow Horace dealt him. Raising his hand to strike the glass, he saw the bloody stump where it had once been. He looked at it and without thinking, used his left hand which was still attached as usual to break the glass and sound the alarm before returning to examine the stump which was pumping out blood in regular spurts. It reminded Harry of an ornamental fountain he'd seen as a child on holiday in a hotel, remembering how beautiful it had been, standing transfixed by the water jets illuminated in different colours. Especially

70

red. Harry looked on the floor for his hand but it was nowhere to be seen. Maybe if he could find it he could just pop it back on before anyone noticed, then everything would be ok. It couldn't have gone far; I'll be sure to find it in a minute, he thought. Gradually he became aware of a high pitched screaming over the sound of the alarm and looked up to see the face of Elizabeth, one of the female research assistants who was contorted in disgust as Harrys blood squirted over her, leaving crazy Jackson Pollock patterns across her face and clothes. What's the matter with her, has she found my hand? The lights were fading and despite the racket Harry felt very peaceful. The alarm and screaming merged into the jazzy sax music he loved so much. The swirling melodies were weaving their way around his head casting their magic. How lovely. I think I'll lay down for a nice sleep. Getting a bit chilly in here…

◆

Ava was ripped from her peaceful sleep by the urgent voice over the Comms of Jordan Harris, the security team director.

'Ava! Are you there?' Startled, she sat bolt upright. The books she'd been studying before dropping off to sleep tumbled off the bed, hitting the floor along with the glass of water. A loud crash filled the room.

Her voice was groggy and confused. 'Y…Yes I'm here Jordan. What is it?'

'We need you down in the Gargoyle labs now! We've had a breakout. A single Gargoyle. One casualty. He's in a serious way. We can't find the Gargoyle. You're needed to help us track him down. We think he's in the cooling plant.'

Jordan's words jolted her out of bed. 'Ok I'm coming. I'll meet you there.' Even though she was wearing only her night clothes, she pulled on her trainers and ran out of the room. After a couple of minutes she arrived at the cooling plant and was met by Jordan and Nicklas Overgaard, leader of Security Team Red. The hum of the cooling system filled the area. 'Right what have we got?' She asked, out of breath.

'A single Gargoyle, 191065N broke out from its pen approximately 10 minutes ago. We don't know how, but Harry Felton's been seriously injured.' Jordan replied.

Ava felt sick. 'Harry! How serious?', she asked.

'We don't know yet……' Nicklas cut in, '…..But there was a lot of blood around. No sign of it forcing its way out of its pen, so we can only guess that Harry opened it, but why we don't know.' Ava nodded, trying to appear calm as her mind took in the enormity of the situation. 'We've tracked it through the lab area. Luckily Harry sounded the alarm before he lost consciousness, sealing the vicinity, preventing the Gargoyle breaking out into the base. Our images and radar show it entering the cooling plant. He's a clever bugger as our infra-red can't pick him up against the pipes, nor can we use the radar in there.' Nicklas looked up at the tangle of pipes and cables above their heads. 'We tried running a remote camera in there. We caught a brief view of him before he ripped the camera off its lead, so we know he's in there somewhere. That leaves you Ava.'

Ava had to put all thoughts of Harry's wellbeing to one side. If the Gargoyle somehow broke into the main cooling system that fed the rest of the base it would be virtually impossible to catch, and could strike anywhere at any moment. 'We've got a problem. 191065N, AKA Horace.' Jordan & Nicklas gave each other a puzzled look as she added, 'I know. Harry's idea. Horace is the only Gargoyle that I can't read. He seems to be able to block me. He's different to the others and appears to have some kind of control over them.'

'So you can't read him. Fat lot of good you are!' replied Jordan. 'What do we do now? Blast him out?'

Ava just about kept a lid on her irritation. No better than that little squirt Walker, who as if by magic appeared right on cue.

'What is happening here! I turn my back for five minutes and all hell breaks loose.' He gave Ava a filthy look up and down. Her hackles well and truly raised. 'Hopeless bunch of clowns, haven't got a clue.'

Two assholes for the price of one, thought Ava. 'The usual levels of restraint and sensitivity on display I see Dr Walker.' Ava was satisfied to see Walker's nostrils flare with anger and his mouth opened to retort. 'Perhaps instead of you lashing out at everyone, let me try first to see what happens and that means YOU!' As she jabbed her finger at Jordan and Walker, 'Being quiet'. They silently acquiesced. Right Miss Matthews, this is your moment, she thought to herself. Take a deep breath and calm your mind.

The years of training made this almost a natural act, as her mind became a receptacle for Gargoyle mind signals. There was a feeling of being in a darkened room filled with mysterious shapes and textures, but this was a mental room, not the real type that evoked such fear in her. It was comfortable here as her mind reached out to make contact in the darkness, searching further in the emptiness, sensing a breeze here and some warmth there but nothing solid. She detected a momentary shape of fear and hate that moved away immediately. Ava recognised it and tried following it in the mindscape she had created. A perceptibly deeper black that subtly stood out against the surrounding darkness was before her as she tried to reach into it. The edge of the shape let her in a little way before it stopped her going further. It needed a light to illuminate its interior.

Walker's unpleasant little voice could be heard in the background. 'What is this mumbo jumbo shit? Can you hear me Uncle Albert...' His mocking was shushed down by the others.

Ava ignored him and cast her mind around. Dim orange lights, like those of the spindly figure who towed the moon away, slowly came into view. Moving away from the shape towards the light she knew it was Billy, and could feel his fear.

'Hey remember me', She coaxed. The eyes looked toward her, trusting yet nervous. 'Come on let me lead you'. As the lights came towards her they illuminated the space and she could see the outline of the black shape. The closer Billy's light got towards the shape, the further Ava could see inside. She was accessing Billy's virtual mind to peer inside the shape of Horace. 'Wow this is advanced stuff Ava. You'll have to document this later and submit it to the Psychic Journal'. There was another shape hovering over her. A benign floating diamond floated gently toward the darkness before it disappeared inside the shape.

'Don't be scared Billy. It's going to be ok', Ava reassured. There was something inside the dark outline. Figures, as they were seen through a gap from above. Billy moved Ava nearer as the figures became clearer. One of them was her! Standing next to her was Jordan and Nicklas, but the focus was on Walker. Ava felt the coiled spring of tension inside the shape ready to pounce upon its' prey.

Ava opened her eyes and saw the Gargoyle emerging from the gap in the pipes above. His body was a shimmering cloak of red and purple, mouth open, teeth glistening, and claws ready. 'UP THERE!' she screamed pointing frantically towards Horace.

Nicklas was the first to react, turning, aiming and firing in a single smooth instinctive movement. Horace who was preparing to jump, let out a squeal as the first bullet struck him in the arm, the next one missed, hitting a pipe causing a jet of superheated steam to erupt out, engulfing Jordan and scalding him. He yelled in pain and instinctively raised his hands dropping his pistol, sending it clattering on the floor, causing it to fire a single shot. The bullet struck Nicklas high on the shoulder of his body armour, spinning him around like a top, ricocheting up and carving out a gash along the flesh just above his ear. He landed with a crash, lying stunned and motionless on the floor, blood pouring from the head wound. The pistol landed at Ava's feet. She picked it up as the jet of steam rapidly filled the room shrouding everyone in a thick white fog that obscured everything. Horace emerged leaping from it onto a screaming Walker, who was knocked to the floor.

'Get him off me!' pleaded Walker as the aqua blue sticky liquid spurted from Horace' wound into Walker's face, its noxious fumes chocking and blinding as he rolled away, quickly pursued by a rapidly weakening Horace. Trying to rise,

Walker stumbled into a wall as the desperate Gargoyle closed in on him, ready to perform a final act of vengeance on its tormentor. Ava took aim but couldn't get a clear view of who was who. There were two outlines in the cloud to aim at. Which one to pick? One to be a hero, the other a murderer.

'Noooooo!' The scream cut through the fog. Too late to think, time to choose. Ava took aim at the figure she thought was Horace and fired. The scream abruptly stopped to be replaced by a groan, then silence.

♦

'She's just not been herself Doctor.' sobbed Danielle. 'She's not my little girl anymore...' Chris put a comforting arm around her shoulder.

Sophia watched her mother pouring all her problems out to Dr Ferguson with a mixture of contempt and embarrassment. Trying to lay the big guilt trip on me again. Usual crap, you'll never understand in a million years the daughter thought. The Doctor moved away from her notes. There was a reassuring manner about her that was backed up by an air of professional authority.

'Mr and Mrs Whittaker. I've examined Sophia and she appears to be a perfectly normal fifteen-year-old girl. I can find nothing whatsoever physically or mentally wrong with her.'

Normal! Some doctor you are Dr Ferguson. Little do you know, Sophia thought.

Dr Ferguson continued. 'I would suggest that the issue is more emotional and that some counselling would be the best course of action. We have some highly qualified professionals here, in Pangea base who I'm sure would be better placed towards a successful outcome. If you would allow me, I'll find the list of consultants who are available.' She turned to the screen and started to investigate the database, her fingers rattling on the keyboard.

Sophia looked across and noticed her parents were looking at her. Her mother smiled at her and she was about to return it when she became aware of a whispering in her ear. Indistinct noises, not quite a voice, not just a sound. It got louder and became a lamenting cry. In her mind's eye was an orange tinted light in the distance. A light blue orb was guiding the orange light towards a dark shape. The orange light shone inside the shape to reveal a tunnel with a light at the end with figures seen from above. Sophia entered the shape. Fear of and hate for the figures engulfed her. One of the shapes turned. There was a flash, she felt a searing burning pain and screamed, not only in agony but also with the urge to kill. Consumed in a cloud, a burning cloud, the face of hate looked her in the eye. He was going to die and he knew it. The face disappeared into the haze, but she knew

74

where he was going and followed, closing in. His throat quivering with a glistening fear that looked so inviting as she plunged at it, before another pain ripped her body apart, tearing through, driving the life out. She was almost upon the face of hate, pain and fear, looking into the terrified piggy eyes before it began to fade…There were other voices, familiar voices. Hands grasping her arms and legs as she tried to fight her way free.

'I can't hold her down!' Sophia's father said.

'Unless you hold her still for a few moments Mr Whittaker I can't sedate her!' Dr Ferguson warned.

'What's happening to my baby?'

'That's it. Hold still, I've got her', the Doctor said.

Sophia opened her eyes and found herself staring into the terrified face of her father, dripping sweat and terror before morphing into the face of hate and pain smiling at her, gently mocking, brandishing a large hypodermic needle. Sinking her teeth into the hand that was holding her arm, a cry of pain echoed through Sophia. The needle moved towards her eyeball, right in the middle of the cornea, getting bigger until it filled her vision, sinking through the lens and inside her eye out of the back into her brain. The noises became slurred and time slowed down. A bright light approached her and a feeling of peace and euphoric calm replaced the terror. The sounds melted, growing slower until the only thing she was aware of was breathing and a sense of peaceful release.

♦

Moving forward cautiously through the cloud of steam, Ava saw Walker laying still against the wall, surrounded by a pool of steaming aqua liquid. The Gargoyle was on top of him and started to move. Instantaneously Ava's finger prepared to squeeze the trigger again as a breathless Walker pushed the lifeless body of Horace away from him.

'You took your time!' Walker said as his head turned to see the smoking bullet holes in the wall a few inches from him. 'You could have killed me there!'

'Yeah, sorry I saved your life,' sneered Ava; 'Better luck next time.'

Nicklas staggered through the fog holding his head as blood ran down between his fingers. 'You saved him. We thought he was dead.' The tone of regret noticeable in his voice.

Ava looked down at the dead body of Horace, whose face displayed a serenity denied to him in life, suggesting he was relieved from the burden of his tormented existence. 'Perhaps he wanted to die and take you down with him.' She said and turned to Walker offering her hand to lift him up, which he took. 'After all who'd want to have you holding the pain button over their head.' She added as she looked at Walker.

A brief expression of shame and regret passed across his face. He spoke softly so only Ava could hear him. 'Thanks for saving my life. Perhaps you're right. It might have been better if I'd died and Horace lived.'

Ava was astonished at the gentleness and honesty in his voice. Maybe this is a new Leighton Walker emerging, she thought just as the old one quickly re-surfaced.

He turned to Nicklas. 'Where's Felton? The fuckin idiot must have been a brain donor at birth. I'm going to have his bollocks served to him on a plate.'

'I just heard over the Comms. He's in the infirmary sir. His hand was severed.'

'Serves him right, stupid bastard. Hope it was his wanking hand!'

Tears of rage filled Ava's eyes and her legs trembled as the shock of killing for the first time, took hold. The thought crossed her mind to empty the remainder of bullets into the obnoxious individual in front of her, but as if possessed by another force she let out a primeval scream and struck him across the face with every ounce of energy she possessed.

The blow knocked Walker off his feet. She stood over him as he looked up at her, raised himself on one elbow and rubbed the side of his face. 'Ok. I'll give you that one, this time', he said to her.

Ava glared down at him, chest heaving, her teeth bared, contemplating her next move before thinking better of it. 'If I could go back over the last couple of minutes, I promise there'd have been a very different outcome...' Walker looked back at her and she knew he believed every word, before she angrily turned away, unable to look at his face for another second, and left the cooling plant, heading off towards the infirmary to check up on Harry.

♦

Eleanor had guessed what had happened as she cleared the broken glass and debris away in the corridor outside the Gargoyle lab. She swept the thousands of small shards of glass into shapes for the automatic collector to pick up. The main commotion had died down a few minutes ago, although occasionally a troop of the security team crunched through, scattering the glass as she stepped to one side. Earlier she had been in the Gargoyle pen area accompanied by a single member of the security team. Not the one who had told her just a bit too much last time, but another almost completely silent one. No joy from him then. The pens were covered, except one where the door was left ajar, moving open very slowly. There was a lot of blood. Everywhere. Up the walls, on the floor in the pen and along the windows. Scuffling noises came from within the covered pens. From a gap in the covering, a small pair of eyes were studying her. A clawed hand gingerly, almost imperceptibly reached out between the bars and drew the cover aside. She could make out the creature's face. A shiver travelled up Eleanor's back as the Gargoyle looked into her eyes, but at the same time she felt a connection that reached down into her being, yearning to be acknowledged. Quickly glancing up at the soldier, who was looking away, she turned back towards the creature and smiled. A flickering shade of green and blue shimmered along the creatures back and into the gloom before the cover snapped back into place and the hand disappeared into the pen. Eleanor took another look at the soldier, who returned her gaze, shaking his head. Don't even think about looking again while he's there Ellie. The soldier's attention was now on his Comms and Eleanor took another look at the pen. The creature, whatever it was, had gone back to the darkness. Well well. At last I've seen one. Whatever had broken out it must have been more quick than strong. It was broken glass as opposed to ripped doors and twisted metal the bigger ones would have surely caused.

Back out in the corridor Eleanor was clearing the last of the glass when something caught her eye. It didn't fit in with its surroundings of glass and plastic that half covered it. It had an off pink, almost grey tinge to it and a splash of red. Moving closer, she shifted the litter away from it, stifling a gasp as she recognised it as a hand, tattered and smeared in blood, the little finger and the top of the ring finger, missing. Shiny pink flesh and ragged tendons hung from its open side. It wasn't the first time she'd seen a severed body part after her time as a combat soldier, but it was the first occasion she'd had to examine one up close. She leant forward and picked it up by the thumb. It was surprisingly heavy.

'Looks like I've found something interesting', she said as she held it toward him. The blank bored look on his face was quickly replaced by disgust as he recoiled, the colour draining from his face.

'What's the matter, never seen a hand before?' She was surprised at her own callousness as the shocked soldier talked urgently into his Comms.

He quickly regained his composure. 'Someone's coming down to collect it', he told her.

At that moment the strident voice of Dr Walker could be heard approaching. 'Of course, there will be a full enquiry Doctor. No stone will be left upturned.' A large group led by Walker came rushing around the corner. Walker was looking at the slight figure of Dr Khan, the research director, as he crashed into Eleanor. His eyes were bloodshot; he had cuts and scratches on his face in addition to the large welt on his left cheek.

'What the.....!', he exclaimed as he fell on top of her. His soft frame felt more like being attacked by a cushion. She pushed him off of her and they got to their feet. Walker looked shamefaced at Dr Khan whose saucer like eyes returned the look.

'Why don't you look where the hell you're going!' Walker shouted at Eleanor.

'I wasn't going anywhere Dr Walker. You walked into me while you were looking in the wrong dir....' Eleanor stopped midsentence and stared in horror at Walker's chest where the severed hand of Harry Felton was hooked by the thumb between the buttons of his shirt.

Walker looked down and instantly flinched, although that didn't do him much good as the hand was stuck fast. He writhed frantically, desperately trying to free himself from the cold dead grip of the detached hand. Not for the first time that morning he cried; 'Get it off me, get it off me!' to the sound of screams and groans of disgust from his entourage.

Eleanor noticed the tall dark skinned figure of Miss Matthews who had a sadistic smirk written large on her face. After a few moments the hand detached itself and dropped to the floor, landing with a rubbery thud. Walker's ashen face turned to Eleanor and emitted a howl of incoherent fury as he aimed a kick. Eleanor avoided it easily as she moved to one side. He jabbed his finger at Eleanor. 'I want your name now! You are fired. Is this your idea of a joke?'

'She didn't do anything other than try to get out of your way.' Eleanor looked towards the voice. It came from the smiling lady, although by this time the smile had vanished to be replaced by a cold eyed stare.

'I'll appreciate it, Miss Matthews if you kept your opinions to yourself.' He turned to Dr Khan. 'Please excuse this unfortunate incident Doctor. The cleaning teams are meant to have cleared up and gone by now.'

'Evidently not Doctor Walker.' Replied Khan in a low soft voice. 'I would say also that is the hand of the unfortunate Doctor Felton.'

'Ahh yes Doctor. Poor Harry. I'm very concerned for the poor lad', Walker said. Eleanor noticed a gasp came from Miss Matthews. 'I'll pay him a visit later in the infirmary along with Jordan Harris and the heroic Sergeant Overgaard', Walker continued. 'I've been tied up hunting down the escaped Gargoyle as well as directing the clean-up.' He turned to Eleanor; 'Dispose of that immediately.' He gestured at the lifeless hand on the floor. 'I'll deal with you later.' he muttered under his breath to Eleanor who raised her eyebrows in mock indifference.

Deal away dickhead, I don't give a shit, Eleanor thought as Walker continued on his way. Ava gave her a friendly smile as she passed. Eleanor returned it.

'Don't worry about him. We all saw what happened. Hope you're ok.' Ava put her hand on Eleanor's arm.

She enjoyed the brief and all too rare moment of genuine kindness. 'Thanks Miss. I've seen off bigger men than him.'

Ava laughed. 'I don't doubt that for a second. Nice to meet you…?' She looked quizzically at her.

'Eleanor Wells, Miss?'

'Ava, Ava Matthews. Nice to meet you Eleanor.' they shook hands before Ava continued on her way with a wave.

Eleanor watched the group disappear off down the corridor, the sound of Walker's pompous voice fading in the distance. She allowed herself a brief smile. Nice to meet you too Miss Matthews. Interesting, she thought. My enemies' enemy is my friend. Could be useful.

◆

He stared out through the narrow gap covering the entrance of his pen. The glass and blood were gone along with the small human with odd coloured eyes who cleaned them up. His mind felt free for the first time since his capture, but a sense of unease and emptiness had replaced it. There was another emotion overriding them. Betrayal by the voice. Its persuasive soft voice had coaxed him to view the mind of the other and enabled her to see through his eyes. There was another there, a different sharper but also frightened presence. Billy had experienced the hate, pain and death of the other through his eyes, but he had also sensed the freedom and the exhilaration of escape. Not the soaring across a shimmering mindscape. Not being in a cage or constrained, but an actual physical liberation. It still contained fear, but the joy of being able to move without restriction had instilled a sense of yearning that would not die with the other. He didn't feel the hate or the urge to kill of Horace. Only the longing to be free with others of his kind. He didn't know how he would achieve it, but he was now aware of the thrilling possibility and he would do something. Not knowing what that something was, Billy sat there in the gloom, but he knew it would come to him eventually.

◆

Despite the painkillers and dressings, the agonising pain from the burnt flesh of Jordan's face and hands didn't stop.

'Superficial first degree burns', he'd been told by Akeely Fergusson.

'First degree my fuckin arse!' he'd replied. 'Feels more like tenth degree.'

'You'll be fine in a few days Mr Harris', Akeely continued unperturbed by Jordan's outburst. 'Try to take it easy.'

'No chance of that.' Jordan responded sardonically.

Never being one to wish his life away, Jordan nevertheless prayed for the end of the current purgatory, but that wasn't going to happen quickly or painlessly. Especially as he would be spending every waking hour investigating how the breakout happened. Even with the comprehensive security measures, there's no accounting for human stupidity. What did Felton think he was doing? Entering a pen containing a lethal creature.

Harry was heavily sedated, but when he'd come around from having the stump where his hand had once been, dressed and cleaned, he told Jordan a tale that frazzled his ragged exhausted nerves. These supposedly reactive brainless creatures they'd captured were capable of foresight, planning, deception and acting. All very human traits, not the actions of primitive bundles of instincts that only experienced fear, pain and hunger so they can be thrashed into sniffing out the desired target. They continued under that delusion, even after they had genetically modified it, updated it's neuroware, and told themselves everything was under control. Not suspecting until it was too late that one of these things had watched, absorbed and processed sensory input, before executing an escape and evasion plan that came within a hairs breadth of success, and it had taken the combined skills of a highly trained team to stop it.

And this was one of the less dangerous ones! God help us if a Gorthon decides to go for a little stroll, or there's a group outing of Gargoyles. Yet this is your job Jordan. You've signed up for this shit and it's on you to do something about it. At least the weak spot at the base of their skulls gave him a minuscule crumb of comfort. Prevention must be the first step but what about if that fails. You've got to prepare for the unthinkable. If a few escape it'll be about containment first, but what if that fails and there's a breakthrough to the civilian areas. With some of the settlers hurt, after being assured they were perfectly safe on the base, they'll realise the lie they've been fed, and the danger they're in. Then the situation could get out of control very quickly. Beyond that there lurked a distant troubling cloud on the horizon of a mass breakout. There must be a contingency plan, a means of escape to a safe area to evacuate the civilians to, while we hunt the Mags down one by one and destroy them. On top of that there's the possibility of rogues and stragglers. The flood of eventualities coursed through Jordan's mind in a relentless stream of disaster. Each scenario playing out in its terrifying entirety.

Jordan looked around the room at those attending the secret meeting he had convened. The leader of Red team, Nicklas Overgaard, tall and lean. The sealed wound on the side of his head testament to the cunning of Horace. Sergeant

80

Montano, leader of security team Blue. Well-built and in his prime despite the flecks of grey in his short dark hair. In contrast there was the smaller bespectacled, not so athletic Ryan Baxter. This was more than compensated for by his unparalleled knowledge of the Pangea's systems, augmented by a fierce intelligence, making Ryan indispensable.

'How's the scratch on the head Nicklas?' Montano's jibe sliced through Nicklas' ego like the bullet through his flesh.

'When I'm as ugly as you Montano I'll worry, but that'll take my head being blown off first and even then it'll still be debatable.' Replied Nicklas gingerly running his hand across the gash that acted as a stark reminder of the mornings terrifying events.

Montano raised his eyebrows. 'Lucky you've got a thick skull, anyway the extra side parting suits you.'

Ryan, not being the military type looked mildly alarmed at the conversation that to the untrained eye was laced with a vicious tension bordering on the edge of violence. 'Hey! I thought you two were on the same side.' he ventured.

'Most of the time, ain't that right Nicklas?' Montano said.

'Depends who's winning at cards.' The deadpan features of Nicklas broke into a broad smile.

'I heard that fat little shit Walker screamed like a baby.'

'I wouldn't know; I was unconscious at the time.'

'Gentlemen. If you please?' They all turned to Jordan. His countenance illustrating the serious nature of the conversation. 'You may be wondering why I've called you three only and in confidence.'

'I should imagine it's something to do with this morning's events sir?'

Jordan smiled at Nicklas. 'Right first time! First of all, what we speak about stays in this room.' The others nodded in response as he continued. 'To be honest, I think the strength and intelligence of the Mags have been completely underestimated and I feel we are woefully underprepared. We need to beef up our capabilities but also devise contingencies in case this happens again.'

'And you think it will happen again?' They looked across at Ryan. 'With respect I thought that was the purpose of the security team and now you're telling me you think you're not up to the job!' The professional soldiers in the room bristled at the suggestion but Ryan stood firm. 'I'm sorry Jordan but that's the impression I'm getting here. It seems to me you have no confidence in the men and equipment you are responsible for. Am I correct?'

Jordan noticed Montano and Nicklas exchanged a brief glance that raised the alarms inside his head. Fuck! This isn't the way it's meant to come out. Think fast or you've lost them. Above all keep your cool. 'Not at all Ryan. I have total confidence that all the men under my command can handle whatever comes their way', he said. Better Jordan, much better. Keep it going. 'But, given our numbers and levels of equipment I feel that we need to maximise our resources in the most effective way possible.' He felt a wave of relief as the nods returned. 'So therefore we need to plan for every eventuality and that includes everything from missed feeding time to a mass breakout of Gorthons.'

'So have you got any ideas Jordan or is that why you've asked us here', Ryan enquired.

Jordan was unsettled by Ryan's directness but he was also reassured at the sharpness on view. 'Well Ryan, we could evacuate, but the practicalities of moving a thousand terrified civilians across a hostile landscape with a toxic atmosphere look pretty much out of reach, so considering your incomparable knowledge of this base I considered you the first port of call. In particular, regarding the service tunnels and how we could put them to good use in an emergency.' He looked directly at Ryan who held his stare, before continuing. 'Also a refuge for people to stay until we bring them under control. So that's why I brought you in.'

Ryan considered Jordan's words carefully before responding. 'The best place for a sanctuary would be the storage areas. There's several smaller ones but there's two main bays. One on the eastern side and the other at the western end of the base. There's also the Eva shuttle bays on the northern side, but most of the supplies for the colonisation phase haven't been moved there yet.'

Montano spoke up. 'And us sir? What's our role in this?'

'I was about to come to that Sergeant', Jordan said and continued; 'I want both of you to select one member from each of your teams. The best you've got. Then Ryan here can take them and show them the Service tunnel network so they'll know it in their sleep by the time he's finished with them. Are you ok with this Ryan?'

'Of course Jordan, but remember the base is huge, so knowing every nook and cranny is beyond mere mortals, which is why I'm responsible for knowing it instead!'

'I wouldn't expect anything else Ryan.' He turned to the sergeants. 'Any suggestions on who you'd put forward.'

Nicklas replied first. 'Fynn Michels sir. No hesitation.'

'A fine choice.' Jordan turned to Montano. 'Sergeant?'

'Denise Auger Sir. In terms of navigation alone she's the best anywhere and generally better than anyone Sergeant Overgaard can offer.'

Overgaard didn't rise to the bait but smiled and shook his head.

'Ok gentlemen. Please proceed with all haste. As soon as Michels and Auger are up to speed we can roll it out to the rest of the teams', Jordan told them.

Ryan raised his eyebrows. 'What about the SPC Jordan. Won't they need to know? Maybe we could use them as well.'

This time it was Montano who responded. 'I wouldn't trust those shithats to find their way out of a field, let alone a complex web of tunnels. Plus of course they're not to know about us or the Mags, so that's a big "No no" Sir.'

Ryan rolled his eyes. 'I never really understood all this pointless interservice rivalry shit.'

'We're special forces.' Nicklas cut in. 'The SPC are specialists in fuck ups.'

Montano laughed. 'At least we can agree on something Nicklas.'

'There's a first time for everything I suppose.'

The meeting broke up amidst laughter. Phew, Jordan, that went better than I expected. That's one more thing off the pile of crap I've got to deal with. For a few brief moments he forgot about the nagging pain as the sense of fear and foreboding eased a little off his shoulders.

8

03:15. Magdur mean time display cast its pale green light across the bedroom as Bruno shifted uneasily. Beside him the sleeping figure of Naomi stirred. He studied her peaceful features with a feeling of disdain. Her beauty was undimmed as her long dark hair lay unfurled across the pillow, but the novelty had long since turned to resentment for Bruno.

'Take them away. They've got heads on them.' Naomi mumbled as she shifted, curling into a foetal position, settling into a new slower breathing pattern.

'I wish someone would take you away. Without the fuckin head preferably.' he whispered to himself.

A frown spread across her face and she caught her breath before slurring 'Wassat...'

He made no reply and remained silently observing her continued slumber. Her constant stirring and mutterings had kept Bruno awake since they finished a frantic humping session, or lovemaking as she preferred to call it, over four hours earlier. Her obvious enthusiasm and skill didn't make up for the fact that he was bored beyond endurance with her and there was no love made as far as he was concerned. Just a biological function satisfied. Her needy insecure jealously swamped his relentless wandering libido, as well as slowly puncturing his overinflated ego.

Back in his quarters at the academy on the final night together with Naomi before the recruits left for their assignments, Bruno hadn't laughed as much in years as they were recalling the events of the previous day in the hearing.

Lying next to him Naomi had propped herself up on her arm, the look of vindication spread across her triumphant expression. 'Serves her right, tried to stab me in the back and get me thrown off the course after I helped her to pass. Lucky I had my big bear to give me the heads up, and did you see her face when I started the sobbing. God I was nearly wetting myself. "Cadet Naomi, Are these the papers?"' Naomi was recalling in the deepest voice she could muster, tears of mirth rolling down her cheeks.

'Yes, your honourableness.' squeaked Bruno in his highest falsetto before he resumed in an affected angry voice. 'I'm gonna get you Naomi, Oooo you little cow you.'

'Silence in court.' She smacked Bruno's naked buttock as he lay helpless with laughter on the bed. 'Guilty as charged! I sentence you to be hanged by the neck until you fuck off.' They both screamed with laughter although Bruno less so. His

84

mind was back in the holding cell during his friendly little farewell visit he had paid Eleanor earlier that morning. Ungrateful little shit. He'd shown her a good time and all she did was insult him. Little Man, little man! From a poisonous midget who'd been put in her place. The audacity of it. It was her own fault and she got what she deserved. Bollocks to her. There was one thing though which had unnerved him as she'd looked up at him from the corner of the cell, nose bleeding and wheezing for breath. The blazing fire of hatred in her eyes. He had seen it before when he participated in the terrorist sweeps during the Water Wars ten years earlier.

*

They had been diverting the water supply from the main feed into their village. It was no good trying to conceal the water store, they would find it. They always did. Bruno's squad were searching the houses, screams and crashing coming from within. One by one the houses were being torched. A piglet hared along squealing through the scene of destruction. A trail of machine gun bullets had chased it along the ground and caught up with it, sending it twirling and wriggling through the air as they found their mark, accompanied by howls of hilarity as the dead pink figure landed with a comical bounce as if it was made of rubber.

'Bacon sarnies tonight lads!' called one of the squad to wild cheers and raucous laughter from his colleagues. The acrid smoke of the burning huts surrounded by the bloodied bodies of those who had resisted filled the air. Glowing embers swirled in the breeze as Bruno stood over the woman kneeling on the ground rocking back and forth, cradling the tiny lifeless body of her baby. A low keening moan was the only sound she made. Sitting next to her was a small child, no older than four or five. Struck dumb by shock, gazing vacantly into space as she trembled in numbed terror, a trickle of blood running from her scalp down her face which was a pale mask of light brown dust with two clear channels down either cheek where the tears had once run. Bruno leant forward, grabbing the crying mother by the hair and yanking her head back. One eye was swollen shut while the other was rolled back, as her mouth lolled open in incoherent grief. A glistening filament of saliva stood prominent in the open empty space between her lips. Bruno pulled his pistol from its holster and thrust the muzzle into her mouth. The moaning went up a level.

Bruno was yelling into her face, trying to make himself heard above the cacophony of flames, gunfire and hover copters. 'Stupid fuckin animal. What's the matter with you people! Tell us where you've hidden the water and we can all go home.' He pulled the gun back and hit her in the face with the butt. The groaning continued unabated. 'Ok no more mister nice guy. You wanna fuck me about, this is what happens!' He said and pointed the gun at the small girl's head.

'One down, one to go! Your choice. Make your mind up. You understand me ok now?' The small girl stopped shaking and turned, looking Bruno straight in the eye, daring him to put a bullet in her head. Her relentless gaze bore into him. The fear had vanished, replaced by the fires of hell that was contained within her dark eyes, burning through him with their loathing and contempt. Her face was blank but the eyes contained the concentrated hate of every human who ever lived, and it was directed at Bruno. Swallowing hard, a tingling fear danced on his jangling nerves. It felt as if it was the little girl who held the gun to his head. He was the victim, not knowing if he'd make it through the next few moments. Tearing his stare away from the small terror and back towards her mother. Shaking her head with renewed brutality, he pulled the piteous face closer to his, filling his vision and blocking the girl from view. 'One more chance, where's the water?', he demanded.

A familiar voice sounded in the distance and caught his attention. 'Hey Sergeant!' Bruno looked around towards the other smiling squad members running back towards him waving their arms. 'We've found it, over by the ditch, hidden in a tunnel. Crafty bastards', one of them shouted.

Although their objective was achieved, his anger continued unabated, turning back to the mother. 'Thought you were clever didn't ya.' She was shaking her head pleadingly.

'No…No…No…'

'This is for wasting my time.' Without looking, Bruno pulled the trigger. The shot tore through the surrounding noise as the lifeless body of the girl was driven backwards into the ground like a rag doll. The mothers' screams filled the air. A sound that could only be made by someone who had suffered the ultimate outrage. The limits of the human voice were exceeded in her shrill grief as she knelt over the broken violated body of her daughter, the blood soaking into the dust behind her shattered head. She turned to Bruno. An animal ferocity erupted across her previously broken features, her teeth were bared, her nails became talons and her face a frenzied mask of hatred as she hurled herself at him. The next bullet from his pistol stopped her as she thumped into the dust joining her children in death. 'Fuckin Animals, the lot of them.' He turned to the silent watching group of soldiers who had stopped in their tracks.

'What'd ya do that for? We found the water. There was no need for that you murdering piece of shit.' It was one of the corporals.

'She went for me, you saw it yourself.'

'After you blew her daughter's head off she was entitled to. They were no threat.' The Corporals face was red with disgust and rage. His chest was heaving. The rest of the squad stood in silence.

'You know they were terrorists. We've got a job to do. It's the only language they understand. Anyway, I'm saving lives. When word gets around we mean business no one is going to be stealing any water, ever. Remember who pay your wages guys.' Bruno ventured a smile, but they turned away muttering to each other. A couple of days later they were all dead in a hover copter crash. All except Bruno that is...The price of crossing him had been paid.

*

But it was the look that had unnerved him. The ghost of the girl haunted him through Eleanor. Not having a conscience helped. Anyway she'd have only grown up a terrorist like her mother. Oh to have done that to the poison dwarf. Never mind she's hundreds of light years away and he had bigger problems to worry about at the moment. Like being screwed over by that worm Sinclair. His mind drifted back to the meeting in the Captains office at the academy.

*

'Sit down please Sergeant.' Captain Sinclair had said, motioning to the other side of the desk in his private office. It was a couple of days after the hearing. Bruno noticed that Sinclair avoided eye contact. 'I assume you know why I've asked you to attend this meeting.'

'I would imagine it would have something to do with my promotion request Sir. After all I've carried out and exceeded every goal you set out during my previous unsuccessful application.' Bruno deliberately stressed the penultimate word as he sat down.

'Indeed, Sergeant. You have far surpassed every objective you were set in our last meeting.' He looked up at the daunting bulk of Bruno across the desk who continued to stare impassively back, before he continued. 'However, the situation has now changed and new factors have come into play.'

'What factors would they be sir?' Bruno tried to keep his voice unchanged but it had acquired a deeper, more menacing quality and the atmosphere in the room changed accordingly.

Sinclair let out a short nervous laugh, but Bruno remained expressionless. 'Well before we jump to conclusions there's good news.....', the captain continued although there was no change in Bruno. 'And then there's other news, which isn't bad, but also isn't as good as the good news, if you see what I mean.'

Bruno raised his eyebrows and his head slightly. Get on with it pussy. I haven't got all day, he thought then said. 'Not sure I follow your meaning sir.'

'Ok, well an opportunity has arisen which I think could benefit all parties involved.'

'Please continue.' Bruno's curiosity was starting to get the better of him.

'I have a former comrade in arms....'

87

In arms? You've only ever filled out forms, Bruno was thinking as Sinclair carried on.

'He's putting together a team for an upcoming trip.'

'Where to?'

'It's not too bad. It's called Magdur. It's the sixth planet of the system and orbits right in the middle of the goldilocks zone around a yellow dwarf main sequence star, Ereus in the constellation of Cygnus, very similar to our Sun as it happens, about five hundred light years away. Initial scans and reconnaissance have indicated a benign environment, again similar to Earth before the Great Heat started in the late 20th Century, although some terraforming has taken place.'

Bruno gently nodded and Sinclair continued. 'Transit is on a planet colonising class C interstellar cruiser, the...' he checked his notes; '.....G.V.S. Arion. It'll be about a thousand colonists and crew, trip should be about six months by tube, so best you top up your oyster card.' Bruno smiled outwardly but sneered inside at Sinclair's pathetic attempt at a joke. 'When you arrive. That'll be when your role comes into effect.'

'Which is...'

'Well, it's planned to last about two years before you are rotated out. Obviously it's a newly discovered planet and everything looks fine, but as we've found to our cost it's best to be prepared in case unexpected circumstances arise. After all, you're a long way from home. So you'll be 2nd in Command of the protection team, to help Colonel Gutierrez. You'll be leaving as Sergeant and returning as Captain Bruno. On the trip there Colonel Gutierrez will be assessing the leadership team, and he has been instructed to appoint you.'

'Thank you sir. But why does it have to be on a relatively undemanding trip, I was hoping to take a senior role in a front line combat unit. Where I belong.'

'I can see where you're coming from Sergeant, and there is an added component which brings us to the...erm... more delicate part of our discussion.' Bruno's face coloured as he tried to maintain his self-control. Not something he was adept at. '......As you know....' Sinclair continued; 'Cadet Mann has been foisted on us from high. In fact her father General Mann has been most appreciative of our role in her development and as a sign of his gratitude he would like us to continue that supportive role, which is where you come in....' The mask of composure was slipping from Bruno's face and he started to shake his head. '....In fact he specifically selected you for this role after Cadet Mann's glowing tribute to him about you. So you will be her mentor and guide on the trip.'

'She's coming? I've got to baby sit a spoil brat and wipe her arse because she's daddy's little princess?' Bruno retorted. He got up and leant across the table over Sinclair who was shrinking back into his seat as the intimidating presence loomed over him. 'I've been in more combat situations than he's got arse licking staff....' the Sergeant continued; '....I'm a decorated war hero. This is bullshit, and respectfully you can stick this promotion where the sun doesn't shine! Sir!' Bruno heard his pulse hammering furiously in his ears and felt the crackle of his knuckles from his clenched fist like a mound of nuts and bolts.

To Bruno's surprise Sinclair found the balls to stand up to him and look him straight in his face.

'Sergeant Bruno! You will get back into your chair immediately before I have you arrested, thrown into the cells, then charged with gross insubordination and threatening an officer.' Even though he towered over Sinclair, Bruno took a deep breath and sat back down. 'There's no easy way of putting this Sergeant, so I'm going to tell you straight...' It was Sinclair's turn to dominate the room while Bruno sat with his head down quietly listening. '.....There have been rumours.....' Sinclair continued '....Rumours of a most unsavoury nature may I say regarding your conduct, both here at the academy but more significantly during your time as a front line sergeant. Stories about war crimes, which if they become public will be a significant problem to the company. You may protest you were only carrying out the instructions of your superiors but they're not going to see it like that and neither are what remains of the free press or the public. These were difficult times and nobody doubts your bravery but your methods appear to have been at best questionable.'

Bruno thought back to the sweeps on the villages. To be carried out with 'Extreme prejudice.' With 'No stone left unturned.' As the company said. He had carried out his instructions to the letter. Anyone who questioned his methods tended to end up KIA (killed in action) shortly afterwards. They knew the score, they signed up and they took the money and the consequences. He'd heard stories that some traitors had suddenly gained a conscience and gone to the press. His name had come up repeatedly. 'These are unsubstantiated reports Sir. Made by people jealous of my recognition and holding a grudge', he offered.

'I'm sure they are Sergeant, but they are persistent and the company have requested that you are taken out of the line of fire until the whole furore dies down. Hence the trip. Otherwise I can't guarantee your position here or indeed your role in the SPC, so it's in the best interests of everyone involved that you accept this opportunity with good grace. I'm sure once all this has been cleared up you can return to your former role, with an unblemished reputation and a more senior position in our organisation.'

Unblemished my fuckin arse! Bruno thought but said; 'Thank you sir, I'll happily accept your generous offer and I'm sorry for my loss of control earlier. I wasn't aware of the full picture before you clarified the situation.'

'Thank *you* Sergeant. I knew you'd see things sensibly in the end. Good luck with your new role. Dismissed.'

Bruno stood up and saluted before leaving the office, resentment churning his insides.

*

The memories still stung Bruno. All those times I've put my ass on the line for the company. Doing their dirty work while they keep their nice pink hands squeaky clean. Out of sight, out of mind. As long as I get it done, they don't give a shit. Fighting for a cause one day and against it the next. All to keep their share price high. I wonder at the amount of money on the company value each death adds. Do the trillionaire owners even notice it anymore? So much money, they might as well be aware of the individual oxygen atoms they breathe or water molecules they drink. But then it's not about money anymore is it? Only the power. The ability to change the lives of millions with a press of a screen. Each person as insignificant as a single atom. Individually worthless but collectively priceless. That's the way of the world Valerio but there's a price to be paid. They make the decisions and there's fuck all I can do about it. I'm on the way to the arse end of nowhere to babysit and save their scrawny necks. What the fuck do I do now? Especially with that sonofabitch Gutierrez and his arselicking lackeys van Dee and Williams. The knowing sly smirks between them when he was around. Their undermining of him when he was bollocking one of their men. 'Don't take it personally private. Sergeant Bruno's only trying to make a good impression for Colonel Gutierrez. ' The barely suppressed sniggers from the men hurt more than any wound possibly could. Even the half-hearted admonishment from Gutierrez himself only seem to rub salt into the wounds. The only one I feel I can trust is Mikey Voronoff. He sees them for the grovelling shits they truly are. Don't worry Mikey wherever I go, you'll be right alongside me while we kick the world's arse. They won't be laughing so much when I'm promoted. I'll break the fuckers back to the ranks. The thought of it bought a small glow of comfort to Bruno, even though a cold edge of uncertainty remained. Again he looked across at the time.

04:02 on the clock. Bruno pulled the sheets to one side and got out of bed. He turned and looked at the sleeping Naomi in the dimly lit room and thought. 'You have brought so much shit to my life, but perhaps I'm better off out of it for the time being'. Bruno dressed and left the room, making sure there was nobody around first. Can't get caught shagging the Generals little princess now. It might be interpreted as taking his instructions too literally. The assessments for his promotion will be coming up in the next couple of weeks. I'm nailed on. What can go wrong? He smiled to himself.

♦

Eleanor toyed with her plate of chips as she absentmindedly dipped them in the barbeque sauce before popping each one into her mouth. After the events yesterday she needed some peace and quiet, moving from her usual position in the Cafeteria to a spot away from the boisterous noise of Counsellor Marcus's fun and games. The cheers and squeals of the children still rang out in the distance, but the words spoken were lost in the general hubbub of the Cafeteria. The white robed figure stood over this small audience gesticulating like an out of control puppet. But it was the sadness in the creature's eyes staring out at her from the pen that dominated Eleanor's thoughts. The eyes were shining out of the gloom, studying her as she stared back. There was something else, that hadn't occurred to her at the time. There was an almost subliminal defiance behind them, a challenge calling out to her in a silent voice. But what was the challenge? To understand, fight, ignore? Only a psychic would know. They would have the requisite skills to connect with the creature, but for Eleanor it was like asking the blind to see and the deaf to hear. What could be the purpose of such creatures? Who would have use for such things? Even a small one had caused havoc; the severed hand was proof of that. What if a big one was on the loose? You didn't have to see one of those to know how big they were. The piles of shit in the pens were nearly as big as her. Even twenty of the small creatures on a high fibre diet and laxatives, with their little pellet like droppings, couldn't produce that in a day.

She smiled at the memory of that plump little bastard Walker's crazy dance as he tried to dislodge the hand without touching it. Fuckin' cheek. Trying to blame me for his own stupidity. Fired my arse! They couldn't get no one else to clear that mess up. Only the lowest of the low like me. Vital but invisible, like the life support systems. They'd soon notice when I'm gone. Even the cleaner Droids couldn't approach my diligence. I could easily do the main corridor and the big pens in under....

'Hey Eleanor, hope I'm not interrupting.' Eleanor looked up into the smiling face of Ava. 'Mind if I join ya!' Her voice had a light almost musical quality to it that drew Eleanor in. Normally a voice seemingly out of nowhere would have startled Eleanor but it was almost as if she expected, indeed welcomed it. She smiled back.

'Please, be my guest Ava.'

Ava placed her tray and sat opposite. Eleanor looked with dismay at the meagre amount of brightly coloured peppers and tomatoes with something that looked like a dollop of boiled shit. How could anyone survive on that? Then again, I suppose Ava doesn't exactly raise a sweat during the day. Eleanor guessed Ava to be in her mid to late thirties. It wasn't so much her appearance, which Eleanor had to concede was pretty good, but her persona. Her self-assurance was obvious, although it could lead to overconfidence or arrogance, but her posture exuded a calm authority.

'I wasn't sure if I should join you, you looked a million miles away', Ava said.

'No please don't worry. I was only thinking about what's on my schedule this afternoon.'

'So, you didn't get your marching orders from our friend then?'

Eleanor held out her hands. 'Apparently not. Mind you, it's not as if they could ask the agency for a replacement is it? Maybe they could email one up as an attachment.'

Ava placed her hand over her mouth and closed her eyes. Her shoulders rocked with laughter as she leant forward. 'Oh my goodness, you are so funny.' She wiped the tears from her eyes and shook her head.

While Eleanor enjoyed the moment, it felt strange to be sharing a laugh with somebody so senior to her. At the same time her company felt the most natural thing in the world. Go with it Ellie. Just let it happen. 'It's a pity we can't attach Mister Walker to the reply and send him back. Mind you I don't fancy sharing an email with him. He'd be climbing all over me like yesterday, the creep.'

Ava's cool professional persona was disintegrating before her eyes as she screwed her face up and blindly put her hand in the small pile of boiled shit on her plate. This time it was Eleanor who shrieked with laughter as Ava examined the mess on her hand. Eleanor noticed the slightly irritated yet puzzled looks of those in their vicinity, who'd stopped their conversations and were staring in their direction.

Ava sighed, cleaning the gloop off her hands as their laughter died down. 'Many a true word said in jest Eleanor', she said.

'Well he's got a track record; I can tell you.'

Ava sat back, the smile on her face gradually fading. 'Really? How'd you know that?'

Eleanor told her of the hushed conversation she'd heard in the corridor a few days earlier between Walker and the young research assistant. 'It looked pretty intense, but I couldn't help noticing the fear in her eyes. I felt a bit awkward to be honest and didn't really know what to do.'

'What did the girl look like?'

'About five two. Blond, glasses.'

'Well well, the sonofabitch. That's my neighbour Liz.'

'You know her?', Eleanor asked.

Ava nodded slowly, lips pursed, eyebrows raised. 'I saw him hugging her shortly after the incident, the snake. She was covered in blood and obviously still in shock and sobbing. His creepy little hands stroking her hair saying "There there" as if he really cared. Knowing him and the way he operates, he doesn't have normal human feelings, only those of a predator.'

'Ahh was she the one who discovered Doctor Felton wondering around in a daze waving a bloody stump?' Ava nodded as Eleanor added, 'Not nice. Not nice at all. I was the one who found the missing part.'

'I must say I was impressed how calm you were Eleanor.'

'Oh, I used to work in a poor hospital as a cleaner once. You'll be amazed what you find lying around, especially after a crackdown by company forces.' Eleanor secretly congratulated herself on her quick thinking. Remember Ellie, you're dealing with a Psychic here, visualising some of the horrors she'd witnessed during her time in the water wars.

Puzzlement briefly flickered across Ava's face. 'Really. You must have seen some sights in your time there.'

'I try to blot them out to be honest Ava.'

'Probably for the best. Some things are hard to deal with... I suppose.' Mmm sounds a bit unsure there Eleanor. Sounds like she wants to get something off her chest.

Ava rested her chin on her hand, looking pensive. 'I've led quite a sheltered existence until recently. Mom and dad's precious little princess, y'know? Privileged upbringing in an affluent part of Manhattan, only child of professional academics, private schools then on to Princeton. Spent a year in Cambridge. Only mixed with the rich kids and so-called elites of society. But I can't shake off the feeling of somehow...missing out...'

'On what...?' Eleanor asked then adding; 'Sounds a bit better than where I was bought up, actually dragged up, on a North London council estate. Alcoholic mother, absent father, two brothers constantly fighting.' Eleanor decided not to mention her special uncle. 'I lost count of the times we were broken into, normally by junkies looking to pay for their next hit.'

'God, I must sound so much like the spoilt little brat.' Ava sat up straight, holding her hand out in a placating gesture. 'I didn't mean to belittle your problems Eleanor, I promise.'

Eleanor smiled and Ava relaxed a little. 'I know you didn't. It's ok. I've had people speaking down to me all my life and I'm good at spotting it...' She reached out and took Ava's hand. 'I suppose there was some excitement, but not the good type.'

'I can imagine. What I meant was… I suppose I had the academic education, the polite society, the material trappings but…' she squeezed Eleanor's hand; '….There's another kind of education, more about life itself, with some gristle thrown in. Where it's not all "just so", where stuff goes wrong, and you've got to deal with it and find a way out or…'

'It's ok Ava, I know what you mean…'

'Because you seem to have that about you Eleanor, I can sense it…'

The alarm bells rang in Eleanor's head as she withdrew her hand. 'What do you mean…?'

'No, no no. I wasn't reading your mind, but I can sense the fierce intellect that burns deep inside you Eleanor. The different kind of education that I'm searching and reaching out for… Something you've got in spades…'

Eleanor chuckled. 'I've been called a lot of things in my time Ava, but never "Intelligent"' Nobody had ever spoken to her like that before, not even Naomi. Her heart swelled. The intense look in Ava's eyes seemed to look deep inside of her as if shining a light in places that had only known cold and darkness. She knew Ava meant every word more than anything in her life. There was an utter certainty to it.

'I've always been the career girl Eleanor. No time for long term relationships. They hardly ever seemed to match up to my lofty criteria and when they did, they were so conventional, so boring. I suppose I've been married to my career all along and didn't realise it.'

'Men are just… bastards.' Eleanor was surprised at the bald statement but liberated by the simplicity of it. 'Out for what they can get and then disappear as soon as they get it.' The shadow of Bruno passed quickly across her mind.

'Hey! Say how it is Eleanor why don't ya!'

'I can't bring myself to trust any of them…' This is getting too serious Ellie. Looking down at her plate, she picked up a chip and dipped it in what remained of the boiled shit on Ava's plate before holding it out to a startled looking Ava. 'Fancy a chip?'

'Don't mind if I do!' Ava took the chip, gingerly examining it, then bit a little bit off the end, before nodding approvingly and placed the rest in. 'Mmmmmm tastes good. They're called Fries where I come from.'

'Chips, fries. Who cares? They look tastier than that rabbit food you've got.' She shoved the plate over to Ava. 'You wanna be like me! Eat these, all of 'em. I gotta go back and do some cleaning!'

'Same time tomorrow Eleanor?' Ava asked hopefully.

Eleanor nodded. 'To be continued.' She turned to make her way back. She looked across at Marcus' playgroup, watching the counsellor as he held his rapt audience, the smiling reverent faces of the children turned as one towards him. Shaking her head gently, Eleanor walked past the group and out of the Cafeteria back to the Lab area. All that nice exterior, bet good old Counsellor Marcus is a right bastard as well.

♦

To: Wilhelmus.schuiling@familyofykdar.com
From: marcus.burgman@galactic_vistas.com
Subject: Re: Progress

Brother Wilhelmus
   Your kindness in your last message has left me lost for words. To hear such sentiments from a great man is indeed an honour I don't feel worthy, but it will spur me on to fulfil my task of bringing the words and deeds of Ykdar to the lucky few upon whose ears they will fall.

As you said, from small acorns spring mighty oaks and I have been tending the saplings which have started to sprout. As you can imagine some need more nurturing than others, but I have the start of a great forest. The most tender of these is Aaron whose eagerness often blinds him to his shortcomings, but he shows great promise. There are others I have been spreading the teachings and love of Ykdar to. The playgroups have been a great success and the ranks are swelling. So much so, that we will be holding our first service in a few days' time. My hopes are high that fortune will smile upon us.

   I was searching through the Tomes of Tadarida a couple of evenings ago and was struck by the story of the young girl, Meean who rode Ias the white swan in search of the cosmic seed of Quatos after the fall of the Cerura. The prophecy foretells that she will one day return to the world of mortals and the time of greatest tranquillity will come to pass, and men will live in peace under the guidance of Ykdar.

It had me thinking that our host star, Ereus, dwells in the old constellation of Cygnus the Swan, and that we could be making Magdur the world of men, therefore could the prediction mean that we are going to the land of Quatos and the prophecy could come to pass on the new world we now inhabit? You could say that the Arion was our Swan that bought us here. I feel the possibility is getting stronger by the day. Perhaps we have our very own Meean here now and she will be shown to me in signs. I will be vigilant in my search and will not fail you.
   Your obedient servant

Marcus

To: marcus.burgman@galactic_vistas.com
From: Wilhelmus.schuiling@familyofykdar.com
Subject: Re: Progress

Brother Marcus

The waters of your words are bringing forth great benefits. Soon the young saplings will branch out in the golden dawn of Magdur. Your gifts are a blessing to us all. Remember how I told you of my early days and the struggles I endured before the breakthrough. You show great promise but there is no rush. This is a long road and not a short sprint. You have done well but do not let vaulting ambition cloud your judgement.

Therefore, I must council caution and patience. Too much water early on can drown the saplings. Do not concern yourself with the prophecies, some of which are only parables that were originally intended to show the peoples of more simple times how to deal with the complex moral dilemmas that we can encounter on life's meanderings. Anyhow was it not spoken that what in fact returned in Meean's place was the darkness of Xerdarr and the dark times that followed? So be careful of taking the Tomes of Tadarida too literally my boy as therein lays trouble. You should try to read between the lines for the real message within.

I look forward with great eagerness to your next update.

May the light of Ykdar shine brightly upon you,

Wilhelmus

9

Confidential
To: Celina.Novak@galactic_vistas.com
From: Brandon.Schofield@Ateus_Industries.co.uk
Subject: Re: Outstanding Issues

Ms Novak

Thank you for you update regarding the progress of the Mag research. Please pass on our appreciation of the tremendous work your staff have carried out so far.

In addition to the sensitive matters we discussed, since you departed Earth, our research has indicated further Nadinium applications in Energy, Quantum AI and most recently Defence, particularly in unit protection, detection and munitions. We feel that the publicity surrounding the negative environmental impact is of minimal concern and our investors are becoming increasingly restless at the falling stock values but we are confident that the announcement of new deposits will restore market confidence.

In relation to the Mags, we would like to remind you that it is of critical importance that their presence in Pangea base is concealed from the settlers at all costs, as any breach would have untold negative consequences. Once the civilians are embarked to the settlements the primary function of your mission can commence.

Finally, we would also like to express our disappointment and concern at the issues and delays in the Mag research. I would have expected your arrival on Magdur to have pushed this phase of the program to a successful conclusion, however this appears not to be the case. They have been sourced from the habitat of the planet and modifications should have been completed. We think it would be remiss of us to not point out the crucial role these entities have in the location of the element Nadinium as well as the success of any future recovery of the significant deposits available on the planet. If there are any unnecessary obstacles, these need to be parked and dealt with at a later date. Time is moving on and progress is not keeping pace. You do not need reminding of the responsibility placed on you and the consequences of failure.

We look forward to receiving your swift response.
Brandon Schofield

Ateus CEO

Confidential
To: Brandon.Schofield@Ateus_Industries.co.uk
From: Celina.Novak@galactic_vistas.com
Subject: Re: Outstanding Issues

Mr Schofield

Thank you for your appreciation of our efforts and I have passed on your kind words to all those involved.

We have experienced significant challenges regarding both the environmental modification and the construction of the settlements. After bringing the APP's back online, the issues resurfaced within a week. I have despatched a team of specialists to establish the root cause, however due to the unstable magnetosphere of Magdur we have had difficulty establishing contact.

Returning to the main topic of our discussion, I fully understand your concerns regarding the challenging timelines. I would not underestimate the ground-breaking complexity of the research taking place. As you know the Gargoyles are sourced from indigenous samples collected at great cost, and the associated modifications and cloning has bought their own associated issues. The same applies to the Gorthon, and not having a live sample only exacerbates the difficulties. It's similar with the new variant, the Bornix, while a triumph of Biobotics, they are also at the cutting edge of our current capabilities, and this brings its own problems.

The issues are not so much on the physiological domain but more in relation to the psychological and in particular the issues surrounding the control of the instabilities found in the Gargoyles and Gorthon (although there has been significant progress in this particular Mag type). The sub types are cloned from samples extracted directly from our primary samples and modified by the DNA developers. Once the desired modifications are modelled, the type is instantiated for three or four generations, each one an upgrade on the previous cycle until the correct level is achieved. A set of criteria are agreed against each type and a series of tests are implemented using specially created Neuroware which is downloaded into the Mag's brain imparting the correct intellectual characteristics as well as instincts to match their specified tasks. Here is a breakdown of each type my teams have designed, its features, tasks and current status.

- **Name:**   Gargoyle
- **Category:** Genetically modified clone
- **Task:**   Precision Detection of Nadinium
- **Features:**
  - Indigenous Magurian creatures. Genetically modified for long range psychic control. To be used en mass for initial detection of Nadinium. Their innate ability to sense Nadinium surpasses all of our remote sensing capabilities. Once they are guided by the Neuroware they have an almost unparalleled success rate. Have the potential for rollout to further worlds where Nadinum deposits exist in challenging locations as well as great abundance. Limited extraction potential, but this is offset by the guidance of the Hyperthon to initiate excavation.
- **Current Progress**
  - After initial difficulties integrating the Neuroware, a recent breakthrough has engendered significant progress. However, this was offset when one of primary samples was allowed to escape by lax security procedures resulting in serious injury to the individual responsible but also more significantly, the destruction of the subject. The remaining crumbs of comfort from this unfortunate incident are that there has been no breach of security and Dr Walker has assured me progress will resume unimpeded.

- **Name:**   Gorthon
- **Category:** Genetically modified clone
- **Task:**   Deep Extraction of Nadinium.
- **Features:**
  - The other indigenous Magdurian creature. Based upon a single sample (dead). Ultra-strong and long endurance. Designed to mine and extract the deep lying deposits of Nadinium. Upgradeable.
- **Current Progress**
  - We are extremely proud and excited by the tremendous progress made in this arena by Dr Chiang and her team. Results have far surpassed expectations. Intelligence is high. Instability levels are nominal. If the Nadinium can be

located, the potential for swift and economic extraction is huge. We feel this could be the template we searched for and could be rolled out company-wide upon successful completion of its mission on Magdur. Additionally our robotics team are in the process of developing an upgrade which we hope will extend its capabilities significantly. Finally and most exciting of all is the emergence of a super Gorthon, the Hyperthon, which will possess the capability to psychically control large groups of Mags, under the auspices of a human controller naturally. Dr Khan will personally oversee this development.

- **Name:** **Bornix**
- **Category** **Hybrid Biobot**
- **Task:** Airborne Long Range Detection of Nadinium
- **Features:**
  o Modified Airborne Gargoyle used for long range Nadinium detection. Able to drop packages to guide the Gargoyles in
- **Current Progress**
  o Satisfactory progress. Reduced instability although still not completely eradicated. Marker Packages seem to contain concentrated acid which while dangerous had the benefit of being detectable at distance by the Gargoyles. We are currently assessing potential applications.

- **Name:** **Hyperthon**
- **Category** **Cloned Biobot**
- **Task:** Multiple Mag communication, coordination and control
- **Features:**
  o Genetic offshoot of the Gorthon designed to direct the Mags in their location and acquisition of the Nadinium. This saves time in developing individual instructions for each Mag type as they are programmed to respond intelligently to its directions. The hierarchy of this particular type will be fed back to the AI as per our previous conversation. We have a contingency of Human.

- **Current Progress**
  - Individual testing passed smoothly, but live integration testing has proven challenging and our teams still haven't established if it's the Hyperthon where the problem exists, the Mags or both. We are making progress but slower than anticipated. One interesting point is our Psychic consultant; Miss Ava Matthews has suggested that the Hyperthon appears to have its own agenda which currently is undetermined. This has been met with general scepticism however, I highly respect Miss Matthews's professionalism and capability and I'm not inclined to dismiss her claims out of hand. However I suspect another force is at work here.

In terms of clouds on the horizon, Base director Alexeyeva has expressed her reservations about the Mags and the potential impact on the civilian population if their existence came to light. As her word is final within Pangea Base, I have no direct control over her actions which is a potential security issue. I would urge you to bring her back into line in your communications, reminding her that now is not a time for inappropriate qualms and that her ultimate responsibility is to the company before the situation develops to our detriment.

Additionally, I was informed by Dr Khan that a safety feature has been included in all Gorthon and Hyperthon in the form of a weak spot in an area the base of their reinforced skulls. He assured me that it would not in all probability be needed and would not have any detrimental effect of their function. While I was not pleased that unauthorised modifications were implemented, the reality of the situation dictated that these modifications could not be reversed, however I directed Dr Khan to remove this unnecessary and unwelcome precaution from the next generation cycle.

In conclusion, we are a little short of our projected landmarks but given the complexity of the project remarkable progress has been made by the team we have in place. I will remind Dr Khan of the timeline pressures and urge him to press his teams to even greater efforts and I have a high degree of confidence that the majority, if not all the tasks they have been set, will be achieved within the allocated deadline.

Yours

Celina Novak

Chief Colonisation Administrator

♦

'I'm not interested in anymore excuses Doctor Khan! I'm thoroughly tired of listening to the litany of shoddiness you offer as progress.' Celina looked along the sofa at the forlorn academic who sat in silence. 'Have you nothing positive to offer me Doctor? Hold ups with Mags, technical incompetence and now you tell me the instabilities that plagued the other Mags have now been found in the Gorthon. Please!'

'Ms Novak.' Dr Khan's voice was quiet and controlled, belying his anxiety. 'These problems are inevitable when we are pushing the boundaries of Synthetic lifeforms and in our case Hybrid Biobots.'

'Will you please refer to them by their correct name Doctor Khan?' Celina cut in browbeating him. 'Indigenous Madurians or just plain old "Mags" for short. "Synthetic lifeforms" carries all sorts of negative connotations associated with the unfortunate incidents that took place a long time ago. I'm surprised that your association with this event hasn't made you aware of the sensitivities surrounding it.' Celina noticed with satisfaction the sting of pain across the normally impassive Khan's features.

'Of course Ms Novak, and yes I'm fully aware of my association with those events, that to me feel as fresh as if they happened yesterday, and which still cause me great pain and shame, which is why, more than anyone, I am aware of the factors that led to them.' His voice grew stronger as he added; 'And as a result I can see those same unfortunate errors undermining our current achievements.' Celina pursed her lips and raised her eyebrows, but Khan did not hesitate; 'The shortcuts you advocate do not take into account any potential side effects. Genetics, particularly when combined with robotics, rarely allows single changes to have a single specific isolated outcome, and making single nucleotide alterations without monitoring for secondary elements is exactly what caused "The Outbreak" as it is popularly known, to occur and I will not be a part of yet another catastrophe.'

Celina took a sharp intake of breath and decided a less aggressive approach would be required. She was taken aback that the normally polite and reticent Dr Khan would be so direct, but she needed results and fast.

'Doctor...' She smiled; 'obviously none of us want a repeat of those terrible, tragic events and I completely understand your concerns. I have complete faith in you as a leader in your field and I'm sure you will make the breakthroughs we need, but we are under pressure to achieve results.' Time to dangle the carrot Celina thought... 'Maybe if we could divert resources from one of the less significant types into the Gorthon, then maybe what we learn from our successes we can apply them to the remainder of types.' Come on old donkey, have a nibble.

Khan slowly nodded his head in response. 'Miss Novak, I feel this is the only option we have to progress and I thank you for your wisdom and understanding.'

Celina allowed herself an imperceptible clench of the fist. Eeyore, my old donkey. 'Thank you Doctor. You're a great and honourable man and I'm sure one day history will judge you with the kindness that has been denied you for so long.' A bit over the top there Celina but the look of pride and satisfaction on Khan's face told her the job was done. As they rose from the sofa, before she offered her hand which he shook.

'I am most appreciative Miss Novak', he said as he turned to leave.

'Likewise Doctor.' Celina responded, satisfied her carrot and stick has worked on the old fool yet again. Academically brilliant, politically stupid, easy to manipulate. 'Before you leave Doctor, just one more thing', she added. He looked back over this shoulder at her smiling face. 'What type are you thinking of cutting back on?', she asked him.

Khan momentarily furrowed his brow as if deep in thought and responded with a single word. 'Hyperthon.' He said as he nodded to himself then turned and left Celina's office without another word.

♦

To: Michelle J. Farrington @ electron.com
From: robert.nash@galactic_vistas.com
Subject: Re: Q&A

Hey Michelle

Things are going swimmingly! Today we had the privilege of a Q&A session with Miss Novak, the chief administrator. She was very reassuring, allaying people's concerns are all feeling regarding the delays in the move to the settlements. I must say she is quite an impressive figure who carries an air of quiet authority. No dull answer-bot either, churning out well-rehearsed platitudes. I'm guessing she must be in her mid-50's judging from her resume on the base infonet, but she carried her age lightly and there a lot to admire in her stylish but understated appearance. Hey! Here's me getting all hot and bothered about a woman old enough to be my mum (more of her later)

Anyway, she told us how proud and honoured she was to be our guide on this great adventure to a new and exciting future. On a less happy note, there was an awful fat man near the front with a shiny bald head who was horrible to poor Miss Novak. Rude questions and unsubstantiated accusations about one of the other colonies poured from his foul mouth, but she took it all in her stride and quietly stated the facts. You really feel when she speaks that underneath her position and responsibilities, she's just like us. She told us the vision for Galactic Vistas is one of perpetuating the human success story across the galaxy and making our dreams come true and received a rapturous round of applause at the end. I was lucky enough to shake hands with her on the way out and it's funny, but she seemed to know me. She didn't actually say anything, but I just felt it. How strange...

How's things your end? Have you heard from Mum? Has she even mentioned me yet? I saw some hair restorer today and thought of Charles. Hope he don't end up like the bald man at the meeting. He seemed very bitter and twisted about how life's treated him. Some people are just so ungrateful.

Love to all,

Rob xx

10

The child's stare bore into him as she held out the bullet. His quivering hand reached and gently took it.

'Thank you.' He examined the bullet, deformed and smeared with the blood that slowly dripped from it.

'You're welcome.' The child smiled as he loaded the bullet back into the chamber of his pistol before raising it once again. She raised her hands to her face giggling in anticipation. 'I'll count to ten this time. Ready?'

He swallowed hard as each new number rang out, crashing on his clanging nerves. Every digit increasing in volume as the countdown approached its inevitable conclusion.

'…Two...One…Ready?', the child said.

The boom of the shot and the crunching impact of the bullet merged into a single sickening entity, that ripped through his being at the same time as it ripped through the child's head, as she slowly fell back into the dirt, laying still as the growing pool of blood spread out. There was no wound where the bullet entered as she opened her eyes as if waking from a pleasant sleep. Suddenly sitting up the girl reached around the back of her head, as though trying to scratch an unreachable itch. A look of mild consternation crossed her face before her eyebrows raised, but as she found what she was looking for, her smile returned. She stood and walked towards him, holding out a bloodied bullet once again.

'Here you are...' She said as Bruno took the bullet and placed it in the chamber of the pistol before he prepared to fire again. 'Don't miss this time' She said to him.

Behind him the sound of spontaneous laughter rippled out. He turned to look as a growing crowd of people were pointing at him, their faces puce with laughter.

'What you fuckin laughing at? You think this is funny!' Bruno's anger only made the crowd laugh even harder. 'How about I stick around between your eyes, so you know how it feels', he said. The laughter climbed to a crescendo. The bulging eyes and protruding tongues added to those doubled up helplessly on the floor, poured rocket fuel on the raging furnace of Bruno's fury. Then it suddenly stopped, and they all looked back at him in silence. There was a shuffling of feet and the crowd parted. A familiar figure emerged and walked confidently forward. The wrath in Bruno's heart withered as the figure approached until she stood just a couple of feet away.

'Hello little man. How's it going.' The casual tone of Eleanor's greeting only added to the terror Bruno felt. Looking down, she added, 'Still little I see'.

Bruno became aware he was naked from the waist down. The tittering of the crowd resumed, as they pointed and nudged each other, giving knowing winks. Trying to raise the gun and blast their smirking mocking faces off their heads, his arm didn't respond. Pushing every ounce of strength didn't make the slightest difference.

Eleanor reached forward and took the pistol from his hand with the same tenderness his mother once took a sweet he offered her when he was a small child. She gently took him by the shoulders and laid him down on the ground. He looked up at Eleanor who now towered over him, blocking out the sun. At her side stood the child. She handed the pistol to the child as the crowd started a slow rhythmic handclap. The child looked over at them, slowly nodded then turned back to Bruno and raised the gun.

The crowd started the countdown with each clap. 'Ten! Nine! Eight....' Speeding faster and faster towards blast-off. Each clap in time with the thundering heart beats that echoed in Bruno's terrified mind. An accompanying 'Woooo' growing louder each moment as the countdown reached zero and the girl pulled the trigger.

'Ahhhhg!' Bruno opened his eyes. The shadows of the room closing in on him, touching his face, their breath chilling his skin. Slowly, he sat up and looked around the room. The lights automatically came on, just bright enough for him to find his way to the bathroom. His heart rate began to slow. 'What the hell was that...', he thought. A feeling of dread and guilt came over him, as if the realisation that he'd committed an unspeakable deed, although he couldn't quite remember what it was. Then the sense of guilt and helplessness faded as the dream slipped from the cache of his short term memory and into the darkness of suppressed fears and desires at the back of his unconscious mind.

♦

'Mikey you are so full of shit, how'd you expect me to believe anything you say now.' Bruno saw a pained expression pass briefly across Michael Voronoff's face, another of the Sergeants from the SPC. He'd formed a close bond with Bruno over the last months of the voyage. A veteran of the Water Wars, he shared Bruno's similar cynical view of the world.

'I'm telling you Bruno; it was her and her sister. They were willing and I was able!', Voronoff replied.

106

A loud barking laugh escaped Bruno as he clapped his hand on Voronoff's shoulder. 'How can an ugly fucker like you have two women at once. You can't even get one at once.' He doubled over; his vision red as he laughed at his own joke. He held his hand out for a moment. 'Ok, ok. So, supposing this cock and bull story happens to be true, I bet they must have been dog rough and desperate.'

'I thought they were pretty hot…', Bruno did not allow Voronoff to continue.

'Yeah, but your hot would be most normal people's piss warm.' After regaling everyone in the Sergeants mess within earshot of his sexual conquests for the past hour, Bruno barely noticed that the others had slowly drifted off one by one, until Mikey was the last one left. Goading the normally reticent Mikey into revealing some of his adventures, he thought it shouldn't take too long before he himself could move onto the next batch of satisfied customers to boast about. He had to admit for an SPC sergeant Mikey was quite a wallflower when it came to the ladies. Perhaps it was the large wonky nose, the pockmarked skin of his famished face or maybe the receding hairline. Bruno liked Voronoff, because he was no threat as well as being a loyal friend with a similar outlook, although he definitely wouldn't go on the town with him in case he frightened off any potential prey. 'Hey, come on Mikey, I'm only kidding. I believe you…Honest…' he said before launching into another fit of self-induced laughter.

'Well it's not as if you win the ladies by your charming wit and sensitivity, is it Bruno? What'd you do when they realise you're an asshole!' This time is was Voronoff's turn to laugh.

Mee fuckin oow you sly bastard, Bruno thought. He couldn't let that pass. 'Yeah! Is that what your sisters told ya?' This time his voice wasn't quite so bold as the overinflated ego had sprung an insidious leak that allowed the hot air to escape slowly.

'No! Your Mum!' roared Voronoff. There was another laugh as Williams and van Dee, the other SPC sergeants remaining in the mess overheard.

Bruno shot a look over, but they continued to laugh even harder and louder, raising their beer in a mocking toast.

'Hey watch it fuckers. This is grownups speaking now.' Bruno pulled his best grimace which brooked no comeback, except this time it did.

'What's the matter Bruno? Ok at dishing it, but can't take it back.' It was Williams who was second in command to Colonel Gutierrez.

'I can take it ok, but only from those who ain't arse lickers.' Bruno responded. This resulted in more laughter from Williams and van Dee.

'So says little Miss Mann's baby sitter. I bet "*daddy*" will be pleased. Such an honourable man is our Bruno... A decorated war hero no less. A shite in whining armour, unless there's any enemy around of course', It was van Dee who countered.

Bruno could feel his shoulders tensing and heart thudding in his ears as another crash of baying laughter burst over him. The open gaping mouths, the gleaming white teeth and protruding tongues all mocking him. The tears running down their cheeks were raining distain on his self-esteem. The pointing, accusing fingers shaking from the heaving shoulders. Bruno stood powerless in the face of their jeering scorn. He could feel his hands twitching, aching to close around van Dee's throat, to dig the nails into the sides of his windpipe, closing his grip and tearing it out in a fountain of blood before turning to Williams and forcing his big mouth open wider and wider, pushing the jaw further back, tearing tendon and cracking bone as the laughter became a gurgling rattle, finally releasing his grip and digging his thumbs into van Dee's eye sockets, the eyes popping, pushing ever deeper into the soft tissue, the fingers around the back of Williams head crushing the skull until it exploded with a deeply satisfying pop.

The vicious fantasies swam in Bruno's mind as Voronoff stepped forward. 'Hey guys, c'mon cool it.' He held his hands out in a placating manner. 'Let's not let a few jokes get out of hand.' He smiled nervously. 'After all we've all got to work together, and you never know when your lives are gonna depend on us.'

Yeah, because if your life depends on me, you're both dead fuckin meat, Bruno thought. Despite his pain, he forced a smile. His hands still twitching, thirsting for blood as the laughter died down. A wise general picks his battles and this wasn't a good time. A tactical retreat, he thought. The hiss of his ego deflating had stopped as a piece of sticky tape was placed over the puncture. 'Hey guys it's only a bit of banter, that's all. No hard feelings eh?', he said. You're not a very good liar sometimes Valerio he admitted to himself, as the forced tone of his voice broadcast his insincerity.

The look that passed between Williams and van Dee told Bruno they didn't buy it. 'Hey Mikey, we were turning in anyway', Williams said as he and his comrade placed their empty glasses back on the bar, before making their way out. A few seconds later Bruno heard their laughter fading into the distance.

'Fuckers...' Bruno muttered and stared at the glasses that stood empty on the bar. The visions of what he'd like to do to their owners fresh in his mind. He turned to a sheepish Voronoff who said; 'Sorry Bruno... I overstepped the mark about your mum.' His Adam's apple bobbed nervously up and down as if desperately trying to find an escape.

For once Bruno's smile was genuine as he offered; 'Don't worry about it Mikey. You gave as good as you got. What's the problem with a few jokes amongst friends.'

Voronoff's Adam's apple abandoned its break for freedom and settled back into the centre of his throat.

'Anyway, I haven't got a Mum. Not since I was ten', Bruno admitted

'What happened Bruno, if you don't mind me asking...'

The long-supressed smells and sounds of the cool evening wafted back into Bruno's memory. The early evening light, the aroma of cooking, his sister's voice...

*

'Give Miss Sprinkles back Valerio, please...' Her doe eyes looking mournfully up at him as he tried not to laugh.

'I don't know where it is Eva, honest...' His grip tightening on her favourite doll.

'It's behind your back, I can see it, give it, give it, give it.' She hopped up and down with impatience, her hands reaching out imploringly, voice trapped halfway between crying and giggling.

He held his hands out, Miss Sprinkles in his left hand while he looked in exaggerated fashion to his right. 'Behind me! Where? I can't see *Mister* Sprinkles.'

Eva lunged forward with a squeal just as Valerio whipped the doll away and held it above his head tantalisingly just out of Eva's reach as he laughed manically.

'Are you two fighting again!' They turned to see their mother standing in the doorway trying to supress a smile.

'Mummy, Valerio's taken Miss Sprinkles again, and he keeps calling her "Mister" just to torment me.' Eva's bottom lip protruded sorrowfully.

Their mother assumed her stern face that she used unconvincingly for such occasions and pointed at him. 'Valerio, stop being horrid, give Eva back her doll now!' She moved her head slightly to one side raising her chin, pursing her lips, eyebrows arched in a challenge. The corner of her mouth quivering as laughter started to gain the upper hand. A blur of movement burst out from behind her nearly knocking her off her feet. The feigned anger quickly transmuted into the real thing as their older brother tore through the hallway on his way out. 'Quintilio Bruno! Where the hell do you think you're off to?', she demanded.

'Football training Mama, gotta rush, I'm running late.'

'Not on an empty stomach you're not!'

'Bye Mama...'

A small cloud of dust was all that remained as the rapidly receding footsteps of Quintilio faded into the distance. Their mother gasped in exasperation, taking a couple of steps in pursuit, before the futility of her actions stopped her in her tracks. She sighed, let out a long breath and stared at the open door. 'I swear that boy will be the death of me…' She looked back at them, Valerio still holding the doll raised above his head, Eva still clasped around his waist in a futile attempt to squeeze him into submission. Their mother reached out with a speed that surprised them both and snatched the doll from his grasp. Eva gleefully accepted her rightful possession, clasping the doll tightly to her chest as she performed a jig of delight. Valerio stood open mouthed as his mother turned to him. 'Valerio, you'll be in deep trouble if I catch you stealing Eva's things again.' The humour had evaporated from her face. 'And another thing while I remember. How many times have I…' She was not allowed to finish.

Valerio felt it before hearing anything. A deep throb seemed to emanate from within his chest, before the rumbling quickly grew to a furious reverberating roar, obliterating every other sound. The air itself seemed to be shaking as the ground under his feet tried to swallow him up while he desperately tried to keep his balance. His mother's mouth worked soundlessly as she staggered towards them. Eva was still clutching her doll, her smile combined with confusion as his mother reached her and wildly gesticulated towards the door. Meanwhile Valerio looked up as a giant crack opened in the ceiling and seemed to vomit the entire upper floor and its contents onto Eva and his mother, before the silent blackness consumed him whole.

It was the thirst that woke him, as he slowly became aware of his surroundings. The pain as he swallowed were shards of glass in his throat. He opened his eyes, but still the velvet darkness persisted. Am I dead, am I blind? There was a noise, a distant keening that called out in the void. He recognised the voice.

'Eva!' His voice croaked as the jagged edges shifted in his throat.

'It hurts' His sister complained.

'Hold on I'm coming…' The realisation that he was trapped dawned on him. It must have been an earthquake. He'd felt the tremors before. They'd been part of the fabric of everyday life, like the occasional rain showers that swept the mountains, but he'd learnt to ignore them. They'd even had safety drills at school. 'Get out of the building, if not take cover under a table or the stairs. Wait until help arrives', they'd been told. He tried to move but he was held by an iron vice that pinned him in place. He could wiggle his left foot and arm below the elbow but that was it. Attempting to lift his head, a sharp object dug into his forehead, sending a spike of pain surging through him.

'Where's mummy?' Eva asked.

A deep sickening realisation washed over Valerio at the memory of the ceiling bursting open and raining down on his mother's head.

'I think she's gone to look for some help. I'm sure she'll be back soon; don't worry, you'll be ok Eva', he reassured the girl.

110

'She's been gone for hours…' She started to cry. 'It hurts…'

Hours! It only seemed like a few seconds ago, Valerio thought but tried to console her, 'I know Eva. You just have to be brave. Have you got Miss Sprinkles? I bet she's not frightened.'

'She can't be frightened, she's only a stuffed doll', Eva replied abruptly.

Valerio tried to laugh but only a strangled rasp came out as once again the darkness enveloped him.

This time it was the tapping on his face that woke him. Am I dreaming? he questioned. He opened his eyes as a drop of water splashed directly into them. Involuntarily, he jerked his head forward as the sharp object dug into the scar tissue of its previous attempt to impale his skull. The water ran down his cheeks and up his nose. The drops became a trickle. Opening his mouth, Valerio desperately tried to consume some liquid. The droplets touched his cracked and swollen tongue as he licked the precious moisture. Just a fraction more, he calculated as the sharp object began to tear at his flesh. The pain was a minor obstacle in his quest to slake his raging thirst. Poking his tongue out into the water, the trickle made its way agonisingly slowly down his throat, feeling the flow slowing before it finally came to a halt. A moaning came from a few feet away. 'Can you hear me Eva?' he asked.

'Muuuurrmy…', came the pained response

'Mummy's coming, I promise.'

'Muurrr…'

But Valerio was helpless. The uncompromising weight pressing down upon him had become rigid and unyielding. The time flowed like thick black treacle, barely moving forward as each second, minute and hour passed with unbearable slowness. He only knew it was passing forward by listening to his heart beat, and even then, he couldn't tell if it was slowing down as death drew him towards its event horizon.

Then he became aware of the barking, followed by the scrabbling above him. This was followed by a voice, like an angel from a dream calling out to him.

'Can anyone hear me!'

It felt as if a cork had been placed in his throat blocking any sound, so he was unable to respond to the voice. There was silence. Then the dog resumed its barking.

A different younger voice spoke. 'They're definitely in there. I know it. Please…' Quintilio!

'We've been digging all night son. I'm sorry but no one can survive five days under the rubble.'

'But the dog! He can sense something.'

'I'm sorry to tell you this but it's probably their bodies he can smell.'

The dog seemed to bark in agreement.

Valerio tried to scream out, still silence.

'Please try, please I'm begging you.' Quintilio's voice pleaded.

'Your family are gone. I know it's hard to take. We've all lost loved ones and my men have been working non-stop. You're just going to have to accept it. There's nothing to be done here, I'm sorry son.', the older voice advised.

Valerio could hear Quintilio's sobs as those around tried to console him. Still trying to scream, not even a groan came out. Valerio reached out frantically in search of something, anything. His finger brushed against a fragment of rubble. His hand stretching out as his little finger gained purchase, slowly scraping it back towards him, before his whole hand closed around it. Lifting it, he knocked it against a wooden beam that lay above him. The dull thuds, distant and muffled, as his arm used up the last of his strength. He could still hear Quintilio's sobs only a few feet away. Stop fuckin' blubbering you oaf and listen.

The voices faded into the distance and all was silent.

Then the barking resumed. Again, voices in the distance. Still the dog persisted. Valerio's arm was burning with pain as he continued. 'Hey Leda, you stupid mutt, come on...' he heard a voice again. His arm was getting weaker but still he pushed it on with sheer will power.

'What is it girl?' The voice was now right above him.

The dog stopped barking as Valerio continued to hit on the wood. 'Come on Leda, it's time to...Hey! I can hear something, there's someone under here. Guys, guys quick!'

Tears filled Valerio's eyes as he continued to knock. 'Hey! If you can hear me, stop knocking' the voice above him said.

His burning arm stopped.

'Fuck! ok start again.'

A feeble couple of clonks was all he could manage before his arm gave out.

'Ok ok we know you're down there. You're gonna be ok, we'll get you out.' Valerio heard just as his strength gave out.

Valerio didn't know how much time had elapsed as he felt the weight of the rubble being lifted from him. The blinding lights shone in his face as hands pulled him upwards. Then the voice. 'He's alive!' followed by sounds of cheers in the distance. As the light shone in, he looked to where Eva had been. Miss Sprinkles was still held in Eva's white still hand that protruded from the rubble. He looked up blinking as someone gently poured some water into his mouth.

*

Even over thirty years later Bruno still recalled the conflict of emotions of the

112

water and his little sister's dead hand. He looked up at Voronoff's face which was a pale sheet of shock.

'She died with nearly everyone else. Only me and my brother, survived', he said.

'Oh my god…Bruno I'm so sorry, I'd never had said anything if I'd known…'

Bruno hadn't thought about them for years, blotting them out until they were pale shadows on his memory. He couldn't even visualise their faces, no pictures, no mementoes, nothing. Only a black hole. Voronoff's hand was on his shoulder, normally something he would have bristled at but at that moment it was exactly what he needed.

'It was the Campania earthquake in 2181', he told his friend.

'I remember seeing it on the news when I was a kid. It was a massive one, thousands dead.'

'It was a 7.9 quake. The biggest in Italian history. Over twenty thousand killed if you include the mudslides after', Bruno informed.

'Fuck, you survived that. You were lucky...' Bruno turned to him and gave an ironic smile. 'I...err... Not lucky in it that way, but you know what I mean.'

He shrugged off Voronoff's discomfort. 'Eva was only a year younger than me. Nine, still a baby really...' He noticed a tear trickling down Voronoff's cheek that was quickly wiped away, but Bruno felt nothing but emptiness. 'My dad was never found. He was out working in the open. Probably caught up in the mudflows that claimed so many lives. Grandparents, aunts, uncles, cousins. All gone. Only me and Quintilio.'

'What happened afterwards, where did you live?', Voronoff asked.

'Oh, we drifted all over Europe, from foster family to foster family. Most were great but I was one angry young man and to be honest a little bastard. I got involved in the street gangs, as I got older, I was bigger than most, so it was easy money for me. School went out of the window by the age of 13. In trouble with the law. Always on the run from the police and other gangs. I did a lotta bad shit but it's all part of growing up. The world eats a lot of people up and shits them out completely fucked up and damaged beyond repair. I happen to be one of those little pieces of sweetcorn that somehow comes out through unchanged.'

Voronoff laughed. 'Then you joined the military and became an even bigger piece of sweetcorn.'

'Well it was that or ending up in a ditch with a bullet in my head. Not much of a choice. The company were on the lookout to harvest raw materials like me. I needed to put my past behind me. No good looking back Mikey. Only forwards. That is until the past creeps up behind and bites you on the arse, which it has a habit of doing.'

'I'll drink to that. Now Bruno which girlfriend were you up to at the last count.'

'Your sister I seem to recall.' This time Voronoff laughed with Bruno. The hot air was slowly being pumped back into Bruno's ego.

11

'Well?'

'I spoke to them about it and first of all they laughed and dismissed it out of hand.'

'Then you must speak to them again!'

'Hold on, hold on. Later, one of them came to me and asked some more questions. He seemed concerned and didn't want the others to think he was weak.'

'A chink in their armour. Most promising.'

'I said to him what you told me to say. First of all, he was reluctant. I tried to calm his fears but he lost his nerve and told me to forget it. He begged me not to breathe a word to anyone.'

'Well you need to work on him. Maybe use your 'Charms' shall we say.'

'I've done enough 'Charming' as you call it already. But then another opportunity cropped up…'

'Continue…'

'Another squad member came to me about it. Same doubts and fears of being seen as weak.'

'What did you do this time? Blow it again!'

'If you're not pleased with my efforts you can always get another to do your dirty work.'

'Forgive me. It's just that we've come so far and now our objective is so close, so tantalising, it's hard to be patient.'

'And yet it's *you* who's always told *me* to show more patience. Please!'

'Ok, ok…. Don't just stand there drumming your fingers and looking away. Speak!'

'You finished? Good, now shut up and listen for once. As I was saying before you rudely interrupted me. A second one came to me expressing interest and doubts.'

'And what was the outcome this time my dear.'

'I told him there was another in the group who had said the same things.'

'Excellent! So you put them together. What next?'

'Not yet I haven't.'

'What?! Please don't tell me that you've just left it.'

'I'm beginning to tire of your insinuations. Do you think I'm a complete idiot?'

'No, but…'

'No but nothing. Now for the last time let me finish. I didn't want to betray the first one's trust. So I told the second that I'll approach the first one and then he'll approach him if he's interested.'

'Very clever. Will you be able to push it along?'

'This is where you come in. I want an event set up in the next couple of days. Then it'll give them the impetus to commit.'

'Splendid thinking. Progress at last!'

'Anything else you might wish to say.'

'What? You want a medal when our objective is not yet achieved.'

'Some small expression of appreciation for all the risks and hardships I've undergone for *your* benefit wouldn't hurt.'

'I'll thank you when... Hold on! Where are you going? Hey don't you walk away from me... Shit!'

12

'**Can** you hear me? Billy…' The pale blue point held its place just in front of him. Its approach repelled yet again. The soft persuasive tones of Ava's words echoed in his mind, caressing his emotions with their soothing reassurance. A black cloak had drawn itself around him that couldn't be breached. From the outside Ava spoke to another. 'He's shut me out. Can we get Harry along? He'll respond then.'

'Felton's not psychically trained, he won't get anywhere near.' The cruel voice sent a shudder of fear and hate through Billy.

'I didn't mean that. I meant for him to actually speak to Billy, or 021161R as you prefer to call him.'

Billy saw the pale blue acquire a dull red halo. The tension was obvious in Ava's voice.

'That's not possible. Felton's security clearance has been revoked pending a review of the breakout incident. Anyway he's still in the infirmary awaiting his new hand to be printed', came the response from the cruel voice.

'Well perhaps he could be accompanied by a member of the security team. It's not as if he's going to break open every cage, with his one hand and usher the Gargoyles out towards the passenger areas', Ava said.

'I repeat his security clearance is revoked. End of story.'

The red became a little deeper, Billy noticed.

'You know something...?, Ava commented; '....I heard a word once, when I studied in England that encapsulates you and people like you perfectly. You wanna know what it is?'

'Genius?' The cruel voice guffawed.

'You certainly are a Genius when it comes to this word, Mister Walker.'

'Go on then Miss Matthews, surprise me with your command of the English language.'

The red halo had become a flaming circle, blazing and drowning out the cool pale blue light that was betrayed by the harsh edge that Ava's voice had acquired. '"Jobsworth." A word that's waited since its first use for you to come into existence and give it perfect form.'

'I've been called a lot worse...', Walker ventured.

'And you've provided me a full list through your liberally foul mouth, but that one sure hits the spot Mister Walker…'

The blue light grew, and with a gentle Whoomph extinguished the flaming ring before returning to its original size. It's glow brighter, shimmering and glistening.

Her voice returned to its smooth calmness although the words still dripped with intent and purpose. 'Billy has closed down because he feels betrayed by me using him to get to Horace. Remember him, the one who I saved you from?'

A silence hung in the air before the cruel one spoke. 'And me and my family will be eternally in your debt Miss Matthews. Please update me on your progress, or lack of it upon my return tomorrow. Thank you for your help and kind words.'

The shimmering light faded and returned to its pale blue hue. The soft voice returned inside his head. 'Billy, I know you can hear me. I understand your pain and anger at being used. I hope eventually you understand enough to forgive me and let me back in.'

Sadness washed over Billy. His fear of Horace outweighed any sense of betrayal but he had a new friend now. One who would never frighten him or sweep him aside. A friend that warmed him, gave him purpose and made him stronger. He turned and looked at the purple light that hovered next to him. Billy could feel it's love glowing and he returned it. There was no need for anyone else now.

♦

They could make out a vague shape floating in the vat of fluid. Sometimes a small part of the shape would come into view as it came into contact with the edge, before it drifted gently back into the red murk. The cables attaching it to the framework above followed its path as it floated aimlessly within.

'Proceed.' The clipped tones of the voice were at odds with the tension in the lab. Reece Coleman looked across at Ava in the control section, who nodded and smiled back. The dark red fluid started to drain from the vat, streaming in rivulets down the smooth transparent interior as the level dropped. It reminded Ava of a wine tasting evening she'd attended as a student back on earth. It's got legs, probably a good vintage, she thought.

'Drainage rate normal, bio markers nominal.' said the voice again. The cables shuddered as they took the strain while the vat emptied, betraying the formidable mass of the creature it contained.

Reece turned to Ava. She could see that his normally youthful face had become more lined, the light of optimism in his eyes had been dimmed by the pressure and responsibility he bore. 'Picking anything up yet Ava?', he asked.

She shook her head. The fluid had almost completely emptied from the vat, although the figure within was still obscured.

'Drainage complete. Withdraw vat', came the advice.

The vat started to disappear into the floor surrounding the motionless shape. Finally, it was gone, the last of the fluid running off, small wisps of steam were curling lazily from the suspended Hyperthon, glistening with the last vestiges of the liquid that had nourished and protected it during its ten-day incubation period. The silence in the control room weighed heavily on its apprehensive occupants. The tubes that had fed the creature were slowly withdrawn from their various orifices. The Hyperthon vomited up a thick yellow fluid, quivering as it did so. Ava noticed the latent power of the Hyperthon, evident in its stocky body that was covered in menacing layers of muscle. The mouth hung slackly open, a snake like tongue protruded, flopping to one side. Its size carried a formidable air of danger. Even though not as big as its fearsome cousin the Gorthon, it still dwarfed the humans that sought to bend it to their will.

Reece let out a long breath, releasing the tension that had been building in him. 'At least we know it's alive. Lower the headset', he said. A silver helmet connected by wires above, descended silently and seamlessly onto the head of the Hyperthon. A large tube protruded from the top of the headset. It contained the killswitch. A depleted uranium slug that would smash through the specially created weak spot at the base of the Hyperthon's skull, killing it instantly. A last resort should things get out of hand.

'I've got something!' Ava's voice carried her excitement although she was trying to remain calm after several months of unbroken failure on the Hyperthon. It was more of a feeling than a definite sense, like being watched or followed.

'Bio markers remain stable.' At least the voice was still calm, thought Ava as her heart beat faster. 'Proceed with Neuroware upload.'

The feeling became a sense and the sense became a gentle light floating about her, radiating benign warmth. The light grew brighter and the temperature increased like the soft late autumnal sun of her childhood, caressing her skin after the blazing heat of the summer months. Ava became aware of a distant noise orbiting her head in a slow pulsating rhythm, synchronised with the light's regular pattern of dimming and brightening. 'We're ok Reece', she said.

'Looking good here Ava. We're ready to go for consciousness initiation', Reece informed her.

The tempo of the sound suddenly increased, rushing faster and faster around her, the light keeping pace until it became one with the sound. The incessant throbbing rhythm increased, merging into a single note, as the light shone a steady yellow. The pitch increased and the yellow glow became whiter, increasing the heat that started to prickle. Ava became concerned. It began to feel like a runaway chain reaction as the energy fed on itself and increased the intensity.

'It's starting to lose control', Ava said and coaxed herself; Try to sooth it Ava, try to bring it down. She sent calming blue waves towards the light and soft harmonies to the increasingly loud note, which had acquired a discordant grating quality, drowning out those she generated. The blue waves were evaporated by the searing heat of the light, like the blazing midday sun of the vast uninhabitable regions of equatorial earth.

The Hyperthon stirred slowly at first, but with increasing intensity began to resist the restraints which were designed to contain twice the strength of the most powerful Gorthon, but the fearsome violence of the struggle far exceeded anything they had ever witnessed or expected. The recently dormant muscles sprang into life with a strength that was terrifying in its suddenness and extent. The mouth opened as the snakelike tongue wafted out, tasting its surroundings with a graceful carefree air that was at odds with its owner. Waves of flickering red and purple danced across the throbbing mass of the creatures' back and flanks. The claws flexed open then closed, exerting a vicelike grip on the restraints, causing the metal to ping and tick, straining in protest as the eyes rolled in a manner that made everyone feel as if the attention of the creature was fixed solely on them. The first whimpers of fear started to sound from the subjects of the creatures menacing stare.

Ava's hand moved toward the killswitch button and she frantically fought off the wall of blue heat and deafening white noise that was starting to overwhelm her. She felt microscopic against the mountainous unrestricted rage of the Hyperthon. Like an ant against a behemoth. The crescendo was deafening and the furnace was melting her mind. Nothing had even come close to this in her experience. It was too colossal to even contemplate.

'Stop the download.' she managed to mumble above the crushing strain.

The grinding squeal of the restraints started to buckle and filled the air as the low otherworldly rumble of the Hyperthon's increasing aggression made the hairs of those present stand on end in nauseating terror. One of the assistants' wobbling legs gave way from under him as he collapsed in a quivering heap. The others were rooted to the spot, mute statues of fear.

Wilting under the onslaught, Ava began to perceive something else. A faint, pure voice on the edge of consciousness. A twinkling pinprick of light in the conflagration shone through despite being dwarfed, and started to cut through the pandemonium. It bought with it a clarity that Ava hadn't thought possible as the relentless power started to yield to the new influence. She knew it wasn't coming from her, but there was no other presence that could have generated anything like it. It felt like the universe itself was singing to both her and the Hyperthon.

The groaning tear of unbreakable elements being ripped apart caused the panicked screaming of those present in the face of certain death and dismemberment to rise inexorably. Reece's voice embodied that fear. 'Killswitch Engage!', he screamed.

A dull thud sounded as the uranium slug fired, obliterating skull and brain tissue in a single shockwave of heat and energy. Vaporising the visceral thoughts and storm of hate that had existed in full force a micro second earlier. The mammoth strength Ava had been struggling against with every molecule of energy suddenly vanished. The resulting unbalanced lurch hit her with the force of a sack of rocks dropped from a clear blue sky, sending her crashing to the ground with a violence that left her disoriented and winded. The pure note continued for a few seconds before stopping in an almost surprised manner, with a little upward whip.

Ava breathlessly looked up to see Reece, the yellow pallor of fear evident on his face. His hands were still trembling as he helped her to her feet. 'It had started to tail off. I could feel it.' She said and looked around at the group of scientists, technicians and the security team. Some were leaning on their colleagues for support while others slumped to the floor in various states of confusion and incontinence.

'Well, that didn't work out too well did it.' Ava and Reece looked around to see Jordan Harris approaching accompanied by Sergeant Overgaard. 'Another couple of seconds and it would have broken the restraints'

'We had no choice Ava.' Reece said and added; 'It was overwhelming you and could have broken you. We did it as much for your safety as to contain the danger.'

'I could feel it coming under control.' protested Ava. 'Another few seconds...', she wasn't allowed to finish.

'Would that have been before or after it converted everyone in the room into puddles of pink goo?' Jordan said and continued; 'We are going to have to seriously look at upgrading our weapons profile. I've never seen anything like that before.' He looked across at Reece. 'I'm sorry Doctor Coleman that I had to order you to bring things to a premature end, but we had no choice.'

'I agree Jordan. We'd run out of options.' Reece looked back at Ava. 'So close Ava, but it failed. We'll have to examine the logs and find out what went wrong, and see what we can improve on. Still, a month's work down the toilet. I fear we won't be ready in time.'

Ava could feel the pain from her side that she must have injured when she fell, and winced as she spoke. 'There was something else there Reece. Another entity that started to placate the Hyperthon and bring it down from the hyper stimulated state. I don't know what it was, but it was definitely real.'

'Well you're the only Psychic consultant we've got on the base, so I don't know where it could have originated.'

'You two can sort that one out yourselves.' said Jordan 'I'm going to call the clean up team in.' He gestured to the hulking figure of the Hyperthon, which even in death still carried a sense of menace.

Ava noticed Jordan turn to Overgaard next to him and spoke softly in his ear. Overgaard nodded in response. Jordan said quietly. 'Excellent. Roll it out immediately', before turning back to speak to all those present and added ruefully. 'God help us if one of those broke loose in the base.' All those present murmured in agreement.

Meanwhile Ava looked out for the first time across the scene. The twisted wreckage of the restraints enveloping the lifeless Hyperthon in crazy angles of splintered and tattered metal. A trail of fluorescent aqua liquid that seeped from a gaping hole in the Hyperthon's head mingled with yellow slime, carved a lazy steaming trail towards the drainage slots, carrying with them the brief story of a creature that had its entire existence contained within a few short moments.

♦

The thunderstorm of agony that Ava was suffering rolled and roared across her side despite the strong painkillers. The constant assault of pain ate into her ability to concentrate. She prided herself on her laser like focus, even when it came to the driest, most stultifying topics. Even at school in Lower Manhattan, before it was swallowed by the Hudson River, she had been able to follow the lesson despite Mister Delgado's best attempts to singlehandedly reduce the subject of mathematics into a rote memory exercise.

Doctor Khan had called the meeting to gauge the progress of each Mag type as well as consultants from other relevant areas. They had worked through several presentations over the past three hours.

Ryan Baxter gave an overview of each module of Pangea base and its component systems. Ava had never fully grasped the scale of their habitat and Ryan's knowledge was truly encyclopaedic. How could humans control such an entity and to her surprise, she found from Kalpana Bhatta the AI specialist, that humans didn't control it at all. Decisions were made by the Artificial intelligence systems that had evolved since the base was first constructed. Using the quantum systems that literally ran every possible scenario simultaneously to return the correct answer and fed it back into the learning algorithms that compared it to previous results before selecting the best option. It was as if they travelled into the future testing each hypotheses and came back with the correct answer 100% of the time, billions of times a second. It didn't tell them how it had arrived at the answer and they didn't need to know. It just produced it. This left Ava deeply uneasy. She'd never understood quantum physics, but then again nobody had ever understood how it really worked, even after over two hundred years of the greatest minds in the world toiling ceaselessly to find out. So Mister Quantum, is there a single equation that encapsulates the universe? Yes, was the answer. Well, what is it? The inevitable question. Dunno, but there definitely is one.

Then there was Magnus Eriksen talking about the base Droids, as well as the planned upgrades for the Mags, bringing them closer to robots than biobots. This really rang the alarm bells in Ava's head. They're strong enough already without it being multiplied. The enhancement prepared for the Gorthon would increase its strength and endurance by a factor of three. This would enable significantly increased range. Ava looked around the room at the attentive expressions and empty nods of those who didn't know anything. She had seen what a Hyperthon unaided could do or the cunning of a single Gargoyle. Even when Magnus announced that the upgrades were still in the experimental phase, Ava's fears did not abate. There was also some mention of Droid upgrades had reached an advanced stage of development and would be ready to roll out in the near future.

She turned to Reece and whispered, 'I hope they do a better job than the current containment facilities or we're toast.'

The Bornix team expressed confidence but were still experiencing sporadic issues, although not to the extent experienced by the Gorthon.

Walker's presentation on the Gargoyles was a point study in fudge, obfuscation and unctuousness. His plastic mask of confidence and authority hid the facts of his cruelty, incompetence and weakness. There had been no sign of the humility or humanity resurfacing. He was quick to point the finger of blame at Harry Felton. 'He's been assigned minor duties upon his return, which won't be for several weeks. I've allocated my remaining staff to take up the slack left by Doctor Felton', he said.

Ava had visited Harry in the infirmary shortly after the incident. She was surprised he wasn't more subdued after such an ordeal. Telling her enthusiastically about his new hand that was being 3D printed. Ava told him of the killing of Horace in the cooling plant. He seemed disappointed that 'Old Walkabout' was the one who survived. She decided against telling Harry about Billy, or indeed of her little tête-à-tête with Walker. That could wait until later.

There undoubtedly had been progress, but there was an air of fear and tension in both the staff and the Gargoyles. Billy had been earmarked for destruction by Walker after he had shut down completely, only to be saved by Ava as she felt it had learnt to mask its signals from her and she wanted to discover how.

'We are ready to start full scale production of Gargoyles within the month', Walker concluded to a standing ovation.

'A month my goddamn ass.' whispered Ava to Reece who responded with a knowing smile.

In contrast to the wild enthusiasm extended to Walker's presentation, the video of the previous day's episode with the Hyperthon was watched, apart from the occasional clearing of a throat or the creaking of a chair, in complete silence.

'One interesting thing to come from all this are the mind logs.' said Reece in his presentation as he continued; 'A single clear line from a separate source detected amongst the noise of the Hyperthon readings.' He turned to the screen of the jumble of frenzied output that told the story of the Hyperthon's initiation. 'If we subtract the Hyperthon's output, we are left with Miss Matthews's.'

A smaller set of data appeared, less frantic but reflecting Ava's desperate attempts to bring the Hyperthon under control. 'And now the interesting part...', Reece went on; 'We subtract Miss Matthews's data...'

Ava's trace disappeared and a single line appeared across the graph, barely deviating from its path. Those present looked at each other. Eyebrows were raised and others shook their head in surprise.

'It started a few seconds after the consciousness upload was initiated.' Continued Reece. 'Thanks to Miss Matthews's bravery and skill we found it, otherwise it would have been lost in the noise.' A small round of applause rippled around the room as all eyes turned to Ava who tried to smile graciously while feeling the burn of embarrassment on her cheeks.

'Do we know where it originated Doctor Coleman?' It was Dr Khan.

'Well, fortunately another apparatus was switched on in the Gargoyle labs undergoing routine maintenance and it also picked up the spurious signal.' We tried to triangulate them. It was difficult but we managed to establish it was from somewhere within the base', Reece replied.

'Where was it from?' Khan persisted.

'The civilian areas.' Reece said flatly.

There was a stir around the room. Khan sat bowed forward with his head in his hands. 'Then our secret is out', he uttered.

'Not necessarily Doctor....', Reece was resolute as he addressed Khan; '....The unusual thing is the exceptional clarity. Both I and Miss Matthews have never encountered such a pristine signal. Our opinion is that the source is artificial as it would be impossible for a human to produce such precision.'

A visibly relieved Khan stood up and bowed to Reece. 'Thank you for this information Dr Coleman. We would like you to investigate the source of this signal further, so we can establish its threat level.'

'Doctor. We've one more thing to show our colleagues'. Reece's voice conveyed the gravity of the next subject. 'If I may....' he turned to the screen.

'....After further analysis of the log, we decided to widen the spectrum and found this.....', It was the readouts of the Hyperthon. Ava and the unknown source were redisplayed in their original configuration. The view zoomed out and a few flecks of interference were displayed, then at the top was another straight line that started when the Hyperthon was initiated and ended abruptly as it was terminated. '.....Ladies and Gentlemen....', Reece continued; '...we have a new signal, on a resonance of five to three. It seems to be in sync with the outburst of the Hyperthon and looks like a carrier signal designed to flip the subject into a state of instability. It does nothing on its own but in concert with the normal waves, it causes a much wider interference pattern leading to the behavioural anomalies.'

'What evidence do you have for this theory Doctor Coleman?', it was the smooth tones of Wen Chiang, team leader of the Gorthon project. 'This could mean anything as far as I can see.' The undertone of sarcasm permeated every word.

Ava noticed how Reece bristled at the condescending manner of Chiang but she knew he was expecting such an attack from the poisonous Doctor. She had noticed Chiang's ingratiating behaviour to Khan as well as her own ill-founded confidence in her own ability. Managing upwards. That was the phrase he'd mentioned.

Reece took a deep breath as he appeared to gather his thoughts. 'Thank you for your question Doctor Chung.' He deliberately mispronounced her name. Her face remained a mask of indifference as Reece continued. 'We've also taken a look at the 191065N incident and the five to three resonance line is there as well.'

'Any more incidents Doctor Coleman?' Chiang asked.

Reece shook his head and said. 'We've only just started looking, but we're confident that we'll find more.'

'I admire your faith in your abilities Doctor, but unfortunately neither myself nor Doctor Khan share your confidence', Chiang sneered.

Khan's head shot round and he looked at Chiang as she continued in her soft smooth confident tones, as if reading a bedtime story or announcing flight boarding times. 'Basing your theory on just two isolated incidences isn't really what I'd refer to as statistically certain, and I see this as a vain attempt to stave off the imminent closure of your mishandled failure of a project.'

Reece's face was a picture of impotent anger as he struggled to find the words to counter Chiang's accusations. Looked around the room for a friendly face, he found numerous averted eyes. Only Ava gave him the support he craved and it gave him the courage required for a counter attack. 'This....!', he said and held out his hand towards his adversary as he continued; '....This is the voice of one of the prime movers behind the Bagama Outbreak.' There was a sharp intake of breath

125

as Reece pressed home the attack. 'It was your recommendations that caused it. Don't you dare talk to me about confidence in my abilities. What have you got to offer? What credibility or integrity do you possess?'. He was indignant while staring straight at Chiang who maintained her impassive exterior despite the onslaught. Nevertheless he continued; 'To be responsible for the deaths of scores of innocent people, just to prove a point...'. He paused briefly and looked at Khan, whose face was crimson with embarrassment and fury.

'I think you've said enough Doctor Coleman', Khan responded as he raised his head and looked straight at Reece. 'We will discuss this further upon the conclusion of this meeting'.

Reece returned to his seat next to Ava who patted him on the hand.

Ava sat and watched in silence with Reece as an unperturbed Doctor Chiang presented her team's findings and concluded with a video of the successful emergence of a Gorthon, christened Titus, from its incubation vat. It was possible to gauge its size by the Lilliputian figures of those monitoring its emergence. The hideous boulder sized head with the beady rodentlike eyes staring out with cold cruelty at its surroundings. The mouth opened unnaturally wide to reveal immaculate lines of murderous pure white teeth, poised to sink into the nearest available flesh and rip it from whatever it belonged to. The arms that sprang from the massive torso were a tangled knot of muscle and sinew that ended in giant slicing claws. The video of its training and statistical charts were, Ava had to admit, a masterpiece of presentation, even though actual evidence of Chiang's claims were in short supply. At the conclusion, a round of applause erupted. This fed Chiang's shameless arrogance and her desperate need for validation. Even Khan seemed impressed. While Ava went through the motions of applause, Reece sat stony faced, arms folded in sullen silence.

'Doctor Chiang....!' Ava's voice raised itself above the noise. Faces turned to look at her. '....Doctor Chiang', she continued; 'could I say that one of the characteristics of the Gorthon is that it appears to have the ability to shield itself from psychic probing.' Her look of self-congratulation was quickly replaced by consternation. 'What have you got to say on this?'

Chiang quickly switched to the attack. 'Miss Matthews. Your lack of ability in your chosen field of expertise reflects more on you than on my achievements. Maybe if you had put the efforts in the right areas you wouldn't feel the need to ask such impertinent questions.' A ripple of laughter spread round the room, some trying a bit too hard to be seen to agree with her.

Khan held his hands downward to calm the commotion as he spoke. 'Ladies and Gentlemen.....' All heads turned to the respected, if limited, academic who continued; '....I would like to stress the absolute need to maintain secrecy and at

126

the same time, I would like to remind you that it's easy to celebrate success before it's actually arrived. We are currently behind schedule, so I urge you to even greater efforts in our endeavour.....' He paused and looked at the silent attentive faces in the room. All eyes were expectantly fixed on him, but he proceeded; '.....You stand at the edge of a new age in Human achievement. You are the pioneers and when the full story is finally revealed, the world will remember your efforts and the benefits it has brought to civilisation. This will be the day when synthetic lifeforms will no longer be a source of fear and ignorance but one of pride.....' The atmosphere in the room crackled as some of the audience seemed to visibly grow with each word uttered, their hands clenched and tears running down their flushed cheeks as Khan continued, the passion in his voice unmistakable; '....I would like to remind you all how far we've come in such a short time, of the personal sacrifices made for the prize that now hangs within our grasp; of the generations who we have followed and now we are forging our own path into the glorious annals of science to achieve an immortality that shall ring throughout the ages. Nobody in the history of the entire human race has witnessed the wonders that you have shone a bright light upon. No matter where you go in life this achievement will stay with you and will be a source of pride, the glow of which will warm your hearts for the rest of your days.' A roar of pure emotion filled the room and people were hugging and shaking their fists at Khan's passionate exhortations.

Ava smiled and joined in but her eyes remained fixed upon Chiang and noted the sly expression of satisfaction with interest. I think you've got a lot to hide Doctor. A lot, and I'm going to find out what it is, Ava thought.

Reece's expression hadn't changed as Ava looked to him. 'I can't stand another second of this shit Ava. I'm off.' He said and stormed off with Ava in pursuit.

They walked through the lobby into the corridor, the commotion of the meeting fading behind them. Ava breathlessly tried to keep up and winced at the pain of her efforts. 'Reece....' she appealed; '...will you just hold on a second.' Reece stopped and turned to her. She took a deep breath and tried to focus. 'Reece you have to be patient....', she said, adding; 'These outbursts only make you look bad.'

'I'll see you in Khan's office', he replied.

Ava looked into Reece's eyes, but he turned and resumed his fast pace. Deciding it was better to let him cool off, she watched him disappear up the corridor.

A hand touched her arm. 'Miss Matthews..' Ava turned to see Magnus Eriksen and Kalpana Bhatta looking gravely at her.

Ava was mildly surprised to be approached by those she considered hostile to her point of view. 'How can I help you Dr Eriksen?'

'We need to speak Miss Matthews', Magnus requested.

Ava was both intrigued and suspicious. Even through the fog of painkillers, her guard was up. 'Of course...,' she said, then asked; 'What about?'

'Not here..' Magnus said and looked across at Kalpana.

'It's important Ava..' Kalpana interjected. '....We wouldn't ask if we didn't think it was.'

Ava knew them professionally, but that was it. They seemed decent enough but you never really knew. 'If it's so important why didn't you raise it during the meeting?'

'I think you know the reason for that Ava', Kalpana responded.

Ava probed their minds and only sensed desperation, and took a deep breath. 'Ok. Come to my room at 15:00 this afternoon', she offered. The look of relief on their faces told Ava all she needed to know. 'I can't promise you anything but I'll listen', she said.

The shuffle of footsteps and the hubbub of voices echoed along the corridor as the remainder of those who attended the meeting approached.

'You won't regret it Miss Matthews.' Magnus smiled at Ava who nodded.

'15:00 sharp. This better be worth my while!', she told them. The noise of the others grew louder. Ava turned abruptly and made her way towards Khan's office, her mind working overtime.

◆

'So they're closing me down!' Reece said and looked across at Ava.

'It isn't like that Reece.' She replied.

The slight figure of Khan stared back across the desk, surprised at the outburst, despite the earlier one directed towards Chiang. 'Doctor Coleman....' Khan began; '....I want to assure you that you are *not* being closed down. All I'm saying to you is that we are diverting resources towards the Gorthon project, while you and Miss Matthews continue to investigate if the extra signal that you propose, is the source of the anomalies that have plagued our research.' He spoke with a paternal firmness that was both comforting and authoritative as he continued; 'Surely you want to get to the bottom of this and what could be more important.' Reece shook his head and shrugged his shoulders. Khan continued, 'I should also add that perhaps a break from the Hyperthon would help with the confidence issues you appear to be the subject of amongst your colleagues. I would suggest that a short time out of the firing line would benefit everyone.'

Ava reached across and put her hand on Reece's shoulder and said. 'Reece. I think we can really benefit everyone if we make the breakthrough.'

128

'But we were so close.' Reece protested.

'I'm afraid that wasn't the impression I had Doctor Coleman.' Khan intoned. 'Deadline after deadline missed. No results of note and nearly a major breakout that would have put the Gargoyle incident in the shade',

'Reece. I'm afraid I have to agree with Doctor Khan....', Ava cut in; '....I think once we get to the bottom of the resonance signal, we can bring benefits across the entire research program. Then we can return to complete the Hyperthon project successfully. Think about it', she invited.

Reece sighed as if relenting; 'Ok, we'll analyse all the signals during the testing phases', he said and added. 'We'll isolate the source of both the human and the unknown and close off the Hyperthon.'

'I knew you would see the wisdom of our approach Doctor Coleman and I would like to acknowledge your professionalism in this matter.' A visibly relieved Khan said.

'Yep, well done Reece. Let's get onto it', Ava announced.

Reece stood up and shook Khan's hand. He and Ava turned to leave.

'Well what do you think Ava?' he said as they exited Khan's office.

'There's a lot of shortcuts taking place Reece, and I don't like it one bit. It's only a matter of time before there's a serious incident and time I'm afraid is the one thing we're running out of.'

They looked at each other and Reece nodded in agreement. 'Let's go', he said as they made their way back to the Hyperthon labs.

13

'**Don't** be scared, these things are a test of your strength and your faith will be stronger as a result.' He looked out to the congregation and smiled. The vastness of the auditorium would have normally dwarfed the two hundred or so present but having them closely packed together near the front magnified their presence and bought a greater sense of unity. The congregation reflected the diversity of the base's population of settlers with all backgrounds, ages and genders present. Even a few soldiers in their civilian clothes were present. Raised up on the stage bedecked with flowers and beautifully woven tapestries of idyllic scenes, the spotlight shone on counsellor Marcus Burgman, bringing to life his shining white robe, interlaced with silver filigree, building to the golden sacred circle adorning the front, matching the golden circle placed at the centre of the stage. His swept back hair, jet black beard and piercing blue eyes complimented his tall upright frame, lending an air of peace and wisdom that drew such devotion from the followers.

He continued in his soft yet strong voice. 'In any new situation, especially as significant as this one, when the moment of truth arrives, and this is no everyday situation, it's only natural doubts will come to the fore. You wouldn't be human if they didn't.' He noted with satisfaction that the majority were nodding in agreement.

A woman from the back of the room spoke up, expressing her concern; 'But what if the planet isn't the utopian paradise we were promised counsellor. We have no idea how long it will be before we can commence the new lives we were promised. We've been kept inside this base for over two months and there's no sign of us leaving anytime soon.' Mutterings of agreement rippled through the congregation as she continued. 'After such a long journey across the stars. It would be unbearable if the same problems that drove us to leave our beloved mother planet reappeared there.'

'Then all the more reason to place your faith in Ykdar the Great Sky Lord and submit yourself to his love and mercy. To treat your brothers and sisters with empathy and compassion', Marcus told her but aimed his comment at the congregation as a whole. Murmurs of agreement grew louder. Marcus never lost the thrill of the moment when the balance tipped and the people were putty in his hands, ready to be shaped according to his wishes. He continued; 'Ykdar will shine the light on our path forward and show us the way. We need to believe in his righteousness and justice, then all will be well.'

The lone voice of the woman was drowned out amongst the shouts of acclamation from the carefully placed followers of Ykdar in the room. Coached to stand and exclaim their love of the great one and the tutor of his love, this was Marcus Burgman, Religious Counsellor and leader of the congregation. The shouts were becoming a mass of noise as the fervour in the room started to increase. The particularly talented followers started to raise their arms with tears in their eyes, beseeching Ykdar to guide their souls along the path to enlightenment and truth. The adulation spread around the room like wildfire as Marcus drank in the moment before raising his hands in a reassuring gesture as the crowd's fervour started to subside.

'Brothers, Sisters! Please, restrain your passion, reign in your spirits', he pleaded. 'Save your energy for the trials ahead.'

A little girl, no older than five, prompted by her parents, ran forward and up the steps at the front of the stage, and hugged Marcus's leg, tears streaming down her cheeks, before stepping back and offering the Counsellor a small knitted doll that was obviously her most treasured possession. Her big eyes looked adoringly up at Marcus, who stroked her golden blond hair. 'Please take it Counsellor Marcus.' she said haltingly through sobs of adulation. Then she returned to her proud, smiling mother who swept her up in open arms.

A big 'Ahhhh.' came from those present. After all who could object to such an expression of pure love from such a beautiful child? Which is exactly as Marcus had planned it. Bypass the reason; go straight for the jugular called emotion. He had been trained well.

'Please, please calm yourselves.....' He raised his voice and the noise died down, and although the hubbub and sobs could still be heard, the passion of those gathered had been lowered to a manageable level. This allowed Marcus to continue '....I would like to thank young Lucy here for her precious gift.' He held up the small orange doll for all to see. There were affectionate laughs, hands clasped over hearts, heads tilted to one side in approval and smiling faces filled the room as the Counsellor, to much acclaim blew a tender kiss to the star struck youngster. Now's the time for the modest, speechless smile Marcus. Don't overdo it he told himself, then proceeded; 'Brothers, Sisters... Children. Thank you for your love and kindness. I'm...', he hesitated to deliberate; Don't forget the sigh, then the slight breaking of the voice Marcus. 'Overwhelmed.' Now nod slowly and purse the lips. There was a roar from the crowd before it quickly abated. You lot are so easy he thought and continued; 'Remember Ykdar loves you. Take that message and spread it amongst your fellow pilgrims because that's what everyone on this planet is. You are all brothers and sisters, pilgrims, pioneers and settlers, starting a new live on a new world, leaving the pain, misery and folly of the old one behind. Now go in peace.'

The music struck up and a mawkish ballad, '*Every Day I Love You More and More*' began playing. Everyone joined in heartily, before they filed out of the auditorium, arms raised, still singing as they left.

He watched from the stage with pride and satisfaction at the smiling faces. You're good at this Marcus, very good indeed and it's getting better each time. Look at their smiling faces, full of joy. Now go forth and multiply, he murmured silently to himself.

◆

They sat in a small circle of chairs leaning inward, except Marcus who was sitting upright to emphasize his position at the head of the group. 'You did well today. I was proud of you all.' He looked around at the group. Antonina with her dark hair and olive skin. Odette, smaller and fair haired. Then his gaze settled on the frail figure of Aaron, sitting hunched between Antonina and Odette. 'But I was especially proud of you Aaron.' he said in a soft voice that was almost a whisper. All eyes in the small contemplation room turned to Aaron, his mouth slightly open and veneration in his eyes. This was the first time he'd been singled out in the post worship meeting.

'Th...thank you Counsellor, I'm honoured.' Aaron managed to stammer in hushed reverential tones before blushing a bright red that was noticeable to all present, even though the room was dimly lit.

Oh Aaron you were always the most credulous of my entire flock you pointless little IT nerd. Though Marcus was silently disdainful of Aaron, he also made Marcus uncomfortable because "the little nerd" reminded him of his naïve younger self. 'However, I would suggest you hold back on the tears a little bit longer', he directed his statement to the boy.

Aaron was crestfallen. 'I... I'm sorry Counsellor. I was so... overcome with love, I couldn't help myself.' A single tear of remorse trickled down his cheek.

Ok Marcus...., the Counsellor silently told himself; ....put him out of his misery and feed him the rest of the shit sandwich. Lovely soft bread at the bottom, a healthy dollop of the brown stuff in the middle and an even lovelier pure white slice to top it all off.

'Dear Aaron. I know your love of the Great One has no limits and I feel that love reflecting the warmth in my heart. I know that such a devoted heart as yours is free with its feelings, but I ask you to think of the higher task in hand. To bring the truth to the masses you need to maintain clarity. Try to control your passion and use your undoubted talents to think of the bigger picture', Marcus advised.

Tears flooded in a torrent as Aaron showed his appreciation. 'Oh thank you Counsellor Marcus for such words of great wisdom'.

Antonina and Odette either side of him embraced the pathetic sobbing figure.

'Aaron…' Marcus said, as the young man, with his bottom lip quivering, wiped away the tears and looked back at the religious leader who suggested. '….Starting from now would be good.'

'Of course counsellor, of course.' Aaron replied. He sat up and took a deep breath then added; 'I just get carried away sometimes.'

Another voice spoke up. 'Don't worry Aaron, we understand your devotion to Counsellor Marcus.' It was the teacher, Leon Jordan. Marcus looked over to him and immediately and silently noted; Oh brother Leon your role is crucial to my plans. To be the leader of education in the ways of Ykdar to the young and suggestible. Their obedient minds ripe for moulding and shaped to our purpose.

'We all feel it in our hearts brother, but we must keep a clear mind for the purpose Marcus has conferred upon us. We are the lucky ones and we desire to spread our good fortune amongst the population of Magdur', Leon offered.

'Well said indeed brother Leon, and I trust that all present, especially Aaron, will take heed of your wise words.' Marcus said, before turning from Leon and addressing the group. 'Let us pray as one.' They joined hands and the sonorous tones of Marcus's 'important voice' as he liked to call it, filled the room. 'Friends….', he continued; '….The great trial of our mission is approaching, and we need to build on our successes. I urge you all to redouble your efforts, spread the truth among the population and raise our numbers so by the time leave this place and move to our settlements they will make up a significant fraction of the peoples of Magdur. Then we will truly be able to create a paradise in a new world.'

'Praise be to Ykdar!' Everyone uttered in unison.

Marcus rose from his seat and held his hands out. 'Now spread our message far and wide, bringing the benefits of Ykdar's wisdom to the uninitiated. Peace be with you brothers and sisters.'

'Peace be with you Counsellor', The smiling followers responded as one, before they stood and shuffled towards the door.

Marcus watched the last of them exit. He remained, alone. After a few moments a tall thin figure appeared noiselessly from behind the curtain at the side of the room. The scarf and black greatcoat made his white hair and pale, translucent skin, seemed almost luminous in the dimly lit room. His scarf and coat seem to float in mid-air. His features, although still appearing young, were bereft of the soft lines of youth. The hardened lines of an addict framed his face. The thin slit of his mouth and deep set eyes complemented the minimalism of his personality.

Marcus sensed his presence and without looking at him spoke, 'Brother Attilio.'

'Counsellor.' Attilio responded in his characteristically soft voice that made even Marcus feel a little uneasy. Marcus remained silent which Attilio took as his cue to continue. 'The chosen one is amongst us, I am sure of it.'

'You have found her? The promised one.' The hope in Marcus's voice betrayed the desperation he felt. The signs were all in place. The trip to Magdur specifically chosen as Ereus lay in the constellation Cygnus, the Swan. The prophecy of the young girl with the Swan would confirm the Sky lord's approval of their plans and would be presented to the followers as proof of his blessing.

'I have heard her voice calling out and see her gentle light. It is nearby', Attilio replied

'But you've not found her yet?', Marcus asked again.

'I've been calling to her; she doesn't respond, but I'm getting nearer every day. It is only a matter of time before she reveals herself to me. I am certain', Attilio said, more with hope.

'And how can you be sure it's her', Marcus sought some assurance.

'There is a swan in flight. I see it as clear as day', came the response.

'Where is the swan?', now it was Marcus's turn to hope.

'Upon her. A mark of some kind', Attilio told him.

'You mean a tattoo? I could have one of those if I wished.' Marcus's irritation was becoming apparent.

'No, it is entirely natural.' Attilio's words adopted a defensive tone. 'I feel you doubt me Counsellor. My word is true.'

'I don't doubt your sincerity....' Marcus lied '....but it seems too good to be true that an ancient prophecy would present itself to us in such an obvious manner. I fear the gods are playing tricks with us. To test our faith.' Marcus tried to look into Attilio's face but the cold features remained expressionless. 'Continue to search and come to me when you have some evidence. Now go', the Counsellor ordered.

Attilio placed his hand on his chest, inclined his head slightly then slipped quietly out of the room.

The cursory tone reflected the cynicism Marcus had toward psychics. He didn't trust them and considered them charlatans. Added to this, the strange haunting presence of Attilio chilled his bones to the extent that, even if Attilio had bought the very tomes of the gods signed in their blood directly to him, the urge to push him away would still be overwhelming.

134

On their first meeting when Attilio had introduced himself, Marcus had been aware of it. A repulsive force that gave him the urge to flee and hide, but the tantalizing information and the opportunity it presented got the better of his abhorrence. Keep him at arm's length until he proved useful. Sometimes solid gold could be found in the least promising locations, the Counsellor figured.

Marcus's thoughts returned to his small flock. A most unpromising crowd, yet the odd flower bloomed in the desert that, with careful nurturing, would become a beautiful garden. The occasional weed would have to be rooted out but it was his to shape and cultivate. A far cry indeed from the cruelty and rejection of the cynical earth and its obsession with material wealth for an undeserving few, while the vast majority were starved and worked to death. The loss of faith through the abuse of position and collusion with the elite to pursue and exploit its historical advantage had corrupted the true message. The people were weak and easily manipulated through their deepest fears, real or imagined. They longed to submit themselves, being meekly led wherever their supposed saviours wished to take them. Never giving a moment's thought as to where they were going, so long as they escaped the monotony of everyday existence. But then new faiths untainted by the excesses of the old ways had started to emerge. They spoke to the people once again even though some acts were regrettable yet necessary for the greater good. Yet this faith had given his talents an outlet and position at odds with the derision and contempt of early life. The bitterness stayed with him even though nearly three decades had passed.

*

'Marcus Bumhole!' shouted Andreas Ziegler. This invited squeals of laughter from the children surrounding him in the playground. His knees shook and they started the rhythmic chant. 'Bumhole, Bumhole, Marcus fuckin Bumhole.' He felt the stinging blow as the bigger, stronger Andreas punched him in the ear knocking his puny frame to the ground and into a puddle, much to the acclaim of those present. 'Look! He's pissed himself.' cried one of the other boys as a shivering Marcus raised himself, the wetness dribbling down his trouser legs. The screeching laughter, especially from the girls watching, was more painful and humiliating than any blow from the cruel fists of Andreas. He looked over with relief to the approaching Mr. Weiss for salvation, and he could have sworn the teacher was laughing a moment earlier.

'Ok, ok. Break it up', the teacher said as his tormentor melted back into the crowd of onlookers. 'Oh dear, another accident?' Mr. Weiss looked down at Marcus wet trousers.

'Why do they hate me so?' Marcus cried to his mother that evening as she cradled him and swayed back and forth. 'What have I done to them?', the boy wanted to know.

'They're jealous of you my darling.' His mother replied, running her fingers through his dark hair, before she held him out in front of her, wiping the tears from his sunken cheeks. Putting her hands on his shoulders and looking him in the eye, she told him. 'Because you're special and one of the chosen few. Don't you ever forget that. The gods will punish them for their cruelty and spite. I promise.' He knew his mother was right. She was always right.

A few days later the gods delivered in spades, just as mother had promised. On the hockey pitch the feverish maelstrom of the game washed over Marcus. The bright sun did nothing to stop the cruel freezing wind that tore at his raw skin and seemed to find its way between his ribs and into his innards, turning them to frozen jelly. His legs were stiff with the cold and unwilling to carry him more than a few yards before his miniscule lungs protested by starving him of oxygen.

The lead fluctuated back and forth between the two teams. Every time the ball went anywhere near him, it was ripped away with a ferocious suddenness he'd been completely unable to comprehend. His shivering white frame brushed aside like a brittle twig with the minimum of effort. Marcus was convinced his own team were passing the ball deliberately weakly to him so he would get obliterated.

'Sir! Why do we have to have Bumhole in our team? He's gonna cost us the game', one boy had complained

'It's about inclusiveness, that's why....', Sir said and earnestly explained; '....His name is Burgman and he's doing his best. Don't let me hear you say that again.'

Despite the teacher's admonition, the boy smirked and skilfully spat in Marcus's ear as he ran past.

Regardless of Marcus's pitiful efforts, the game stayed level. Then in the dying moments he somehow found himself alone in front of the goal. Standing there, an irrelevant almost forgotten figure, the ball broke loose from a melee and skittered towards him. Feet turned in, slack shoulders slumped and hockey stick hanging limply from one hand, suddenly he was the decisive figure on the pitch. The complete and utter certainty of scoring the winner electrified him as he sprang into life. His moment of redemption had arrived. The adoring crowd would sweep him off his feet in their unbounded delirium, as they carried him shoulder high from the pitch chanting, 'Marcus, Marcus, Marcus!' No Bumhole this time. The hero of the day.

Then a voice sounded behind him. 'Bumhole, leave it. It's mine!' He recognised the voice of his nemesis, Andreas Ziegler. But nothing was going to stop Marcus thrashing the ball gleefully into the gaping, open goal. The trampling of Andreas approaching from behind grew louder, ready to steal the glory that was rightfully his.

'Fuckin leave it Bumhole or you're dead.' hissed the spiteful voice.

The ball was nearly upon him. The roar of anticipation of the crowd filled his ears. This was it. This was his moment. No one was going to rob him of it now. He drew the hockey stick back, barely noticing a slight clonk before bringing it forward, thwacking the ball perfectly with all his might. It flew towards the welcoming vacant goal. It was on its way and no force in the universe could stop it now. Please just hold life there. Savour the moment; drink it in, he thought as the ball continued on its inevitable progress goalward. When it hit the billowing net, a primal scream erupted from Marcus scrawny frame. No one would have thought this possible even a few moments earlier. Time stood still and the world was silent, as arms raised aloft in magnificent conquest, he turned to welcome the congratulations of his thankful teammates.

But the silence was real and the only thing that was still was the prostrate, traumatised figure of Andreas Ziegler, blood gouting from a hideous hole where his eye had been a few moments earlier, before it met the full force of Marcus's stick coming in the opposite direction. The scene he observed tore the legs away from his moment of glory, and a new, stronger emotion manifested itself. The thrill of triumphant vengeance over his antagonist enveloped Marcus and it took all of his feeble self-control not to laugh out loud. Everyone was frozen to the spot except the teacher who came rushing to the aid of the stricken Andreas. The look on his face told Marcus that the wound was every bit as serious as he'd hoped it would be. Then he was enveloped in another strange sensation. It was as if the gods had spoken to him personally. 'See my child, we told you all would be well.' Mother had told him he was special and he knew she was right all along.

*

Marcus smiled at the memory of his first communication with the Great One, as he closed the contemplation room at the back of the auditorium. Turning and facing the busy concourse with its pristine white walls interspersed with gleaming glass and metal of the shops that the company had thoughtfully converted to make the settlers feel at home, he started to make his way back to his living quarters through the crowded throng. Even though his robe was hung up in the contemplation room, he still cut a distinctive easily recognisable figure and several people offered him warm greetings. He always responded with a small nod to match the modest smile, hand placed on heart. 'Peace be with you Counsellor.' they would say. He liked that, particularly when the pretty girls said it. There was nothing about sins of the flesh in the books of wisdom and in his

137

opinion, they seemed to extoll the virtues of free love. None of the perverse self-denial that had caused so much harm in earlier times, he told himself. Looking around at the empty smiling faces consumed with the pointless purchases of frivolous trinkets, his contemplation continued; Idiots, they're not going to help you when you finally get to the end of your journey, and reach the settlements. A captive audience if ever there was one. You should be considering the meaning of your existence instead of frittering away your time and money. The evils of consumerism had been a major distraction from the true word and the rapacious multinationals that fed it were emptying the minds of the young in particular. Buy this, do that, wear these. Yes, keep looking there while we continue quietly removing just enough money and hard won liberties for them not to notice. Until it was too late of course.

He'd become aware of a different path shortly after he'd escaped from the dark clutches of his mother's smothering attentions. It was the day the smiling man with the wide staring eyes and crazy hair handed Marcus the leaflet in the street.

*

'There is another way!' proclaimed the headline on the leaflet that was thrust into his hand. He had noticed the man on a few occasions on the corner near the shops before, but had taken no notice. People passed him by, almost oblivious to his existence as if he were a ghost or a wisp of smoke. But on this occasion he'd caught Marcus's eye, and was on him in a flash. As Marcus studied the literature before him, the man spoke. 'Have you read any of our material before brother?' His warm friendly manner immediately drawing in Marcus.

'No... No I've never had the privilege my friend.' Privilege, privilege! Where did that come from? Marcus asked himself.

'Well brother....' the man continued before Marcus had time to think '....what do you think of the appalling inequality in the world....? Where privilege is handed on a plate to the genetically engineered super rich and their cronies, while the rest of us suffer the consequences of their voracious greed'. Though he answered his own question, he asked again; '....and what do you think could be done to cure the ills of modern society?'

'Well I've never really thought about it, to be honest. I'm too busy trying to scrape together a living to consider stuff like that.' Marcus said and looked in to the cheerful confident face in front of him.

'Yes brother that happens to everyone. Too oppressed to get their heads up and look around and notice what's happening to society and the world in general.'

'Hard to disagree with that.' Marcus ventured, still unsure.

'Look..., the man said and continued; 'We're holding a meeting this evening at the local scout's hall if you're interested brother. Eight o'clock.' He raised his eyebrows to question. 'See you there?'

Marcus nodded, although he was still unsure. 'Ok, sounds interesting. I'll give it a go.'

'Splendid stuff!', satisfied, the man thrust his hand out and as Marcus took it, he asked; 'and you are…'

'M...Marcus. Marcus Burgman.' Marcus answered but immediately questioned himself; Why did you give your surname you idiot! He can track you down now.

'Max, or Maximilian Sanger if you want the full version.' The man introduced himself and let out a loud bark of a laugh that momentarily startled Marcus. Max placed his hand on Marcus's shoulder. He felt the latent power of his grip as he looked Marcus in the eye, seeming to search his soul. 'You won't let me down, now will you?', he said. It was more of an encouragement than a question.

'No. I'll be there.' Marcus replied then continued on his way, trying not to run. Looking down at the leaflet, he turned back to Max who by now was trying to engage someone else in conversation.

Marcus screwed the leaflet up and was about to throw it in a bin, but something inside stopped him. Not knowing what it was, he couldn't throw it away. Returning the scrap of paper to his pocket, he continued on his way.

That moment changed his destiny. This was the happy accident life had been saving up for him. Attending the meeting on a whim. Max had spoken first, before the main attraction Phillip. His calm persona, smooth blond hair and aquiline nose exuded a peaceful authority. When he started to speak, Marcus knew this was the moment he'd been waiting for. Recognising the clarity of vision, the truths hidden in plain sight that he'd been too blind and stupid to notice all along.

Within a week Marcus was handing out the leaflets himself. The route forward was clear. Soon he was standing up on the stage at the meetings extolling the virtues of the cult, for that's what it was. He was living and breathing the beliefs. Women were drawn to him for the first time in his life, and he liked it. There was the lord's work to do and he needed all the help he could get spreading the word of love. As he read the literature, watched the films and listened to the preachers, he inculcated a sense of purpose. It became his whole world and his mission was to bring the enlightenment to the masses. To spread the truth to the ignorant. Soon his whole world was contained within the cult. All his wages and meagre savings were willingly given to the cult, who in turn reassured him they would look after all his earthly needs, while he now lived in the commune, although he didn't mix with non-believers, unless he was recruiting them.

Then one day it all changed. Stumbling across a discarded document while digging out some leaflets. The title in bold ran across the top of the crumpled coffee stained page. '*Crackpot Religions: 16 Steps to creating your own belief system. Guaranteed Profits!*' He would have dismissed it as a hoax, except he recognised some of the language used in the talks, and then there was the familiar distinctive script of the handwritten notes scattered at various points.

"Say the world and all that is in it has been created by some kind of Great Creator"

"Invent "Sacred scriptures" based around the Great Creator, full of parables couched in vague yet important sounding language."

"Equate your religion with "Goodness" and the "Absolute and total truth" while dismissing all other viewpoints as "Evil""

"Use "Warped Logic" to point out the superiority of your religion to other religions."

"Proceed to "Indoctrinate" converts using standard brainwashing techniques normally creating a sense of fear of "Non-believers""

Finally, he saw the following…

"When sufficiently indoctrinated/brainwashed, extract money from the converts again empathising their goodness factor with the great creator"

As he continued to read the document in mute horror, tears welled in Marcus's eyes and his hands shook with rage and betrayal as his throat constricted. Then there was clarity. In the meetings, he'd noticed the sly looks between Max and Phillip and thought it was the understanding of great men sharing their wisdom. Then there were the smarter clothes that were passed off as the 'Public face' of the cult. His anger boiled over during one meeting, when he confronted them with the document and evidence of their rapaciousness. Condemned as a heretic, a disbeliever, he was cast out. No clothes apart from those he wore, no money, no home and no friends.

The following day, arriving at work and discovering he'd been sacked for gross incompetence, he left, and wandered the city, a pale shadow, relying on the kindness of strangers. A few days later while trudging the lonely streets, he heard a familiar laugh behind him and turned to see them climbing out of a sleek limousine, entering a glittering, expensive restaurant. Max, hair tied back, sophisticated glasses, looking tanned and healthy, donning a luxurious designer suit to complete the transformation, and alongside him, Phillip in an open necked white shirt. Both accompanied by stunning women he'd never seen before, on the very evening they'd normally allocated for "meditation and peace". He tried to speak to them, but they affected not to know him as their private security hustled him away. The repudiation of Brother Marcus was complete and their lies were naked before him.

The following evening, standing silently in the rain, Marcus looked up at the house where he'd spent the past year of his life. The warm glow coming from within, reached out to him, but never quite arrived. Singing could be heard and the voices carried the joy he had once known that was now denied to him. Scratching the symbol of a rival cult they'd been conditioned to fear on the door, he blocked them, before he poured the petrol, bought with his final remaining pennies, through the letterbox quickly followed by the lighted match. The whoomph of the flames blasted back through the small gap as he turned away. The first screams could be heard as he turned the corner, and after a few minutes, sirens were sounding in the distance. Max and Phillip would be enjoying the warmth of Ykdar's' love very soon.

Walking all night, Marcus arrived outside his mother's home. As he was about to knock on the door, he put his hand in his pocket and pulled out two pieces of paper. The first said 'There is another way!' He screwed it up, cast it bitterly aside as it was quickly snatched by the wind and carried into the night. The next one was entitled 'Crackpot Religions'. Considering the document for a moment, with its scrawled handwritten notes of those now consigned to the flames, he folded it neatly and placed it carefully back into his pocket, subconsciously patting it before taking a deep breath. Then, he stepped forward and knocked on his mother's front door.

*

'Counsellor, we are so pleased to see you!' Marcus was shaken out of his reverie. A couple of his congregation approached with beaming smiles. Responding to them with his standard modest "I'm your grateful servant" platitude.

'We were so inspired by your wise words earlier today', one of his admirers said.

'The Great Lord will always favour the pure souls.' Marcus enjoined and parroted; 'and his light will show us the true path we must follow.' He noticed the awe and wonder his words had on the couple, then looked beyond them momentarily at the different faces in the crowd. Most of them were complete strangers to him and the teachings of Ykdar. So many ripe for plucking he thought. All that was needed was a catalyst, something to draw them to him. Even though they were starting a new life on an untouched planet, relatively few were attending. Something had to happen and soon, before the flock were scattered across the new world where the job would be a hundred times harder. The voices of the couple barely registered but Marcus was an expert in feigning interest. Then he saw her, an apparition. The girl with the sleepy eyes. Long raven black hair, tall and the figure of a goddess. He'd spotted her a couple of times previously and tried to catch her eye, but they had a far off glistening dreamlike quality to them. Marcus had never seen such a vision of beauty. Surely she was sent by the gods. He decided from the first moment he saw her, he had to have her. Making his excuses to the couple, he moved towards her, mouth dry with anticipation.

14

'**C'mon** Sophia! Stop shuffling. You're holding us up.'

Sophia heard her mother's voice but couldn't seem to be able to respond as quickly, as she trundled slowly behind Mum, Dad and Jasmine in the shopping concourse. Eventually she responded blearily; 'Coming Mum.' The medication that was supposed to help moderate her episodes, as they were referred to, made her drowsy. Everything seemed to be happening in slow-motion, a befuddling blanket, suffocating yet enabling even though time passed as normal. The voices and feelings in her head had dulled but not disappeared. A few days earlier she'd heard a piercing distant cry, angry and scared. Despite another trying to interfere, she had reached out to it before it stopped as suddenly as it had started. There was still the other whispering, searching voice.

The sedatives had dulled the visual component but the sounds remained. Sophia recalled the pain and the flash, the face of hate and the orange light, the cloud and the needle coming towards her eye. It was hard to tell what was real and what was part of her imagination. The face of hate had cruelly haunted her dreams. She'd prayed for the visions to disappear. It was always the same plump face that transmuted into her father's then back again to the cruel face. Speaking harsh words and inflicting pain. The darkness of the cage. The girl with the different coloured eyes looking at her with sadness and fascination. Sometimes the blue orb gently floated off in the distance. Oblivious as she hid from it, like the whispering voice that called out during waking hours.

Her parents looked at her differently now, almost scared, since the episode in the surgery. Her father's hand had taken a couple of weeks to heal from the savage bite inflicted. 'Like a cornered animal, fighting for its life.' he had said. Her mother just irritated her. Looking and spontaneously bursting into tears, always seemingly angry towards Sophia who felt like a stranger in her own family.

Only Jasmine understood. She told Sophia what had happened in the surgery. 'You were ok one moment, the next you went completely crazy and jabbering like a maniac. It was terrifying, I remember your teeth. Like a Tiger or a T-Rex. But the most frightening thing was the strength. Poor dad, you threw him off like a doll when he tried to hold you down. The blood from his hand was everywhere. He was screaming in pain. Mum was screaming, I was screaming. It took two huge security men to hold you down while the poor doctor sedated you. The room looked like a tornado had passed through it. Poor Doctor Ferguson. Her legs wouldn't stop wobbling after.'

Sophia felt particularly sorry for Akeely Ferguson. A lovely lady, calm, kind and Sophia shed a tear of regret when she heard the effect the incident had on the Doctor. Describing what she had seen during the incident, Sophia asked if Jasmine had felt anything. Nothing. Not a thing. It seemed she was hyper sensitive to the signals.

Sophia anxiously looked around the concourse for her family who had disappeared among the multitude. Scared and at the same time relieved to be free for a short time at least from mother's smothering attentions.

'Are you lost miss?' The voice startled her but she still reacted slowly, turning to see the vaguely familiar man. His shoulder length hair and calm features were at odds with the piercingly blue eyes that made her nervous with their intensity. There were no signals coming from him, only a stark emptiness.

Sophia frowned, 'Do I know you?' she responded in a slightly slurred voice.

'You may do my dear', he replied. He reached forward touched her arm. His hand was ice cold. Sophia recoiled from him but managed to avoid snatching her arm away. 'I'm sorry; I didn't mean to startle you', he said.

Sophia forced a smile that seemed twisted and unnatural, lips feeling like rubber that had been glued to her numbed face as she spoke; 'That's ok. I didn't mean to be rude, I was daydreaming as usual. I appear to have lost my family.' There was a slightly dazed look in the stranger's face.

'Everyone living within the walls of Pangea is your family my dear.' What a strange thing to say Sophia thought. As the stranger continued. 'We are all brothers and sisters on this journey to a better world.' He continued.

'Yes I suppose we are.' Sophia laughed nervously, 'I'd never really thought of it like that.'

'We need all the family we can get in this situation.'

'Situation? What situation? Has something happened?', Sophia asked with some urgency.

'Of course not. I didn't mean it like that. I merely meant about the adventure we are all undertaking and the unknowns it may contain', he said, trying to allay her fears.

Sophia's addled brain was having trouble processing the meaning of the stranger's words, although there was no difficulty interpreting the feeling of embarrassing awkwardness he exuded.

'Ohh I think I see what you mean', she said, longing for the conversation to end, casting her eyes around searching desperately for her family.

'But then life is a journey, and I know of a family you can share it with...' the stranger suggested, his voice lowered, becoming more serious.

'There you are! I've been looking everywhere for you. Just wandering off like that.' The sound of her mother had rarely sounded as welcome. Danielle Whittaker turned to the stranger, 'Why, hello Counsellor Marcus. I hope she wasn't bothering you.' Adopting the raised false sounding manner that Sophia referred to as her "official voice", reserved for people she felt were higher up the social ladder than her.

'Of course not Sister. I was in the process of helping this delightful young lady find her family, that's all.' Marcus gave her a sidelong glance and the suave quality of his voice was very disarming. Sophia noticed her mother was actually blushing at the creep. 'And I can see you are her mother although you could easily be mistaken for her sister.' He was massaging the mother's ego. Sophia felt her stomach turn in a nauseated fashion. A slick salty taste filled her mouth.

'Why thank you Counsellor. You're such a charmer', Dannielle responded. The gorge rose in Sophia's throat as Marcus took her mother's hand and kissed it, while she laughed in a flighty way that reminded Sophia of the full bosomed Georgian women she'd seen in films, half expecting her to produce a fan and flutter her eyelids coquettishly. Ohh Reverend. You mustn't. I'm a Ladeee you know. Danielle turned to Sophia and spoke in her common voice. 'Are you ok dear? You look like you've seen a ghost.'

'I'm ok mum. I'd just like to lie down for a while.'

'Ok, better make our way back...', Dannielle said, then turning to Marcus and resuming the silly tone she'd adopted, added; 'A pleasure meeting you Counsellor.'

'A pleasure to meet you Missis...?'

'Whittaker! But you can call me Danielle, and this is Sophia.'

'An honour to make your acquaintance Danielle, and of course young Sophia.'

A wave of nausea rose in Sophia's throat as she fought the urge to recoil, but she managed to keep a neutral expression before turning away. 'Please feel free to come along to one of our gatherings', Marcus invited.

'Oh undoubtedly Counsellor, undoubtedly.' Danielle said, turned to see Sophia had left, and giving Marcus a final wave of her hand, she quickly caught up her daughter as they made their way back to the living quarters.

'What a charming man.' Danielle intoned breathlessly.

'Please just shut up Mother.' Sophia replied through gritted teeth. 'Let's find Dad and Jasmine.'

Marcus watched the pair disappear into the crowd. Well you broke the ice and it went well. I think the girl likes you, he thought then turned and continued on his way. He was thinking happy thoughts for once.

'Yes! You *were* flirting with him Mother.'

'I was doing something you seem unable to do. Being polite!' retorted Danielle. 'The Counsellor is a well-respected man, and you would do well to note that.'

Sophia looked up at one of the large telescreens dotted around the concourse. The newsreader was looking out earnestly while the strip at the bottom of the screen rolled across the latest news. Sophia observed with envy the perfect face, hair and outfit of the newsreader, which was a pity as she thought Patricia Fernandez was arrogant and rude. She turned to Danielle and gestured to the screen. 'Remember when Jasmine saw her and tried to speak to her', she motioned towards the newsreader.

'Yes I remember only too well. How embarrassing. I told Jasmine to leave her alone, but she didn't listen', her mother said.

'That's still no excuse for her to be so rude to Jasmine', Sophia opined.

'She wasn't rude. Can you imagine every person you see wants to talk to you all the time and find out your views on what they happen to be thinking? I felt a bit sorry for her in a way', Dannielle replied.

'That didn't stop you from shouting at her when she made Jasmine cry....', Sophia recalled. It was the irritated hiss and the flash of the eyes toward Jasmine that sparked the outburst that embarrassed Danielle. 'What was it you said....?,' daughter asked mother, although she gave the answer; '....Oh yes, I remember "What's the matter, she's only saying 'Hello' you stuck up bitch. Just because you're Patricia Fer-fuckin-nandez you think you're better than us and your shit don't smell." That didn't sound too sympathetic did it now?' Sophia reminded her mother.

'Shut up Sophia. I'm warning you.' Danielle's embarrassment at losing her temper in public lingered fresh in her mind.

Sophia continued regardless, digging her nails that little bit deeper; 'The look of shock on her face. Its lucky Dad was there to drag you away. I noticed that a bit of the old South London accent you reserve for special occasions slipped out. I'm sure your new admirer, Father Marcus or whatever his name is wouldn't have been too impressed.'

'Your medication appears to be wearing off. It'll be time for the next dose very soon', her mother warned.

This time it was Sophia's turn to hiss in irritation.

The flames of argument flickered as they searched around for the others. 'Where the hell are they.' muttered Danielle under her breath.

'Language Mother, the Counsellor may hear you', Sophia said sarcastically. Danielle narrowed her eyes and glared at her daughter before responding but the only thing Sophia noticed was the deafening whispering coming from inside her head. Every word indistinct but feeling like sandpaper. Whoever was sending it was near. Very near. It had a sense of direction and was searching for her, calling incessantly. It felt like every face was turned her way, seeing and knowing. Then she saw him standing against a wall, only twenty feet away. A young man with a shock of pure white hair, watching with a malignant intense focus. Sophia knew it was him, a lighthouse sending out its beam through the darkness.

'Sophia! Are you listening to me?' Her mother's voice cut through the noise in her head.

Don't respond, he'll spot you, Sophia told herself. A slow nod placated her Mother while she contemplated. I need to shut him down. Concentrate on making it smaller, quieter. The serrated edges of the voice began to smooth. The face of the white haired man looked suddenly unsure, the intensity replaced by consternation. It's working! The painful deafening whisper rapidly receding, shrivelling, disappearing until it was crushed out of existence. The ease and suddenness of it shocked and elated Sophia, as she dared to glance over at White Hair once more. Hands covering his ears and nose bleeding, he wore the expression of the shock and fear of one who had opened a small cupboard and had suddenly been confronted with something so gargantuan that it was beyond his comprehension. The eyes were frantically searching around for a target that was no longer there. Sophia's mind was pristine. I've obliterated him. I can stop the voices. They can't hurt me anymore. She silently celebrated.

'Are you sure you're ok darling?', again her mother interrupted her musings.

Sophia responded to her mother's concern with a smile and hugged her tight. 'I love you mummy.' She sobbed with happiness, 'and I'm sorry...' She saw her father and Jasmine approaching and noticed the astonished joy on their faces. She felt better now. Better than at any time she could remember.

15

To: Michelle J. Farrington @ electron.com
From: robert.nash@galactic_vistas.com
Subject: Re: Hi

Hey Michelle

We are still awaiting the go ahead for our move to the settlements. We're told that the terraformers are transforming the atmosphere at full speed and it won't be long now. It's lucky that there's so much to keep us occupied, especially the kids. The Auto cinema has been a real blessing. It can't be that long before we set out on the final stage of our long journey across the galaxy. Sam has started to make some friends at last and Amy is putting a brave face on things. She still misses her family and worries about the situation back home, if we can still call it that.

Galactic Vistas have provided us with everything, even a counsellor called Marcus. He really is a wonderful man and has certainly soothed any ruffled nerves. I didn't know about him until a couple of weeks ago, when Heath told us about him and we went along to listen to what he had to say. It was a joyous occasion with music, stories about Ykdar the great sky lord and finally Marcus himself spoke. I've never quite seen such adulation, but listening to his words struck a chord in the hearts of those who attended. I wish Mum was there. It would have cheered her up no end. I can't wait until the next gathering. Hopefully there'll be a few more there next time.

Ollie is still having fun. He's made a new friend, Darren the play leader at the Cafeteria. I personally find him a bit scary being a rather large man, but he's like the pied piper and the kids love him. Maybe Marcus could learn some lessons from him.

Love to all

Robert

16

Ava stared in wide-eyed shock at the two contrite figures sitting across the table.

'You've got to be kidding me!' Magnus and Kalpana glanced briefly at each other. 'Please, tell me again in case I've missed a step.'

It was Magnus who spoke up. His uncompromising voice wasted no words, only the facts as he saw them. His blue eyes held Ava in their cool considered gaze. 'We've been holding back on the upgrades for the Gorthon and Hyperthon. As far as we're concerned the Mags have the potential to cause serious damage once on the planet surface, not just in terms of the safety of the settlers but also in terms of the eco system. These things are a disaster waiting to happen. The anomalies are being pushed forwards without being resolved. The enhancements only multiply their power and that's something I'm not prepared to countenance.'

'That's what I thought you said...' Ava intoned. She saw a lot of truth in what Magnus said, but she couldn't bring herself to admit it in front of them. At least not yet. You've gotta play this straight down the line Ava. One step the wrong way and all hell could break loose.

Then Kalpana spoke. 'Miss Matthews, we have agonized over speaking to you. We wouldn't have come here unless we were desperate.' She leant forward her hands almost reaching to out Ava as she continued; 'We have put everything on the line here. We are at your mercy, but we can't see any other way forward. We don't know what to do for the best...' Her voice broke at the last word as a tear trickled down her cheek. Magnus took Kalpana's hand and gently squeezed it. He turned his gaze back to Ava who could sense Kalpana's anguish and the sincerity of her words.

Ava nodded gently to herself, desperately trying to stall for time and put the ball in their court to draw out the remainder of what they had to say. 'So, what do you intend on doing? Because I can't see any way through this, and unless you've got any good ideas I can run with, this is going nowhere', she said to them.

'The Droids', the hesitancy in Torben's voice echoed Ava's disbelief.

'You're gonna have to give me more than that, I'm afraid', Ava rejoined.

'Hear me out, Miss Matthews....', Magnus appealed. Ava raised her eyebrows inviting him to continue. He obliged; '.... First, the Droids, they can easily be adapted to prospect for the Nadinium. Guided by micro satellites, they can home in on the richest deposits. They might not have the same endurance as the Mags, but they are more inherently stable and are not going to turn on the civilian population and massacre them in the blink of an eye. Their first impulse isn't to rip the nearest human into tatters.'

Ava shook her head. 'I'm still not convinced Magnus,' She said.

Magnus slapped his hand on the table. The sound ripped through the peace of the room like a gunshot, as he stated; 'I'll tell you their big advantage over the Mags shall I? It's called an 'Off' switch. Any moment if we like, we can just press a button and the Droid stops whatever it's doing. It doesn't try to hide or escape it just stops.'

'But isn't that possible with the enhancements. We can just immobilise the Mag's', Ava suggested remembering how the Hyperthon had been 'neutralised' by the uranium slug the previous day.

'You were there when the Hyperthon almost broke loose. Do you think an upgrade is going to stop one of them if it sets its mind to break its restraints?', Magnus argued.

'Then what about the AI on the Droids being hacked? They could end up being just as dangerous and out of control as the Mags. Have you considered that?', Ava asked. A chill passed over Ava as the memory of the close escape with the Hyperthon lingered fresh in her mind. The sense of remorseless purpose and implacable menace, the white heat of the flames and squealing tones dragged like a rasp across her memory.

For what seemed an age both sides stared across the table at each other. A shroud of silence hung heavily in the room, waiting for an answer to step into the light. It was Magnus that spoke first, just above a whisper. His voice seemed to come from within Ava's head. 'A dark force is lurking amongst us, waiting for its moment to strike, and we are it's deliverers', he said and continued; 'I've watched those videos and I've looked into the eyes of evil.....' He leant across the table and held out his hand just in front of Ava's face, his finger and thumb millimetres apart. '...It's that close, I can feel it.'

Ava could see his eye staring unerringly back through the gap between finger and thumb. The dim shapes of Ava's dreams and visions rushed back through her, blown by an icy wind from somewhere out in the darkness, jarring her thoughts and sending a chill of fear into every corner of her mind. 'Look....', she said; '...I don't doubt your sincerity, but just suppose for a second that I decide to act upon your concerns.' Kalpana shot a look at Magnus, who remained focused on Ava. 'Not that I'm saying I will....', Ava continued; 'But suppose I did. How do you think this will go down with Khan, Chiang and Celina? They'll rip you both to shreds and have you thrown in jail. You need to demonstrate why you think the Mags are unstable. At the moment they think the incident with the escaped Gargoyle was human error. No more, no less. A one off caused by the carelessness

150

of a lax individual not paying attention. You can mention the foresight and planning by the rogue Mag, but that's the line they'll take and they're gonna stick to it like glue.'

'I see your point Miss Matthews but...' Magnus acknowledged but Ava held her hand out to interrupt him as she continued.

'Hold on a second. Let me finish.' Magnus made to speak but Kalpana placed her hand on his arm while Ava continued. 'You need to push forward suggestions for the Droids that are demonstrable, to show a greater degree of reliability as well as efficiency....' she told them. '...All this at the same time against the opposition of the whole of the Mag development teams who are just aching to show what they can do. Remember, the Mags are their babies and they're not gonna just give up on them without a fight. In its current form your proposal has nowhere to go. So, you need to bring something to the table, if you want me to help you. Correct me if I'm wrong.' She could see their shoulders sag in resignation as the reality of her words sank in. Throw them a lifeline, don't let them sink without trace, she thought. Let them know you're on their side, or at least not hostile. Take a deep breath Ava, here goes... 'What was it you said about the Mag enhancements. I didn't quiet hear it...', she asked, trying to assuage their feelings.

Magnus frowned momentarily, opened his mouth to speak, hesitated as the light of understanding flickered across his face. 'I... don't recall mentioning the Mag enhancements.' He said and turned to Kalpana. 'Do you?'

'I don't remember you saying anything Magnus. I think Miss Matthews must be hearing things', Kalpana concurred.

'Yes, the medication I'm on can sometimes cause me to hear things and sometimes it causes me to forget things as well...' Ava said and smiled. The two of them smiled back knowingly. Ava added; 'In fact, I don't even have any recollection of this meeting.'

Magnus smiled at Kalpana and turned back to Ava. He nodded gently and they got up and left the room without another word.

Ava sat for a few moments as she took in what had just happened. There was a curious feeling of nakedness, of being exposed and being able to do nothing about it. In her mind, a giant darkness was crossing the landscape, rushing at them just as the moons shadow during an eclipse blots everything out, swallowing up the light, leaving only the blazing shadow staring down like a giant hole in the sky. Death's dark dominion was spreading its wings and heading this way. Ava felt what Magnus felt when he uttered his warning. It *was* close, very close.

♦

Ava had difficulty concentrating after the meeting with Magnus and Kalpana earlier as she studied the readings on the screen. Exhaling a long, deep breath, she turned to Reece. 'It's hard to disagree with your findings.'

'You look sceptical Ava…'

'No, I believe you. I just want to be sure. So, sum up to me once again. What do we actually know for certain…?'

'Well it's been difficult trying to pin it down during certain periods. The signals are weak and sporadic. I was looking at the plans for the area where the pure signal was originating. He pulled up the layout for those levels and explained; 'It seems to be mobile. Randomly moving around, but only within the civilian areas. Then I noticed something else. It remained stationary for about 8 hours, and also seemed to enter a different mode. The signal retained its purity, but the frequency went through a repeating cycle.' Now it was getting interesting, Ava thought as Reece's voice turned to a whisper. 'These are REM patterns. The source is asleep, which means it isn't artificial. It's human'.

'And you can't pin down the exact location.' Ava inquired, as she struggled to contain her excitement and keep her voice steady.

'I'm afraid not Ava. We're only able to tell it's moving by the Doppler shifts in data. When it's night-time they stop moving, although they increase in regularity.' He looked up at her quizzically. She noticed a pleading in his eyes that required vindication, but also a hesitancy, as if there was something else troubling him. 'There's another thing I wanted to speak about Ava…'

'Well! Don't just leave me hanging there Reece. Out with it.'

'….The 5:3 resonance appears to be originating from outside Pangea base. Almost from the planet itself. It occurs whenever there is a significant increase in Mag instability….'

'What evidence have you got of this Reece?'

'I was trying to triangulate it but wherever I pointed it came from all around, except one direction. Up.'

'So why don't we perform a long-range EVA and take a look. What's stopping us?'

Reece threw his hands up in exasperation and asserted; 'Because they don't think there's anything out there, so there's nothing to investigate….'

'What the hell! Why not? *I* believe you Reece. It at least warrants some further investigation.'

'It's exactly what I've been telling the others, but they dismiss my findings out of hand.' The relief in his voice was evident as he added; 'At least somebody thinks I'm telling the truth. It feels like they don't want to hear what I've been telling them because they don't want it to be true. It's so frustrating.'

Ava was incredulous. 'So, you're suggesting the unknown signal is a natural phenomenon, and that senior figures know about it and are trying to put you off the scent. Why?', she asked.

'Your guess is as good as mine, but it's not beyond their capabilities to keep rather dark secrets from large numbers of people is it?' Reece replied.

'But the Mags are here to prospect for Nadinium and as they've not exactly got a particularly good reputation, they don't want to alarm the settlers', Ava pointed out.

Reece grabbed Ava's arm. Eyes wide open, the intensity in his face reflected the gravity of his conclusion. 'Then why would they keep it from us who are aware of the Mags, unless it was something even more alarming to conceal. You tell me an alternative reason? He asked her.

'First of all, it's a pretty stupid error. Maybe someone wanted it to be found. Then that raises a completely different set of questions', Ava surmised.

'Not only that, but they obviously never thought I'd find anything and now I have, they're scrambling to cover it up....' Reece's voice returned to its more reasoned normal self. '....Ava....' he was earnest; '....I'm telling you this because you're the only one I can trust and whose opinion I respect.'

Ava's heart warmed at the sincerity of Reece's sentiments and she smiled. 'Thank you Reece....' she said then advised him; '....Maybe you can start by letting go of my arm as it's starting to hurt.' Reece withdrew his hand and laughed. Ava continued;'....We need to keep this quiet for the time being....', she suggested; '....You don't know what they'll do if you find out something they don't want you to know. It never works out well for those who speak the truth to power as we know from back on Earth.'

Reece nodded. 'Agreed. I'll return to them and say I made a mistake with my analysis.'

'Good thinking. Then we try to see who we can trust, identify those who will possess the relevant knowledge and take it from there. I've got someone in mind who would help us.' Ava smiled as she thought of Eleanor and her world of hard gained knowledge. 'Now it's my turn to reveal secrets.'

This time it was Reece's turn to be impatient. 'Pray tell Miss Matthews.'

'I'm as sure as I can be there's another Psychic in the base', she said.

Reece's mouth formed an 'O' as he looked at Ava in shock, before he stammered. 'So that confirms my findings on the signal...'

'Yes. There was a purity to it that I've only ever seen once before.'

'Really. When was that?', he asked.

153

'When I was a student. They spoke to us about the natural Psychics', she said. 'I thought they were only rumours.'

Ava shook her head slowly and explained. 'No, they're real enough. Just extremely rare. The gentle strength of the signal added to what I heard and saw when I was trying to control the Hyperthon had me thinking. The power of the Hyperthon was incredible. A wall of flame that nothing could withstand. Then the voice started. A sparkling point was in the distance. A twinkling star of the purest colours flickering in and out of vision. It was beautiful...' Ava caught her breath as the memory washed up on the shores of her mind. The undefined emotion evoked by a beautiful piece of music, poetry, or a sunset that has stirred the hearts and minds of people since the first civilisations arose, flared in Ava's heart, causing the prickle of a tear to dance on the edge of her eye. She blinked and took a slow breath to bring her emotions back under control.

Reece put his hand on Ava's arm again. This time with compassion. 'Are you ok Ava?' he asked her.

She nodded then continued. 'Then the Hyperthon started to relent. A solitary note from the star and the fire cooled. A butterfly turning back a hurricane with a single flap of its wings....' she pursed her lips momentarily but persisted; '....Then Jordan pushed the button and the Hyperthon was dead. A moment later the voice stopped...' Ava didn't know how long the silence lasted. It could have been a second or a minute as time solidified. The only thing she could feel was the steady rhythm of her heart beating.

'Then you fell off the seat and nearly broke your neck.'

Reece's voice shook her out of her contemplation, and she turned to him. 'Indeed! And it still hurts now...' She put her hand on Reece's. 'I'm ok.' She smiled. 'But I think the natural Psychics are more common than even I previously thought and we've got one here with us. I'm not surprised they keep it under wraps, considering the history of their treatment.'

'Why? What happened?', he asked her.

'Well the power of a Natural far exceeds anything that I or the Mags can hope to reach. Even after all my years of experience. There was a young boy in Cameroon who was discovered. He was taken by the company "For his own protection" to be examined. A few months later he died in mysterious circumstances. Nobody quite knew what happened. They tried to pay off his family as if he were a piece of property. The family weren't having that, and started asking some awkward questions....', she paused briefly before asking; '....Do you remember the tragedy where there was a carbon dioxide pulse from a lake bed that seeped down into a village, killing everyone and everything in their sleep? The lake sat over a volcanic vent where the CO_2 welled up, but it was kept

154

at the bottom by a layer of salt water. Supposedly there was a landslide into the lake that disrupted the salt water layer, which released the CO_2 that wiped out the village. Strangely enough, that was where the boy's family lived, then died. A bit too convenient I'd say, especially as some people thought that the landslide was no "accident". But if true, it shows the lengths people will go to cover up inconvenient facts. So whoever this Natural Psychic is, they are wise to keep quiet about it.'

'Can you try to contact them? Will they know you're trying?' Reece asked.

'It's unethical and I'd love to meet him or her, but I don't think it'll be anytime soon. If they can control a Hyperthon with that ease imagine what else they're capable of.'

'You should at least try Ava. What have you got to lose?'

'I don't know yet Reece. In the meantime, we keep all of this under wraps. Also you've got to cool your temper. Don't shoot from the hip because Chiang has got under your skin again. You're playing straight into their hands.' Ava told him then got up to leave the room. As she reached the door, she turned, looked at Reece and reminded him; '....Anyhow if you tell anyone I'll know. I'm Psychic as well remember!' Reece smiled and Ava was relieved he saw the joke as she exited and closed the door, making her way back to the Hyperthon containment area as her mind fizzled with possibilities. Some exciting, some more frightening.

◆

They watched the screen in silence as the video showing the Hyperthon emerging from the vat played out. As before, the steaming liquid rolled off the dormant creature before the silver cap lowered itself on to the head. Ava briefly glanced across at Reece whose gaze was fixed intently on the images before him.

'You will now observe the primary interactions with the Hyperthon....' The smooth, feline voice of Wen Chiang broke the silence. '.... My colleague Dr Fink has downloaded the suite of Neuroware, and the subject is now aware of its surroundings.'

The video showed the Hyperthon slowly looking around, not in the way of a new-born but a fully aware sentient being that comprehended the situation perfectly. There was an air of silent, patient menace about the creature as it turned to the camera and looked directly into the lens. The face stared out from the screen as if it could see into the room. Its tongue flicking out, tasting the air in search of weakness and fear.

An ominous silence lingered momentarily before a forced round of applause burst out dispelling the tension. It was led by the usual obsequious members of Dr

155

Khan's team. Chiang's modest smile was offset by the sly, knowing glance she directed at Reece, his face a picture of complete shock that hadn't changed since he discovered that Khan had handed control of his Hyperthon project to Chiang, who had in turn delegated it to the equally ambitious Mandy Fink.

'I would like to offer Doctors Chiang and Fink my sincerest congratulations on this magnificent achievement. This is the breakthrough we have yearned for since we departed Earth', Khan said.

'Thank you Dr Khan.' responded Chiang with a small nod, addressing their project director in a fashion that he felt was a mark of the deep respect he commanded. She continued, 'As you are now aware, we duplicated the technique that was applied to the Gorthon, completely eliminating the aggression issues that Doctor Coleman struggled in vain for so long to overcome. We were only too happy to help our esteemed colleague out of his difficulties.' Mocking laughter rippled around the room, again led by the ingratiating individuals trying just that bit too hard. Reece smiled but Ava noted with concern there was murder in his eyes as Chiang summarised; 'After extensive analysis we could find no further evidence of the signal hidden in the Hyperthon's noise and the 5:3 resonance appears to be a false trail.'

Ava spoke up, 'These are indeed impressive results Dr Chiang and I hope the issues are resolved, however I would like access to both the Hyperthon and Gorthon subjects to verify your findings.' She noticed Mandy Fink's raised eyebrows but Chiang remained impassive. Ava continued; 'There are characteristics that a trained Psychic such as myself are able to pick up that cannot be identified purely by using instrumentation.' She looked over at Dr Khan, 'So with your permission?'

Khan nodded his assent and announced; 'To conclude Ladies and Gentlemen, I have the pleasure to announce that we are proceeding with the first stage of Mag implementation along with the full upgrade program!' This was met with even wilder applause than the previous announcements. With the exception of the aghast Reece and Ava, cheering broke out and resonated around the room, with team members embracing and slapping each other on the back.

A lone voice cut through the commotion. 'Excuse me!' The hubbub died down and all heads turned to Reece Coleman, who was unable to contain himself any more. 'I need to say something.' He took a deep breath. 'I'm not going to mince my words here. This is bullshit. All of it.' There was a gasp from those present. Before anyone could intervene, he stood up and continued, staring accusingly at Chiang. 'These discredited methods of Doctor Chiang have been used before and failed, as the dead of Bagama could testify. We considered this approach at the very beginning with the single nucleotide modifications and they didn't work....',

He paused then addressed Chiang directly; '....In line with your track record, you are not curing the problem. Only covering it up, and I dread the consequences.' Then he turned to Khan pointing his finger. 'And you! Doctor Khan, do not want to hear what we've said. Sack the impartial advisers and replace them with toadies. The lazy way out that's caused the fall of empires throughout history and we're next. You only want to hear what suits you, and you only surround yourself with liars and flatterers, who never for a second question anything you say, while all the time...'

'Reece! That's enough!' Ava interrupted him. Although she agreed with everything Reece had said, she could see his career vaporising before her very eyes and had to save him from himself.

Reece closed his eyes and took a deep breath.

Khan's voice was calm but the sheen of sweat and ruddy colour of his face betrayed the deep anger and bitterness he felt. He informed Reece; 'Doctor Coleman. You should leave the room immediately and do not return. You are dismissed from your position with immediate effect. I will not be spoken to in such a manner.'

Reece looked around the room and said indignantly; 'You miserable excuse for scientists and human beings are going to get everyone on this planet killed...'. Shaking his head slowly, he added; 'You all know it and not one of you has the guts to speak up.' He turned to see the guard who gently led him from the room.

The noise picked up again in the room but this time it was more subdued. Ava looked over at Chiang being consoled by some colleagues as the crocodile tears trickled down her cheeks, but the traces of the smirk that remained on her face could not conceal her true emotions.

17

Confidential
To: Brandon.Schofield@Ateus_Industries.co.uk
From: Celina.Novak@galactic_vistas.com
Subject: Re: Outstanding Issues

Mr. Schofield

We are in business! Dr Khan pulled it out of the fire and we have started Mag production with immediate effect. The instability issues that plagued this project have been completely resolved. The upgrade has exceeded expectations.

The average time from initial mixing until the Mag emerges and complete operational readiness is five days. We are looking to scale up to full capacity after the first run when production will be fully automated. Our weekly production target is as follows:

- Gargoyle: 100
- Gorthon: 5
- Bornix: 20
- Hyperthon: 10

All the above have been sourced from the Primary samples and are pristine.

The Hyperthon project is still on target and full control of the Mags from a single source is a realistic prospect. We are confident the enhanced applications of the Hyperthon project are within our reach and will initiate the preliminary steps at the earliest opportunity.

All primary targets have been achieved and we are at the early stages of selecting our first test subjects from the base population.

I will keep you abreast of our progress and any further developments that may occur.

Yours
Celina Novak
Chief Colonisation Administrator

18

Only the dim blood red glow accompanied by a low throbbing rumble broke the silent blackness. Ava searched about for any other signs. She picked up a dull hue of purple that hovered on the edge of perception, otherwise there were none to be found. As far as she was concerned the lack of signal was a sign in itself that the Gorthon was concealing something, but that wasn't going to convince the sceptics. Trying to move around the mindscape, she found herself hemmed in the restricted space created by the Gorthon. Occasionally the rumble would subtly increase in tone, before returning to its regular throb, or there was a slight change in the shade of deep red like the flare of a blaze over the horizon. This is what it must be like in the womb she thought. She knew there has to be another way in but had no idea how.

'Anything?', Chiang asked.

Ava opened her eyes and turned to Chiang. 'Nothing means there's something there as far as I'm concerned.'

'I like your thinking Ava.' laughed Mandy Fink who inferred; '....Create something out of nothing in the absence of any evidence.'

Ava ignored the slight and continued to address Chiang. 'It's hiding something.'

Chiang rolled her eyes in mock exasperation. Ava gestured through the glass panel to the area where the restrained Gorthon was held. The grey glistening mass rested passively inside the restraining harness as delicate shades of colours flickered fleetingly across the expanse of flesh. Malevolent eyes gazed out from the grotesque head. Absorbing its environment. Weighing up the possibilities and calculating. Biding its time and waiting for the right moment to arrive. A brief glimpse of the lethal rows of teeth added to the perception of the total killing power that could be unleashed at a second's notice.

'How can you tell me there's nothing there?', Ava asked.

'Because you can't find any evidence to fit your hypotheses.' replied Chiang. As usual her voice remained smooth, but Ava could sense the shadow of unease that lurked just beneath the surface. 'Sometimes we can want something to be true so much that our mind plays tricks on us by disregarding inconvenient facts and only focusing on the things that reinforce our preconceptions', Chiang theorised.

'It sounds like you're speaking to yourself Doctor Chiang. Also we can ignore things that contradict our preconceptions', Ava remarked. Chiang's involuntary sideways glance told Ava she had struck a raw nerve in the seemingly imperturbable Doctor. As she added; 'Like the 5:3 resonance for instance.'

'We found no evidence whatsoever that it had anything to do with our current difficulties.' Chiang responded, her eyes flicked nervously from side to side, her words possessed the careful deliberateness of a script agreed beforehand by accomplices in a misdeed.

Ava sensed the deceit in Chiang's heart and knew she wasn't going to get any kind of admission, but addressed the Doctor directly; 'I'm all too aware of the enmity between yourself and Reece. It obviously runs quite deep. I can't excuse his outburst, but I do share his concerns.' Chiang nodded to herself as Ava continued, 'I'm only offering you my expertise that comes from my considerable experience, and in that light I'm telling you now that the Mags are hiding something. I don't know what, but every part of my being tells me they are, and it's in everyone's interest that we get to the bottom of it. In this case, absence *is* evidence and I'll be including that in my report to Dr Khan. Looking at Titus out there I'm sure you'd agree that you wouldn't want to meet him in a dark alley late at night.'

Chiang's laugh broke the tension. 'Ok Ava, I get your point. You can continue to monitor the Gorthon and Hyperthon, and I promise to take your findings on board', she offered, putting her hand on Ava's arm in a surprisingly friendly and open manner. This led Ava to speculate that maybe the cool exterior was a guard against Reece Coleman' hostility.

'I appreciate that Doctor Chiang, and after all, despite our professional differences, I wouldn't want you to come to a premature end at the hands of Titus.' Ava said, and noticed the reality of her words interlaced with the concern in her voice had a sobering effect on those present, except Mandy, who was either unaware of their gravity or feigned indifference. One way or another they would all find out soon enough.

◆

The waves rolled through Billy's mind in a Tsunami of ecstasy. The technicolour orgy of feelings and emotions lifted his thoughts to a higher dimension, looking down upon himself, seeing the whole of his inner being laid out bare. The good, the bad and the downright terrible. To control and adjust according to his will. No longer weak and afraid, a new feeling of power resonated within Billy that made every cell in his body ring with a new sense of power and purpose. Only the Purple stood above him. He had guided it into the dark heart of Titus's inner sanctum and allowed it to delve deep into the fire of the Gorthon'

160

psyche, planting the seeds of discord that will grow into the strangling vines of hate. Now he was reaping the reward of his deeds as the mindscape extended into the distance. He could see every colour flickering, hear each whisper and feel every thought. To zoom into any point at will and delve deep within. A small part of him still tried to hide from the new reality of his existence. His weaker old self with the unwelcome thoughts were drowned out in the blaze of his triumphant elevation. They would soon fade away, to be obliterated by the purple light that had guided him to this point. Its power over him complete, as Billy waited with relish to complete the next task allotted to him.

19

'**I** spotted some SPC there but still not enough. Also no sign of our primary objective.'

'It's a start. His closest friend still appears uninterested. The others are still too unsure to approach him directly. We've got to be careful and not show our hand.'

'So, we need to try more persuasive methods.'

'I told you, I'm not doing that. Anyway it's too risky if our main target found out. How about you use one of your friends to get to him, then draw him in.'

'Hmmm. Let me think.'

'There must be some, especially the less secure ones.'

'I got just the one.'

'Who is it?'

'She's one of the pretty ones and one of the most committed.'

'You can trust her?'

'Of course. I trust my disciples implicitly.'

'Then we should engineer a "Chance" meeting at the earliest opportunity. Can you arrange it?'

'It'll be the first thing on my list after this. Anything else?'

'I want this to be over now. I've had enough of the double life and yearn for everything to be out in the open.'

'Well that may not be possible for a while, but it will happen.'

'When?'

'Eventually. Remember the darkest hour is before the dawn, so have faith.'

'Faith is what got us into this situation in the first place.'

'And it will triumph over adversity.'

20

Reece Coleman' face stared out at Celina. The small screen with its high brightness settings gave a mask-like appearance to the fear that dominated his features. 'What do you mean "Until further notice." I've committed no crime and yet here I am. Held in detention like a common criminal for the past 48 hours. For what?', he insisted.

Celina tried to keep her cool. Reece had been deemed too high a security risk after his outburst and dismissal. Despite Ava's protests, Celina and Khan decided to secure him until the settlers had transported to their new habitats.

'Doctor Coleman. Let me reiterate that this is only a temporary situation that will be resolved once the settlers are safely relocated', Celina tried to assure Reece.

'Well how long will that be? The settlements won't be ready anytime soon, and you know it!' Reece's pleading voice was stuck in a high whining pitch that had started to irritate Celina as well as making her uncomfortable.

'It won't be too long; I assure you Doctor Coleman.'

'But I...', Reece's protest was interrupted.

It was Celina who cut in; 'Thanks for your understanding', she said. Seeing Reece's mouth lolling open in dissent, she reached out quickly and switched the screen off before he could reply.

Reece was right to be afraid, although he didn't appreciate the full gravity of his situation. He knew too much and had flown too near to the sun. The wax holding his wings of safety together had started to melt and he was about to plummet to a painful end. His dogged persistence added to his high levels of intelligence, while desirable for a scientist, had counted against him. He'd reached the stage where his knowledge was a danger. Luckily they'd managed to contain it. He was easy to goad, and it gave that fool Khan the chance to sack him, atoning for his stupid error in letting him investigate the 5:3 resonance in the first place.

Now they had him where they wanted him, what next? Celina's thoughts turned to darker possibilities. Even the team working on the Mags had been kept in the dark about the source of the 5:3 resonance, so anyone even suspecting its existence was a danger. There was only one permanent solution. She had been mulling over it during the past couple of days. Reece's persistent questions and demands for more information had been deflected, but his constant digging was getting too near to the truth. Even the sudden and frankly suspicious change of tack since his arrest had not lowered Celina's sense of alarm. She shook her head. You pay diamonds, you get geniuses. No good complaining once they started to put those highly skilled minds to work. A pity really. In retrospect she regretted not having Reece in on the 5:3 resonance from the start, but then again, he was a dangerous combination of intellect, free spirit and integrity that wouldn't fit into this dangerous and morally questionable area of research.

How to put her idea into effect, Celina pondered. There were few trusted enough to carry out such dark deeds. Jordan certainly wasn't one of them. Another of her mistakes. Too many scruples for a soldier. How about a nice little accident, but not in his cell? There wasn't exactly a lot that could be pointed to. Fell off the low bed and hit his head on the softened wall? Of course the finger of suspicion would be pointed at those who held him. Suicide? Maybe, but how, in the cell. Just happened to find a handy length of rope to hang himself with. The cell was a problem. Maybe releasing him and placing him under house arrest would work. Good lateral thinking there Celina. Then what?

Celina contemplated. There had been one particularly unsavoury individual she had been watching, with the requisite qualities to carry out the task, given the correct motivation. One of those characters with the cool minded brutality for such an assignment. Celina had read Bruno's confidential dossier with that in mind. Certainly the rumours of extrajudicial actions carried out on behalf of the company showed no sign of scruples whenever they coincided with his self-interest. I'll speak to his superiors and leave the details to Mister Bruno. I'll leave Reece to stew for a couple of weeks before releasing him where, after a few days of self-recrimination, he could no longer bear the consequences of his actions and takes his own life. Such a tragic and premature end to a promising career. Genius had tipped into madness.

Celina smiled to herself. It set her casting her mind back to the conversation with the company's CEO, when she had been assigned to the Arion trip.

*

Being shown into the inner sanctum of the company and the surprisingly understated office of its leader, Celina gazed out across the panoramic views, the dazzling steel and glass monuments to money, thrusting triumphantly skywards. The sun reflecting off their polished exteriors, the ribbon of the river snaking its way through the heart of the city.

Brandon Schofield sat at his desk staring intently at his screen. After a few moments he looked up and stood, before shaking Celina's hand and gesturing for her to take a seat.

'Celina, thank you for attending at such short notice...', Schofield began; '....First of all, congratulations on your successful application. It's a defining project and I'm sure you're aware of the fundamental importance Ateus Industries places on its success. The responsibility is high, but the rewards are even higher.'

'Thank you Mister Schofield. It's an honour, and I won't disappoint you.' Celina replied.

Schofield spread his hands, placing his fingertips together. He looked pensively over the top of his small rimless glasses, before smiling reassuringly at Celina. 'Please, now we're colleagues, call me Brandon.' His smooth shaved head and meek appearance belied the senior role he occupied. Celina estimated he must be one of the ten most influential and powerful people on the planet. Access to him was closely guarded and he wouldn't have requested her presence unless it was of the highest importance. Knowing that under his open manner and amiable demeanour, there lurked a sharp mind filled with a darker purpose. Celina swallowed nervously and said; 'Of course... Brandon.'

The invitation of calling the head of the Company by his first name filled Celina with trepidation, making her feel as if she'd crossed the Rubicon into a secret society from which there was no escape.

Oblivious to Celina's misgivings, Schofield continued; 'I'm sure you're aware of the sensitive nature of particular aspects regarding the Arion's mission and your role in it.'

Celina nodded and replied; 'You can count on my absolute discretion.' She had been well coached in the art of high level interviews. When to remain silent, when to speak and ask questions. She knew of the secret nature of the Mag research, the different types and of course, the Nadinium deposits found on Magdur. The richest found anywhere in the known galaxy. Not only the vast quantities uncovered but also of the highest quality. The Planet had been purchased as part of a batch by Ateus Industries under the Orion Arm Treaty of 2161. Also, she was aware of the reputation of Hybrid lifeforms and the chaos that would ensue if their existence on Magdur became known.

Schofield's voice became quieter as he spoke again. 'I've asked you here to discuss some additional information of the highest sensitivity', he said. This time Celina sat impassively as Schofield added. 'There have been further findings about the nature of Nadinium.'

'Nothing surprises me with the applications of this miracle material. It seems almost too good to be true sometimes', Celina answered.

'Well it's certainly blown any expectations we had out of the water....' Schofield continued; '....The theoretical limits are constantly being rewritten. Which brings me to my next point. It was discovered that those who were researching Nadinium, and handling the concentrated levels identical to those found on Magdur over an extensive period, suddenly displayed significantly increased levels of intelligence and memory.' Celina raised her eyebrows in amazement and leant forward in her seat. 'Of course this was before the furore about the health and environmental impacts....', Schofield went on; '....But there was another side to the story. They also demonstrated a sudden and dramatic acquisition of psychic capabilities where there had previously been none.'

Celina nodded approvingly. 'How was that discovered?', she asked.

'Serendipity my dear....', he offered and continued to elucidate; '....They were working in the same university as the Institute for Psychic Applications, when one of the subjects walked near some of its students who were honing their skills, by sending each other test messages. You know the normal pranks students like to play on each other. At that stage the students would be expected to score thirty to forty percent. Anything above fifty is unheard of. Remember the record for a trained psychic is seventy-two percent and even that was a one off. The subject was walking across the common room and blurted out the correct answer. After the laughter died down they fired more messages and then they stopped laughing. The individual with the Nadinium exposure regularly exceeded ninety-five percent.'

'That's incredible. So how did they link it to the Nadinium?', Celina asked, genuinely interested.

'The stories around the university were rife....', Schofield went on; '....Then a colleague of the original subject also displayed the same symptoms. She spoke to her supervisor. The tutor of the students spoke to the supervisor who put two and two together.'

Celina shook her head in disbelief before replying; 'All these years we've been searching for the rarest of the rare, a natural psychic, and now we've discovered we can produce them on demand. The possibilities are limitless.'

Schofield let out a long sigh and said. 'It's not quite as simple as that Celina.'

The balloon of Celina's excitement suddenly developed a small hissing leak that slowly deflated her initial enthusiasm. 'How do you mean?', she asked.

'Well life has a habit of taking away with one hand and giving back with the other', Schofield answered. Celina tried to process the significance of the reversed metaphor as the CEO carried on; 'First of all the Psychic ability dropped off sharply when the exposure to Nadinium was stopped. Second, even when they were exposed, they didn't display the same characteristics as the Naturals. For instance, they couldn't send anything detectable out. On the other hand, they were highly susceptible to mind control.'

Celina was now puzzled. She asked; 'But surely with their increased intelligence, they would be aware they were being controlled and therefore resist it.'

'Well spotted Celina, but the added bonus is that they were completely unaware they were under control...'.

Celina noticed Schofield's wry smile as he let the words hang for a few moments. Her brain quickly computed the huge implications of Schofield's words before she managed to stammer. 'You're telling me we can have mass mind control on demand?'

'It certainly seems that way', he said matter of factly.

She took a few moments to regain her composure, before she could think clearly again, as more questions were fired at her overworked brain. 'How does this relate to the Mags and the trip to Magdur with a ship full of passengers', she asked.

'You are aware of the planned capabilities of the super Gorthon and its ability to control several Mag types simultaneously....', Schofield said, then informed her; 'Well, there were further findings from our initial trip to Magdur. As you well know Psychics refer to the medium known as the Mindscape. Not being a Psychic myself...' Celina laughed on cue as Schofield continued. 'I wouldn't really know this. Normally the objects in the mindscape emanate from a specific source, such as a Psychic or indeed a Mag. However, before they were forced to evacuate Magdur, our Psychic researchers discovered an independent object existing in the mindscape that had no source. Its strength was unprecedented, far in excess of anything generated by man or beast. It's been labelled "The Source" for want of a better name.'

'Did they discover the Source's origin?' Celina ventured, quickly assimilating the new name into the conversation.

'It seemed to emanate from the planet itself, although this is only a preliminary theory, we think that the high concentration of Nadinium is a factor.'

Celina nodded. 'That would figure...' Before she continued, 'So what are the implications for our research Brandon,' carefully adding Scofield's name to continue the façade of familiarity.

If you think back to earlier in our conversation, I told you about the variant, the Super Gorthon. Remember 'It's primary purpose is to have control over multiple Mags creating a hierarchy. Of course, the super Gorthon itself will still be under our direction, but it will make the mid-level decisions and automatically assume the individual complexities, releasing the burden from the human directors', Schofield explained. 'Well we plan to add another level of control over several super Gorthons, using the Source by gaining control and directing it. It's part of Magdur and the Nadinium is part of Magdur, therefore it stands that the Source would know where the richest deposits of Nadinium lay and can guide the Mags to them. I've been assured that this is theoretically possible, by our leading experts in Psychic research.'

'Very impressive, yet I feel there's more to come., Celina insisted.

He answered her without hesitation; 'Indeed there is. When on the surface of Magdur, The Source will execute its primary function of super Gorthon direction and control in the detection and recovery of the Nadinium. But here we come to the more delicate area of our little discussion.'

There was a pause as he looked expectantly at Celina, who knew he was waiting for her to respond.

'You're going to use The Source to exert mind control of a sample population exposed to Nadinium', she guessed.

Schofield looked at her and nodded almost imperceptibly. 'It's our most closely guarded secret Celina, and you are one of a select few in its possession', he told her.

She could feel his stare boring into her, the jovial demeanour cast off to reveal the true darkness within, she thought.

 Schofield continued; 'We want data on the effect both physically and psychologically on the test subjects. These can then be fed back so we can plan our next steps in this great adventure. I'm sure you are aware of the lengths we will go to protect this information and the consequences for anyone who has unauthorised access to it…'

*

Celina stared at the blank screen she had been talking to Reece on only a few moments earlier. Schofield's words were still ringing in her ears as the memory of the meeting almost a year previously remained fresh in her mind, particularly the implications for Reece and all those who saw under the veneer of the world of those who controlled it. But now she had to prepare. The existence of The Source in the form of the 5:3 resonance was now in danger of becoming common knowledge, and that has to be stopped at all cost. Decision time was fast approaching and Reece Coleman' fate could wait a few more days.

168

21

Ava lay in her bed as she looked around the familiar surroundings of her dimly lit quarters. The strain and pressure of the Mag development had taken its toll. The breakout of Horace, the clashes with Leighton Walker, the emergence of the Hyperthon and the visceral terror it had spread across the mindscape. On top of this were her growing concerns of the direction of the Mag development and the unavoidable feeling of impending doom. Each one chipping away at her nerves, wearing them down layer by layer.

Tired from her exertions of the past few weeks, Ava began to drift off to sleep. The nightmares that had plagued her first weeks in Pangea had abated, and sleep had become a blessed release from the stresses and strains of the responsibility that weighed so heavily on her shoulders. Faint whisperings of a faraway voice reaching out to her and the blood red of the Gorthon's mindscape played across her memory before fading into the black wall of her dreams. The relaxation and carefree world of slumber enveloped her like a warm comforting blanket, holding the world of Pangea at bay for a few hours at least. In her dream she was floating gently above the planet, looking down at the fluffy welcoming cloud tops, getting nearer as she swooped over them before the deep blue of a lake surrounded by lush grassland came into view. A peaceful warm breeze washed across her face. She was starting to dive down, the wind blowing through her hair, faster and faster, increasingly out of control. Starting to tumble, she began to feel nauseous and disorientated. There was a sound in the distance like the incessant call of an exotic bird. A flock of flamingos were heading straight for her. The call contained a voice, but they were dissolving along with the remainder of the dream into a greyness that rapidly started to fade to black. The voice became louder, the black became total and a flashing red light was slowly circling around her.

'Anti-Gravity Alert! Anti-Gravity Alert!'

The calm voice of the alarm was in contrast to the befuddled state of Ava's senses as her heart hammered in panicked protest. The room was completely dark except for the flashing red light that gave random frozen pictures of her surroundings at confusing angles. One moment the edge of her table, then paper floating like a swarm of butterflies surrounding her. Even though she was now aware of what was happening, she still struggled to calm her breathing and fight down the terror that threatened to engulf her, as she span helplessly in the centre of her room with nothing to gain purchase on. The alarm continued in its reassuring voice. 'Anti-Gravity Alert!'.

'Ahhhh! Just shut the hell up!', Ava shouted, lashing out in impotent frustration, taking deep breaths until she inhaled a glob of water that had been floating in the darkness, leaving her coughing and retching. The alarm voice stopped, almost in obedience to Ava. Everything that wasn't secured down, including furniture was swirling around the room, participating in a crazy free for all dance of her possessions. Just as she was in a particularly awkward attitude, without warning everything crashed back down to the floor. She barely had a moment to realise what was happening but she braced herself as the floor came up to meet her with a thud. A loud tearing sound came from her shoulder, immediately followed by a white hot flare of sickening pain, as a heavy solid glass ornament struck her on the head, leaving her lying senseless on the floor.

When she came to, she wasn't sure if she'd been unconscious for seconds, minutes or hours. There was a banging on the door.

'Ava. It's Liz! Are you ok in there?'

'Yeah, I'll be there in a second.' Ava answered and, using her right arm, tried to raise herself. A lightning bolt of white agony shot mercilessly through her as the bone of her arm scraped against the nerves of her shoulder. The shock of the pain drove the air out her lungs, before she vomited and collapsed back down, landing her already injured ribs on the glass ball that had struck her on the head. Gasping in paralysed agony, a scream of rage welled up inside her. 'Fuck, fuckin, fuck fuck!', she shouted. Spit sprayed in impotent fury as she kicked out at the bedside table sending it clattering against the wall, breaking one of its legs and leaving a jagged splinter in her shin. The insistent knocking on the door continued.

'Hold on! I'll get help', Liz offered.

'No wait! I'm ok.' Ava said. Managing to raise herself using her other arm as the relentless stampede of pain thundered over her. Feeling giddy and close to tears Ava, desperately clutching her injured arm to her side, stumbled over to the door.

The expression on Elizabeth's face told Ava all she needed to know. People were being led or carried along in various states of injury.

'Well you don't look ok to me. I'm getting you to the infirmary.' Elizabeth, apart from some coffee across her t-shirt, appeared unscathed. 'But let's sit you down first', as she guided Ava back into her room, pulling up a chair and sitting her down on it.

Ava winced with pain. She looked up in the mirror and saw the open gash on her head with blood liberally running down the side of her face. Instinctively, she put her hand to the wound and stared uncomprehendingly at the glistening, slick redness that covered her hand.

'On second thoughts don't move, I'll get a medic', Elizabeth suggested

'What happened?', Ava asked her.

'I'm not sure but it seems like a lighting failure occurred, and the Anti-Gravity was activated throughout the whole base. Lucky the backup systems worked, otherwise we'd all still be floating in the dark.' The rest of Elizabeth's words were lost on Ava who had a single thought in her head. Were the Mags secured?

'Ava, are you ok', Elizabeth asked again.

Ava looked up at Elizabeth and told her; 'I'm just a bit shaken that's all.'

Elizabeth turned and summoned the medics from the wall panel. Then she turned back to Ava and explained; 'They're a bit overwhelmed at the moment Ava but they'll be here as soon as possible.'

Ava could feel the first prickling of tears. Swallowing hard and looking down at the vomit on her nightclothes, as the pain was doing laps around her head, while it played the drums on her ribs. She coughed. The top of her arm scraped the nerves once again causing her to scream even louder this time. Feeling cold and ill, sweat was pouring down her face. Her lip was trembling as the first sob burst out. As the tears became a flood, Elizabeth took her hand trying to reassure her. 'Hey, it's ok to cry.'

A big weight, not just of physical pain, lifted off Ava's heart. Sometimes it's not good to be so controlled Ava, she silently told herself.

'I'm sorry Liz.' Ava said. There was a compassion in Liz's eyes that Ava hadn't seen in a long time. So much work and professionalism had turned her into an emotionless robot. She remembered seeing her being hugged by Walker as she cried, still covered in Harry Felton's blood.

'How are you now? You know, after the thing with Harry', she enquired.

Elizabeth's eyes looked down and she slowly shook her head as she explained; 'Well I'm not the important one, Harry is, but at the time, it was pretty shocking to be honest. After all it's not every day you see the severed stump where someone's hand once was. I must say Dr Walker has been a great comfort to me and very supportive.'

'Yes I noticed. It's a pity he doesn't extend that to everyone', Ava intoned

'He's not as bad as people make him out to be.' There was a slightly defensive tone in Elizabeth's voice.

'Well I won't hold my breath...' It took all of Ava's self control to leave it at that.

The intercom sounded and Ava was relieved to see the medic on the monitor. The sense of relief washed over her as she wiped the tears from her cheek with her good hand. The door opened and the medic approached smiling.

'Great to see you again Miss Matthews!', he greeted.

Ava wasn't in the mood for jokes or annoyingly cheery voices. 'Just fix me up and get me back on my feet.' She responded grumpily. The medic rolled his eyes, but Ava didn't care, just wanting him to shut up and the pain to end.

♦

The pain in Ava's shoulder was numbed by the painkillers which in conjunction with the mild concussion she was suffering, made it harder than usual to follow what people were saying. Crying like a baby the previous day, despite the sedation, she suffered pain that she never thought possible as her dislocated shoulder was put back in place. It left her feeling faint and nauseous as the popping of the joint being reinserted added to the roaring agony, causing her to scream so loud she temporarily lost her voice. Perhaps it was a punishment for the profanities that forced their way out of her mouth in her moment of desperation. Despite the pain she felt, there was also a tinge of shame at her loss of control. Added to that, the thunderous headache and the indignity of crying while having the gash on her head glued back together left her in an irritable and fragile state. God I've had the hell knocked out of me over the past few days, she thought. Normally she would have been under observation for twenty four hours but this was anything but ordinary. She was listening to Ryan Baxter, the chief engineer stepping through the series of events that had led to the power failure.

'So remind me. What is a CME again?' It was Celina cross examining Ryan after his presentation.

'Coronal Mass Ejection. Trillions of tons of charged particles ejected from a star. Most pass harmlessly into outer space without interacting with anything before they dissipate and lose energy.' Ryan replied in his usual calm assured manner and continued'; 'If a CME heads towards a planet with a magnetic field, they're channelled in through the magnetic poles, which on earth are aligned with the geographic poles. Now if you've got the equivalent of an entire year's energy output of Planet Earth slamming into the upper atmosphere, anything in the way is going to get pretty seriously fried. This is the cause of the Aurora seen from the extreme latitudes back home.'

'But we're away from the polar regions, so how does that affect us?', Celina asked him.

Unruffled, Ryan explained; 'Well, we've discovered that the magnetic field of Magdur is undergoing what is called a polarity reversal, which means that the magnetic field of the planet is shifting from north to south and vice versa. This happens on Earth but not during the past hundred thousand years, so it's the first time it's been observed.'

'That's all very fascinating Ryan and I'd normally be very pleased for our scientific colleagues, but how does that explain what happened yesterday?' Impatience was evident in Celina's voice.

Ryan clarified at some length; 'At the moment, the polarity of Magdur is tilted at a fifty-degree angle, and we've discovered that Pangea Base we is currently right on the edge of Magdur's north magnetic pole. Added top that the planets magnetic field seems to be considerably weaker during this reversal.' A swell of consternation moved around the room as Ryan continued. 'We hardened our electronics as standard procedure otherwise the base would be dead, but even so, there was a lot of damage to our systems, although they're all fixable. We were lucky to escape so lightly, but I can't say how another such event would turn out. This time it was the anti-gravity being activated and the lights failed. The fusion power plant immediately tripped, but we seamlessly switched to backup power and disabled the anti-gravity, thanks to the preparation work of my colleague Floyd Pearce, which saved a lot of lives. We're working on the getting the fusion reactor back on line, but restarting it after an emergency shutdown isn't a five minute job. Kalpana reported that apart from a few small glitches the AI was not seriously compromised. There was not so good news from Magnus. Some of the Droids were completely fried and it'll take at least a couple of weeks to get back to where we were before the incident. It also seems to have impacted our reserves of entangled electrons, which has significantly impacted our ability to communicate with Earth. Finally, the Mag containment areas were unaffected in terms of security. The only problems were caused by the nutrient liquids escaping from a couple of vats, but this was cleaned up quickly with no damage to the Mags contained within them. Overall, considering what hit us, we got off pretty lightly and this is thanks to the contingency planning of the engineering teams.' He smiled at Celina, the glowing pride in his team obvious.

'So what are the chances of another CME hitting us?' This time it was Myra Alexeyeva who asked.

'I would say that depends on the Sun Spot cycle of Magdur. If it's at maximum then I expect more events, although I don't know what the odds of another one coming towards us are. Nobody can answer that one.' The cool professionalism of Ryan reassured everyone present. The unparalleled knowledge he possessed more than supplemented the database and AI systems. He had the gift of being able to distil the most convoluted of problems into its essential elements and knowing what to focus on. Something, despite their prodigious power, no amount of AI's could hope to match. They were good for large boring tasks that required levels of concentration and precision beyond the abilities of any individual, but they lacked those most human characteristics that Ryan possessed in abundance. Insight and compassion.

'Thank You Ryan.' Celina nodded her gratitude to the engineer as he left the room before she continued. 'Fortunately there were no fatalities. Lots of injuries but none life threatening.' She looked across to Ava and smiled. 'I trust you're on the mend Miss Matthews.'

'I'll live.' replied Ava through gritted teeth.

Celina continued. 'I agree with Ryan, we were lucky this time, but I think we need to take some precautions, so we'll have to monitor Ereus and if any CME's make their way toward us, we should shut down all but essential systems. We should have about four days' notice. Are you ok with that Myra?'

The director nodded her approval and replied; 'I think that'll be the safest course. Let's hope it doesn't reoccur, but if it does at least we'll be prepared.'

With that the meeting broke up. Ava had barely been able to follow proceedings and she staggered back to her room to continue her suffering in peace and quiet.

22

To: Michelle J. Farrington @ electron.com
From: robert.nash@galactic_vistas.com
Subject: Re: Luxury detention

Hey Michelle

I was thinking back to when we looked down on our new home for the first time. I have to say there were tears in my eyes, but I wasn't alone in that. It made me think that's how earth must have once appeared. The clarity and purity of the colours took my breath away. The greens and the blues each in a thousand shades and tones. No dark smudges or yellowed browns. No scars across the landscape or billowing smoke. No scorched endless deserts. Only tranquillity and peace. It seemed to call out to us to embrace it. A whole new world waiting for us to start a whole new life. I looked across at Frank Cunningham and Martin Preston, my two colleagues. Normally you can't get a word in edgeways, but they were standing there with their mouths open and tongues hanging out. There was a strange faraway gaze in their eyes. They were clearly in awe.

But the promise that new world held for us has started to lose its allure here in Pangea base. Don't get me wrong. It's pretty luxurious for basically a metal sphere, but oh to feel the breeze on my face and the sun's warmth in my bones. We don't know how long it'll be before the atmosphere is breathable and we're finally shipped out to our new home, where we can walk the land in freedom and safety. But not yet. I've been putting on a brave face for Amy and the boys, but I've got a strange sick feeling at the pit of my stomach that all is not what it seems. An air of controlled hysteria is starting to creep in here. I'm surrounded by friends and family but I've never felt so alone. It's a completely unexpected emotion and very unsettling.

I think even the staff are feeling a bit strange. You remember Darren, the play leader who Ollie has befriended. I heard he had a punch up with the Chef in the staff bar area. Luckily the kids were nowhere around but instead of being the large cuddly figure of fun, he was drunk and the Chef (who is a bit of a prima donna from all accounts) was goading him about his weight and lowly position. Darren didn't take it too well and thrashed the poor chef to within an inch of his life. So now it looks like he's going to get fired, which has made him drink even more. It's all happening here...

I'll try to write again when (if) we hear anything about our final settlement.

Love to all,

Robert

To: robert.nash@galactic_vistas.com
From: Michelle J. Farrington @ electron.com
Subject: Re: Luxury detention

Dearest Robert.

There's no easy way to tell you this. Mum passed away yesterday morning from a heart attack. Her neighbours found her slumped in the lounge. The Homebot was still charging and didn't sound the alarm but there's nothing anyone could have done. Time had caught up with her. The medic said death would have been instantaneous and she wouldn't have suffered.

I'm sorry to be the bearer of bad tidings, but although she acted angrily towards you, deep down you know how much she loved you.

There's something else you need to know although news coverage has been restricted. Three days ago there was a limited nuclear exchange between Utopian Prospects and Altumanina Industries. It was only a matter of time before the unrestricted greed of these rogue companies spilled over into madness. Only a run on their share prices pulled them back from a full scale war. Over six million dead and four cities reduced to radioactive dust. All over the control of water supplies in Asia Minor which were thousands of miles away from the cities. The fallout spread for hundreds of miles, so there's bound to be more casualties. They've tried to minimise the coverage so the news is only fragmentary. After more than 200 years, the nuclear genie is well and truly out of the bottle once again.

It's been a bad few days. I'm beginning to regret not joining you.

Last night, after I'd cried myself off to sleep, I dreamt we were back on holiday in Hayling Island with Mum and Dad. It was beautiful and peaceful. I cried even more when I woke. The world feels a very different place today.

Stay in touch and take care. Hug Amy, Ben and Ollie for me.

All my Love,

Michelle.

To: Wilhelmus.schuiling@familyofykdar.com
From: marcus.burgman@galactic_vistas.com
Subject: Re: Our time is approaching

Brother Wilhelmus
Please excuse the brief nature of my communication but I have much to do and not much time to do it!

Although I am anxious as anyone to press forwards to our final settlement, I also feel that every day it gets closer the more chance of our mission's failure becomes a reality. At least while people are in Pangea and are concentrated, the greater the opportunity, which must be grasped with the utmost vigour, and I for one am impatient to push ahead with the Great Lord Ykdar's work. I can feel the great one watching over my shoulder as I write, and it is of great comfort to me.

Our numbers continue to grow with each passing day. This is reflected in their devotion towards the Lord Ykdar. Their love seems to have no boundaries, and this is reflected in the passions displayed during our gathering (with a little encouragement from my disciples). Naturally there are some doubts amongst them but with the right guidance I'm sure we shall create a new paradise on the virgin lands that await our presence.

We are hearing troubling rumours of terrible events back on earth. I thank the Lord Ykdar we are far away.

      Your humble servant
      Marcus

To: marcus.burgman@galactic_vistas.com
From: Wilhelmus.schuiling@familyofykdar.com
Subject: Re: Arrival

Brother Marcus
The moment of truth has arrived and for the pilgrims of Magdur a new world is awaiting. You only have to close your hand and it is yours in the name of Lord Ykdar. You are the new Thumis leading his people, the Strix to the promised land of Tadarida where purity and peace await. You will truly go down in history as one of the founding figures of Magdur and one of the great pioneers of the expansion across the galaxy, starting a new chapter in the human story, fulfilling its destiny amongst

the stars away from the hell left behind.

Do not concern yourself about the storms of evil and darkness sweeping the earth. Focus on the task in hand. The eye of history is upon you my son and I know you will not fail.

Wilhelmus

23

Titus gently pulled at the harness as he watched the coming and goings of the humans through the bars of his compound. It felt looser that the previous one, that seemed to chafe against him causing him fly into a rage, sending the humans into a frenzy of activity. He'd awoken with a looser fitting one a few days earlier and the pain had stopped, although he'd still acted up. Just to scare them. The enclosure still hummed with the strange metallic smell. He'd learnt it was best not to touch the bars after the last time. The burning pain and the sparks had been enough to deter him for now. Sometimes he could see the pale blue orb approaching in his mind's eye, but by now he'd learnt how to trap the light in a corner so it couldn't have a good look around, trying to probe his secrets and intentions. It was a while before feeding, and even when it happened it was never enough, but he suspected that there was something in the food because after some meals he would awaken in the restraints and the light blue light was trying to float through. He would send the trap to the light and hold it easily.

The previous day had seen Titus plunged into darkness, except for the bright red sparks that flew off the bars. They were coming towards him, but soon realised it was him moving toward them. Bracing himself for the inevitable pain, he gently bumped into them in the darkness, but he felt nothing. Unable to understand why the room was floating about him, Titus grasped the bar and lowered himself down to the floor, grimly hanging on, as his legs drifted lazily. Instead of giving him a feeling of limitless power, the cold metal object on his back had become rigid and unyielding. Then the lights came back on and his legs slammed into the ground. A second later, the humming sound started again and his whole body was sizzling in spasms of excruciating agony. A burning smell filled the compound and smoke appeared to be coming from his claws. His hands were stuck fast to the bars as they were paralysed with the shock. The melting flesh was acting as a glue. Watching with an almost detached interest despite the carnage being inflicted on his nervous system.

A sound caught Titus's attention. 'Turn it off! Now!' The puny pink shape shouted. A deafening roar of pain and anger burst out of Titus, seemingly from his very core, as if all his body was generating the sound. The pink shape staggered and collapsed to the floor, placing its hands on his head in a vain attempt to block out the blare. Its legs were moving in a random uncoordinated fashion that did nothing to move it away.

'Turn the current off the bars!' it shouted.

The pain stopped as suddenly as it had started. The smoke wafted lazily up from Titus' still burning hands, small flames licking his flesh but there was only numbness now. Pulling his hands away, there was a sickly smell of burnt flesh as he left great chunks of his skin shrivelling away on the still red hot bars. He looked at the raw weeping things that had once been his hands with yellow and aqua gloop sliding off in slippery elastic loops.

The pink figure stood on the other side of the bars, blood running down both sides of his head, staring up at the towering mass standing over him. Another display of power was called for and Titus let forth a guttural thunderous roar that made the air reverberate in front of him, causing the pink figure to collapse into a jelly like heap. Raising his arms, he smashed them against the bars, bending them outward with a titanic crash. Another blow and one bar was sent flying out, somersaulting and clanging it's way along the passage in a crazy random dance that led away from its cage. This time they would give way. Drawing up his strength for the final blow, before bringing it down on the bars, but the humming sound started louder than ever and this time there were bigger, bluer sparks and flames as the maximum current flew up Titus' arms, throwing his gigantic mass backward to the rear of the compound, sucking the last of his energy, leaving him motionless on his back.

Reflecting upon on the events of the previous days, a new emotion became apparent to Titus, disquiet. He wasn't sure what to do about it. The humming and smell of the bars continued as he drifted off to sleep. In the darkened landscape of dreams, a gentle purple light had surrounded him, slowly permeating through his skin to gently draw out his innermost thoughts, holding them before him to examine. An opening appeared in the purple glow and from the other side, a cool breeze washed softly over his face. In his world of meat and metal, there was no concept of softness, as refreshing air filled his lungs, sweeping through his whole being, creating a new emotion, a yearning for something different to the empty existence. Titus moved towards the opening, taking another breath, drinking in the feeling and letting it dance through his mind in a carnival of light, colour and freedom.

When Titus woke up, the dream had vaporised, leaving a few half remembered wisps that lingered momentarily in his consciousness. It left him with only the outlines of a feeling. Looking at the stark surroundings of the pen, he noticed bars had been repaired. He looked down at his hands. The pain had disappeared and the flesh had regenerated, leaving them looking almost identical to before the burning. It would soon be time for the probing again, the voices, the needles, the pain. Then it hit him. The metallic smell was gone and so was the sound. Moving toward the bars, the pink shape was nowhere to be seen. There were others across the area looking into one of the other compounds, deep in conversation. A click sounded from behind him. His head shot around at the sound but nothing was to be seen. A half remembered smell of freshness wafted through his mind as he slowly reached out to touch the bar, expecting the pain to ignite him once more. His hand trembling in anticipation and fear. A faint shimmer of purple momentarily played across the metallic surface as he made gentle contact, ready to pull back at the slightest signal. The coldness of the metal travelled up his arm as he grasped the bar. Quickly, he withdrew his hand before it was spotted. He craned his neck forward to see if he'd been spotted and gently knocked his shoulder against the door, which gave way and gently swung open.

The sight of the outside world, unbroken by the bars, was new to Titus, as was the sound that suddenly filled the compound area. The figures were running away shouting in terror, as Titus moved quickly through the inviting gap that the door had occupied moments earlier. Somehow he knew things would never be the same after this, but the intoxicating smell of liberation filled his nostrils as he took a deep breath before letting out a shattering roar and moved towards the lab area.

◆

Eleanor looked up and down checking the gleaming floor of the corridor she'd been cleaning all morning. It was the longest one and she was pleased with her work, although not as pleased as when she had spotted Naomi Mann amongst the shoppers in the mall earlier that morning. She'd pulled her cap down over her eyes and watched Naomi while she, oblivious to her nemesis' proximity, looked idly at the various shoes for sale. Eleanor smiled at the first sighting of her prey as she planned out her next step on scaring the shit out of her.

Eleanor looked up and for some obscure reason thought of Johnathan Gough as she glanced up and down the corridor. There was a loud unfamiliar sound coming from inside the lab area. A groaning howl from a thousand trumpets echoed through door. Then screaming, crashing and the shattering of glass. A loud thumping came from behind her on one of the doors. The ashen-terror filled face of Khan frantically banging his hands on the glass, pointing down at the lock. Next to him, desperately looking over her shoulder was Chiang. Both were shouting with voices muffled, pleading for Eleanor to let them out. She could see debris flying in the background before more faces appeared at the window, crying and imploring. The crashing and trumpeting became louder as Eleanor frantically pressed her hand against the scanner. The red line lazily worked its way up her hand as the people behind the window became a sea of pleading faces pressed up against the glass.

'Please enter PIN.' said the display. Eleanor punched in her number. The door didn't open. 'Incorrect PIN. Please enter correct PIN'

Eleanor wasn't a lip reader but she could have sworn she saw one of the faces say 'What the fuck are you waiting for?' She punched in the numbers as the roaring and screaming got louder. One of the faces was suddenly whipped away from the window as the red circle jauntily whirled around. The rest of the faces were squeezed into the bottom corner, as a red mess thunked against the glass and slowly slid down, leaving a trail of innards in its wake. There was a buzz, then a click and the door opened.

The deafening pandemonium burst out of the room as several sets of fingers hauled the door open. Eleanor recognised the whippet like shape of Mandy Fink shooting out through the narrow gap. Eyes bulging and teeth drawn back like a plastic skull from a cheap souvenir shop as she sprinted down the corridor in a blur of frenzied movement. As the door opened wider, a thrashing mass of limbs and outstretched fingers strove to get through the open space before a giant claw ripped through them, leaving a red trail of gore. Severed limbs, heads and giblets slipped through the open door. Eleanor reached out and took the arm of one of the thrashing, desperate survivors, as a blast of sound from behind the bodies nearly knocked her off her feet, her ears ringing in protest. This was followed by the metallic groan of the door being violently wrenched from its hinges before she was thrown against the opposite wall. The floor cleaning machine she had been using a few seconds earlier, landed on top of her. Looking down she found she was still holding the arm, minus its owner.

The great shadow burst through the space that was once the door, sending glass and twisted metal flying in all directions. There was no noise apart from her ragged breathing. Eleanor looked through the gap to see a huge pink grey foot before her. Its pearl white claws smeared with tattered fragments of human flesh. There was a low growl, more like a series of deep clicks from the clock at the end of time, that could be felt rather than heard. She'd heard that sound before while cleaning the compounds. Laying still, not daring to even twitch a muscle, watching the foot move away, hearing the thud of the footsteps along the corridor. After a few seconds, as the thuds faded into the distance, she lifted the cleaning machine off her. A long rod of metal that had been perched against the wall on top of the machine, scraped sideways along the wall, landing with an echoing, bonging clang that repeated with every bounce before coming to rest. The thud of the footsteps had stopped.

Eleanor looked along the end of the corridor that was filled by the massive shape of the Gorthon. Its legs poised to propel it forward in an instant. The rippling sinews of the muscle under the iridescent skin stretched taut over them. The dark beads of the eyes were fixed on her as she slowly rose to her feet. The lower jaw stretched open, as the two lines of murdering teeth glinted white and red in the harsh lighting. The clicking growl started again.

Eleanor looked desperately around for an escape, remembering the small cleaning closet just twenty yards back along. The clicking grew faster and louder before the full orchestra of the trumpeting roar slammed into her eardrums with the force of a drill as the Gorthon moved towards her at demonic speed. Her scream was utterly lost in the hurricane of sound. She started to run, although her legs were numb with panic. The thudding footsteps quickened as the charging Gorthon closed in on her. The silver door of the closet was slightly ajar. The grunting breaths of her pursuer were a few feet behind her and closing as the clacks of the claws on the polished floor rattled out its imminent arrival. Too late. It was on her. Eleanor waited for the final ripping blow before oblivion and death. Make it quick, she thought and took one final glance over her shoulder. The face filled her vision just as the pounding feet momentarily faltered and the gargantuan body slipped, crashing to the shiny ground.

Diving through the gap into the closet, she slammed the door shut behind her, pushing the lock up. Inside was engulfed in complete darkness. A moment later a crashing boom filled the small space as the door bent inwards. A shaft of light shone through the gap. The eye of the Gorthon peered in as the door shook from the force of the roar. A clawed hand started to pull at the open gap and the door began to tear away from the frame with a metallic screeching. She grabbed onto the inside in a futile attempt to keep the beast at bay, as the face came into full view. A look of triumph in its eyes. Loud bangs sounded and sparks flew from the door. This must be the final few sinews holding the door on, thought Eleanor, but the roar was momentarily cut short as she could hear shots and shouts in the distance before it was redoubled. The door crashed back on Eleanor, throwing her against the wall. The giant steps thundered off in the direction of the shots, leaving her limp in the darkness, dust and silence.

◆

Ava removed the sling. Her arm was still sore and stiff. It could be moved without too much pain, although it was still restricted. Looking in the mirror, she examined the scar on the side of her head. It was a couple of inches long and still tender to touch. Her concerns over the Gorthon were still valid. There'd been her first disturbing dream for a while the previous evening. The feeling of being trapped and the roaring was all she remembered. Maybe it was the medication, or maybe the medication supressed it. Either way it had been a restless night. She'd

183

been given a few days' minimal duties to recover, but being a workaholic, she decided to put the spare time to good use and catch up on some studying.

Ava looked across at the base's time on the wall display. It was just past midday. A couple more hours work, then she'd make her way to the Cafeteria. Sometimes she'd meet Eleanor there and was surprised at their connection. They spoke for long periods about anything and everything. How could someone with her intelligence be a lowly janitor? Maybe people from London didn't have the same opportunities as those from New York, but it felt strange. She seemed professional and organised. Disciplined even, Ava thought. But Eleanor had brushed off her observations with platitudes about not having the right breaks at the right time or not studying. Ava tried not to use her powers on friends, but her curiosity got the better of her and she felt guilty about it. It didn't tell her much anyway apart from Eleanor concealing something, but that was the same for just about everyone over the age of five. Still they had become firm friends and she enjoyed Eleanor's refreshing company. She never asked about the Mag's and Ava never mentioned it. It was odd that someone with her intelligence would be so incurious about her daily surroundings.

Ava turned back a few pages of her studies. She'd been reading and nothing was going in. C'mon Ava. Focus, she told herself. Then it hit her. A wave of aggression bursting out of the deep red surroundings. A wall of flame engulfing her. The shock of it caused her to gasp. At that moment the security alarm sounded. Rushing over to the screen connected to the Labs, she saw a high view from one of the cameras, which was the default when nobody was directly contacted. The lab appeared to be deserted. Noticing the odd shapes strewn around, Ava zoomed the camera into one of them. It looked like a large brown snake. Ava narrowed the view and stepped back from the screen. Fear pierced her heart as she took another look at the intestines draped languidly across a work surface. Something flashed across the screen. Drawing out to the wide view, she recognised the unmistakable shape of the Gorthon moving towards the door where a small group of survivors were huddled, cowering in terror. They were struggling to get through the door and blocking it in their desperation to get out. The Gorthon struck them with an almost casual swat of the wrist, as the bodies gave way like wet tissue paper, scattering in various directions. The Gorthon ripped the door off and smashed its way through, before disappearing through the hole. Then she noticed the voice that had been calling for the past twenty seconds.

'We've had a breakout in the Gorthon labs. All security teams immediate assistance!'

She forgot her nausea, terror and pain and sprinted out of her quarters, making her way to the Labs and the carnage.

♦

Ava crashed into the wall of the corridor as she slipped on the wetness beneath her feet. An electric shock of pain burst from her shoulder and made her feel faint. She leant against the wall for a couple of seconds to recover.

'Are you ok Miss Matthews?'

She looked up at the voice. It was Sergeant Montano from Blue security team.

'Yes, thanks. Just a bit winded that's all', she answered.

'No survivors, I'm afraid. I've dispatched a team to check the remaining Mag's', he told her.

Ava noticed Montano's complexion was a waxy yellow, reflecting the deep primal terror they all felt, although she bore the added weight of responsibility for her part in the creation of the nightmare that had been unleashed.

She looked past Montano at the tangled mass of ripped, smashed human innards, limbs and heads. Chiang and Khan who had both been sliced in half were joined at the waist in death in a grotesque parody of their closeness in life. Chiang's face was still a mask of calm indifference. Ava's mouth filled with a salty taste and a thick sensation filled her throat. The horror of the reality they now faced and must be solved filled her with the urge to run away and hide, but they had no choice. They had to face it down any way they could. Having witnessed the power of the Hyperthon close up, the memory had burned itself so deep inside her that even when her eyes were shut, she could still see it as clear as day. The violence of the Gorthon was several orders of magnitude higher, making the Hyperthon seem like a pet gerbil in comparison. The fact that she and Reece were proven right gave her no sense of vindication, and even if it did, Khan and Chiang were in no position to hear it.

A loud crash sounded a few yards along the corridor and a battered silver door flew open. All heads bolted around to look where the noise came from. Fear crackled in the air. A thunderstorm ready to burst. The security team sprang into action. One of them pulled a grenade and readied to lob it into the opening.

'Blue team, Stand by!' The strong voice of Montano cut through the fear that spread like wildfire through the team. They gingerly moved towards the opening. 'Show yourself', he ordered. A scraping shuffling sound came from within the closet. The clicking of cocked guns filled the air. 'Hold!' Montano commanded his team this time and edged toward the opening.

A shaky voice sounded from inside the closet. 'Ok, ok. Hold fire. It's Ellie. The Janitor...'

The sigh of relief filled the corridor, but the fear filled faces found no respite. With tears filling her eyes, Ava ran towards Eleanor and embraced her.

'I'm ok, I'm ok...' Eleanor was trembling and, apart from a bloody nose and a scrape to her head, she was unharmed. She stood back. 'Ava, what the fuck was that thing? What have you created?'

Ava looked down in shame, shook her head and admitted; 'Death and lies...'.

'All the other Mags are secure in their compounds sir....!' one of the security team reported to Montano. '....It's a single rogue. Reports tell us the Gorthon has broken into the Civilian areas with multiple casualties.'

Ava felt she'd been punched in the stomach. Her worst fears had been realised and there was no undoing this, no turning back.

'Blue team on me!' Montano bellowed then turned to Ava. 'At least we know where to find the fucker.', he said before he turned and ran back down the corridor towards the Civilian area. The tramp of footsteps and the jangle of equipment filled the air as Ava and Eleanor followed. Ava thought to ask what the Janitor would be able to do, but she suspected she already knew the answer. In the distance she could hear roars, gunfire and shouts.

♦

'What is the matter with them? C'mon girls!'

'Sorry Mum. Coming.' Sophia had noticed the change in her mother's demeanour since the daughter had been able to block the signals. The irritation mock, the raised voice ironic, the looks warm and loving. Sometimes she'd noticed a distant rumbling in her mind, but it felt isolated and harmless. The probing continued but she kept it effortlessly away.

Sophia noticed the intensely coloured hologram ads floating above as she glanced behind her. The brightly lit mall flanked with the shops and restaurants, could have been in any city on earth. Any city that is, which hadn't been swallowed by the relentless march of the deserts and abandoned to those who didn't have the money for permits to gain access to the steadily shrinking temperate areas with their gleaming towers and lush forests. The throng of shoppers flowed around Sophia and Jasmine.

They were heading towards the Auto Cinema to watch another iteration of her favourite generated film. They were never the same twice, but always geared towards maximum excitement, with new twists and turns. You could watch the same film, with the same basic story a dozen times and it'd never be the same. Sometimes a happy ending, other times a sad one. One character may be the lead, the next, a completely different one would dominate. Sophia wasn't even sure if

186

the actors actually existed, such was the realism. Probably cheaper than real actors, but without the tantrums. They'd have to get proper jobs like everyone else. How could people watch the same film repeatedly in the old days. It must have been as boring as shit. Still, she wished the world or just her life could be rerun until it turned out just right. Save it when you get to a good part. Restart and keep trying until you get to the next good point. Then they wouldn't be stuck inside a glorified tin can on a far off planet after fleeing a broken earth. Perhaps some people had run it and it had turned out well for them, at the cost of the other 99.9% of the population.

Sophia noticed a few people were staring back behind her. A look of bewilderment and unease on their faces. A distant screeching could be discerned. In the mindscape there was a growing heat. An approaching fireball hurtling towards her, and before she could respond, it struck her dumb and rooted her to the spot.

'Sophia, what's that noise? I'm scared.' Jasmine was pulling on her arm. The noise grew. Crashing, howls and smashing getting louder, as Sophia stood, a mute witness, wanting to shout a warning, but her mouth was paralysed. Knowing what was coming even though she'd never seen it, she'd always known it had existed. People staggered from around the corner, some helping others who had blood pouring from various wounds. Terrified mothers were carrying crying children. The fire was incinerating Sophia's mind.

Even though people were fleeing past her, Sophia remained as still and silent as stone. Jasmine's increasingly frantic shouts and tugging on her arm had no effect.

'Sophia, what are you waiting for? Come on. RUN!', Jasmine said, though the last word was cut short by a colossal reverberating roar that seemed to split the air with its violence.

A dismembered body was hurled through the air before crashing into a wall and flopping lifelessly to the ground, blood oozing from the stump of the neck where, until a few moments earlier, the head used to be. Gunshots rang out as a soldier came into view, backing off and firing upwards before he stumbled backwards over a prone figure behind him. He let out a final pitiful yell as the huge shape of the Gorthon pounced on him, breaking him backwards and twisting the soldier's broken body in two, before slamming them into the ground. The legs momentarily twitching before they stilled permanently.

The Gorthon looked around and finding everyone else gone, turned its malicious purpose and menace straight towards Sophia and Jasmine, who held on to her sister, refusing to leave. The power unstoppable in its intent. Jasmine squeezed her sister screaming; 'No! No! No!'

187

Sophia closed her eyes, the roaring of the Gorthon and the yelling of Jasmine filling her ears as she waited for the final blow. Then there was quiet, broken only by the frantic wheezing breaths of Jasmine and the crazy thudding of her pulse in her ears. Is this death? Is this how the end feels? She opened her eyes again. The black eye of the Gorthon, surrounded by the monstrous face, was inches from her. It was coolly considering her, as if trying to perceive this new and curious object before it. The low clicking rumble of the growl reverberated in Sophia's chest. There was a strange calm that exuded from the massive head. It reached out and softly caressed her arm. The giant claw displayed a tenderness diabolically at odds with its primary purpose. The fire in Sophia's mind was subsiding as the two of them contemplated each other.

The Gorthon's momentary calm dissipated as a familiar voice shouted behind Sophia. 'Get away from my girls you fuckin monster'.

The Gorthon's face lost its momentary serenity as its true purpose was restored. The full fury of its mass was turned on Christopher Whittaker who was running toward the beast wielding a metal pole above his head, closely followed by a howling Danielle. A swift blow of the arm from the Gorthon turned both of them into a spray of blood and tattered flesh that splattered over Sophia and Jasmine. A shriek erupted from her younger sister as a numbed Sophia turned to see the huge back of the Gorthon heading away, to be met by the sound of more gunfire. Looking down at the motionless bodies of her parents, a dark hole of grief opened in her mind, sucking her down into its depths.

♦

Eleanor's lungs were bursting and her legs were burning. Even though she'd tried to keep in trim since being thrown out of the Corps, keeping up with the Blue team had left her and Ava trailing in their wake. They'd seen the first bodies after a couple of minutes and they led a bloody trail straight to the Gorthon. A scene of even greater carnage than the one they'd left behind in the labs greeted them as they turned the corner into the shopping mall. In the midst of the bodies were two young girls frozen in shock and covered from head to toe in blood and entrails. Medics were searching amongst the casualties for any survivors but all they had was a mush of mangled body parts.

By the time Eleanor and Ava caught them up, Blue team had met Red team led by Nicklas Overgaard, still bearing the scar from his encounter with Horace, and Jordan Harris, the security team director who was speaking to Montano and Fynn Michels.

'It's heading towards the residential area....', Jordan said, adding; '....Once it gets there the carnage will be total. Red, cut around the flanks and head it off.'

Beside Jordan was the leader of Robotics, Magnus Eriksen. He spoke up. 'If we can't kill it straight off, target the weak spot at the base of its skull. Get to that and we'll at least slow it down it and give ourselves a fighting chance.'

'Ok everyone you heard Magnus.....' Jordan cut in; '....We'll pursue directly and slow the Gorthon down. Right let's go!'

'Turn on the anti-gravity, that way he won't be able to move.' Eleanor said as all heads turned towards her.

'We've got the fuckin cleaner giving out orders now have we?' Retorted Jordan. 'Thanks for your bullshit advice Miss but that slows us down as well. Now kindly fuck off, do the job you're paid to do and clean up the mess behind you.'

'Not if we coordinate and everyone is secured first.' Eleanor shot back.

Magnus and Nicklas briefly spoke to Jordan who turned to Eleanor and said. 'Brilliant idea! Contact control and see to it. Right let's go!'

Eleanor caught the amazed look from Ava out of the corner of her eye, but pretended not to notice as they set off after Blue team once more.

♦

The shouting and cries for help had ceased as they caught the monster up. Only the Gorthon and the fighters remained with the dead as their sole witnesses. One side would walk out victorious, and currently the rampaging Mag was the red hot favourite. The way to the residential areas was clear and until Red team intercepted it, Montano and his team were the only hope.

Three troopers cut around the side of the Gorthon, and blocked its path before opening fire. The Gorthon barely seemed to notice as it casually swatted them aside in an eruption of gore, before it continued the pursuit of juicier quarry. Bullets flashed and ricocheted off the mighty creature's impenetrable back, presenting more of a danger to the shooters than the target.

'He's barely noticing them....!' shouted Montano in desperation as he turned to Ava and continued; '....We've got to stop him until Red arrives or he'll kill everything in his path. Try to patch into its mind. You've done it before, and you can do it again!'

'I don't know if I can, it nearly broke me earlier.' Ava replied, adding; '....but I'll give it everything I've got.' She took a deep breath and closed her eyes, immediately jolted and sank to her knees, groaning while holding the side of her head. Her face grimaced with the strain as Eleanor watched her friend's desperate struggle.

The remorseless thundering of the Gorthon's footfalls slowed, then came to a halt, as if a distant memory occurred to it as it turned slowly, and looked straight at Ava. One of the claws on its foot seemed to be marking time, tapping out a couple of beats before it too stilled. There was almost a look of recognition and irritation on the terrible features that passed for a face. The rumbling resumed the ominous rhythm from deep within its throat. Drawn by the siren call of Ava's mind, the creature hesitantly started towards its source, gradually increasing its speed, oblivious to the firestorm as every gun opened up on it. The ground shook with the power of the charging juggernaut. A trooper hurled a grenade which exploded just in front of the Gorthon, briefly slowing the onslaught. The trooper threw another, aiming it at the head. This time a swipe of the hand batted the lethal package straight back. It bounced off the wall, before rolling towards Ava, who was still involved in a battle of wills with the Gorthon.

Someone just had time to shout 'Grenade!'.

Eleanor hurled herself at Ava knocking her sideways. In that moment, the air itself seemed to groan with the blast as Eleanor felt the breath driven out of her lungs. At the same time, she felt the tearing bite of fragments ripping into her back and head, as Ava screamed in pain. Despite the agony, Eleanor turned to see the intact Gorthon moving almost casually towards them. It seemed to recognise her from earlier, and was intent on renewing old acquaintances.

'Oh god help me! I can't see. Please help!' Ava cried, holding her face as blood streamed between her fingers, her legs vainly kicking in pain. 'The dark, not the dark! Pleeeeeease!'

The desperate cries were the only sound as Eleanor's attention was focused on their approaching doom, oblivious to the scattered groaning members of Blue security team. The mouth of the Gorthon drew back revealing the rows of shining white certain death. It took a breath and let forth a roar that reduced all who it struck into a state of helpless insensible shock.

All except Eleanor who looked across at the still body of a trooper a few feet away. If he was alive or dead she couldn't tell, but what she could see was the fully loaded and cocked gun on the ground next to him. Slowly, she leant across, her eyes fixed on the Gorthon. *Ahh, Ellie grown some fuckin balls at last* said a familiar voice in her head. *Won't do you any good though, you're going to be a puddle on the floor in a few seconds.* Her hands closed around the cold metal as she pulled the gun up to eye level and took careful aim. *What good is a peashooter against an elephant. Might as well piss on him for all the good it'll do.* The rumbling started again; her finger squeezed the trigger. The juddering recoil felt comforting against her shoulder as the rounds struck home in the Gorthon's eyes.

190

A new sound came out of the beast. This time a startled yelp as it recoiled in blind pain and shock. Then a scream such as had never been heard by human ears rent the air, before the Gorthon lashed wildly out in all directions, twirling and stamping. The giant feet narrowly avoiding crushing the casualties of the grenade.

Didn't expect that, did you voice? Well you can fuck off. She took the opportunity to grab a spare magazine of ammo from the dead trooper. Shouldering the weapon, she ran across to Ava who had lost consciousness, while the staggering Gorthon performed its wild dance of pain. Grabbing Ava by the arm, Eleanor dragged her out of the way, dumping her roughly around the corner half a second before a foot came crashing down onto the space she'd vacated.

Montano, blood running from his ear and mouth, slowly clambered to his feet. 'You didn't learn that cleaning floors, did ya!' he grunted as he helped her to remove some of the casualties.

Shots sounded from the far end of the area as Red team finally arrived. Instead of hurting it, the bullets seemed to infuriate the Gorthon as it headed towards the retreating Red team.

The fire died down and Eleanor saw her chance, noticing the harness the Gorthon was wearing. If she could get close enough there was a chance of firing straight into the weak spot that was barely visible just above where the neck joined the base of the skull. *Still not finished, you crazy bitch Ellie.* I wondered where you'd gone. Thought I'd shut you up for good. *Lucky shot, bet you don't get lucky again,* came the response.

The pain from her wounds was making her faint, but deep within, Eleanor found the strength that a thousand nights of pain and tears had given her. Taking a deep breath, she ran towards the rear of the tottering creature. In a single leap she jumped up on the towering back, gripping onto the harness. The Gorthon turned around in surprise as Eleanor clung on, her legs swinging out, striking the wall. Some bullets flew off the skin, narrowly missing her before she heard a distant voice.

'Hold your fire! Hold fire!'

The arms of the Gorthon reached frantically behind, trying to rid itself of the new torment. With her free hand she took aim at the weak spot and squeezed the trigger. The rounds struck the reinforced skull but none found their mark. Eleanor shouldered her gun as she hauled herself up, desperately trying for a better aim. The shaking increased in violence and she was beginning to lose her grip as the strength in her arms began to fail.

'C'mon Ellie you can do it, don't fail me now.', she encouraged herself. She dug her foot into the base of the harness and pushed herself up in a final desperate effort. Her trembling hand closed around the gun as she once again took aim and pulled the trigger. The beast let out an almost tearful groan as a single shot struck the edge of the weak spot, as the magazine emptied and her gun fell silent. The last of her strength left her arms as her hold failed, but instead of falling to the floor she found herself heading weightlessly towards the wall. The upside down image of the Gorthon floating helplessly past just as she struck the wall, rebounding back towards the thrashing ball of deadly fury. Quickly changing the magazine, Eleanor pointed her gun in the general direction of the Gorthon and blindly fired. The close proximity of the bullets caused the Gorthon to squeal in pain and rage. The gun's recoil slowed Eleanor down, but still she was heading inexorably towards the crazed monster. One of the claws hurled around in a wide arc, as Titus blindly sought one last act of vengeance on his tormentor. She managed to twist her body, feeling the breeze of death pass a couple of inches from her face. The gnashing teeth were closing in, the mouth opening in welcome for the final morsel. There was an explosion of Aqua that ripped through the head of the Gorthon blasting into Eleanor. Coming gently to rest, she was face to face with the glistening white spear-like teeth and empty eye sockets of the dead Gorthon.

Eleanor shrunk back in horror and disgust, then kicked herself away. Feeling cold and weak, red globules of blood which she knew were hers floated in front of her. Out of the corner of her eye, she caught a brief glimpse of a round shape. She turned and saw the severed head of one of the Gorthon's victims drifting gently past. Its fixed distant gaze, stared out at her from the land of death. The voice was silent as her vision greyed and then darkness welcomed her into its open arms.

24

The heavy hand of terror pressed down on Bruno's overworked mind as the ear-splitting blare of the alarm and the feeling of fear of the unknown still resonated inside his head. Shots, explosions and roaring in the distance. Then there were the screams. Gutierrez had gathered them together and they grabbed their weapons. The sickening feeling of running towards fuck knows what, the sight of the huge thing laying in a pool of aqua liquid mixing with streaks of bright red, merging into each other. The bodies, the parts of bodies the different liquids from the bodies strewn around in random patterns centred on the dead thing. Bruno didn't recognise what it was. He'd heard rumours back on earth about synthetic lifeforms and outbreaks but thought they were exaggerations. To borrow the old phrase, he dismissed them as 'fake news'. Well there was nothing fake about this. This wasn't a rumour. This was real! It was happening now, in front of his eyes. The medics were attending to the injured and covering the dead. Some of them could have been scraped up into a bucket. He walked up to the dead thing with holes where its eyes once sat. The limp mass of smooth glistening flesh dominated the space around it. A silent menace oozed from every dead pore, threatening reanimation at any moment. To leap back into life once again, tearing flesh and ripping souls in two. Even though he knew it was dead, an instinctive fear kept him from approaching too close. It reminded Bruno of a beached whale he'd seen as a youth, when he'd lived in France.

*

Bruno was looking out over the scene. The tide was out, water glinting in the sunlight off the hundreds of whale corpses that stretched as far as the eye could see. Whole pods washed up. The cries of seagulls filled the air along with the stench of death and decay as they circled their unexpected bonanza. Curious onlookers climbed up over the mountainous piles of dead blubber and flesh. The smell overwhelmed his protesting nostrils as he watched in the distance a group of people who were trying in vain to drag one of the helpless creatures back out to sea. The sporadic flaps of its tail sending them sprawling in all directions. Why are they even trying? Stupid brute doesn't even want to live. Supposed to be as intelligent as us? My arse! That's why they're committing mass suicide and hardly anyone ever sees them anymore. Their days are numbered and we live on, because we're not brainless.

A seagull was perched on the head of the dead colossus preparing to take a peck at the empty socket. A nearby dog started barking furiously, causing the startled bird to abandon its meal and take flight. Its giant wings casting a shadow across the features of the dead whale. There was a rumbling gurgling sound in the distance. The dogs bark increased in frequency and intensity. Bruno aimed a wild kick at the dog before falling over, laying there laughing, looking up at the giant silhouette of the carcass. The gurgling morphed into a groaning whoosh. A deafening farting sound ripped the air as a gushing spout of red and brown erupted from the split bloated body of the whale. Blocking out the sun, reaching to the top of its arc before lazily falling back down to earth.

He heard the shouts and laughter as people fled the fountain of blood and guts, just as the first of its contents came splattering down on him. Starting to scream, a mushy lump filled his mouth, choking him as he scrambled to his feet against the red onslaught. Reaching into his mouth, he dragged the disgusting mass out before staggering back into the sunlight. Looking down at his hand, still holding the crunchy slop, he opened it to see the half-digested, half rotted head of a fish. The open mouth, the empty sockets surrounded by white flesh staring accusingly back at him. A surge of nausea consumed him as he threw it away. His bowels emptied into his trousers and he let out a groan of disgust before he vomited the entire contents of his stomach in a pitiful retort to the whale. Collapsing back into the sand, he heard another sound. Sounds of disgust, then laughter gradually increasing as a crowd gathered to look at the boy who got too close.

He angrily turned to the sea of faces. 'What you laughing at you fuckin' bunch of arseholes!' he screamed at them, but that only seemed to make them laugh even more, before a policeman appeared from amongst them. He approached Bruno and put his coat around him before leading him through the baying mob of laughing faces back towards the town. Bruno looked back at them and shook his angry fist. 'One day you'll shit yourselves when you see me and I won't forget or forgive. I promise', he said. They laughed even louder. The memory still stung, and even though one day he did return, nobody even remembered or cared. They had bigger things to worry about by then.

*

'Over thirty dead so far and counting.' Voronoff looked over at the body of Titus and asked; 'What the hell *is* that thing?'

'I don't know Mikey, and I don't want to know, but we have to know, because if there's any more of those inside the base with us we're eyeball deep in the shit', Bruno replied.

'I heard one of the troopers from the security team climbed on its back and disabled it before they managed to kill it', Voronoff said.

'Well he's one brave son of a bitch. Is he still alive? I'd like to meet the guy and shake his hand.'

194

'She, Bruno. She.'

Bruno raised his eyebrows in surprise. 'Well in that case I'd like to meet her, then fuck her, then shake her hand after!' His cruel laugh was shared by Voronoff.

'She's a casualty and is in the infirmary. Not serious I heard.'

'Well I'll take her some flowers first!', Bruno offered.

'Sergeants! On me. Now!' It was Gutierrez. Naomi was by his side looking a pale shade of green, struggling to control her shock at the scene before her. Bruno and Voronoff winked at each other before they made their way over.

'Mind sharing your little joke with the rest of us Sergeant Bruno?' Gutierrez asked, the dislike in his voice obvious.

'Sorry sir, just some nervous laughter. I meant no offence or disrespect sir.' Bruno's tone was dutiful but not submissive. Gutierrez had made it plain from day one that he found Bruno an unwelcome imposition, especially replacing a trusted colleague in the process. Bruno didn't care as long as he got his promotion.

'I'd be careful as to who sees your nervousness at the moment. It could spark a riot if the wrong person notices it.', Gutierrez said, as Naomi shot Bruno a quick look. He said nothing.

The Colonel continued. 'Right, we've been instructed to maintain law and order over the next few days. Things can get quickly out of hand, so we have to stay on the ball. First of all we need to…'

A breathless soldier came running over, stood to attention in front of Gutierrez and saluted. His face pale with shock and grief.

'Yes soldier?', Gutierrez demanded, his irritation at the interruption barely concealed.

'Regret to inform you that Sergeant Williams was killed a few minutes ago, singlehandedly fighting the monster sir.' His bottom lip was trembling.

The start of a whimper escaped Naomi before she managed to bite her lip. A tear trickled down her cheek. Jeffrey Williams was well liked by men and officers alike. There was a sharp intake of breath by the other Sergeants. All except Bruno who had clashed with Williams after he called Bruno out as the bully and coward he truly was, making no secret of it. Bruno just about managed to keep the smirk off his face as his mind immediately computed his chances of being the next in line to take Williams' position.

Gutierrez took a deep breath then dismissed the soldier. The Colonel was struggling to maintain his self-control as he looked around at the shocked faces before him. He told them; 'That is indeed a terrible blow men. Jeff Williams was a much loved brother and I feel your pain, but we have to put it to one side for the moment and carry on.' He glanced at Naomi who swallowed hard and took a deep breath. 'There'll be time enough for tears later. For now, I need you to stay strong

195

and focused', he added. The Sergeants nodded and even Bruno found himself joining in as the exciting new world of possibilities raced through his mind. 'There is a high likelihood of law and order breaking down, and this is not the time or place for that to happen....', Gutierrez continued; '....We need to organise ourselves into squads providing security at key points throughout the base, as well as providing patrols to reassure the civilians.' He looked around at the men before him. 'We need to step up quicker than we anticipated, but as you know I have total faith and confidence in all of you. I need a new senior Sergeant....'. His eyes passed over Bruno and his gaze settled further along the line. '....Van Dee, report to me afterwards. The rest of you dismissed.'

Bruno stood frozen in disbelief as the other sergeants returned to their duties. The role promised to him had just been handed to someone else. 'Sergeant Bruno? Dismissed!', Gutierrez repeated.

'Sir may I speak in private for a moment?', Bruno requested.

The Colonel rolled his eyes and sighed silently to himself before approaching Bruno. 'Make it quick', he said, the impatience in his voice apparent.

'Sir, I was under the impression that I was earmarked for the senior Sergeant's role. Not Van Dee.'

Gutierrez stood back, his face red with anger 'And where did you get this information from?', he asked.

'Captain Sinclair sir. Back at the Academy.' Bruno struggled to keep the pleading tone from his voice.

'Well Sergeant Bruno.....' Gutierrez replied through gritted teeth; '....I'm not answerable to, or aware of any little secret deals between yourself and Captain Sinclair but as far as I'm concerned, the very fact that you've sought to gain advantage from the death of one of your colleagues while his body is still warm makes you, in my view, singularly unsuitable for such a role. In fact, I'm seriously considering breaking you back to the ranks, and the only thing that's stopping me right now is the fact that I need everybody focused totally on the tasks in hand, and that includes you, so you can take your secret deal and shove it up your arse. Do I make myself clear Sergeant Bruno?' His voice had been increasing in volume and he nearly spat Bruno's name back into his face.

Bruno kept his eyes fixed on Gutierrez and thought to add something. Normally he used his considerable size to loom over officers in an oafish way that attempted to intimidate, but even though the Colonel was considerably smaller than him, Bruno knew that Gutierrez's taut wiry frame was more than a match for him.

'Is there anything else Sergeant....?' Gutierrez asked before adding; '....or do I still have to massage your bruised ego.'

A sharp voice sounded from a few feet away. 'Colonel Gutierrez!' They turned to see two Troopers approaching, accompanied by van Dee, still basking in the glow of his rapid and unexpected promotion. The older one stepped forward and offered his hand to Gutierrez. 'Jordan Harris, Security team director and this is Sergeant Overgaard.'

Gutierrez gave Jordan a blank stare, ignoring the offered hand before he let out a derisive snort. 'Security Team! Is that what you call yourselves?' He turned and pointed his finger at the scene of carnage. 'I don't see a lot of security going on there. Only the dead and injured you were supposed to protect.'

Jordan quickly withdrew his hand and clenched it into a fist, his face turning purple. Nicklas stepped forward but Jordan placed his hand across him. Nicklas' eyes were fixed on Gutierrez although he spoke to Jordan. 'Sir! Are you going to let a fuckin shithat speak to you like that!'

Van Dee, stung by the familiar insult given to members of the SPC, raised his gun and pointed it straight at Nicklas' head. 'How about you getting your head blown off by a shithat.'

Nicklas smiled and walked calmly towards van Dee. 'I thought I'd move a bit closer in case you missed...Shithat.'

Bruno watched with a mixture of contempt and satisfaction as van Dee's hand shook, while beads of sweat formed on his forehead.

'What's the matter Shithat, still too far away?' Nicklas said and took another step forward. In the blink of an eye, he expertly swept up his arm and grabbed the barrel of the gun, moving it away at an angle and ripping it from van Dee's grasp. At the same moment he raised his foot and planted it squarely in the Sergeant's chest before shoving him over, sending van Dee sprawling on the floor. Nicklas calmly examined the gun with a practiced eye. 'Your weapon is dirty sergeant. There's some brown substance on the trigger...' he said. He walked towards the prone figure and tossed the weapon towards him. van Dee caught it in his trembling hand. 'Point a gun at me again, you'd better use it properly or it'll be the last thing you ever do...', he warned, adding; '....Oh and don't forget to switch the safety catch off next time.' He turned and walked back to Jordan's side.

Jordan looked at Gutierrez and said. 'Colonel. We require some of your men to learn the service tunnel network. Sergeant Overgaard here will be their instructor.'

Bruno bristled at the superior tone of Jordan's voice. He looked across at Gutierrez who declared; 'The SPC don't hide in tunnels like rats Mister Harris.'

Jordan momentarily glanced at van Dee climbing gingerly to his feet. With a smirk of satisfaction, he said scornfully; 'Yes, rats are fearless and intelligent so I see where you're coming from Colonel.' Gutierrez's teeth gnashed with

197

impotent rage as Jordan continued without pause. 'This is a direct order from Miss Novak, so I require an immediate response if you please.' He raised his eyebrows and pretended to nonchalantly examine his nails. Gutierrez took a deep breath, his jaw working angrily. 'Now would be good Colonel.' Jordan added without looking up.

Bruno felt Gutierrez's gaze fall on him. A sneer of contempt on his face. 'Take Sergeant Bruno. One of my finest.' Gutierrez said, the irony unmistakeable in his voice.

Jordan smiled and looked at Nicklas whose face betrayed no hint of emotion then he ordered; 'Thank you Colonel. Sergeant Bruno, report to Sergeant Overgaard at 08:00 tomorrow.'

Bruno opened his mouth to protest, but decided he'd pushed his luck far enough for one day. Despite his displeasure, it was obvious that Gutierrez was relieved to rid himself of an unwelcome problem. 'Any questions Sergeant?', he asked Bruno.

'No sir, I understand completely', Bruno replied. He could feel the burning of humiliation on his face as he saluted, turned away and walked off, all eyes on him as he was reminded of the walk back along the beach with the policeman's coat draped over his shoulders on that sunny, smelly day long ago. This time there was no defiant shake of the fist.

◆

Darkness, sounds. Confinement... Ava's world had been swallowed whole by terror and despair. Even through the sedation, she'd known. Fighting the fireball of the Gorthon had taken everything out of her. It was just enough to get its attention sufficiently to turn. That's all it took, and then to taunt it, to draw it to her. As the melting wall of heat approached, it was destroying her. Her mind withered to a shrivelled husk. Hearing the explosion, Ava vaguely felt the blow of Eleanor covering her, the ripping of the fragments in her body. What she recalled more than anything was the white hot needles of pain in her face and eyes, the redness then the darkness. She knew. She knew right then that was it. There was no way back. The silence of the doctors when they examined her told Ava everything. Her psychic ability, like her eyesight, had deserted her. Burnt out.

That was yesterday. Laying trapped in the blackness as Akeely Ferguson spoke, the words sounded strange and distant. A recording of another disconnected conversation from a faraway room, reaching down into the depths of Ava's desolation. She was part of it and yet detached.

'We've removed all the fragments from your face and limbs, but Ava I have to tell you, the damage to the eyes is extensive.' Akeely's gentle compassionate voice didn't soften the blow as she continued; 'The fragments didn't only cause superficial damage. They appear to have impacted the retina and optic nerve.' Ava felt Akeely's comforting hand on her arm and felt the tears run down her cheeks.

'So that's it. I'm trapped in a prison of darkness for the rest of my days', Ava remarked.

'Not necessarily, please don't despair Ava', the doctor offered some solace.

'It's pretty difficult not to at the moment!' Ava immediately regretted raising her voice, but she was unable to moderate her tone. 'I wish more than anything Eleanor had let me die. I should be grateful, but I hate her at the moment.'

'I'm sure you don't mean that Ava.'

'I fuckin do!' Ava's own vehemence shocked her as much as it's intended target.

'It's early days Ava. Both physically as well as emotionally. Your life has been turned upside down, but think if you hadn't stopped the Gorthon how many people would be dead now. Scores? Hundreds?.....', Akeely tried to assuage Ava and explained; '....It had already slaughtered twenty-eight innocent people in just under ten minutes. There are people alive now who'd be dead if you hadn't stopped it.' Ava had been too deep in the hole of misery to consider that before. The revelation momentarily stopped her grief in its tracks. 'What you did was the bravest and most selfless thing I've ever heard of...', Akeely continued. Even through her blindness and grief Ava could hear the emotion in the doctor's voice; '....You took on an unstoppable physical nightmare and turned it away from its intended path. You willingly placed yourself between it and its prey, regardless of your own safety, unarmed! I couldn't have done that. Everyone is talking about Eleanor, but you were the real hero in my view.'

'I was one of its creators! If only I hadn't been such a spineless jellyfish, if only I'd made them listen...', Ava said. Finding it hard to breathe between sobs, the hard rock of guilt weighed heavily on her heart. The rush of events was a blur, but even while it was happening, the feeling of responsibility drove her to put it right. She reasoned; '....You say I did all that because you think I'm some kind of hero, but I had no choice. It was partly my creation. I was so *professional*, so *focused*! I didn't stop for a second and think about what could happen if one of these creatures broke loose. I should have known after the Gargoyle broke out. But I didn't, and now nearly thirty people are dead. Because of me, and my stupidity. Khan and Chiang are the lucky ones. They're dead and their guilt rests on my head. No one else.'

Akeely was silent for a few moments as if she were gathering her thoughts then argued; 'They'd have gone ahead anyway. Regardless of the warnings. If you didn't cooperate they'd have got someone else.' Ava continued sobbing but was listening. 'Ava, these are early days, and the pain and irrational guilt are swamping you at the moment, but I say two things to you.' Akeely's voice was returning to its authoritative best now. Her hand gripped Ava's arm even firmer as she spoke. 'First, you are not responsible for all this. You acted in good faith and bear no responsibility in my view. Second, I swear I will do everything in my power to restore your sight. I promise, and I know it can be done. Please believe me when I tell you that', she implored. Ava stopped sobbing but was still unable to speak. She sighed and gently nodded. 'We'll speak again tomorrow.' Akeely said, releasing her grip.

Ava heard her walk away, leaving her to contemplate the past few minutes. What use am I to anyone now? A blind ex-psychic. Totally dependent on someone else. I can't even find anything to kill myself with, she despaired.

She'd tried to pick up on those around her. Nothing. No background noise, no shapes in her dreams, no sounds. Only the void. The terrors of the dark forever. Not a single photon will ever register again, no colours, no shades no smiles. All my life has come to this. I wish I was dead, I wish that Eleanor had just left me to die at the hands of the creature. A moment's pain then peace. Not the life of torture I face now. I hate her. She deserved to die. Not me. My life's work counts for nothing. Ava wanted to cry, but she was an empty broken shell, continuing her contemplation.

Akeely's only telling me that because she wants to let me down gently. Softening the blow. Give me some hope then gradually let it fade. But she was also right. There *are* people alive now who'd be dead in a parallel universe where I didn't act, or someone else was the Psychic consultant. The Gorthon would still have escaped. In *that* universe, the consultant resigns, refusing to partake in the madness of the Mags. The horror would still have taken place. But *this* is the place I inhabit now. The universe where I'm blind and helpless.

Ava's mind flashed back to the faces of Chiang and Khan. The placid features of Chiang. The slightly puzzled, almost disappointed countenance of Khan, with the glazed empty stare of the sightless eyes. The small dribble of blood trickling from his mouth at odds with the catastrophic injuries inflicted on the rest of him. She should have felt they bought it upon themselves, but it was more they were blinded by the prize, prestige and pressure. It was all academic now. The Mag program was over. There was no conceivable way it could continue after this. Even the company couldn't cover this up. Word would get back to earth somehow.

Her part in it would be known. She'll never work again, even if she had her eyesight and psychic powers fully restored.

'Time for your medication Ava.' The voice of the nurse startled her out of her thoughts. Not wanting to think anymore. The pain from her wounds were grating on her nerves, as the hiss of the injection and the cool soothing feeling spread throughout her, as she floated softly down into the welcome world of oblivion.

♦

Eleanor's hand was shaking. It hadn't stopped since she regained consciousness the previous afternoon. Sometimes it would be quite violent, other times barely noticeable. Enduring the pain emanating from all over her body, arriving in waves, sometimes from where the fragments had been removed, then from her shoulders and finally her head. It sounded like the Gorthon's roar in her ear. But the real source of her pain was her hand, or more precisely, what she had done with her hand in opening the lab door and letting loose the Gorthon on it's rampage. It shook with the elephant of guilt that stood on her shoulders, crushing her down little by little. Eleanor looked around the room at the other patients. *All your fault Ellie* said the voice. *If only you'd thought for a second then all those people would still be here. Innocent women and children, all dead and mangled because of you.* Don't you think I know that, don't you think it's the only thing I've thought of since, she retorted silently.

A young girl, with no apparent injuries, laid on the bed opposite. She was as still as stone, staring at the ceiling. There was a companion, another girl a couple of years younger who sat there silently holding her hand. They looked similar. Eleanor guessed they must be sisters. Ava laid at the far end, her eyes bandaged.

Eleanor had seen the doctor speaking to Ava earlier that morning and heard the sobs. Approaching Akeely, she enquired after Ava.

'Its best you don't try to speak to her Eleanor. She's not herself at the moment.' Akeely smiled reassuringly.

'That's understandable doctor.' Eleanor replied then asked. 'What's the chances with her eyes? Will she see again?'

This time Akeely looked ruefully at Ava and said; 'It's tough but there is a chance.....' then turning her attention back to Eleanor, she continued; 'So believe it or not you are quite lucky. We removed over twenty grenade fragments from your back and head. You would have been ripped to shreds at that distance if you were standing, but you managed to avoid the worst of it. You also dislocated your wrist and some fingers. On top of that, a badly bruised shoulder and finally concussion, so we're going to keep you under observation for a day or so.'

201

Eleanor looked at Akeely. The strain and horror of the past day was evident on the doctor's face. Looking like she hadn't slept in all that time Eleanor thought, then said; 'Thank you Doctor. I don't feel lucky.'

'Well Miss Wells....', Akeely responded; '....considering everyone else who came into direct physical contact with the creature is dead, I'd say you are incredibly lucky, as well as incredibly brave or crazy. I'm not sure which.'

'Crazy I think. I don't know what possessed me. I didn't even think about it.'

'Well you're lucky to be alive.'

'One last thing doctor. My hand. It won't stop trembling.' Eleanor told her.

'Yes I can see. There's no nerve or muscle damage.' Akeely said. Taking Eleanor's hand and examining it. 'I think it's more that you're in shock', she said.

Eleanor nearly laughed; 'What?', she exclaimed.

'I can see it in your face and hear it in your speech. Seemingly alert, yet disconnected and vacant. There are different levels.' Akeely told her then gestured to the girl lying still in the bed, adding; 'Young Sophia there for instance.'

Eleanor looked at the mute figure.

'Both parents killed before her eyes as they distracted the creature from her and her sister. Yet not a scratch, but the wounds are deep and probably incurable.....'. Akeely shook her head and continued; '....She's the one I'm most worried about. The creature by all accounts was inches from her face, yet for reasons unknown to anyone it left her and her sister unharmed. Physically that is.'

'Yes, we ran past them. Covered in blood and holding each other.', Eleanor pointed out.

'Whereas, yours will start to wear off in a few days. You just need time and rest, maybe speak to someone....', the doctor said then asked; '....Have you got any close friends?'

'Yes. Ava.'

'Well she's not in a position to speak to anyone presently, and I certainly wouldn't recommend you talk to her. I'm afraid she harbours an irrational hatred towards you at the moment', Akeely told her. Eleanor gasped and tears filled her eyes. 'I'm sorry, but Ava wishes she was dead, but you saved her life. Strangely enough it's quite common for people to turn on their saviours at times like this, so don't take it personally. It's part of the recovery process. She'll be ok with you... Eventually', the doctor made clear. Eleanor took a deep breath and nodded. Akeely smiled and, looking over her shoulder spotted someone. 'Looks like you got a visitor. I'll be off' she said.

Eleanor wiped her eyes as she watched Akeely leave the room, then turned to see Montano standing before her, covered in wound dressings and his arm in a sling. Eleanor approached him and put her arms around him. It felt strange and went against her reserved nature, but it also felt good, and at that moment she needed it.

'Ow. Be careful Eleanor.' Montano flinched back half smiling 'I'm a wounded war hero.'

'Oh I'm sorry Sergeant! I forgot myself.'

'Please, call me Raph. Short for Raphael, Montano invited.

'Ok Raph. How are you?'

'Not bad considering. The wounds are more emotional than physical. Six men dead.' He looked down and a shadow passed across his face. 'Six brothers smashed and ripped to death by that abomination.' He took a deep breath as he contemplated the events of the past day.

'And it was all down to me.' Eleanor said. Feeling the weight of the words as she spoke them.

Montano looked up. 'How so?' He asked, his gaze piercing.

'I let it out.' Eleanor sobbed as she admitted; 'They were banging on the door, pleading to be let out. I didn't realise, I overrode the lockdown. When the door opened it burst through, and then....' The rest was lost in her tears.

Montano put his hand on her shoulder and said; 'Hey! Look at me.' Eleanor's eyes met his as she heaved another sob. 'Did you see what remained of the door after?', he asked. Eleanor nodded. He inquired again; 'Did you see it? A mangled twisted piece of metal lying on the floor. Did you see the hole in the wall?' This time Eleanor shook her head as he continued; 'Well you didn't make that hole. The Gorthon did. Titus did! Not you. Even if you had left the others to die you would have only delayed it by a few seconds. Nothing could have withstood that, nothing in this world. So you can forget that shit about it being your fault, because it wasn't.' Eleanor looked at Montano and she knew he was right, but she took no pleasure in it. The burden of guilt lifted slightly from her, leaving its deep imprint on her... The shock and the desolation still remained. The slow clicking sound of the Gorthon echoed in her memory. 'On the other hand....', Montano went on; '....I've never seen anything like you. Super cleaner. I don't know what you are but I'm as sure as shit you're not what you say you are!' Eleanor opened her mouth to protest, but Montano held up his hand, 'Hey Whoa lady! Your secret is safe with me. I ain't gonna mess with you!'

'I did what I had to...' Eleanor said, too flustered to respond properly.

Montano wasn't hesitant in his praise; 'Well, you did it brilliantly, if I may say so! Special Forces elite fuckin Janitor hit squad. I thought you were gonna give the ceiling a good wipe while you were up there riding the Gorthon! Give its ugly great head a little polish.'

203

Through her desolation, a shriek of laughter escaped Eleanor. Missing the mockery of the forces, she liked Montano. It was liberating. Regaining her composure, she spoke, 'I was thrown out. On trumped up charges...', she told him. He was looking at her and she felt herself blushing.

'That's for another day Ellie....', he said and held his hand out. Taking it, she squeezed it. 'Faced down death together and came through. Friends for life', he said. They looked at each other and Eleanor smiled.

'Who took the kill shot....?', she asked '....I saw its head explode but I don't remember anymore after that...'

'I managed to get a depleted uranium armour piercing round into a sniper rifle....', Montano explained; '....It was too near to aim through the scope, so I pointed and hoped for the best. I noticed you were on a one way trip down its throat so I had to act fast.'

'So I owe you my life.'

'We all owe you our lives Ellie. You and Ava. How is she? I heard...', he was interrupted.

'Miss Wells!' A familiar voice from behind her broke in. Turning, Eleanor saw Leighton Walker waddling towards her, followed by his small entourage. 'The hero of the hour no less!' Walker said, extending his hand. Even though he was acting nicely, Eleanor still felt an instinctive repulsion. She took his hand, which felt cold, weak and clammy, and shook it as briefly as possible while feigning a grateful smile.

'I was just in the right place at the right time.' She looked around for Montano to rescue her, but he was nowhere to be seen.

'Nonsense nonsense. Such monogamy...' One of Walker's entourage leant forward and whispered briefly in his ear. A look of irritation flashed across his face as he hissed 'I *said* "Modesty", idiot.' The obsequious smile instantly returned as he looked back at Eleanor. 'You really *must* claim some of the credit. I heard about your bright idea from our friend here.' He gestured to a bemused looking Jordan behind him, who sported a black eye as well as a wound dressing on his left cheek. Walker continued with the false sincerity. 'Still, better than the last time we met, ay!' He let out a bleating laugh and roughly put his arm around Eleanor. The fingers squeezing just that bit too hard as Eleanor flinched in disgust and pushed him away, sending him slipping backwards before crashing on the floor. 'What the f...!' he managed to mutter. Everyone looked at Eleanor who stood agog.

'Mister Walker!' they turned to see Akeely. 'What the hell are you doing to my patients?', she demanded. She stood over the prone figure and said. 'She has suffered a serious shoulder injury and you're pulling her around like you're in a judo match!' Eleanor quickly raised her hand to her shoulder. Akeely turned to Eleanor, barely able to suppress her laughter. 'Are you ok Eleanor?'

'Yes, Yes I think so.' Eleanor replied in her most injured, just managing to suffer the pain voice. 'I'm sorry Doctor Walker. I didn't mean to… The pain…'.

'Don't you worry about him Eleanor....' Akeely cut in before she turned to a shamefaced Walker as he slowly pulled himself to his feet. She told him; 'You'll do well to treat my patients with care from now on Mister Walker or you'll have me to deal with, and I assure you, you won't want that. Now get out of the infirmary!'

Walker eagerly nodded 'Yes Doctor, I'm sorry Eleanor I didn't...'

'Now!' repeated Akeely more forcefully as the browbeaten Walker started to withdraw followed by those in train.

As they shuffled out of the room, Jordan approached Eleanor. His face was grave with a hint of shame. 'Eleanor....' he began; '....I owe you an apology for the way I spoke to you earlier. It was disrespectful and arrogant.' He shook his head and his voice quivered with emotion. He continued; 'What you did was unbelievable. I've never seen anything like it in my life. You saved everyone. It would have killed all of us, and your quick thinking about the Anti-Gravity was a stroke of genius.'

'There's nothing to apologise for Jordan, you were under tremendous pressure. At least you took my advice', she replied.

'Thank you Eleanor, you're very generous. Just one thing if I may. Where did you learn that? The cool decision making under pressure and decisive action. The bravery. The list goes on.' He smiled and extended his hand which Eleanor took and shook, not squeezing too hard. 'If you ever want a place in the security team you're in straight away', he proffered.

'You're very kind Jordan....' she neatly sidestepped the question '....but who'll clean the Labs now?', she asked.

'Good question! I don't think there's going to be a lot to clean after yesterday. I've heard rumours the whole lot is being shut down and the Mags destroyed. So, it looks like we're all out of a job.', he told her.

'Somehow I don't think it's going to be as simple as that.', she said.

'Neither do I Eleanor. Neither do I.' Jordan replied. He shook his head slowly and continued; '....The worst thing is that we're outgunned by them at the moment. If we'd been told fully of their capabilities, we'd have seriously upgraded our armoury. It's going to take some lateral thinking on our part.' He looked at his watch. 'I've got to go Eleanor. Think about my offer.'

'I will, I promise', she said as Jordan left. Eleanor looked over at Ava. She knew what Akeely said, but she couldn't just leave her. Eleanor walked carefully towards Ava but couldn't tell if she was asleep or not.

'I know you're there, Eleanor', Ava said.

Eleanor flinched. 'Ava. I…'

'Do me a favour Eleanor….', Ava interrupted her. '….I'll be ok eventually, but for the moment please leave me be. I don't want to talk. I'll tell you when I'm ready.'

'Ok Ava let me know. Please.' Eleanor replied as she beat a careful retreat.

It's funny where life takes you Ellie. You've had more people being nice to you in ten minutes than the rest of your life put together, Eleanor's thoughts were punctuated. *Yeah that won't last long,* said the voice. *You'll all be dead as soon as the rest of those* Mags *break loose, and even if you ain't, Bruno ain't gonna stand for you being around for long. He's bound to have seen you on the broadcasts through the base.* Well, Eleanor mused; I'll have to make a change of plan. Now for the first time in your life you actually have people on your side, don't waste it but also don't abuse it. But then what? Even if they admit everything. *Like fuck will they. As soon as you open your big mouth it'll all go wrong. Crazed, revenge thirsty bitch. That's what you'll come across as. Hell hath no fury like a conniving little whore denied her prize. Probably tell some cock and bull story about how you seduced him to try and pass the course. You're fucked Ellie and you know it.* But *I* know that's not true. Naomi betrayed me, why I don't know and he raped me for fun. I can't kill them and how do I get enough people to believe me? What else is there? Set them up for something they didn't do. That would be sweet, but what? *You're far too stupid Ellie. Even if you do dream something up they'll laugh at you. Hardy fuckin ha har!*

Eleanor walked back over to her bed to try and get some rest. Her hand was still shaking.

25

Aaron lay face down on the bed heaving and convulsing as he sobbed uncontrollably. Tears soaking the pillow and knuckles white as he gripped the sheets with the desperation of someone dangling from a precipice. A ball of acid ate away at his insides, destroying him from within. No amount of tears could relieve him of the great burden of grief and fear that he felt. He was one of the few who had seen the face of the beast and lived. The livid flesh of the creature, rippling with malicious intent, reaching and ripping out the hearts of those who witnessed its blood soaked parade, overloading every sense, searing an indelible impression into the memory and polluting every other remaining thought with its presence. Aaron groaned and writhed in a desperate attempt to throw off the feeling of hopelessness that enveloped him, but to no avail. Each time he closed his eyes, it was there, staring back. Looming over him, poised to consume every last shred of his flesh in a single gulp.

'Please please please. No more!' His voice was hoarse in its pleadings. Unable to drive the images out of his mind, recalling how he cowered in the corner as the monster slowly, deliberately cast its gaze around the shopping mall, before moving on through the tangled mass of corpses, limbs and entrails. The moment he saw the foot of the creature disappear around the corner, he fled back to his room and trembled in abject terror. First of all, he hid under the bed but claustrophobia only magnified the raw agony caused by the tortured kaleidoscope of images raining down upon him. The sweat streamed off his emaciated body as he sought a moment of peace. Holding his quivering hands together in supplication. 'Please, brother Marcus rescue me from this hell. I don't want to be weak, but I can't help it. I'm so scared. I don't want to die.', he pleaded.

Aaron fixed his stare at the illuminated clock next to his bed, trying to focus purely on that. The pale green light somehow seemed to take the edge off his state of extreme agitation. '13:15' Just over an hour since the Monster had roamed. The panicked screams and thundering of running feet outside his door had long since ceased, as silence once again reigned. Gradually, he managed to slow his breathing with only the occasional sob breaking through, as he dared to close his eyes once more. Blessed darkness welcomed him in and he breathed a sigh of relief.

In the distance an orange light hovered. Considering it for a few moments, he decided it was no threat. It slowly approached and Aaron opened his eyes again quickly, fearful that the visions would return. He glanced at the time. '13:20' Five minutes. Closing them again, this time he floated in the blackness that held him in its embrace. The light was nearer and he could feel the gentle warmth soothing his mind. The fear was receding, the terror of earlier, drifting into the distance, the visions replaced by tranquillity as the light surrounded him, lancing the pulsating boil of fear. Aaron embraced the light as it merged with him and they became one, experiencing a peace he had never known. A feeling that he was accepted and loved for who he was, and not what someone else wanted him to be. This time there were tears of joy. The visions and feelings of the beast's rampage gradually shrank before disappearing completely in a gentle puff, cast out from his memory, never to return.

He could feel a pulsating rhythmic beat. Drums beating out a tattoo that gradually increased its volume. He became aware of someone calling his voice.

'Aaron! Aaron! Are you in there! Please answer me!'

His eyes snapped open. The knocking on the door incessant and a voice could be heard from outside. He looked at the clock. '17:35'. Over four hours had passed.

'Hold on!' Aaron wearily climbed off the bed, feeling drained and shaky, his heart leapt as he opened the door.

It was Antonina. His eyes drank in the splendour of her beauty as the object of his forlorn hopes stood before him. The expression on her face told him something was badly wrong. He had a vague feeling of danger and disorientation but was unable to pin it down to anything specific. She moved forward and put her arms around him. The earnest intensity of her embrace confused and excited Aaron. 'Thank the great Ykdar you're safe. I thought you were among the dead.', she said.

'Dead? Who's dead?' A strange sense of guilt enveloped Aaron as if he had unwittingly committed some unknown crime. Antonina's tone brooked no argument that something terrible had indeed happened, but he was totally unaware of it. 'Has there been some kind of accident?' he asked.

She stepped back, and with her hands still on Aaron's frail shoulders, looked into his eyes before inclining her head slightly to one side, adopting an expression of mild bemusement. 'I was told you were last seen in the shopping mall. You're telling me it wasn't you?'

He frantically worked his memory but there was no recollection. 'I've been here all day. ...asleep.' Even as he said the words he felt unsure. A void had appeared in his mind that could only be perceived by the space around it.

Antonina frowned and sounded doubtful. 'It must have been a hell of a sleep. Didn't you hear anything? You look exhausted.' She took a deep breath and gazed deep into his eyes. 'Aaron....', she uttered; '....I need to tell you something and

208

you have to show courage. For me.' Aaron could feel himself shaking and nodded hesitantly. 'A terrible vast creature ran amok in the shopping mall earlier today. It killed a lot of people before it was eventually bought down and destroyed'.

Feeling a stab of terror as if a long suppressed fear were unleashed, a vague roaring echoed in his mind before a soft note overlaid and suppressed it. Looking back into Antonina's eyes, he urgently questioned her. 'What kind of creature? How did it get in here? Are there any more?'

'We don't know. People are saying it's a Synthetic Life form.'

Aaron's voice rose in alarm 'A Synthetic! Like the ones that killed everyone in that place in Australia. What's it called again?'

Antonina nodded and answered; 'You mean Bagama. That's what I thought.'

'And now they're here, inside the base with us. How?', he asked urgently.

'Nobody knows. It came completely out of the blue. Counsellor Marcus has called a meeting for 18:00. We are all to attend. He says we need to stay calm and clear headed, so no crying, understood?', she emphasised the last word.

Aaron could feel himself blush but Antonina's presence and embrace gave him strength. He swallowed, nodded and vowed; 'I'll be strong... I promise.'

'Good Aaron. We'll get through this.' She said and smiled reassuringly. Despite his fear, a small shiver of excitement tingled down Aaron's spine. His heart was racing, but he wasn't sure if it was through fear or pleasure.

Antonina stepped back out into the corridor and turned to Aaron. 'Don't be late and remember, NO CRYING!', she warned him then turned and was gone.

'I'll be there', Aaron muttered to the empty space where Antonina had stood a few moments earlier, before he closed the door and let out a long breath. The last couple of minutes possessed a surreal dream-like quality. How could I have just slept through all of this. Searching his memory, only the black void remained, still and unyielding.

◆

Marcus could see the fear on the faces of those in the room, as the tension swirled around them in a suffocating fog. Tread carefully, he thought, it'll only take a single wrong word to send them spiralling into the depths of hysteria. I need to take control of this situation as quickly and seamlessly as possible.

The moment a breathless Leon Jordan had burst into his living quarters telling him of the events in the shopping mall, his calculating mind instinctively sprang into action, weighing up the opportunities presented. A sense of fear, real or imagined was one of the primary objectives presented in 'Crackpot Religions'. It opened up a whole world of limitless possibilities. Once people are scared enough, the more can be done to manipulate those fears. In the face of fear, it is a psychological fact that people's most primitive and selfish instincts dominate. The first step is to make them think you are the only one who could possibly be their saviour, so a sense of calm authority is crucial. Ensure the voice is soft but strong and clear, soothing raw nerves. Once they are drawn in then it's time to encourage them to think they possess the power for their own salvation, whilst at the same time carefully manipulating them and the situation to your advantage. Appeal to emotion and override reason. That way they lose the capacity for rational thought as well as awareness for the consequences of their actions. Make the things most important to them feel under maximum threat. Vehemently dismiss any opposing viewpoint as obvious lies concocted by malicious enemies bent on their destruction. Create your own orthodoxy so every utterance becomes about what it represents to the congregation rather than what it objectively means.

*

After receiving several reassurances from Leon that the beast was no longer at large, Marcus pulled on his white robe and rushed like a concerned parent to the scene. He was stopped by one of the Troopers at a cordon set up by the perimeter of the carnage.

'I'm sorry counsellor, you can't come through. It's not safe yet.', the Trooper told him.

Although a rush of fear flashed across Marcus's body, he could not be seen to show it.

'Then all the more reason to let me through brother. People are in need', he said and tried to push his way past the Trooper.

The Trooper was splattered in blood and his face was pale with shock and fear. He placed his hand on Marcus chest. 'Sir, I'm no longer asking. Stand back now.'

Marcus rose up to his full height and looked down on the Trooper, aware of the crowd of onlookers. Satisfied the story would now spread, he gently removed the trooper's hand from his chest. 'Brother. You're going to have to either shoot me or let me through for I will not be prevented from going to the aid of those in need, no matter what the danger.' He said it in a loud enough voice for all around to hear. 'Now let me through', he ordered the soldier.

The Trooper looked uncertain. 'One moment.' He spoke briefly into his Comms then nodded slowly. Looking back up at Marcus, he said to him; 'Ok. You are free to pass sir, but at your own risk.'

Marcus felt his legs tremble as he received the unexpected news. He'd gambled on being stopped and forcibly removed, creating a suitable spectacle of his selfless devotion to the settlers, whilst displaying a flagrant disregard for his own safety. 'Thank you brother.' He turned to Leon who was accompanying him and added;

210

'And my colleague will join me.' Leon turned a distinct shade of green and flinched in fear, the hint of a refusal passing across his face. Marcus leant forward and whispered in his ear. 'Be strong in this hour of need brother.'

The Trooper let out a snort of irritation and motioned them through. Marcus heard him mutter under his breath. 'Go ahead, It's your fuckin funeral.'

Marcus gulped but maintained his composure, forcing his quaking body one step at a time towards the scene that awaited him.

He shuddered at the memory. The mountainous creature, the blood, the bodies, the entrails. He'd moved amongst them offering comfort to the injured and dying. Even Marcus's cold heart ached at the scene before him. Some were surrounded by medics working frantically on them, others covered by a sheet. The uninjured just sat there, numbed in shock, staring into space as people moved around them.

*

Marcus shook himself out of his melancholy and reminded himself there were bigger, more important tasks at hand. The door to his contemplation room opened and they looked to see Aaron, his eyes red and face drawn, silently entering. Marcus groaned inwardly. When will this poor excuse for a man develop some backbone? How can someone go through life like a frightened little mouse, constantly flinching at the slightest misfortune? Completely unable to cope with anything other than the mundane. Marcus bit his tongue, smiled and said; 'Brother Aaron. I am pleased you have seen fit to join us.' Aaron acknowledged him with a small nod, but remained silent. Marcus looked around at the grave faces. Leon, Antonina and Odette amongst them, listening intently and waiting. 'Brothers and sisters....', he began; '....we have endured a grievous ordeal. Our fellow pilgrims have been violated by a creature from the depths of hell. A monstrosity, an abomination that has run amok spreading terror before it and leaving death and despair in its wake.' He felt satisfaction as they nodded earnestly while he continued. 'Some of our flock have lost their lives, some injured and others have lost loved ones.' He let the last words hang for a few moments before pushing on. 'But we have to be strong for them and put our own fears and feelings to one side, for the burden of leadership will now fall upon our shoulders.'

'Counsellor Marcus, is it true that you put yourself in peril to comfort the injured and dying?' It was Odette who asked.

Leon answered; 'He did indeed sister. He fought his way past a guard who tried to save him, but Marcus ignored his appeals and without hesitation, placed himself in harm's way. I was privileged to accompany him and his bravery gave me the strength needed to see it through. See how he has spilt his own blood in the protection of those in need.'

Marcus looked down at the blood he had carefully smeared on his white robe as he wondered through the casualties. He said; 'You're too kind brother Leon, but I was merely fulfilling the role that fate has bestowed upon me and I was grateful to have you by my side.'

'Ykdar's blessings be upon you Counsellor Marcus', Leon responded. A hubbub of approving noises sounded around the room as he added; 'We are truly privileged to have you as our guide.'

Marcus wore his usual expression of humble gratitude and smiled benignly. 'Thank you brothers and sisters. I will now devote every waking hour to the benefit of everyone on Magdur with all the strength I possess.' He said, noticing a few of the disciples were weeping. To his surprise Aaron was not one of them. 'But my personal wellbeing is of no concern to me....', the Counsellor continued; '....it is the good of others that is important. Even those who knew of the beast, allowing it to cause such suffering.' Gasps sounded amongst those present. Before they could intervene Marcus went on; 'But that does not mean that they shouldn't pay the price for their incompetence, arrogance and worst of all, lies.' They were back on side again, he noticed.

'But how do we ensure that justice is served if they are surrounded by armed guards?', Leon asked.

'Indeed brother....', Marcus agreed; '....We can't do it alone, but we do have our fellow settlers. They will look to us for guidance after the treachery cruelly perpetrated upon them, for we are the only source of truth open to them.' He held his hand out in front of him and clenched it into a fist, as he carried on; 'How can we look them in the eye if we fail them now? How can we shrink from the task of leadership that has befallen us? They would tear us down from our position if we, for even one moment, even considered compromising our unshakable resolution. Ykdar himself would cast lightning bolts from the very heavens down upon our heads before hurling us into eternal damnation, if for even one second, we deviated from our true purpose.....' He could feel the group leaning in toward him, hanging on to his every utterance, trying to drink in his very words. Their rapt expressions telling him he had them in the palm of his hand and now the moment was right to strike. He raised his voice; 'For I....!', he thumped his fist on his chest. '....I would rather suffer the most brutal of deaths and be ripped limb from limb rather than fail them.' Breathing hard, he felt like he'd left his own body and was looking down on himself from above. The sound of his voice didn't feel that it belonged to him as, raising his fist above his head, he moved towards the climactic clarion call. 'So let each one of us pledge their very being to the task before us, leading the masses forward, for we hold their salvation in our hands and will never relinquish it while there is breath left in our bodies!'

A crash worthy of a fully grown Gorthon ripped through the small room, as everyone present shouted their acclamation. Crying, hugging and thumping each other on the back in a display of solidarity and determination that only a few moments earlier Marcus was convinced they were not capable of. He maintained his expression of calm determination as his piercing blue eyes cast their gaze around the dimly lit room. But inwardly he was thrilled with gleeful satisfaction as he realised his first real step to total control had been successfully concluded.

♦

Marcus looked up from the book. The pale spectre of Attilio Schiavone floated in the gloom before him. His white hair and ghostly features hung like living smoke, staring out from the half imagined shadow world he occupied. Looking deep into the hearts of those he observed, probing for weaknesses, drawing out secrets and gaging strengths. Marcus had learned to control his sense of repulsion in Attilio's presence, but he was unable to shake off the feeling he was being observed from inside.

'A traitor? Within my disciples?' Marcus tried to intimidate Attilio by staring at him, but he may as well have tried to frighten a cloud. Attilio looked back in silence. 'Does this come from the same place as the prophecy about the young girl with the swan markings?', Marcus asked, leaning forward in his chair to try and provoke a response, but the unsettling stillness continued. He noted with irritation the same scarf and coat from before. Why does he dress like we're living up a mountain? Does the fool think he can threaten me by dressing as a spirit of the underworld? Finally, his patience snapped. 'If you have nothing further to say then this conversation is at an end.'

Marcus rose from his chair to leave. The exhilaration of the gathering was fast souring into doubt and despondency. The opportunity to be able to decode the thoughts and actions of friend and foe alike has been too good to reject, but so far all he'd received was illusions and riddles. And yet... He couldn't dismiss the feeling that there was something to Attilio's claims despite his better judgement.

'As you wish counsellor.' Attilio said and added. 'I have no desire to offer my services to one who doubts them.

Even though the words were not what Marcus hoped for, he felt a measure of relief that Attilio had actually responded.

Marcus grasped the opportunity to elicit more from the strange man in the room with him. 'How can I not doubt when you bring only empty words and excuses unaccompanied by even a single shred of proof?', he asked.

The merest hint of dismay moved swiftly across Attilio's face as he responded. 'The prophecy is amongst us, I am sure. Only such an individual would have the power to nearly break me. She was there before me and crushed my puny attempts to get her to join us.'

Marcus shook his head slowly in mock sympathy. 'Well how convenient....' he said and continued; '....You say she's here but cannot point to her despite your self-proclaimed powers. There's always something just stopping you people isn't there? Just that last obstacle which requires some extra funding to break through to the truth.' He could see the façade of Attilio's inscrutability beginning to crack. It just needed another blow to rip it wide open, so he carried on. 'And when I'm unwilling to waste any more time on this drivel you mysteriously change tack and invent another story about treachery within my group. You really do take me for a fool. Now get out of my sight!' Wincing inwardly at the last words, cursing himself for letting his mouth run ahead of his brain for once. He looked at Attilio. The cracks had closed tight and the emptiness returned.

'I know you have killed those who betrayed you and cast you out.' The softly spoken words hit Marcus like a thunderclap. 'I've seen the flames and heard the screams...' Attilio added almost as an afterthought. The ground had been ripped out from under his feet and below him a void dropping into an eternity ready to devour him. For once, Marcus was lost for words, unlike Attilio who noted; 'I know the one you need is here at your bidding.' Marcus could feel himself shrinking as this time Attilio who towered over him advised; 'I see into your heart counsellor and I know you believe me now.'

'I... I don't know what you're talking about. How dare...'

'Fear not counsellor, your secrets are safe with me. After all I want the same thing as you.'

Marcus quickly regained his composure and asked; 'Which is?'

'Control.' Attilio responded. Pausing before continuing; 'We both have complementary gifts. I see into the hearts of men. You speak to the hearts of men. Together we work to establish control.' His cold face broke into something people would call a smile and others something more sinister as he added; 'You can be the voice and I can feed that voice with information.'

Marcus found the smiling Attilio even more menacing. Control Marcus, strength and control. Don't show him any weakness, he told himself. 'And if you are correct and it is control I seek, how can you help me establish it....?', he enquired before suggesting; 'I need more than just rumours, more than half truths. I need facts. Have you any hard facts on who the traitor is, if they actually exist that is...?' He knew Attilio could sense his weakness but he forced himself to exude calm determination. 'When you can give me that, then we are in business and maybe we can discuss further steps. But time is of the essence and the beasts are on the march. What have you got to offer me now?' His former boldness returned with every word uttered, pushing aside any fears and doubts. Knowing Attilio had picked it up and had returned to the back foot.

'I think counsellor, that you are not in a position to be making demands. You have been given a small glimpse into the array of abilities I command. Now I put it to you. Will you meet my asking price?', Attilio challenged.

'*You* make threats to *me!*' Marcus slammed his hand down on the table and stood. Moving forward, the anger surging through him, as he reached out, closed his hand around Attilio's cold clammy throat and drew his face to a few inches from Attilio's. He had not suffered so much and fought so hard to be held over a barrel by a trickster, no matter how convincing. Seeing fear in the face of Attilio, showed Marcus that control of the situation had returned. He spoke in a low controlled voice. 'If your claims about your so called powers are true, then you're already well aware what I'm capable of, and what happens to those who cross my path.' He tightened his grip and moved even closer. 'If you don't want to join them, then I strongly recommend that you get me what I want very quickly. After all, for all your big words, a dead ex psychic is no use to anyone.' Marcus noted with satisfaction the strangled squeak of terror that escaped Attilio's constricted throat. The superior self-assurance that so infuriated Marcus, had melted away like snow in springtime, as the pale complexion transformed into a deep scarlet. Attilio's tongue protruded and eyes bulged as he reached up in a pathetic attempt to break the stranglehold that was squeezing the life out of him. Marcus released the grip enough for a small trickle of air to make its way into Attilio's screaming lungs. 'Does not being killed satisfy your impertinent demands?', the Counsellor asked. Attilio nodded frantically. 'Good, then our business is concluded.'

Marcus opened his hand, letting Attilio slump to the floor, the sound of his rasping breaths filled the room. Turning his back and returning to his chair in a studied display of indifference, Marcus resumed the book he was reading when Attilio had entered his room. After a few moments he looked up. 'You still here? You're beginning to outstay your welcome.' he said, the carefree breezy tone in stark contrast to the murderous words of a few moments earlier.

Attilio slowly climbed to his feet, swaying unsteadily and holding his throat. His glazed eyes fixed on Marcus who returned it with an air of nonchalance before dismissing him with a small flick of the wrist. Attilio drunkenly staggered toward the door, looking warily over his shoulder as if he half expected Marcus to pounce again.

'One last thing.' Marcus almost laughed as Attilio jumped with fright at the sound of his voice. 'You have until this time tomorrow to provide me with some

215

useful information which I can act upon...' Attilio nodded. His eyes red and mouth lolling. 'Good', said Marcus in an unnerving kindly manner. 'Now run along, before I strangle you with your stupid scarf.' He said and returned to his book. He paid no further heed as the door closed behind Attilio. He looked down at his clenched, shaking fist and gritted his teeth before angrily muttering under his breath, 'May the sky lord eviscerate him if he fails me.'

26

To: Michelle J. Farrington @ electron.com
From: robert.nash@galactic_vistas.com
Subject: Re: What have we unleashed??
Dearest Michelle

I remember Mum saying to me once upon a time to 'Be careful what you wish for.' Naturally being a know it all teenager, I sneered at her words of wisdom. I wish I could tell her now how right she was. When I received your email, I didn't feel how I thought I would upon hearing of her death. I felt a strange, almost selfish sense of relief, as if the burden of guilt I've carried had been lifted and the last vestiges of the past had been cut loose, ready to drift off into the mists of time. But now… Now I would hold her closer than I ever held her as a child. To tell her she was right all along and I was wronger than wrong. If there is an afterlife and Ykdar's words are true, I yearn for it after what I witnessed yesterday.

Blood and terror. A creature shaped by men but ripped out from the very depths of my darkest nightmares, moved amongst us, dealing out death in a display of wanton reckless cruelty that I never thought possible. Nearly thirty people at the last count met their end in the most violent and terrifying way. A synthetic, like those from the Bagama incident all those years ago. The very things they promised would never see the light of day again, were unleashed on the unsuspecting civilians, wreaking havoc and smashing lives into oblivion. Only the swift actions of a hero saved us from total carnage. Amy, Reece and Ollie were returning to our quarters when the outbreak occurred and suffered minor injuries in the crush to escape. They were the lucky ones. I was working and immediately rushed down to see if they were safe. The feeling of relief when I saw them was overwhelming. But it didn't wipe out the sights I saw whilst making my way to them. What remained of people who a few minutes earlier were as alive as you and I, were left in mangled, splattered mounds of flesh so that it was difficult to tell where one body ended and another started. Then I set eyes upon it. The thing that had unleashed the nightmare. It lay dead. A mountain of flesh that even in death cast out a cloud of menace whose shadow froze the hearts of even the bravest amongst us.

The story circulating is that it was part of an abominable experiment that went wrong, while others say it broke in from outside and there are more, many more lurking and waiting to pounce. To have escaped the rampant greed driven cruelty of earth and find that we've been plunged into an even worse nightmare is too much to bear. The fury amongst the population of Pangea at the deceit and betrayal at those responsible is pretty combustible at the moment. I would like to tear the hearts out of those who are responsible for this outrage, but there are more important things than my anger to deal with. Here we are, stuck 500 light years from home on a hostile planet that potentially contains a darkness and evil too terrible to contemplate.

At the moment we crave guidance and there is only one person amongst us who can provide that. The man I told you of previously, Counsellor Marcus is the one. We have a gathering in an hours' time. He will guide us, for only he possesses the wisdom and vision to lead us out of the nightmare we inhabit, and bring us safely to the paradise we were promised. I fervently hope he will deliver us.

Pray for us all

Robert

27

'**We're** down by twenty, including six dead. The SPC suffered one casualty. The numbers don't lie; we're going to have to draw on some of their bodies, to maintain the levels necessary to enable the service tunnel contingency.' Nicklas stared back at Jordan, as he kept his expression neutral. The livid scar above his ear still prominent, seemed to glow redder as Jordan explained his plan. He knew Nicklas well enough to sense his doubts. 'I sense some… scepticism, sergeant.' Nicklas blinked a couple of times.

The usual decisiveness in Nicklas' voice was notable by its absence. 'I like your plan in principle sir.'

Jordan let out a long breath and raised his eyebrows. 'I can feel a "but" coming somewhere along the line sergeant.'

'But they're shit sir.'

Jordan was shocked by Nicklas' directness. 'Shit? Who's shit?'

'The SPC sir. They're useless, the lot of them sir.' Nicklas' voice had taken on an indignant tone that to Jordan bordered on whinging, and once the dam of frustration had burst, nothing was going to stop him. 'I've seen them up close and none of them would even make the second week of trooper selection...' Nicklas continued; '....They lack basic soldiering skills. They survive on bravado. On top of that they're stupid and lack discipline. Only yesterday one of my men tried to tell them to...'

'Enough enough! I get the general picture.' Jordan interrupted. He was irritated by the tiresome interservice rivalry that had blighted his career, but he had to admit Nicklas had a valid point. 'I know where you're coming from Sergeant but they're all we've got, so we'll have to make do I'm afraid.' Despite his annoyance at what he considered petty whining from someone who he thought should know better, he forced himself to soften his voice. 'Sometimes in life we're served a nice juicy shit sandwich, but being an elite trooper means you've got to take a nice big bite and swallow it down. That's why you're the best and that's what you're trained to deal with.' The flattery didn't work as irritation flashed across Nicklas' face. Jordan smiled paternally and placed his hand gently on Nicklas' shoulder. He could feel the tension in Nicklas' wiry yet muscular frame. 'Think of them as a kind of armed militia....', he advised the sergeant; '....You've dealt with that kind of situation before. Flatter them, soothe their egos but always let them know who's in charge.' The tension in Nicklas' shoulder eased a little. Good, thought Jordan. Mission accomplished.

'There's one of them who is a particular asshole. His name is Bruno.', Nicklas intoned.

Jordan's patience was rapidly wearing thin. They're like a bunch of squabbling children. A momentary wish to kick Nicklas in the testicles almost found its way to his foot. He stopped it in the nick of time. Remember Jordan, calm authority, he reminded himself. 'And what particular issues do you have with this "Bruno" sergeant?', he asked

'Thinks he's god's gift, both to the SPC and the female population, sir.'

'We've all met individuals like that sergeant. It's doesn't matter, do the usual and let him think it was all his brainchild. As long as he does it, you probably won't have to deal with him anyway.', Jordan advised.

'There's other things as well sir.' There was a moment's silence before Nicklas continued. 'There's stories about him. Atrocities, from the water wars.'

'What kind of atrocities are we speaking about here sergeant?'

'Whole villages torched and the inhabitants "dealt with" if you see what I mean. Only rumours, but there's a lot of them.', Nicklas replied.

'No actual proof though?' Nicklas shook his head. 'Sergeant...', Jordan said; '....I'm tiring of this, and even if all the stories are true, we still have to deal with the fuckers. As they're the only ones within several hundred light years, you're going to have to put your personal misgivings to one side, cut the bullshit and get it done now! Do I make myself clear?'

'Yes sir.' replied Nicklas through gritted teeth. Jordan cursed himself for losing his patience but he'd had enough.

'Good! Get to it. Dismissed.' There was a hint of regret as Jordan watched Nicklas walk away. Sometimes Jordan, even those you trust and respect the most, need putting in their place. It's called the loneliness of command. Get used to it. It's going to get a lot lonelier over the next few days.

◆

The shaking of Eleanor's hand, like the physical pain of her wounds, had relented a little, but the emotional rawness remained, despite Montano's words of comfort. She knew he was right, but still the relentless rhythm of guilt beat in time with her heart. There was a small spark of pride in the insane bravery of mounting the beast, but it felt like it had been someone else, and the real Eleanor, whoever that was, had watched from a safe distance. Then there was the rejection of her by Ava. She'd seen it before after combat, when a sole survivor of an ambushed unit had turned on his saviours for not letting them die with their comrades, and had to be dragged, kicking and screaming from the scene, harbouring an irrational hatred for days after until the shock wore off and the self-loathing began. She didn't understand, but it was real enough. Looking across the ward over the past day, she'd seen the silent bandaged figure of Ava blindly accusing her for her predicament. *See Ellie, even the only true friend you've got within five hundred light years hates you now. What does that tell you about yourself? Spreading poison wherever you go. Soon the whole world will know the real Eleanor Buckley, oops sorry Eleanor Wells.*

Walking past Ava on a couple of occasions, the compulsion to approach was almost too much, but she'd learnt by bitter experience to respect peoples' wishes as an act of self-preservation.

Eleanor was in the dining area of the infirmary. The telescreen sounded in the background. A few tables were dotted around, with only a couple occupied. She stared at the coffee that Montano had brought her a few moments earlier, hardly daring to touch it. The ripples told her what her eyes didn't, but her heart knew, that the hand still shook with the burden of guilt.

'Well if I wanted silent contemplation, I'd have become a Buddhist monk.'

She looked into gentle humour of Montano's eyes. 'Sorry Raph, sometimes it comes back to me.'

'I can see that, and I'm trying to shake you out of it. Obviously, I'm not doing very well.', Montano opined.

'Well, I'm not one of your security team buddies who you can punch on the arm and everything will be...' She stopped, seeing the look of pain that had quickly replaced the kindness on Montano's face. *Fucked up there didn't you Ellie.* The voice returned .... *He lost his brothers in arms and you're stamping on his balls with your big size ten boots. And you think Ava is playing the bitch...* 'Oh shit, I'm sorry Raph... Sometimes I think I'm the only one.', she quickly intoned.

He reached across and took her hand. It had the same pleasing closeness as a couple of days earlier. 'We're all hurting Ellie.' His smile had quickly returned.

'I know, but I've hurt for most of my life and I should be used to it by now!' Montano laughed. Eleanor noticed with admiration the flash of his white teeth against the olive sheen of his skin.

'It's only natural that you try and protect your thoughts and feelings from others. What you would do with the same information would be completely different to what another would. That's what make us human. That's what makes us individuals.', he counselled.

'I'd never really thought about it before, but it's obvious when I think about it....' Eleanor said and continued; '....I suppose it would explain why certain individuals will screw you over, while others would help. It's the betrayal that kills you...You think you know someone, and they seem everything you'd like in

221

a person, then it turns out you don't really know them at all, and by then it's too late and you're fucked...' This time Montano was sitting quietly, eyebrows slightly raised, inviting Eleanor to continue. Looking around to check they weren't being overheard, she confessed; '....I was raped...as a child...' Eleanor paused, feeling as if she'd been turned inside out, her darkest secrets and deepest fears had been revealed to the whole world. The feeling liberated and terrified her at the same time. Sharing this with Montano had the unsettling intimacy of stripping naked in front of a lover, for the first time. Scary but necessary. 'And then I was raped again a couple of years ago.', she added. The only outward sign from Montano was a couple of rapid blinks. Eleanor continued her confession; 'Until recently I'd been driven by an undimmed rage that just ate away my insides, despite the warnings, despite the better part of me telling me to drop it, that vengeance wouldn't wipe the memory clean, that the past cannot be undone and yet I blotted it all up, because I didn't want to hear it. Only the violent fantasies of what I would do when I caught up with the perpetrator were in my mind.'

'Can I make the assumption that at least one of them is inside the base with us now?', Montano surmised.

Eleanor nodded slowly and said; 'The first one, he's dead...' She felt Montano's eyes bore into her and added quickly. 'It wasn't me...My older brother found out and took matters into his own hands. He's doing a life stretch...Rotting away on my behalf. He should have been a warning. But I never heeded his words.'

'You can tell me, but I can think I can guess who it is...The obvious military training, the false allegations, the rejection. They all add up Ellie...' The air between them seem to thicken as the breath caught in her throat. 'One of the SPC I would say....' Eleanor nodded again, the cloak of her past being peeled back little by little. 'Who?', he asked.

The poisonous mass that had grown inside Eleanor was waiting to be cut out, but the spectre of her brother Nathan languishing in jail hung before her. 'I can't...', she told him; '....I want to, but I can't. You'll kill him and then I'll have two wasted lives on my mind.'

'You're right I would. Without thinking I'd cut his throat, but as you say what good will it do. That's the dilemma, retribution or justice.', he admitted.

Eleanor let out a long, exhausted breath and said. 'I'm tired Raph. Tired of hating, tired of being angry and tired of killing.'

'You've seen action in combat zones?'

'During the water wars....', she explained; '...Africa, south east Asia, Indian sub-continent, South America and Northern Australia. All over the world really. Humanitarian work, other times on operations. Sometimes I'm not even sure

222

which side I was on. The things I've seen and done. The cruelty of humans to their brothers and sisters' beggars belief. Whole communities exterminated on the say so of executives insulated thousands of miles away, or some crazy cult in the next village. Sometimes we got there in time, others too late. You could almost hear the culprits laughing as they drove off, a good day's pay for a good day's work.'

'We've all been there Ellie....', Montano conceded; '...Some didn't think about the implications of what they did and just took the money. No questions asked. I count myself amongst them. Look at how we protected the Mags until it was too late. Turning a blind eye to the dangers despite what we knew all along. We've all got blood on our hands and while we can wash it off, the stench will linger forever.'

'That I agree with. But we're the ones in a position to do something about it.'

'That's dangerous talk Ellie....', he told her; '...I'd be careful who I'd say that to if were you.'

'There are a lot more dangerous things on this fuckin planet than my mouth.'

Montano cautioned her; 'The right word in the wrong place and the whole thing will go up in a massive shitstorm, so be careful. Especially as you're seen as a hero now. People will hang on to your every word. When people are scared their most primitive instincts emerge. They become more self centred, more driven by impulse and rumour, to suspend their belief if they feel someone will save them and that someone is you, whether you like it or not.'

'Me a hero? Please Raph, you're pulling my leg.', she said.

'You think so? Well look behind you at the screen.'

Eleanor's head shot around to view the screen. The familiar short mousey hair and the odd coloured eyes were staring back at her. All in the dining area turned to face Eleanor. Her stomach lurched as if she'd placed her foot on a step that was longer there. The urge to dive under the table and hide was overwhelming but also futile. Looking across at a smiling Montano, a familiar, yet unwelcome voice spoke. *Well well well, looks like your cover's blown Ellie.* Her face was burning as more and more eyes set on her. She took a deep breath and muttered. 'Fuckin hell...'

28

'**I'm** telling you now Mikey, if I ever get trapped with one of those things, fuckin shoot me. Rather that, than being eaten alive by one and shit out of the other end.'

'As long as you promise to do the same for me.'

'What? Shit you out my other end, or shoot you!'

'Just put a fuckin bullet in my head, that's all..'

'Only if you shoot me first!'

'Har dee fuckin har Bruno.'

The smell of fear still lingered in the air, but generally it was quiet. The calm before the storm thought Bruno. Once people are over the shock of the mornings events and process them, the anger will start. But Bruno had more important things on his mind than a few dead civilians, such as being lied to about his promotion prospects and them being stolen by a weasel like Van Dee. Being humiliated by that son of a bitch Gutierrez just rubbed salt into the wounds. He would get his just deserts, just when he least expects it.

Voronoff interrupted Bruno's thought processes. 'What 'ya thinking about Bruno? You look pretty pissed off!'

'Ah, you know me. Usual shit.' Bruno tried to appear carefree and nonchalant but Voronoff knew him better.

'Yeah, not a care in the world, apart from being trapped inside a base on a hellhole of a planet with indestructible monsters on the loose that'll liquidise us on sight. What could possibly go wrong.', Voronoff intoned.

'Don't worry, we've got sir's little favourite, Van Dee to save us all from them, so everything's going to be fine. My arse!' The anger still burned away beneath the surface, glowing through Bruno's thin veneer of indifference.

'I know what you mean. You do all the dirty work and someone else gets all the rewards. It's like we're too good at our jobs and unpromotable, because we'd make those above us look like the incompetent weaklings they actually are.'

'Well said Mikey....', Bruno guffawed. '....Couldn't have put it better myself.' He lowered his voice and continued; 'Although I shouldn't speak ill of a fallen comrade, Williams was first amongst them.' He was slightly dismayed to see the look of shock and disapproval on Voronoff's face and rapidly tried to backtrack. 'I didn't mean that I wished him dead, but you said as much yourself Mikey.' Good thinking Valerio, put the emphasis back on him, he thought.

'Well we all say stuff in the heat of the moment that we regret later, but I'd be careful who I repeated that too if I were you Bruno...' The normal cheery tone of Voronoff disappeared.

Bruno decided to lighten the tone. 'Point taken Mikey, point taken. Anyway, now I'm rewarded by following that fish brains, watsis name again... Overgaard around the service tunnels looking for escape routes so we can hide quicker.' He still smarted at being classified as a 'Shithat' and had quickly come up with the label of 'Fish Brains' much to the general amusement of the SPC rank and file. That couldn't hide the shame of van Dee's pathetic attempt at confrontation with the Troopers, as well as the almost casual fashion he was neutralised with minimal effort. He knew, regardless of the blame for the creature's breakout, he had a grudging admiration for their skill and bravery in eventually bringing it down. The idea in turning on the anti-gravity was a stroke of genius. None of the SPC would have even thought of that, let alone put it into action and successfully executing it. What I could do, leading half a dozen of them, he thought wistfully.

Voronoff continued, 'Mind you, from what I heard, the 'Mag' as they call it, was one nasty piece of work. Bullets pinged off of it like hailstones, but not a scratch, until one of the security team managed to get in a head shot with an armour piercing round.'

'Yep I heard. Some guy called Montano....', Bruno supposed and went on; '....I'd never heard of him, but that's no surprise considering we weren't even aware of the Mag's or the security teams until Gutierrez's briefing. There's masses of them, and different types as well. Big, small, fat, thin and some who can fly as well.' He remembered the pictures from the briefing and some of the names. 'Gorthon', 'Gargoyle', 'Hyperthon' were the ones he remembered. 'Mind you....', he added '....I don't buy all that shit about them being there for "our protection", I thought that was our job!'

Bruno casually looked up to one of the telescreens that were dotted throughout the Civilian areas. The face of Patricia Fernandez reading the news stared earnestly out. Bruno couldn't help admire the dark almond shaped eyes, framed by the luscious locks of her raven coloured hair, as his eyes wandered down towards the ample cleavage at the bottom of the screen. He turned to Voronoff and adopted his big bad wolf smile that he reserved for particularly stunning women. 'Hey, look Mikey....', he said; there's your girlfriend, Patricia.' A look of shame and displeasure spread across Voronoff face, but Bruno persisted; 'Now that's someone I could fuck for a living. Pity she's outta your league Mikey. What was it she said to you again?'

''Very funny Bruno, just drop it will ya!' Voronoff's face turned a shade of red.

225

Bruno continued to prod mercilessly, 'I remember; it was something like "Fuck off creep or I'll call security". Poor Mikey, your dreams shattered. Should have left her to a real man, like me...'

Voronoff shook his head ruefully at the memory of his humiliation and turned his nose up. 'You're welcome to her....', he said; '....the stuck up bitch. I was only trying to get her to pose with me for a picture. You'd have thought I'd asked to squeeze her tits the way she reacted.' He shook his head and muttered something to himself that Bruno couldn't understand.

Bruno laughed at Voronoff's discomfort. 'Hey Mikey, only pulling your leg', he said then asked; 'Anyway how's that little hottie you've been screwing the past few days?'

Voronoff's head shot around, eyes wide open. 'How'd you know about Antonina?' He screwed his eyes shut, immediately cursing himself.

'So that's her name. I have my sources Mikey.' Bruno smirked. 'Anyway it's your bit of fun. Just beware. As someone once said to me long ago, when the dick gets hard the brain goes soft.'

'Just a pity you never put it into practice Bruno!' A loud bark of laughter escaped Voronoff. 'Touché Bruno!' A triumphant smile returned to his face.

'Yeah yeah, fuck you Mikey', Bruno tried to laugh it off, but he hated having the tables turned, and Voronoff's swift retort stung him.

Suddenly Voronoff stared back up at the screen, a look of excitement on his face. He pointed and said; 'Hey look! Up there on the screen, that's her!'

Bruno casually glanced up. Eleanor's face stared back at him from the screen, before it was replaced by the roving reporter. Bruno recognised her instantly, even though his befuddled mind didn't want to.

Voronoff continued; 'Super Janitor they're calling her. Doesn't look much to me, more your type I think Bruno.' He looked across at Bruno whose face had drained of colour, leaving a pale mask of shock.

'It can't be! How the fuck did she...?', Bruno couldn't quite finish his question.

'Well you look to me like you're already in love Bruno.', Voronoff mocked him.

Bruno quickly gathered his wits, fumbling for an excuse. Being an accomplished liar helped. 'I err... Yeah. Sorry, thought I knew her for a second.'

'Not another one of your ex-girlfriends. I'm sure you make this shit up!', Voronoff postulated.

Bruno felt a flash of anger, but kept a lid on it, and said; 'You know how it is Mikey, you lose count after a while, or maybe in your case you've still got a few more fingers to go before you get to that stage. Anyway I'm sure she'll be an ex-girlfriend pretty soon.' He inwardly congratulated himself on his quick thinking and coolness under pressure.

'Ha fuckin ha! Hope your dick drops off', Voronoff scoffed. There was a few moments silence between them as they continued their patrol, before Voronoff spoke again. 'Back to your frustrations earlier. There's someone I know who may be able to give you some advice on that. Some of the guys were talking about him a couple of days ago, before the shit exploded everywhere and hit us smack bang in the face. Marcus, the counsellor. They said they felt a bit better after listening to him. Talks a lot of sense from all accounts.'

'I know the guy. With the beard, women always talking to him like the sun shines out of his arse.', Bruno surmised.

'The very one....', Voronoff interjected and continued; 'Well from what they said he's striving to build a better society here on the Magdur. One where people find their progress based on ability and humanity, not because they're a bastard or an arse licker.'

'Yeah dream on. That'll never happen. It's always been survival of the fittest and the fittest normally refers to the arse lickers!'

'Well I'm not so sure. I was impressed...', Voronoff wasn't allowed to finish.

'So you've seen him then!' Bruno said. He saw Voronoff's face turned crimson and added; 'I bet you went with the hottie didn't you?'

'Well... Yes I did first of all, then I told the others about him,' Voronoff reluctantly confessed. 'I went along to find out what they were talking about. I've got to say it was quite impressive. He spoke a lot of truth. You know the kind of stuff that's so obvious that you don't even notice it until it's pointed out to you. Why don't you come along? There's a gathering this evening. We can go after we're off duty', he invited.

'I don't get taken in by that fairy tale shit. Telling people only what they want to hear always comes back and bites you on the arse in the end', Bruno responded.

'So you're embarrassed, I understand.' Voronoff rolled his eyes in a gently mocking gesture.

Bruno turned to Voronoff and stood just that little bit closer. 'Do I look embarrassed? Mikey...' He said Voronoff's name with a little hint of menace that he reserved for those he felt were a notch below him and wouldn't stand up to him.

Voronoff backed away slightly. He said, rather sheepishly; 'Hey, I didn't mean it like that, I was just saying some people feel a bit awkward with that kind of thing. Look, I'm sure an open minded guy like you will be able to make his own decisions.' Bruno was a sucker when people appealed to his vanity. 'Come along this evening and I'll even introduce him to you', Voronoff offered.

227

'So, you know him?', Bruno asked. Again the idea of the counsellor having the privilege of an audience with the great Bruno caressed his ego. Perhaps I can give him a few tips, he thought, then acquiesced with his comrade's suggestion; 'Ok I'll go, just to shut you up!' He let out his favourite false laugh when he felt he was making a concession, clapping his huge hand on the top of Voronoff's shoulder, in an almost subconscious dominant way, as if to say I'm above you. I have power over you. You are mine to control.

Voronoff, as usual, was blithely ignorant of Bruno's subtle psychological manipulations. 'Excellent! You won't regret it', he promised.

'Ohh I think I will.', Bruno said.

They both laughed, but Bruno's mind was galloping with the thoughts of Eleanor. Was it her? What was she doing on Magdur? What to do about her? Three shocks in one day. None of them nice. Mind you with the lack of promotion that made the clinging attentions of Naomi redundant, the only thing to worry about now was their framing of Eleanor, but she was in it almost as much as he was. He had his own dirty little secret he'd kept from Naomi. What would she do if she found out? Her weak dependent nature and fragile confidence made her unpredictable. She'll have to be handled carefully but, one way or another, her days were numbered.

◆

'It *was* definitely her! If you could stop blubbering for a few seconds I'll explain!'

Naomi looked up, her nose running and eyes red from crying. 'Well you're used to death and destruction. I'm not!', she said.

Her voice had acquired a hysterical edge, which Bruno had seen all too often, and was all too aware of the unpredictable consequences if it was allowed to develop. Daddy isn't here to save his little princess, is he? Only poor fuckin Valerio. 'You need to calm down and stop being so hyper. You're an officer in the SPC now.', he reminded her

'Don't you tell me to calm down, especially when you're the one seeing things! Anyway you're imagining it. How could she possibly be here?', she was incredulous.

'I saw her face staring back out of the screen at me, as plain as day. She even had the different eye colours.', he explained.

Bruno had been in shock for the past hour. Looking at Naomi's face, he could see, even through the angst and terror, her scepticism was obvious. He needed proof. Her breathing had slowed, as she struggled to control her emotions. Her voice softened as she asked; 'So tell me what happened again?'

He stared back at her. You're gonna have to be careful here Valerio, he thought. Her situation has changed and she doesn't even realise it.

He tried to access the infonet, but all he got was a screen with a message. 'Error 404:'

'The infonet is blocked', he said and turned to Naomi, adding; 'I'm sure it's deliberate.'

'You can't say that. How about routine maintenance. It could be an innocent explanation.', she suggested.

'Either way, I'm as sure as I can be it was her...', he argued; '....The hair was longer, but the face was the same, plus there was the odd eye colours. How did she get here? She's even kept her first name and only changed her surname from Buckley to Wells.'

'It sounds like your mind is working overtime and fitting the facts to meet your forgone conclusion.', she contended.

'You've got a lot to learn young lady.'

'Don't patronise me! I've had that all my life, people thinking they can talk down to me like I'm a child and I'm not taking it from you.'

Bruno muttered to himself, 'Ever thought there might be a reason for that...?'

'What? What did you say? I heard. I'm not as stupid as you think.'

Yet another pointless argument over nothing. Bruno shook his head wearily and decided to get back to the main topic. 'Let's assume for a moment it *is* actually her.' He looked at Naomi who stood with her lips pursed and arms folded, letting out a snort of irritation before Bruno continued. 'Why would she be on here?', he asked.

'Perhaps she wanted a reunion with old friends and have a cosy chat about the good old days.' Naomi responded testily.

'Oh yes. I would say that's definitely on the agenda, but not in the happy get together way.....', Bruno's voice took on a hard edge. '....What was one of the first things they taught you at Academy, assuming you can actually remember anything you learnt there.' Again there was an irritated silence before he reminded her; 'Put yourself in the mind of your adversary. Think what you would do if you were in their position.'

'I'll tell you what I wouldn't do in her position. I wouldn't waste my life chasing someone halfway across the galaxy over a failed course. I know her better than you ever will, and she's not that crazy. Driven yes, but not mad. She'll get a job for private security or even as a mercenary, but as a cleaner? You can't be serious.', she reasoned.

Bruno thought carefully for a few moments. He knew the reason she was here, but he had to give Naomi some plausibility to Eleanor's presence, as well as scaring the living shit out of her of course. 'Well, in that court room I saw crazy....', he recounted; '....Murder was in her eyes, when she saw you take the stand. Desperation when she started accusing me of all that crazy shit. What about when she found out she'd failed. She would have killed me if she could. Is that the mind of a stable person? She's the kind of nutter who'd cut someone's throat over losing a game of cards.' He could see the first seeds of doubt in Naomi's demeanour.

'So, you think she'll come after us if she's here. Are we in danger?', she was clearly anxious.

'Remember how I discovered her trying to screw you over, so she would get the champion recruit? When people are prepared to go that far over such a small thing, there's no telling what they are capable of..', he didn't finish the sentence.

'So, what can we do about it? She'll expose us if we confront her directly, and if she's the one who stopped the monster, she can do no wrong in everyone's view. Even if we told them all, it's our word against Eleanor's and who would they believe? Us or her?' She, like him, knew full well the answers to her questions.

'Exactly. That's why I'm saying we have to think about our next steps and tread very carefully', he cautioned.

'We can try to discredit her, without her knowing. But let's see if we can find out if it's actually her first.'

'How about we take some flowers and visit her in the infirmary. That'll be nice. I'm telling you now. It's her!'

'Who's being stupid now? Anyway how do we get close enough? You can't even visit anyone you know in there.', she informed him.

'I dunno. But I'll think of something,' Bruno said, shaking his head in dismay, but the wheels of his mind had been turning all along and an idea was forming to rid himself of two turbulent priestesses' in one go. Naomi would be easy to manipulate, but Eleanor was another matter. Get them in the same place at the same time, but how?

He turned to Naomi, 'I want you to be sure it's her, just to prove to you I'm not making it up. Keep watching the Telescreens. She's bound to come up.' He felt his life depended on outwitting Eleanor, and in that case, there was only going to be one winner in that situation, and it wasn't going to be that poisonous little bitch. He shook his head. Two more fuckin years on this shithole of a planet before I'm on the next flight home. It was the first time he'd ever wished his life away...

230

29

The sea of anxious faces looked toward Marcus as he stepped into the spotlight. The whisper of the audience diminished to a deathly hush. A sense of expectation lingered as the silence assumed that peculiar physical quality unique to a large gathering, pressing its weight down on everyone in the auditorium. He could sense the fear that pervaded those in attendance, a fear that was his to mould to his advantage. His white robe shone in the spotlight almost casting its own shadow as he beheld the scene before him. Nearly a thousand faces turned to him in expectation, awaiting guidance and salvation. This is it Marcus, your moment, what you've worked towards all your life. He took a calming breath, then spoke.

'Brothers and sisters, I can understand your fear....' He began '....I can understand it because I feel it too.' He saw some heads nodding. 'But what I feel more than fear is the hurt and anger of betrayal.' A few voices murmured in agreement. His followers were doing their jobs well. Not pushing too hard, playing it just right. Even that blibbering idiot Aaron was sticking to his instructions. 'Those in whom we have placed our trust, as well as the lives of our loved ones, have not only lied to you, but have placed us *all* in mortal danger.', he continued as the voices were rising. 'The terrors of the Earth, along with its associated lies and corruption have reached out, to sink their poisoned claws into our hearts, before ripping them out!' The voices became shouts that quickly escalated into a crescendo of anger, fuelled by jangling nerves, egged on by the followers. 'We have witnessed what their monstrous creations are capable of, and we are not going to suffer the fate of the abomination's helpless innocent victims!' The audience became a single furious entity that could easily race out of control.

Even Marcus was taken aback at the power of his oratory. Rein them back in Marcus and be careful, only a few prods can send them into frenzy. Play it carefully, pick your moment, he reasoned. He held his hands out in a calming gesture, but the clamour continued unabated. 'Brothers, Sisters! Please!' His voice carried the power of authority and control as the crowd quieted once again, allowing him to resume; 'And yet who are those who inflict such fear upon us? What is special about them that they have control over us?' Again the nodding heads told him he was striking the right note. 'They are but men.', he said.

'And Women!' Shouted a middle aged man near the front. A spontaneous ripple of laughter eased the tension and Marcus allowed himself a smile.

'Ah women as well....', Marcus continued; '....But they are just people. Flesh and blood. Not supreme beings with omnipotent powers, not elected, no one voted for them except their genetically enhanced taskmasters who are surrounded by the trappings of power, who stay hidden in the shadows while their minions do their bidding. Those whose companies wield vast amounts of power and who are only answerable to their shareholders, where profit is their only motive. Elected governments replaced by company boards, parliaments by AGMs, countless millions of lost lives cast aside onto the scrapheap in the interests of a few elite super rich, who rape the earth and its population while giving nothing back to it'.

'Thieves! Tyrants!' A few shouts arose from the darkness at the rear of the auditorium.

'But there is one thing we have that they'll never have in a million years.', Marcus suggested. He paused. There were intrigued expressions throughout the congregation, filled with anticipation, teetering on the very edge of realisation. Keeping the momentum going, he slowly raised his right hand, holding it almost in a claw shape, ready to reach out and grasp the future that was just in front of him. Marcus resumed his oratory; 'The single thing that binds us together in belief, compassion and mercy. That fills our hearts with the faith of thousands, the warmth of the eternal light of love. The thing I speak of, is the majesty and love of Ykdar! The Great Sky Lord himself!' His hand was above his head as he clenched his fist.

'Let us bless Ykdar! The Sky Lord!' Right on cue Aaron leapt to his feet.

'We submit to his greatness.' This time it was from the other side of the congregation. One of his favoured female disciples taking her cue from Aaron the foolish.

Within a few seconds, the shouts and exclamations spread around the auditorium in a conflagration of passion and exultation. A red haired woman ran onto the stage and threw herself at Marcus's feet. I don't remember her or asking her to do that! He thought and looked down at the tear stained face, contorted in the throes of an almost sexual ecstasy. The thrill of excitement tingled over Marcus's loins. Don't get carried away Marcus. We don't want anything poking out of the robe do we now. Tearing his gaze away from the rapturous face and the associated erotic thoughts, he waited for the commotion to die down.

'I hear his voice in my prayers, and he tells me to remain calm, I hear his wisdom and he tells me to be patient.', he told his congregation.

'But how can we be patient oh Counsellor?' shouted a voice from the back 'When the beasts are scratching at our door, ready to drink our blood!'

Well done my faithful one. Stoke their fears. His thoughts raced as he turned to face the speaker. 'There is another way my brother. A different path from the lies that drip down from the poisoned lips of the servants of immorality, who want to turn your fear against you, to tie you down with chains of terror. There is a way

232

built on justice, cooperation and respect. A way that rewards the righteous and sees those of us who are natural leaders take the hand of those who need guidance, to show them the path to truth and the rewards they so richly deserve.'

'But how Counsellor? Please show us!'

Keep them intrigued Marcus, don't give it all away. Leave them wanting more, he surmised silently and answered; 'All in good time brother, all in good time. Be patient.' He turned to the rest of the congregation and held his arms out, palms turned upwards. 'I am your servant brothers and sisters. What are you wishes? Please instruct me.'

'Tell the evil doers! Tell them our demands!', a boisterous voice called out, followed by murmurs of support.

'And what are your demands my family?', the Counsellor asked them.

'Destroy the beasts. Kill them all!!!!' A chant started, 'Death to the beasts! Death to the Beasts!' It reverberated around the auditorium.

Marcus closed his eyes, letting the sound of the mob, as that is what it had become, flow over him as he bathed in the splendour of the power and control he had craved all his life. The choreography had gone better than he could have ever dreamed. The hours of practice with his following had paid off. They had served their purpose well. He had arrived, had seized the moment with both hands, and only death was going to prise him away from it now.

♦

Alone backstage, Marcus was shaking with excitement, his robe drenched in sweat. Reaching into his pocket, he retrieved the old key he always kept as a reminder, running his finger gently along it's jagged edge, wondering what his mother would think if she saw her Marcus now. He could hear her voice.

*

'You're special and one of the chosen few. Don't you ever forget that.' He remembered the haggard withered creature that opened the door to him that night and welcomed him in from the rain. The sunken eyes, the knobbly crooked hands with the long yellowed nails. Her shock of frazzled grey hair that gave the appearance of a recent surprise electrocution. The hugs and tears reserved for her long lost son. Her love overpowered him. He told her of the cult, but omitted the fire, he told her of lies he'd been fed and how they took his life over.

'I knew you'd return to Mother one day and now we'll always be together', she'd said. Marcus was fed his favourite food from childhood. She'd even kept some of his toys and showed them to him, half expecting him to play with them. He tolerated her attentions as he slowly regained his strength.

233

'This is where you belong my dear. You'll never want to leave mummy anymore will you?'

'Of course not mother, why would I ever leave this paradise.' He lied. But she meant every word. Literally.

The following morning he'd woken to find his bedroom door locked. At first he hammered on the door, but it was reinforced. Eventually her voice sounded from the other side. It was for his own protection. He needed to be kept safe from the cruelty of the world, she reassured him.

Food and water along with the bucket were left in his room each morning. Then there was the constant tiredness and strange hallucinations. The terrifying dreams. Sometimes he'd woken with a bright light shining in his face. Her voice sounding from the darkness behind the light.

'Don't worry my prince. I will protect you. It's all for your own good. Mummy would never hurt her special boy.' Her face would appear over him. Sometimes metamorphosizing into the face of one of the cult members. 'We are waiting for you Marcus to join us, down here in the flames.' As the hands reached to him, pulling him down before the face reverted to the spectre of his mother. Looming over him in the darkness with the needle moving closer, as he felt the pain of the injection, before returning to the twilight world between life and death. There was a hazy awareness that he was fading away. Becoming a ghost, a shadow, a half forgotten afterthought. Ceasing to exist as a person.

A small glimmer of his former self flickered deep in his soul. He clung to it with all his remaining energy, a piece of the wreckage of his life floating in the storm of his existence. His strength slowly failing as the cold sank through him, numbed fingers slipping from the shrinking flotsam as the infinite depths beneath his feet waited to welcome him.

Emerging once again from the darkness, her hands gently caressed his matted hair. 'You know this is for the best my darling.', she said while she bought the needle forward, glowing in the dim torchlight. Holding the syringe upwards to examine it, she methodically flicked it to remove the bubbles from the murky brown liquid. Her smile revealed the broken rows of brown crooked teeth. 'Here comes the big aeroplane. Open wide...'. Through the mist Marcus knew what he had to do. His final chance before extinction. Smiling weakly, holding held her hand, Marcus drew the needle to him. Her bony arm relaxed in response and she smiled benevolently. 'That's right my darling. You know it's good for you', she reassured him.

The gleaming point of the needle moved closer, a small droplet of fluid shimmered on the end. 'Thank you mummy.' Marcus croaked before he pushed back with the final vestiges of his strength, the needle striking his mother's jugular before discharging its contents. Her smile became a contortion, the eyes opened in shock, before they rolled back as her skeletal body slumped across him, shuddered, let out a long wheezing breath, then was still. The torch dropped to the floor and rolled under the bed, filling the room in an eerie red glow as her grip failed and Marcus slithered into the blackness.

Marcus was woken by a searing pain that rang every nerve ending, accompanied by uncontrollable shivering. His throat burned with thirst and the tongue was swollen, the light blinding as he opened his eyes. The cold bag of bones that had once been his mother was surprisingly heavy as it rested across him. Raising his hand and shielding his face, he slowly opened his eyes once again, making out the bones through the redness. Then he became aware of the smell. He moved his hand slowly away. The shaft of daylight shone bright against the wall next to the bed, illuminating the purple features of his mother's dead face. A scrabbling noise came from the floor. Moving his head, he saw a large rat feasting on the rotting flesh of her leg. Its jet black eyes shot up in challenge at Marcus as it drew back its mouth, revealing blood soaked incisors, emitting a loud hiss. Marcus let out a scream of rage and disgust in response as he pushed the shrunken carcass off him. The rat scurried out of the way just in time to avoid the corpse, before it fled the room pursued by the scarecrow figure that had once been Marcus.

He felt frail, a final heartbeat away from death. But for the first time since the bedroom door was locked on him, he was able to think clearly. The doors to the outside were padlocked shut, the windows barred and screwed down, trapping him inside. There was no communication to the outside world as mother didn't want to allow the evil influences to pollute her pure sanctuary. The electricity had long ceased to flow. He tried to drag the putrefied corpse of his mother out of the room, but the stench and the rats drove him back.

The rats returned each night in ever increasing numbers, drawn by the irresistible odour of death that permeated every corner. They became more adventurous as if they could smell Marcus's weakness. He survived on a small packet of stale biscuits he'd discovered between the cushions of the rancid sofa. The water came from the tap in an agonisingly slow dribble. He left a cup under the tap which took an eternity to fill, each drop a moment nearer to salvation, before his patience snapped, snatching the cup and gulping down the meagre contents with a desperation that only the truly thirsty could ever appreciate. Sleep became increasingly difficult, as each evening when darkness fell, the scrabbling figures returned. He cowered in a corner wrapped in a blanket, and armed with a meat tenderiser to fend off the increasingly bold rodents that ransacked the house, eating everything. The shuffling's increased in volume and frequency as they threw themselves at Marcus, who was by now the last edible thing left in the house. The shapes could be half seen by the moonlight that shone in through the barred windows and off the glistening matted fur while they scurried busily to and fro. One was tearing at the blanket. Marcus bought down the tenderiser crunching its head, ending its days with a loud squeak. But they kept coming in waves, relentlessly wearing him down until daylight and respite came, leaving him lying exhausted, surrounded by the furry dead, casualties of the previous night's battle. But he knew they would return that evening for the next round and each day he was fading away.

The biscuits had been devoured, and the raging hunger that consumed his every thought made even the previously inconceivable, desirable. The shining flesh of the dead rats took on an alluring luscious quality. His trembling hand pulled back the black fur, as he tore the wound open to reveal the delicious pink flesh underneath, before he hesitantly took his first nibble. The stringy meat was a succulent feast that his taste buds rejoiced in. Any pretence of humanity was abandoned, as he devoured the furry banquet, tears of desperation and shame ran down Marcus hollow cheeks as he tore flesh from bone, before cracking open the ribcage, to lovingly slurp the innards in a single gulp, wondering to himself whether the rat was one of those that had eaten his mother, and was he eating any of her? He shut the thought out of his mind where it lurked just out of sight, patiently waiting to return during a moment of weakness or doubt.

Working his way through another couple of courses of rare steak a la Rattus Norvegicus, Marcus could feel his strength beginning to return. He had to escape, but no matter where he looked, the keys were nowhere to be seen. Every drawer, cupboard, recess, jar, shelf was examined. He couldn't survive on rat forever, even though an ever increasing supply appeared each evening; but it was the thirst that was killing him, as the tap dried up squealing its final drops in protest. The daytime heat made the house unbearable, while he shivered under his blanket in the night after licking the condensation that had formed off any surface he could find. The increasingly desperate efforts of the rats to add him to their macabre menu kept him warm. Then they decided to attack en masse, lining up like an ancient army, forming up to attack a besieged fortress, waiting as they gathered in increasing numbers. Time lost its meaning as the rats and Marcus regarded each other in the darkness while the rodent legions prepared in menacing silence.

The quiet was shattered by a loud thumping then the crash of glass followed by gruff voices. The groaning of bending metal drove the rats into a fever before they scurried from the room. Marcus tried to shout, 'In here!', but all that came out was a husky croak. It was met with the desperate screams of the intruders from the kitchen as he went to investigate. The rats had found fresher meat. A figure ran past Marcus frantically clawing at the creatures consuming his throat, knocking Marcus against the door to his former bedroom, which flew open with a loud boom. Looking inside one last time at the pile of bones, with the grey electrocuted hair, covered in a few rags of clothes, laying undisturbed next to the bed, he noticed something and moved closer. A shiny metallic bundle sat in the middle. Marcus leant forward, ignoring the increasingly sinister gurgling coming from the hallway, and picked up the bunch of keys that had been lying untouched. Looking at the object of his search, he felt nothing as he left the bedroom. He opened the kitchen door, to witness a thrashing figure desperately writhing on the floor, wearing a living coat of rodent fur. Behind him Marcus saw the crowbar lying on the floor and the bent back broken bars of the window, curtains flapping lazily in the wind that flowed into the place that had been Marcus's prison. Putting the keys in his pocket, the rats paid him no heed as he made his way past the human bait ball, across to the opening and slipped easily through to the outside world, leaving the screams and squeals behind him. As he made his way down the alley and out into the deserted street, the rain started to fall. It felt good on his skin, really good, and he opened his mouth to the heavens. The gods had provided once again in his hour of need.

◆

To: Michelle J. Farrington @ electron.com
From: robert.nash@galactic_vistas.com
Subject: Re: Marcus the great
Dear Michelle
We truly are in the presence of greatness. Our prayers have been answered. The chosen one is amongst us. I speak of the Counsellor. We held a gathering today the like of which I've never experienced before. His words washed over our anguished minds in a soothing balm. Driving out the fears that have paralysed us since the beasts' outbreak. He speaks truths so obvious that we don't even realise they exist until he shines his light on them. The lies and betrayal of those in whom we placed our trust did not escape his wrath and are left smashed upon the ground. How could we have been so foolish to believe them. The fear of death has left me, to be replaced by hope and even if I was to die, I'd willingly lay down my life for Marcus this minute rather than live a thousand years under the heel of those who have abused our unquestioning trust.

Our path is clear to us now. Follow Marcus, destroy the beasts and their creators!

Praise Ykdar The Great Sky Lord!
Robert

30

Bruno looked up at the rear seats while the auditorium emptied. The hysteria of a few minutes earlier was dissipated by a hearty rendition of '*Every day I love you more and more*'. The clumsily played, out of tune acoustic guitar and accompanying tambourine were drowned out by the thousands of passionate voices, exuding a feeling of solidarity that took Bruno aback. His normally imperturbable senses had already been battered into submission by the phenomenon of Counsellor Marcus's oratory. Oh to have that kind of effect over people. I'd lead armies to victory against any opponent with that kind of charisma, he thought. He didn't give a shit about Yakydar whatsisname, or the outrage at the deception by the Company and the Scientists. He'd been lied to all his life, and had learnt it was better to allow himself to be carried along with the tide of mistruths, rather than swim in a futile and solitary stream of truth against it. Anyway, what was true, except the latest set of selected facts from those who happened to be in charge had decided to feed you. One day they would be violently opposed to something they had passionately advocated the day before. As far as he was concerned, truth was whatever you chose it to be, and the effect of Marcus words had on those around him looked pretty real to him, though he was pretty sure the chicken necked creep that jumped up and started the shouting off was a plant. The woman dragged away from the stage however, looked pretty authentic as far as he was concerned. I'd like to learn that trick from you Brother Marcus.

Bruno turned to make some flippant comment to Voronoff, but his friends' normally good-humoured countenance was replaced with the red face and bulging neck of an unswerving fanatic. Bruno looked further along the row at the SPC squad members joining those around them in various stages of wrath with protruding eyes, shaking fists and snarling teeth. All except Janssen, who was slowly feeding a pie into his mouth. No chewing was involved, only the slow steady conveyer belt-like progress as he fed it into the gaping hole on its way to pastry heaven. Jansen's glazed trance-like features acted as the eye of the storm, oblivious to the maelstrom of fury that whipped around him, the pie being the centre of his attention.

Bruno observed around him. Those who weren't shouting worked their jaws angrily. Then the spell subsided and relative calmness returned. Now the angry heads were nodding in agreement, a hopeful smile was on their faces. This man was one worth following, to hitch a free ride on the juggernaut of faith and devotion that Marcus inspired.

'Beats listening to Gutierrez drone on doesn't it', laughed Voronoff, beads of sweat covering his face.

Bruno turned to face him. He looked along the row of comrades wearing a look of flushed satisfaction, including Janssen who was wiping away a few crumbs from around his mouth. 'Incredible. I've never seen anything like it. To have that kind of power over so many people takes a special talent...' he said

'You wanna meet him?', Voronoff asked.

'Fuck yeah! Of course', Bruno answered immediately, inwardly admonishing himself at his over enthusiastic response, betraying his desperation to make an impression on this man who could raise him to the status and prestige he so craved.

'Well let's go then. He asked me to bring you along.', Voronoff told his friend.

'Me?' replied Bruno, raising his eyebrows and pointing at himself in surprise.

'Yep, You!' Voronoff replied, jabbing his finger into Bruno's chest, as he laughed.

♦

'Welcome brother, welcome.' Marcus made his way through the milling entourage of disciples straight to Bruno who was introduced by Voronoff. 'I've heard a lot about you Sergeant Bruno and it's an honour to meet such an outstanding individual.'

Bruno gave an embarrassed laugh as Marcus offered his hand. Marcus placed his other hand on top of the sergeant's shoulder. Normally Bruno's prickly pride would have bristled at such a gesture, but he was enjoying the flattery too much to care, with the counsellor's piercing eyes looking straight into his, trapping Bruno like a rabbit in their headlights.

'Thanks Counsellor, I'm sure they were exaggerating.' Although he believed every word and more, but a strange thing happened to Bruno. For the first time in his life he felt an admiration that wasn't based on fear or status, but charisma.

'Nonsense brother. Sergeant Voronoff here is one of our most valued, respected members and his words carry a lot of weight.' Marcus said as he looked across to a nodding Voronoff who held his hand on his heart, struggling to fight back the tears. Marcus placed his arm around Bruno's shoulder and invited; 'Come my friend, we have much to discuss.'

He led Bruno alone to his private contemplation room. There were two easy chairs either side of a low table. Marcus motioned for Bruno to be seated. 'How did you find our little gathering Sergeant Bruno?', he asked.

240

'Please just Bruno will do.' Marcus nodded and Bruno continued. 'It was like nothing I've ever seen.' He noticed Marcus frowned slightly before he added, 'In a good way may I add!' The counsellor's smile reassured Bruno. 'How you held everyone with the power of your words really impressed me, and I'm hard to impress!'

'Well Bruno, we live in difficult times and they've just become a whole lot more difficult. People need guidance and strong individuals to provide it and that's why I've asked to meet you.'

Play hard to get Valerio, keep those legs firmly crossed and buttocks clenched tightly, Bruno told himself as he responded to Marcus's encouraging words. 'I'm grateful Counsellor, but why me?'

'Well, I'm aware of your history Bruno. Decorated war hero, respected comrade and a charismatic man who leads by example. An envious set of attributes and worthy of great recognition.' Even though Bruno had heard these words countless times from the mouths of flatterers, friends and brownnosers, it seemed to mean more coming from a man of equal standing who could command a vast following. 'But I also see a man who has been unjustly denied the rightful opportunities he deserves by those who don't hesitate to place him in harm's way, as they reap the acclaim and its associated rewards while sitting safely behind a desk.'

Bruno felt the sense of injustice, that had been growing inside over the years of hardship, overflow as if erupting from a bursting dam. His heart pounded and his breathing quickened. He looked down to see his protruding knuckles whiten as he gripped the side of the chair. Every grievance, every stolen opportunity, encapsulated in a few words.

He swallowed hard then asked. 'How do you know these things counsellor. Was it Mikey?'

'Partly Brother, as well as from the men alongside him....', Marcus spoke assuredly; '....They look up to you, while they resent those higher up. But I can also sense the profound discontent of one robbed of justice. A great man blunted by the words and deeds of those who would send you to your death. Those who see you as a threat wish to be rid of you.' He was leaning forward in his seat, his voice quiet, yet strong and clear, resonating in the small room as if it were filled with a thousand souls.

Bruno swallowed faster, his bottom lip trembling as he listened intently while he looked downwards, the words killing and lifting him simultaneously.

Marcus went on; 'Who would be the one leading the troops against the hordes of monsters in the knowledge of certain death? You! Willing to spill his blood to save his comrades. You!'

Even though in reality Bruno would be unwilling to spill even a drop of piss to save his comrades, unless he directly benefited, the heroic visions conjured by Marcus's silver tongue made him giddy.

The Counsellor continued to laud Bruno. 'But then who would people look to in their moment of crisis, to drag them back from the edge of the abyss. To save them and lead them forward. You!'

Bruno sat in silence for a few moments, having never felt quite like this before. A beggar who had found a bag of gold, or one who had been born in a cell, feeling the cool breeze of fresh air and the warmth of the sun on his face for the first time. He could sense Marcus's gaze as the Counsellor's hand rested on his shoulder once again. Marcus spoke softly, almost a whisper. 'You are that man Bruno. The one we've been waiting for.'

There was something strange tickling Bruno's cheek. His hand touched the wetness there, and moving it away, looked in astonishment on the first real tears of his life. Feeling weak and ashamed, yet liberated, he looked at Marcus and knew this was the person he'd waited his entire life for. The one who could transport him to the position the world owed him. He'd never felt love for anyone apart from himself, but he felt something toward this man with the strange piercing eyes. Trying to think of something deep and profound as a reply, about how he'd gratefully accept the great role that fate had bestowed on him, all that came out was. 'Don't tell the lads I've been blubbing. They'll laugh their fuckin arses off.'

'Fear not brother, fear not. That'll stay between us, I promise.'

Bruno felt a strange urge to throw his arms around Marcus. What's happening to me? I'm like a lovestruck teenager. He took a deep breath, wiped his tears away and laughed, the kind of carefree laugh that was alien to him. 'Ok Counsellor. How can we work together?', he enquired.

Marcus smiled, stood up and said. 'All in good time Bruno.' He extended his hand. Bruno stood up and took it. 'We will speak again soon', the Counsellor assured. He gestured to the small drinks cabinet and invited the sergeant. 'Maybe something to seal our newfound friendship before you leave?'

'Thank you Counsellor but I must be going. I'm on duty in an hour and need to see to some tasks beforehand.' Bruno responded.

Marcus smiled again and nodded. Bruno sensed a hint of irritation. Too bad, I let him have a quick fumble on our first date and that's as far as it goes, he thought before he said; 'Till we meet again Counsellor.'

'Indeed Bruno. I look forward to it very much and I'll be in touch.' Marcus said.

Bruno saw the glint of triumph in Marcus's eyes as he turned and left the room. Shutting the door behind him, he closed his eyes, letting out a long breath in the quiet of the lobby. Then he opened them, turned and saw Voronoff standing before him.

'Bruno. You ok?' The usual tone of bravado in Voronoff's voice was gone, replaced by concern.

Without thinking, Bruno stepped forward and hugged Voronoff. The only time you normally grab someone like this is if you're gonna kill or fuck them, he thought, but it felt strangely comforting. There was a slight gasp of surprise from Voronoff, before he returned Bruno's embrace, patting his back.

'I assume it went well then.' Voronoff said as he stood back and smiled. 'How you feeling?'

Bruno could feel the tears pricking again. 'Like I've just lost my virginity!'

'Well I thought you still were a virgin Bruno.' A howl of laughter burst out from both of them and they turned to leave. Bruno relished the feeling of happiness, but he knew it wasn't likely to last long.

31

Well, that was easier than expected, Marcus thought, watching Bruno and the soldiers leave together. The skills he'd acquired over time were finally beginning to bear fruit. Knowing which buttons to press can get anyone to do anything, and you certainly have the gift for that. Whether it's the multitude or individuals, they can be shaped to your purpose if you know what to lean on and what to avoid. Appeal to emotion, not reason. Find out what they want more than anything else, then promise it, and more to them. Hold it to them as a shining vision. Avoid details. Make them think that your need is theirs. Take them beyond what they want, to what you want, then their wishes and desires are subordinated to yours.

The words of Counsellor Wilhelmus played around in Marcus head.

*

'Please, take this Brother.' Marcus looked into the kindly face while sitting in the doorway wrapped in a soaking blanket. His shivering hands gratefully accepted the coffee, steaming hot and sweet, that was proffered to him. As he sipped the liquid, the heat flowed into him, bringing back life to his frozen, emaciated frame. The rain continued to fall, splashing off the balding head of the counsellor as he stood over the filthy huddled figure of Marcus.

'You look like you need more than coffee my friend; we can give you shelter and food, if you wish.' Wilhelmus said then, motioning to the two ladies accompanying him he offered; 'My sisters and I will provide you with new clothing, a warm bed and a roof over your head until you can get back on your feet.'

Marcus had heard similar things before from the man with the leaflets. He sat still and finished the remaining coffee before shaking his head.

'As you wish brother. We are here if you need us.' Wilhelmus said with a compassionate smile. 'Peace be with you', before he disappeared off into the rain with his companions.

Marcus had forgotten how long he'd been wondering the streets once more, returning to the same doorway that provided a measure of protection from the weather each evening. The days merged into a monotonous grey sameness, broken by the passing glittering wealth of a cosseted few and those who benefitted from them. The world existed as a cycle of day and night, busy and empty, cold or wet. The sodden polystyrene cup was left out in front of him for the kindness of passing stranger's to drop a few spare coins. Sometimes he would find a cup of coffee left there for him. Then there was the not so kind stranger's. The ones who relieved him of his scarce pennies. The groups of drunken young men who urinated on his face while he slept, for the amusement of the equally drunk and tittering young women that accompanied them, before they staggered off into the night laughing at their comic genius.

He spent the late evening waiting for the day's out of date food to be dumped. Marcus had no use for frozen sausages or lasagne, but the slightly mouldy bread or rotten fruit gave him enough to keep going for a couple of days. He'd found a fruit pie once, and quickly stuffed the glittering prize into his ragged overcoat.

'Oi! What you taking you thieving fuck', a man's voice disturbed him. Marcus turned to be confronted by the man. 'Put that back. You should pay for it, like the rest of us.' The sneering mouth exuded selfishness and cruelty.

'It's been thrown away, nobody wants it. I'm not hurting anyone', Marcus protested.

'That's not the point thicko! We could all wait until the food's "out of date" and then take what we want, but no! Some of us work for a living and actually pay for things.' The man gestured to the bins and ordered; 'Now put it back.'

'I'm not taking from anyone. It's not your shop or your food. I...' Marcus felt the pain of the blow and his body didn't have the strength to resist, as he collapsed back into the bins. 'Please don't...', he tried to plead but the cruel kick in his ribs drove the breath from his lungs, while the man laughed and prepared to administer the coup de grace. The vicious smile was all Marcus could see.

'Hey! Leave him alone!' The man turned towards the voice, before giving Marcus a kick in the testicles and spat in his face as he ran off into the anonymity of the city's streets. The whoops of joyful laughter echoing in the distance. Footsteps approached Marcus. 'Brother, are you ok? Let me help you to your feet', said the kind voice of Wilhelmus as a gentle hand took his, and pulled him to his feet. Marcus noticed the crushed fruit pie still under his coat. Trying to stand, a sharp stab of white blinding pain seared through his body, causing him to double over in agony. A wracking cough shook his body.

'You have blood coming from your mouth brother, let me get you to someone who can tend to your wounds', Wilhelmus suggested.

'Thank you but I can't afford a doctor.'

'Don't you worry about that. I know someone who helps us at the hostel. He's a good man.'

'Can I take my pie?' Marcus asked.

'Of course brother of course!' the kindly man said and laughed. 'I'll even heat it up for you.'

The warmth and peace of the hostel embraced Marcus like a long lost friend. The doctor saw to him with a tenderness that only existed as a distant memory.

He'd cracked a couple of ribs and had a bruised kidney, but the most painful thing was the site of the skeletal figure staring back at him from the mirror in his room, as he stripped to take his first shower in months. The filthy yellowed skin covered in scabs, sores and bruises, knees wider than his thighs, the ribs showing through on his chest. The hollowed out face with the bulbous eyes and protruding brown teeth. The lank straggling hair that hung limply from his knobbly cranium, the crazy exploding beard that seem to sprout in all directions. He'd seen films of "Concentration Camps" and the walking dead that took place over two hundred years before. He'd remembered film reports of the Great Heat in the south with the famine and wars that followed. Here was one of those figures that had travelled through time and space, stepping out of the screen and was coming towards him. Shuffling toward the mirror for a closer look, the increasing details revealed new horrors as he eventually came face to face with the thing that was once Marcus Burgman. He put his hand to the mirror trying to touch the face of the stranger that was himself, before looking back at the pile of stinking rags that was all he possessed.

A neat pile of clean new clothes lay folded on the bed. Next to them a small dented box marked, 'Mrs Rudyard's Mixed Fruits of the Forest Pie: Medium', and resting on top of it, a folded piece of paper, crumpled faded and torn. The edged curled, words barely legible, "Crackpot Religions: 16 Steps to..." He'd nearly forgotten about the document and only when he emptied his pockets did he find it. The last piece that seemed to speak to him from another life that was an illusion, shaped by others to mould him into their vision. To empty him of the real Marcus Burgman, replacing it with their thoughts and imaginations, but looking back up there, was the light in the eyes that told him there was enough left of him to shape himself to his own vision. Not as the manipulated puppet of others but as the puppeteer, pulling the strings and shaping the world to his purpose and not the other way around.

He remembered his gift for speaking and how those who were now ashes had held him in high regard and looked up to him. He could put that to good use. But then he realised he'd need some help first as he looked around the room and heard the water running, the steam billowing out of the bathroom. He turned his back on the figure in the mirror and walked toward the shower, ready to wash the old life away. The rain outside had stopped, and the sun shone in through the window.

♦

The reflection stared unerringly back from the bathroom mirror. His hair and beard jet black. No grey showing. No need to apply the dye yet as he smiled to himself. Looking a trim, fit and tanned Marcus. A man in the prime of life in more ways than one and at the height of his powers. It's strange how life can drop someone like Bruno onto your lap. Careful planning, getting the right people in place to move things along, a few flattering words and he was eating out of the palm of my hand. A little research goes a long way. He'd been looking for an 'Enforcer' type for a while and cultivating the soldiers from the SPC seemed the obvious place to start. Having disciples with the wherewithal to lift the personal records of each member and looking carefully through the NCO's seemed a good place to start. Knowing how to read between the lines. Somebody with Bruno's track record of service hitting the old glass ceiling told Marcus all he needed to know.

'An unrivalled ability to carry out orders no matter how difficult', *'Ruthlessly efficient'*, *'Relentless in his pursuit of perfection.'*

Like a machine that goes on and on when pointed in the right direction. Just what I need, especially as he thinks he's in charge of me, the fool. Rule number one; When dealing with egotistical idiots, always let them think it was their idea.

Marcus had waited a long time and was looking forward to working with Sergeant Bruno and his merry men. They can do his dirty work amongst the SPC. One heaped teaspoon, add hot water, stir and et voilà! Instant private army, ready to smooth his path and dispose of those who didn't meet with his approval, as well as seeing off his enemies. Plan ahead Marcus, not one step but several, put the small pieces in place ready for the large ones, on and on ad infinitum. Think of it like a recipe, a dash of treachery here, a sprinkle of manipulation there. Always new fresh ingredients brought in from the most perceptive of suppliers.

The soft alluring voice with a hint of petulance summoned him from the bed. 'Marceee... What are you doing in there? I'm waiting for my reward for bringing your special present. A girl only has so much patience.'

'Coming!' he called back. The sonorous tones replaced by a gentle voice.

'Not yet I hope. That's my job you naughty man.'

Marcus smiled to himself and returned to the bedroom. The girl lay on the bed, dark wavy hair spilling luxuriously across the pillow. He looked on the gentle curves of her body and shook his head in admiration. Has the lord ever created a more perfect combination of beauty, brains and cunning?

She looked up at him coquettishly, pouted her lips and said. 'I thought you were going to stay in there forever. I was going to have to come and get you.'

'Why would I keep my temptress waiting, after all you've done for our cause.' Marcus replied. He touched her cheek and gently ran his fingers to her mouth where she gave them a playful nip. 'Anyway, how can I resist the woman who brought me Valerio Bruno.' He leant forward and gave Naomi Mann a gentle yet passionate kiss, as he prepared to move on to the main course for the evening.

32

Antonina stood before him. Even in the dim light, Aaron could see the rise and fall of her chest as her breathing increased with the passion they both felt for each other. Her hand reached out and gently caressed his face, causing every nerve ending in his body to sing in a heavenly choir of pleasure and excitement. He raised his hand and placed it on hers, sensuously running his fingers over the back of it. The knowing smile that is shared between lovers spread across her face as she took his hand and placed it on her breast. Aaron's knees were knocking with excitement and his breath was coming in short gasps. He could feel the fullness of her under the fabric of her clothing. She seemed so...alive, as if the power of the universe was contained within her, waiting and ready for him to take whatever he desired. Only a millimetre of material stood between him and her naked flesh, as the heat of her body radiated on his hand.

'Would you like me to take it off... Aaron?', she asked playfully. The sound of her voice made him giddy with excitement and anticipation. He gulped hard and nodded as if his life and all those he knew depended on it. Pulling her dress from her shoulders, it seemed to melt away revealing the olive sheen of her perfect complexion.

'I want you Aaron, I've always wanted you and now you're here my darling.', she said.

He reached out. The silken smoothness of her skin felt delicate and yet firm as once again his hand caressed the perfection of beauty before him. Lowering herself to the ground, as his eyes drank in the perfect peach-like roundness of her breasts, the swell of her hips, before settling on the goal he had sought since he first set eyes on her. His clothes seemed to have magically disappeared as if he had undressed in a trance. His pale bare body exposed before her, his excitement obvious as her eyes lit up in anticipation of him. She closed her eyes, waiting for the ecstasy of their union. 'Love me Aaron. I've saved myself for you and now I want to feel you inside me. Hurry please. I can't wait a moment longer', she gasped gently.

He moved towards her, his body one big throb of lust and longing. In his moment of ultimate paradise and triumph, Aaron sensed a movement in the gloom beside him. A hand roughly closed itself over his nose and mouth before shoving him violently to the floor. Over him, looming out of the gloom, the smiling face of Marcus looked down.

Marcus pointed to Aaron's loins and laughed. 'Out of the way loser. You think that sad little twiglet of yours is going to satisfy her. She needs a real man for that.'

Aaron tried to speak but no words came. He watched as Marcus lowered himself down onto Antonina as her legs wrapped around him, sighing and shuddering with pleasure as Marcus grunted with each methodical thrust of his hips. An orange light appeared above Marcus and Antonina, bathing their intertwined bodies in a warm glow. Aaron could see the sweat glistening on Marcus's muscular back. He wanted to plunge a knife into it, the love he once felt transmuting in an instant to an incandescent burning rage of hate.

'Ohh Aaron, you're so strong, so big, so hard …' Antonina cried in that soft voice that seemed so near that it was almost as if she were whispering into his ear, feeling her urgent breath roaring like waves crashing onto a shingle beach. Marcus looked over his shoulder at Aaron and winked cheekily as he increased his speed. Aaron wanted to tell her, warn her of the imposter. Tears of jealousy and frustration coursed down his cheeks, a strangled shout finally escaped his throat but her cries of pleasure filled the air, drowning him out as they reached a screaming crescendo, before leaving her helpless and limp on the ground.

Marcus stood, dusted his hands together as if he had completed a difficult, but necessary task, then let out a satisfied sigh before casually strolling towards Aaron, leaning over him and smiling the familiar smile Aaron had seen so often.

'Remember Aaron, I can take anything I want, anytime I want, and there's *nothing* you can do about it.' Marcus said. He reached and gave Aaron a couple of playful slaps on the cheek. His blue eyes seemed to look deep into Aaron's heart and saw the hate that lurked there. The self-assurance that had been so apparent faltered as a seed of doubt was planted. The orange light hovered over his shoulder almost silhouetting Marcus against a deeper darker shadow.

The low clicking growl came out of the darkness as the Gorthon stood over Marcus, who's face now melted into a mask of manic terror as the scything claw swooped down. Marcus's cry was cut short as the razor sharp edge reached his throat and severed his head with a neat 'schhipp'. His decapitated body slumped silently to one side while his head went the other way, landing next to Aaron facing him, eyes still blinking in surprise, mouth open in silent apology. The Gorthon examined his handiwork before sauntering off back into the shadows that lay beyond.

Aaron sprang to his feet and stood over Marcus's severed head as it still continued looking up at him. The orange light illuminated a tear that trickled down Marcus dead cheek, as Aaron let out a roar of savage triumph. The light seemed to shine brighter. The light that had shown Aaron true power, beyond words, beyond feeling, beyond belief. The light moved closer as Aaron opened his mouth and then swallowed it. All around him was now bathed in the purple glow that embodied the exultation of victory and a sense of being one with an infinity of voices that now existed within him. He knew that he could travel through time and space in an instant. Be anywhere at any time.

He looked down at Marcus head and thought. Look at you and your plastic gods you sad, sad, sad little man, and aimed a kick at the dead face still staring up at him. As his foot made contact with the dead squishy flesh, a jolt of searing pain shot up from his foot and a loud boom rang out. Aaron let out a howl of pain as the books rained down on him, before the shelf next to his bed slowly tipped over and crashed down. He just managed to curl up into a ball and avoid serious injury, sustaining just a few cuts and bruises. As the dust settled in the room, he looked up at the picture of Marcus hanging on the wall. The piercing blue eyes appeared to follow Aaron around the room, sharply reminding him of the Counsellors seemingly omnipotent presence. Somehow he felt it could peer inside his innermost thoughts and dreams. It was required property for all followers of the Great Sky Lord Ykdar. The pain of the bookshelf had driven out the dream from his memory buffer and he felt a vague troubling sense of resentment and doubt towards his leader and messiah.

A loud knock sounded on the door and the familiar voice of Antonina sounded from outside. 'Aaron, Aaron are you ok in there?'

He looked down at his pyjama bottoms and noticed something poking through, before turning back to the door, and smiled to himself.

◆

Billy looked down on the green light Aaron had become from the mindscape. He was now under Billy's control and ready to do his bidding and better still, he was completely unaware of it. An empty vessel waiting to be filled. A new toy to be switched on and pointed in the right direction. The Purple would reward him with its gentle light. The multitude stretching out across the mindscape, hundreds, if not thousands of Mag's sitting silently, like Aaron, ripe and ready to fulfil their destiny. The moment would arrive soon. Very soon...

◆

Her mouth was moving but Bruno couldn't make sense of what she was saying. The words had a strange whooshing quality and her lips were moving differently to the sounds they uttered. The girl laughed, or at least her face said she was

251

laughing, as a hiccupping coughing noise rang out. She took his hand and smiled tenderly.

'sti rouy nrut tahw od uoy tnaw ot od won yddad.'

Each sound was preceded by a 'sssss'. The words were vaguely familiar as if she spoke a wonky version of English, but as he thought he understood a word, it slipped away like a wisp of smoke on a summer breeze.

'I...I can't understand you darling, speak slowly', he said.

She frowned and stamped her little feet in frustration as a trickle of blood ran down from the bullet hole in her forehead. 'I dais sti rouy nrut yddad', came her response. She placed her tiny arms around Bruno's muscular thigh and squeezed it as tight as she could. He gently stroked her soft hair, the love he felt for her total and complete. The freshness of her smile and beauty of her brown eyes made the sun shine brighter and the flowers smell sweeter. 'I evol ouy daddy', she said.

'Daddy?' Bruno exclaimed. 'Yes I'm daddy!' He scooped her up with one arm and held her close, the fragility of her tiny body was too precious for words. The thought of her even suffering the slightest harm or discomfort unbearable. He kissed the pure soft skin of her rosy cheek. I want this feeling to last forever, I never want to let her go.

The whooshing quality of her voice remained, 'Daddy era ew playing eht backwards emag.'

'You're speaking backwards baby, that's it!', Bruno realised.

'Yes daddy, the backwards game.'

He understood her as a switch flipped in his mind. The sounds now made sense.

'Now it's your turn Daddy.' She produced the gun and handed it to Bruno.

Bruno froze with terror and dread. He couldn't lose her; he couldn't hurt her. The sound of blood rushed in his ears and he could feel his racing pulse thundering in his temples, each beat a giant footstep of doom. His hand closed around the cold metal as the tears welled in his eyes.

'No, No, No. Please I can't. Don't leave me my baby', he pleaded.

She looked up at him and wagged her finger disapprovingly.

'Daddy, It's your turn', she said.

Bruno pointed the gun at her head, his finger squeezing the trigger. Each microscopic movement matched by a scrape or a click of the firing mechanism. Desperately trying to stop it, his hand disobeyed him on it's one way trip backwards. He gritted his teeth in a frenzy of effort, spittle spraying as his breaths became increasingly desperate. His mouth opened and let out a helpless scream. 'Don't go please my angel, Daddy loves you, Daddy is sorry, Noooooo! Not my baby. Pleeeeeease!'

'It's your turn daddy.' repeated the little girl implacably.

252

The resistance of the trigger gave way and the hammer drove the firing pin into the cartridge. A distant roar raced over the horizon, the air shimmered as it was displaced by the blast wave approaching them. The flames spurted out of the barrel followed by smoke. Then she was gone.

The abyss of despair swallowed Bruno whole. There was no turning back, no chance to make it right as reality dawned on him in an instant: a sledgehammer destroying him utterly.

33

Confidential
To: Brandon.Schofield@Ateus_Industries.co.uk
From: Celina.Novak@galactic_vistas.com
Subject: Re: Mag Outbreak and next actions

Mr Schofield

As you're aware, events have moved beyond our control. The current status is as follows:

- 44 dead comprised of:
  - Research Lab technicians: 10
  - Security team: 6
  - SPC: 1
  - Civilians: 27

- 63 injured of which.
  - Research Lab technicians: 2
  - Security team: 14
  - Psychic: 1
  - Janitor: 1
  - Civilians: 45

- Status of the injured.
  - Critical: 17
  - Serious: 26
  - Incapacitated: 15
  - Minor Injuries: 5

We've omitted the security team and research lab casualties from the official figures as we don't want to alert the civilians to the scale of the Mag research.

If it wasn't for the quick thinking bravery of a janitor (yes, you read it correctly), things would have been a lot worse. All security protocols have been broken and the civilians are on the edge of hysteria. The SPC has been mobilised to maintain law and order.

Preliminary enquiries points to the power failure three days ago, leading to a breach of the single containment pen which was damaged by the Gorthon, Titus. The door was not forced and a mechanical malfunction was spotted after the Mag attacked the door on a previous occasion. In addition the lockdown procedure was overridden and containment precautions were inadequate. A major review has been expedited into an immediate upgrade for the remaining Mag's containment as well as transportation and production.

We are holding a press conference tomorrow. Our first objective is to contain the situation and not to let the existence of the remaining Mags be known. The main challenge with this of course is the population of scientists that the civilians are now aware of and indeed are hostile to. The question being asked is why so many scientists for a single Mag? Therefore, I propose that we admit there are other Mags within Pangea base but minimise the numbers as well as emphasise the heightened security measures in place. As a further precaution, we have blocked normal email communications for the civilians to and from earth and replaced them with AI correspondents to allay any suspicions. Only priority traffic will be permitted until it's deemed safe to resume normal services. Naturally we'll be scanning the contents of outgoing emails for any signs of dissent. As a fallback position on this we can quote the legitimate reason of the entangled electrons being corrupted after the last CME.

In terms of the reason for the Mag's presence inside the base, we are going to inform them they are here to assist in construction of the settlements, as well as helping in the search for raw materials. The secrecy was due to the adverse publicity of synthetic life forms and we didn't want to cause the public any undue concern, but planned to reveal the Mag's existence upon arrival.

Now the difficult part. The breakout. I propose a culprit is conjured that we can easily pin the blame on, using standard scapegoating procedures perfected in the 20th and 21st Centuries. Preferably one of the dead who was destroyed by their own handywork. We are looking into which one we shall select by fabricating evidence. Remember we must avoid the accusation of lax security and background checks, therefore it must look like the act of a lone wolf. Preferably radical political motivation with anti-company sympathies. All possible blame must be deflected away from the staff and company. Our prime candidate is Dr Wen Chiang who was considered lofty and arrogant amongst her colleagues. We are putting the appropriate measures in place.

As you know, we are keeping a close eye on the CME's (Coronal Mass Ejections) from the parent star Ereus and in particular their interaction

255

with the skewed magnetic field of Magdur which contains the potential to cause havoc. It took nearly a week to get the Fusion Reactor back on line after the last incident. We have contingencies in place if the situation demands.

On the upside, Mag production is being geared up and heading towards full capacity.

Current Mag count stands as follows:

- Gargoyle: 117
- Gorthon: 9
- Bornix: 26
- Hyperthon: 6

If there are any updates I will inform you at the earliest opportunity.
Yours
Celina Novak
Chief Colonisation Administrator

Confidential
To: Celina.Novak@galactic_vistas.com
From: Brandon.Schofield@Ateus_Industries.co.uk
Subject: Re: Mag Outbreak and next actions

Ms Novak
Thank you for your update regarding the current situation which we at Ateus industries are closely monitoring. Naturally we are concerned at the recent developments and although we place no blame on you personally, we would like to remind you of your responsibilities in maintaining the integrity of the Mags. All other considerations are secondary up to and including the staff and civilians. All measures are authorised, including the use of lethal force and the imposition of martial law.

We are relieved that the casualties amongst the research lab staff are not terminal and can be absorbed internally, incurring the minimal impact on Mag production. As the research phase of the Mag project has been successfully concluded and we are in production mode, the lab staff had already fulfilled their primary purpose, therefore losses are not as serious. It was fortunate none of the production staff were harmed and there was no decrease of Mag output. Security team casualties are to be expected and they are trained to operate with a reduced capacity model. Civilian deaths, while regrettable, have minimal bearing on the success or failure of the Mag project and are of little consequence.

I would also suggest that the situation can be exploited in terms of the power of shock and the disorientation of the civilian population, by taking advantage in accelerating the test run of the new social model of disaster society, where the population are quickly frightened into accepting previously intolerable policies and in particular, the environmental and health impact of prolonged exposure to Nadinium. This could then be rolled out amongst other colonisation projects and accelerate its application on earth.

I concur with your email precautions and recommend that potential rabble rousers as well as their followers are neutralised as a matter of the highest priority.

Finally, I will pass on my recommendation of the cleaning company the janitor was sourced from to my colleagues here.

I await your next update with great anticipation.

Yours

Brandon Schofield

Ateus CEO

♦

'I don't give a shit if you think it's a great question. For the third time of asking, will you just answer it!'

'We are aware of the concerns surrounding our research and I'd like to assure everyone that…..' The rest of Celina's words were drowned out by the shouts of anger from the seething audience.

Myra looked across at Celina whose face was flushed. The bright lights in the auditorium made the audience difficult to see, but the anger was unmistakable. Nearly everyone who could attend did, and those who couldn't were watching on screens across the base. The panel of Celina Novak, Myra Alexeyeva, Jordan Harris and Leighton Walker, who was only there to add scientific gravitas and told by all to keep quiet unless directly questioned, faced the audience impassively.

The woman questioning Celina spoke again. 'So let's get this right. We've got a bunch of extremely dangerous creatures somewhere inside this base, similar, if not identical to those that have caused mass casualties back on earth. This minor detail was concealed from us until one of them escaped and killed 28 of our fellow settlers, and this is all for our own good. Have I missed a step somewhere?'

Celina was flustered. 'Let me repeat….', she said, trying to reassure the audience; '….The few remaining prototype Mags are being held in suspended animation until we decide how to proceed now the situation is under control.'

257

A roar of anger and derision burst from the audience. A man with unkempt hair, looking like he'd just climbed out of bed, spoke up.

'Under control? Under con fuckin trol! If this is a joke, it's not very funny. Nearly thirty people dead don't sound very under control to me, or anyone else here', he shouted.

'The Mags are here to help explore Magdur and help you settle. We were aware of the sensitivity surrounding Synthetic lifeforms and were going to inform you when you'd settled', Celina declared.

'Typical arrogance! Caught with their pants down again telling lies and even with their ass hanging out, they still can't come clean. Do you think we're a bunch of children and the truth must be hidden from us otherwise we might be a bit scared and cause trouble. I wonder why you omitted to inform us before we landed here. Well funnily enough, we are scared now. In fact we're absolutely terrified and all you can do is sit there with your stupid official face and silly voice telling us everything is ok and under control because it's all for our own good', the man argued. 'You act like you know, but you don't know shit.'

The colour was draining from Celina's face. She was losing control and Jordan, worried she was about to faint, popped his head above the parapet.

'Everyone's emotions are running high and we understand your fear....', he posited. '....Especially as it was our job to contain or kill this thing.' His authoritative tone took enough of the edge off proceedings. Celina gave him an almost imperceptible nod as he continued. 'But firstly, I'd like to pay tribute to the bravery of Eleanor Wells, the janitor who almost single handedly bought the Gorthon to heel before it was finished off by one of my team. She is currently recovering from her injuries in the infirmary and a lot of people here wouldn't be alive now if it wasn't for her quick thinking and incredible bravery.'

A few people started clapping, quickly joined by others who stood and some cheers broke out as Eleanor's face appeared on the screen. Jordan let the ovation die down, giving himself some thinking time before continuing.

'This was a freak event....', he told them. '....It should never have happened and those whose complacency allowed it have unfortunately paid with their lives.' He looked across at Celina before taking a deep breath then continued. 'It has also come to our attention that there may have been some deliberate acts involved.' There was a gasp throughout the audience. Again Jordan let it hang for a moment before he added; 'Encrypted documents on the folder of a senior figure were uncovered that pointed towards hostile acts. I can reveal no more than that'. There was a silence amongst the audience before a lone voice spoke up.

'You forget something Mister Harris.' Jordan looked puzzled and raised his eyebrow. A large, bald older man stood up. 'We've been fed this bullshit for longer than most of us can remember.....', he said and continued; '....Every time things don't go as planned or something is revealed, there's an attempt to divert it from the real causes. It's never your fault is it. Always someone else's fault or due to unforeseen events. Never being honest and accepting responsibility. The fact that an entire military unit was saved by a bloody cleaner worries me to be honest.' He looked around and this time addressed the audience. '...Or that a person who created these things, now for some reason wants to destroy them, us and themselves, seems a bit implausible to me. It sounds more like "Don't examine our mistakes. Look over there at the scapegoat we conveniently conjured out of thin air". The thing is that people trapped inside this base with these....things, are not the easily manipulated sheep you seem to think we are....', he argued. He held their attention as they remained silent, listening keenly. He spoke honestly with heartfelt convictions. '....All we want is to start a new life away from the lies that now define mother earth, where profit is supreme....', he persisted. '....Where corruption and nepotism are rife, where blind obedience and mediocrity are desirable traits so those above don't feel too threatened by those beneath them. Where they can fuck up and fuck off after filling their bellies at the trough of greed, to be replaced by someone even more stupid and arrogant than they were, who has to clear up the mess left by their predecessors, who *they* conveniently blame and so the whole self-perpetuating circus of bullshit continues. As long as they're insulated from the effects of their decisions that's ok and fuck everyone else. A planet run by cunts for the sole benefit of cunts.' There was a small stirring at the language used in a public meeting. He noticed this, paused then continued; '....I apologise for my choice of words, but they're the only ones strong enough to describe them. And you....!', he turned and pointed to the panel on the stage and carried on; '....are their stooges. Sent to soothe us with empty platitudes, but you know we're right. But all we want is a clean break from the planet that you and your friends raped with your greed and malice. We didn't come this far to be lied to yet again.'

Again spontaneous applause burst from the audience. The bald man sat back down while he was heartily patted on the back by those surrounding him, except the lady next to him who rubbed top of his head and kissed him on the cheek.

As the applause died down, all eyes turned to the striking figure in the shining white robes who stood in the centre of the audience, arms out and hands down in a calming gesture. There was the familiar hush before Marcus spoke.

'First of all before I speak, I'd like everyone to take a moment to think about those who have lost their lives in this tragedy....', he intoned and went on; '....No matter what their role, they had people who cherished them and it's important to remember them.' There were some quiet sobs, otherwise total silence for a few moments. 'Now I think we need to consider what it is we want next....', Marcus maintained; '....Having widely consulted amongst my brothers and sisters, top of that list would be security and safety.' He looked around the audience at the heads nodding in agreement. 'The one thing that would guarantee that, would be the removal of the evil creatures that have stained our promised utopia.' A few voices murmured in agreement but the majority remained respectfully quiet. Celina and Jordan looked at each other aghast as Marcus added; 'I'm sure these things were created with the best of intentions, but after the recent events how can we hold them in anything other than fear and suspicion.'

Then Jordan spoke. 'We've ceased research and the small number of prototypes creatures will be returned to earth for further development, but we're not going to destroy them. They are no further threat to anyone.'

'Mister Harris.....', Marcus addressed Jordan;. '....I know you are an honourable man and act with the best of intentions but you disregard the words of the people at your peril. I certainly wouldn't want anyone to take matters into their own hands, but people are frightened and frightened people do desperate things. Things that, upon reflection, they may come to regret, but at the time feel is their only option.'

Across the other side of the room Aaron stood up.

'At least there is someone in authority on this planet who has the best interests of the settlers at heart and is prepared to tell the truth. Death to the Beasts!', he asserted.

The cry was repeated around the auditorium. Marcus looked around the room, briefly catching the eye of Naomi, sitting near Bruno before his gaze returned to Jordan staring out at him. A smile briefly flickered across Marcus's lips.

'You see Mister Harris. People are scared and they look to you to do the right thing. I would consider your next actions very carefully indeed if I were you', the Counsellor cautioned.

Jordan looked helplessly out as the crowd's anger continued unabated. Marcus held his arms out in his well-practiced way to calm them. 'I think we should give our esteemed friends on the panel some time to reconsider their position, before we reconvene tomorrow.', he suggested.

'They're not my friends but I'd certainly like to see them steamed', called a voice to much laughter and hoots of derision.

Jordan wasted no time in seizing the opportunity afforded him by Marcus and promptly stood. 'The meeting's adjourned and will meet again tomorrow at the same time. Please leave in an orderly fashion.', he said as he turned to the others and quietly mouthed, 'We are fucked...' They all nodded in agreement.

34

'**We** have them on the rack brothers and sisters. Look at their desperate eyes, how they swivelled from side to side. You can almost hear their brains whirring away.' Marcus spoke. There was a laugh from the small group gathered in the contemplation room as he continued. 'Our efforts over the past couple of days have presented us with a once in a lifetime opportunity.' He looked around at the faces huddled closely together. Leon was nodding in earnest agreement. Although there was fear, there was also excitement that their moment had arrived. 'Think back on Earth how we were struggling, how our message was unheard....', Marcus continued; 'The dark days where there was no hope and only our faith bound us together. But we struggled through, and we formulated a plan to travel on a voyage together to sow the seeds of a new pure society.'

'We know that counsellor, but...', It was Aaron who spoke up. He seemed to have gained confidence over the past few days but he was also Marcus's single point of concern amongst the group of closest followers. He didn't possess the quivering fear that had once crippled him, instead, it had been replaced by a difficult questioning nature that had started to grate. When he had been selected to join them, Marcus had thought he would be the easiest to shape to his purpose, but what had emerged did not please him.

'But what, brother Aaron? Please share your thoughts with us.' Marcus responded icily and fixed Aaron with his steely blue gaze which used to be enough to cow anyone who crossed him.

'I'm uneasy at the way we are...' Aaron appeared to be searching for the right words. Marcus had to suppress a snort of impatience as Aaron finally asserted; '....Leading the congregation.'

'Well of course we are leading them brother. That's what leaders do.' An edge of irritation had crept into Marcus's voice that he didn't intend.

Aaron persisted 'Perhaps I chose the wrong word counsellor Marcus.' He seemed to be emboldened and continued. 'You tell us that we are being lied to by the leadership of the base, and rightly so, and yet I feel that we are also being...'.

'Dishonest? Brother Aaron....?' Marcus hissed. This dissent must be crushed at source, he reasoned. 'You put us in the same category as those lying snakes that claim to lead us? Do I understand you correctly?' The normally moderated voice of Marcus was replaced with a vehemence that shocked even those who had previously heard it on the rare occasions it was used. An uncomfortable air permeated the room. Marcus noted with satisfaction that Aaron's face was flushed as all eyes turned to him. But still Aaron stood his ground.

'No Counsellor....', he enjoined; '....I wasn't going to use that word. I would never use that word about you.' Marcus smiled to himself, but Aaron would not be browbeaten. 'But my point is, we say that we are escaping the lies of earth, and yet we stand up at the given keywords and shout the phrases you have given us. The words you put in our mouths. These are not the things you teach us to believe, and yet I feel we are manipulating the congregation and playing on their fear. That's' what makes me uneasy. I want to be pure in thoughts and actions.'

Marcus had anticipated such a moment, but it surprised him that a snivelling weakling like Aaron was the one to express it. Did it reflect a wider view amongst the following? A broad smile beamed from Marcus's face as he stood and leant over Aaron to embrace him.

'Oh brother Aaron. Forgive me. I have misjudged you.' As Marcus stood back up, he noted with satisfaction the look of puzzlement on Aaron's face. 'We all share your wish for purity and it's heartening that you express it so', the Counsellor said. The others around the room broke into smiles. 'Of course we're not deceiving the congregation, but guiding them....', Marcus continued; '....Overcoming their trepidation, and the leadership we are all showing encourages them to lose their fear. And you my brothers and sisters are the expression of the Lord Ykdar's will. To take heed of his words and convey them to the masses. Why do you think we have arrived at this moment of greatest opportunity now? Because of his guidance.' The glazed wondrous smile returned to Aaron's face. 'Think of the words that were spoken today....', Marcus went on; '....If we hadn't initiated those thoughts in their minds, the words would not have come forth from their mouths, and all of you were doing the Great Lord's will. Now let us embrace!' They all rose as one and Marcus worked his way around the room embracing each in turn until at last he came to Aaron. Marcus looked into his eyes smiling benevolently. 'My purest disciple.'

Once again the tears flooded freely down Aaron's weak face. But looking at him Marcus was already seeing him in the past tense, as if he were viewing a picture of his dear long lost mother. The only difference was that Aaron hadn't been lost yet. But that would happen soon enough.

The warning Attilio had given him earlier that morning was true. Aaron was the traitor within and would be dealt with. The charlatan had come good at last.

♦

'You have a gift my boy and you must use it to do good.' Marcus listened intently to the words of Wilhelmus. He had become the kindly man's assistant in his work of assisting the homeless scattered across the city.

'Thank you Counsellor. I try to please you and the Great Lord Ykdar.' He felt love for Wilhelmus but even now he was moving beyond the benevolent aims of his mentor.

Wilhelmus had allowed Marcus to speak at some of the services and told him he was captivated with his ability to hold an audience in the palm of his hand. Wilhelmus was also aware of the effect Marcus had on the younger ladies of his commune. In particular, young Naomi Mann who they had rescued from the hell of addiction. But the year Marcus spent in the community of Wilhelmus had given him the stability he needed to strike in a different direction.

As the year passed, Marcus found that he and Naomi were closer. Not only ideologically, but physically and emotionally. She told him how she had fled her tyrannical father who wanted to push her into the military, recalled the hell of living in the streets and of the attacks and the abuse. He and Wilhelmus had rescued her from that. But also, she shared his vision for the world. Where money would not hold the people hostage. Where the teachings would be paramount. But he knew that they had to have a plan. A series of steps that was provided in 'Crackpot Religions'. The steps dictated a plan to recruit followers for their pure vision. To draw them in with words and capture them with a sense of obligation and loyalty. Social isolation and group polarisation where people only mixed with those who agreed, so they are more afraid of the outside world than the constraints of their own community. No room for dissent.

But it was difficult to be isolated on a planet of twelve billion, increasingly squeezed into two narrow bands either side of the uninhabitable hot zone that straddled the equator. Then there was the migrations made possible by the miraculous discovery of The Tube and the terraforming of new planetary homes. The opportunities offered were unbounded. The restrictions of earth cast aside. Marcus had tried to recruit from other branches of the Lords Ykdar's' family but he'd been rejected time and time again. Then the day arrived which nearly killed him, but also showed him the way forward. The day the militia arrived at his door.

The location didn't help. Trying to achieve isolation to enhance the group had its drawbacks on this occasion. Maybe someone tried a bit too aggressively with one of the larger cults. It certainly wasn't because they were a threat with just twelve members living in the old manor house. But Marcus smelt danger when the group of vehicles approached during the evening prayer meeting. He sent one of his followers out to investigate. He was met with shots and shouts as the grenades crashed in through the windows. Marcus dived onto Naomi and pushed her through the door, just as the explosion tore through the room. He looked back to see five of the group lying dead. The remainder staggering around, some screaming, others groaning incoherently. Brother Timothy looking passively at his intestines that hung limply from a hole that was once his stomach, trying to stuff them back inside in case anybody noticed first. But no matter how he tried they just kept slipping back out again. Marcus was about to move forward to help him, when the shots ripped into Timothy as the Militia member sprayed the room with bullets. Timothy performed a brief jerking dance before he fell to the floor dead, like a puppet with the strings cut. The passive expression remaining fixed on Timothy's face. The thick wooden door protecting Marcus and Naomi. The figure started walking toward the door and they moved away just as he appeared.

'Is that all of 'em?' said another voice.

'I thought I heard something.'

There was a screaming and one of the other Militiamen dragged Sister Anja by her hair. 'Hey look what I found!'

Marcus could hear Anja's laboured breathing. 'p... p... please don't hurt me. I'm no threat.'

There was a loud thud as one of the men kicked Anja in the stomach. 'Shadup bitch!' A wheezing groan was the only response. 'You fuckin talk when we tell ya! Got it?' The groaning had been replaced by a whimper.

Marcus turned to Naomi, her face a pallid mask that surrounded her bulging eyes. She was shaking as a burst of laughter came from the other room, followed by the sound of clothing being ripped and a pleading voice. 'No, no please don't.'

A loud slap sounded, followed by the second voice. 'I thought we told you to shut ya mouth. Looks like she needs a softening up lads. Who's first!' A loud cheer went up which was met by even louder screams.

Marcus looked down at his trembling hands. Never in his life had he felt so powerless, so miserable, so empty. He considered bursting in and grabbing a gun and mowing them all down. Tears of impotent rage ran down his cheeks as the rhythmic clapping started along with the 'go, go, go, go!' Anja's cries filled the house as Marcus quietly led Naomi out of the room to the cellar. The calls for help, the clapping and the shouts fading into the background.

Marcus had discovered a 'priest hole' in the cellar when he first moved into the house. A small recess with a hidden door that catholic preachers had hidden during the reformation. Seven hundred years later it had found new occupants.

Anja's screams dulled to a muffled distant sound. There was an occasional rise in the cheering and cries, but it gradually died down, ending with a single shot. A loud boom reverberated through Marcus's nerves as the door to the cellar was kicked open. The thump of footsteps coming down the stairs and the harsh voices.

264

In the pitch black he put his hand over Naomi's mouth as a keening groan crept out. Her breathing coming in snorts through her nostrils.

'Make a noise and we die', Marcus whispered in her ear. 'You wanna end up like Anja?' He felt her shake her head. The footsteps came closer. A knocking sound on the wall made its way towards them, moving closer. Then he reached the secret door. Another knock even louder.

'Hey hurry up down there! We ain't got all night. Reukers told us get in and out quick.'

'Hold on I think I've found something.' Marcus blood froze. He was having trouble breathing. His tongue seemed to swell in his mouth, suffocating him.

'Look, we've got to go. Now!', the brushing of a hand sounded against the outside of the door. 'You found anything?'

There was a pause then an irritated hiss as the footsteps moved away and started up the stairs. Marcus let out a long agonised breath. There was the sound of something tumbling down the stairs followed a moment later by a deafening explosion. Splinters of wood filled the small void as Naomi let out a scream. Choking smoke filled the priest hole. Marcus pushed the door open. Better to die by shooting than choking to death. A loud scrape reverberated around the cellar. The glow of pre-dawn light hesitantly shone through the broken slit window, as they stumbled towards it to gulp in some fresh air. The sound of the vehicles crunched along the drive as they sped off into the distance. The cracking and roar of flames could be heard from upstairs. They rushed up the stairs as the fire took hold. Past the naked and battered body of Anja, sprawled across the contemplation room. The look of unendurable horror frozen on her dead face. A neat bullet hole in her forehead. Some huddled in a corner, embracing in death as Marcus and Naomi burst out into the open.

They ran and looked back at the inferno that was once their home. Turning to see Naomi sitting motionless on the grass, he looked down to her empty shocked face. 'This will be avenged. I swear by the blood of Ykdar they will pay. Their guts will be spilled on the ground and they will beg for death', he vowed.

Naomi looked up at him. Her face blackened and hair matted. 'Yeah? Really? How you gonna do that? Preach them to death perhaps?'

Marcus knew she was right, but not for long. He pulled out the little plastic wallet containing 'Crackpot religions' and peeled out the paper.

> *10. Ruthlessly crush any hint of dissent like humour, initiative, awkward questions or disobedience. A good time to employ "Enforcers" of the religion.*

The name they had said, what was it again...Marcus racked his memory. Come on, come on, come on Marcus think, think... Reukers! That was it. Well Mister

Reukers you sound like just the type of person I need on my side. I'm going to find out a bit about you and your methods before I eventually relieve you of your vital organs one by one.

'The Lord Ykdar will provide an answer. I know it', Marcus said as the germ of an idea started to take shape. 'Use whatever materials are to hand...' he said quietly to himself as the flames popped and smoke rose into the early morning light. The glowing red embers swirling around before they drifted lazily on the wind and across the river. Naomi's face illuminated by the bright red glow of the inferno looked expectantly at him. 'I know what to do...' he said gently to her.

◆

'Did you think about me while I was at the Academy?'

'Why would I not think about you?'

'Don't answer a question with another question. You know how much I hate that.'

'I only do that when I hear a stupid question.'

'I thought of you. Often. Particularly when Bruno was on top of me humping away like a big smelly bear.'

'I hope you shouted in ecstasy at the appropriate moment.'

'With the utmost enthusiasm. Don't you feel jealous about that brute fuckin me?'

'I knew it was for the greater good.'

'And did you fuck anyone while I was away?'

'Of course. I told you I would. But it didn't feel the same.'

'How noble of you.'

'You asked. If you don't like the answer, don't ask the question. Anyway, why should you have all the fun.'

'Fun! Is that what you call it? Carrying a fifty-pound backpack and weapon in the pissing rain and pitch black is not fun. Having to navigate, having Eleanor Buckley shouting at me. Calling me a "snivelling failure". That's not fun either.'

'Still, you won top recruit. It can't have been all bad.'

'I did what I had to. I looked through the records. I selected the most ruthless one and I fucked him. All while screwing over somebody I actually looked up to and considered a friend.'

'Why did he set her up like that? Did he say anything?'

'He told me she was going to have me disqualified, so she could win top recruit. As if! He really takes me for an imbecile.'

'Naturally you were appropriately alarmed and credulous.'

266

'Of course. I had to go along with the whole charade. It was the worst part. Even worse than Bruno slavering his sweaty smelly mass all over me like a horny baboon. Don't laugh! It's not funny.'

'It's the way you put it.'

'Well, I deserved an award for my acting. Sobbing like a damsel in distress. I surprised myself, I must say.'

'But what made him do it?'

'I think he fancied his chances with her. Bit of a challenge after an easy lay like me. But I think he bit off more than he could chew with her. She probably rejected his advances. Might have kicked his ass by the look of it.'

'What, a tiny thing like her?'

'You saw what she did to the monster. Bruno would be a piece of cake after that. I noticed he was limping for a couple of days before the court martial. Probably kicked him in the balls!'

'Well you did it my lovely. We got our man and we've got our Militia. All thanks to our clever Naomi.'

'Getting the posting to Magdur was easy. A few words with Daddy and digging some dirt and he's ours, the sweaty bastard.'

'I know. Frightening off the other candidates for the position of counsellor was actually fun. The thing is, I didn't expect to actually be so scary, but we can use it to our advantage. So, this Eleanor. She's on Magdur, inside the base with us now?'

'Yes it was definitely her. I caught her watching me while I was in the shopping mall a few weeks ago. I looked her up on the base personnel file. Eleanor Wells. She only changed her surname. But why? Why would she become a stowaway on an interstellar voyage to a planet, 500 light years from home over a failed course? That's what I can't understand.'

'There's obviously more to it. Shall I get someone to befriend her?'

'Well nobody can get near her at the moment. She's in the infirmary. But I bet she knows who you are. You could be her friend. The mighty Counsellor Marcus Burgman. Master of Magdur.'

'You may laugh, but did you see them when I was speaking?'

'I was very proud of my Marcee. You surpassed yourself my darling. Brother Wilhelmus was right. You do have a gift.'

'She'll be dazzled when I speak to her. "That nasty Bruno hit me sir." "Don't you worry your pretty little head Eleanor. Uncle Marcus will take care of him."'

'She won't be that easy. But talking of Bruno. What are we going to do about him? I can't have him fucking me forever! I'd rather die.'

'I know, but we can't have him blowing our cover.'

'Can't you get him sort of... killed? A bit...?'

We'll need him for the short term until I establish control. Meanwhile I think you need to get on board with his lot. You can keep a watchful eye on him. I'll be rid of him as soon as we don't need him. I promise.'

'Please. How much more do I have to go through? Haven't I done enough already.'

'We can't do it without him at the moment. We'd never have got this far without you. Killing the remaining few Mags will establish me as unsurpassable leader. We overthrow the council and take control of Pangea base. Magdur is our oyster. To establish a new society. We'll be like the pilgrim fathers landing from the Mayflower.'

'Marceee. You're not talking to the congregation now. I've heard it all before remember?'

'Well I have to practice on somebody.'

'You're a genius.'

'I know, that's why you love me, my little shrew.'

'Err, what's your hand doing there?'

'Nothing at the moment. Why where do you want it to be?'

'Higher...'

'As you wish my sweet...'

35

To: Michelle J. Farrington @ electron.com
From: robert.nash@galactic_vistas.com
Subject: Re: They are liars!

Dear Michelle

Just a quick note Michelle as a lot is happening. Our leader, our saviour had the liars on toast. They were snivelling squirming little weasels as he tore their mealy mouthed lies into little shreds. I've never seen Cunningham and Heath so angry, but Preston just sat shaking his head, the weakling. I'm glad Amy and the boys weren't here to witness it. It's scary enough already. There were some rabble rousers (The foul mouthed fat man in particular from the meeting with that Novak) but Marcus rose above the abuse and drove a knife into their cold hearts. At the end they were sitting there like a row of nodding dogs with vacant eyes. Our moment is fast arriving!!

I'll send you an update in the next couple of days.

Bless the sky lord and hail Marcus! Our Saviour!

Rob xx

36

The first lesson in service tunnel navigation wasn't going well. They stood in a semi-circle facing Nicklas who asked;

'Bruno, I'm asking you again. What is the quickest service tunnel route from section A5 to D7?' It's easy.'

Bruno shrugged, turned his mouth down and raised his eyebrows in mock confusion. 'Dunno, maybe you could enlighten us.' He looked over at the SPC guys and winked. A few titters rippled through the tension. He could see Nicklas' face getting redder as the vein on his forehead pulsated. Like a teacher trying to lay down the law to a difficult classroom, Nicklas had tried to impose his authority, and like countless others over the years, had his efforts thrown laughingly back in his face.

Nicklas had given Bruno a simple task to remember. His patronising tone had rubbed Bruno and his squad up the wrong way from the first minute. The session wore on and the jokes and titters wore away at Nicklas' patience, still Bruno didn't sense any danger. After all, there were ten of them, each more than a match for the eel of a man.

'You think you're the real deal don't you, standing there in front of the bunch of losers you call a squad....', Nicklas said and continued; '....I hope you get stuck in the open when the shit hits the fan, because it will, mark my words.' The giggling had stopped, replaced by mutterings of dissent and contempt. 'And you, chief fuckwit.... I can't wait until you come up against a fully grown Gorthon. You'll shit your knickers and start crying for mummy.'

'What did you call me, fucker...?' Bruno could feel the expectant stare of his squad. There was no way this could be allowed to pass. He drew up to his full height and strode towards Nicklas, his fist drawn back ready to splatter his face all over the room. As he got within reach, a whoosh of air was driven from his lungs as Nicklas drove his fist into his solar plexus. The strength in Bruno's legs drained away and he collapsed to his knees gasping for air. Looking up at Nicklas who was now standing a few feet away, with the hint of a smile on his face, he thought; This wasn't how it was meant to be. I'm twice as big as him, this can't be happening. Even though Nicklas was twice as fast, one punch should have done the job. But it didn't because he couldn't land one. In fact, he'd got nowhere near him.

Nicklas' wiry lean frame walked towards Bruno and leant down, looking into his puce face, with the mouth open, desperately trying to draw breath and repeated; 'I said you are a fuckwit.'

Bruno looked into the steel grey eyes. The words that had started the fight seemed a lifetime ago, but could have only been ten seconds in a far off land of a different reality. The land where Bruno's rule was undisputed. The land where Nicklas' words were met with disdainful smirks and crafty winks amongst the SPC. That was then. A lot had happened since, as the stunned silence of the SPC rang out, only the scuffling of feet and the occasional clearing of a throat could be heard. When the flash point came, it was sudden and brutal.

Now Bruno looked up into the eyes of his adversary. He caught a shadow out of the corner of his eye, as the metal pole smashed down on Nicklas' head. The look of calm contemplation replaced by the contortion of shock. A boot swung up into his face sending a spray of blood arcing into the air. Nicklas instinctively curled up into a ball, as the remainder of the squad rained down kicks and punches on him.

A swell of triumph burst inside Bruno's chest as he staggered to his feet. 'Hold it!', he said and raised his hand. 'Don't kill him. Yet...' The thrashing, thudding impact of the assault stopped as suddenly as it started.

Nicklas uncurled from the protective ball, looked up at Bruno and smiled. 'Quite the hero when you're backed up by your mates, aren't you little man...?', he spat the words out disdainfully.

A roaring sound started to fill Bruno's ears as his vision became a single red circle in the distance. The humiliation piled upon humiliation drove him to an eruption of rage and violence as this time his fist found its mark. The cracking and crunching of Nicklas' nose was music to Bruno's ears. Looking down at the bleeding unconscious figure, he drove a kick into Nicklas' ribs before spitting in his face.

'Don't mess with the SPC Fish Brains.' He turned around to his squad who stood silently watching. 'C'mon let's go, enough of this hide and seek shit.' They turned as one, leaving the room to the unconscious, bleeding Nicklas.

37

Ava's patience was beginning to wear thin. The sound of Elizabeth's voice was grating on her raging heart and broken soul, as the words seemed to penetrate beyond her ears and brain, to her inner core, stabbing mercilessly at the raw nerves that hummed with pain. It wasn't so much what she was saying, but the 'thank goodness I'm ok' tone that rasped across her fresh suppurating wounds.

'I'm telling you; it was pure luck that we escaped alive, another couple of minutes and we'd have joined poor Doctors Khan and Chiang', She said.

'"We"? Who's "We"?', Ava felt the momentary silence, before Elizabeth responded.

'Doctor Walker and myself of course...'

'Yes, it really is a big consolation to me to know dear Leighton is alive and well.' Ava retorted sarcastically. 'I can now face the future with fresh optimism in my heart.'

'There's no need for that. I thought you'd be pleased we're ok', Elizabeth replied. The sharp manner of Elizabeth's voice was a welcome change to the self-satisfied crowing that irked Ava so much.

'I'm pleased *you're* ok Liz.'

'But not Doctor Walker?', Elizabeth asked her.

'I'm not *as* pleased as I am that you are ok. But one less death is always welcome news I suppose, despite how I feel about him.' Ava said.

'You suppose. Really? I don't detect much... magnanimity in your tone....' Ava could sense the tension in the air before Elizabeth continued. '...Oh well *I* suppose some people are uncomfortable with the mantle of saviour, especially at such a cost to themselves.'

Elizabeth's words were the spark that ignited a flame of fury that flared up to consume what little patience remained in Ava's tortured mind. 'WHAT the hell do you mean by that?' She demanded. Shocked by the sound of her own voice Ava went on; 'What I'd like to know is why you're defending him? Why is it anytime I say anything, even slightly critical of your beloved Leighton, you suddenly come over all protective about the goddamn son of a bitch?' Despite Elizabeth's sharp intake of breath Ava continued. 'I'd love to know what hold he's got over you. The man's a slime ball and YES I would have picked the little creep to replace any of those poor people who died.'

One of the nurses approached.

'Excuse me....', she said; '...Can you keep the noise down please. You're upsetting the other patients.'

Ava heard the sound of Elizabeth's chair scraping back as she stood. 'It's ok nurse I was about to leave.' She turned to Ava 'I understand you're going through a tough time at the moment and I'll leave you to recuperate. You're plainly not yourself. I'll see you tomorrow when hopefully you'll be in a more positive frame of mind.'

Ava deigned not to answer.

'Time for your rest period Miss Matthews.', Ava felt the nurse's hands on her arm while the syringe injected its cold sleep into her. Elizabeth's footsteps faded into the distance while the first glimmerings of remorse began to shine on the horizon of her conscience as Ava drifted off to sleep.

♦

'Your physical wounds have healed Eleanor, but the mental ones... That's going to take a while longer as we both know.'

'So, I'm free to go Doctor?' Eleanor let out a sigh of relief.

'Yes, but you're going to have to take it easy for a while. No fighting with gigantic all killing indestructible monsters. Try to avoid that kind of thing if possible.', the doctor advised.

Eleanor laughed. She found it strange that over the past few days, when she'd faced unimaginable danger and had been plunged into an apocalyptic situation, that laughter returned to her life. Montano's visits had helped, but there was a sense of relief which was strange in the circumstances. Even the voice had been subdued. *Enjoy the fun Ellie, because the shit's gonna hit the large propeller pretty soon, and you're in line for a big fat mouthful.* Maybe, but I feel like a large stone of guilt has been lifted from my chest. *Yeah...To be replaced by an even bigger one dropping out of the sky and squashing your tiny head. Anyway what about the* Mags? *You think they're just gonna lay down and die? No way Pedro.* She'd watched the meeting at the Auditorium, and felt her face burning with embarrassment when her picture appeared on the screen, the ovation echoed in the infirmary, pretending not to notice as her ID photo stared back at the base. *Well look at Ellie, proper little celebrity now aren't we. Even got your own stage name Miss Buckley, ooops sorry...Wells. Like a porn star. Well I won't be doing the money shot with ya!* Eleanor's cover was well and truly blown, and it was only a matter of time before Bruno and Naomi exposed her. What were you thinking Eleanor? Chasing those two all this way? What did you really expect to achieve...., she asked herself. What a mess. *Yep. I agree with you on that Ellie. Exposed as the crazy lying bitch you've always been and returned to earth in chains. It's all over*. Not necessarily. There's a window where I could expose them. Ok it won't be as good as slowly castrating Bruno and cutting Naomi's lying tongue out of her stupid head, but at least there'll be some justice. *So ya think people are going to believe you just because you killed a big fuck off monster.* Well I won't let them dictate the agenda this time. I'll make sure they're on the back foot. *So people will look at Ellie the vengeful twisted figure and think she'll stop at nothing for her own vindictive ends.* No. I'll tell them that I wanted to work my passage to Magdur and a new life. I didn't know they were on Magdur. *Ohh what an incredible coincidence. I'm completely sure that everyone will meekly take it at face value and not ask any awkward questions.* You got a better plan? No? Good, thought not. Now shut up and fuck off. *Yeah fuck you as well Ellie.*

'Eleanor?' Akeely Fergusons voice momentarily startled her. 'Are you ok?'

'Sorry Doctor. I was just thinking about Ava.' The lie came easily to Eleanor. She'd become well practiced at living them. *See! Lying fuckin bitch, just like I've been saying all along. Nobody knows you like I do Ellie...*

'Of course. She's your friend. I understand.' Akeely adopted a concerned air as she spoke; 'I can tell you how she is physically, which is that her wounds are healing as expected, except the eyes. There's no prospect of her seeing again in the short term. Maybe in a couple of years, but we haven't got that sort of expertise on Magdur, so she'll have to be casevaced back to earth. As far as the psychological aspects, I can't tell. She's taking food and drink, which is a good sign. But she's just lain on the bed for the past three days and hardly said a word to anyone. The only exercise are trips to the bathroom, otherwise completely silent and inert, apart from the steady stream of tears trickling from under the eye dressings.'

'Should I try and speak to her yet?' Eleanor's heart was heavy for her only friend before the outbreak. She wasn't going to abandon her.

'That may be an idea Eleanor. I'll speak with her first.'

All your fault Ellie, all yours.

I thought I'd told you to fuck off.

♦

The nurse was standing over her examining her eyes. The torch glinting and she could even see the reflection of her retina, as pink and fresh as a slice of Salmon. Ava wanted to tell her, but even when the words came out, the nurse blithely ignored her.

'Ok Ava, I'm just going to replace the dressings now.' The nurse turned her back and went to the trolley.

'I can see you. Why are you not answering me?'

'Here we are. Ok if you could raise you head slightly for me.' Her cheery tone exasperated and infuriated Ava.

'Are you deaf? There's no need for this. I can see you perfectly well.' Ava wanted to raise her hands, but no matter how hard she tried they wouldn't move.

The nurse spoke to someone on the other side of the ward. 'I'm just dressing Miss Matthews's wounds. I'll be over in a min...', She jerked violently before looking down at her blue nursing scrubs where the blood soaked claw was protruding from her stomach. Her mouth sagged open as the blood surged out from it. A ripping, sucking sound accompanied the claw, slicing up through her chest while her arms spasmed frantically. It exited just to the right of her neck, letting her body peel open like a ripe fruit, the contents slipping out in a glutinous mess, before she sank to the floor.

The pink and grey shape loomed behind her, skin shimmering in waves of red and purple. The low rumble interspersed with percussive clicks made Ava's trembling body reverberate. The empty sockets where the eyes had once been seemed to be the gateway to eternity. She could see the darkness contained within them as they moved closer. The mouth drawn back in a surreal imitation of a smile, revealing the gleaming teeth, silver strands of Mag saliva drawn out in angelic harp strings across the opening. 'I've come for you Ava. I've taken your eyes and now the rest of you is going to follow'.

The pins and needles started in Ava's hands, spreading up her arm, across her chest, closing up her throat and restricting her breathing. Raising her numbed arm, she reached out to the hideous face before her, touching the cold clammy skin, sending a shiver of revulsion through her. Spreading her fingers out, obscuring the features, she wrapped her hand around the rapidly shrinking head of the Mag.

'You've taken all you'll ever get from me. I won't give a single atom more', before she started to squeeze, feeling the satisfying crack of the Gorthon's skull, its body shuddering and withering away. Diminishing to a husk and shrivelling down to a dry naked nub, before vaporising in a small puff. A sense of strength and invincibility coursed through Ava's being, as she opened her eyes to darkness. The mindscape was slowly returning, obscured. There was something. The blankness of the past few days had been replaced, by what, Ava couldn't tell. Each hour it became clearer. More vivid.

Where did it begin? Where did the feeling come from? It seemed familiar but it evaporated like a half remembered childhood dream that disappeared as the sun shone through the blinds, filling her room with it's warm golden light. There was no start, only a white noise growing over the last couple of days. Then the face appeared. It was talking but the voice was muffled and out of sync with the lips.

The face looked grave and attentive. Sometimes another face would appear, younger, red eyed and pale faced. The background was washed out and hazy, still the voice was distant. Then there was the Gorthon, filling her vision, looking... inquisitive, then blood. Everywhere. The faces would return, then it was blank again. So it had continued in a cycle, but slightly different, each time clearer than the last. She had also noticed she could switch the visions on and off at will. Not that Ava kept them off for any length of time, preferring them to the blackness of the sightless prison that was now the inside of her head.

At that moment the grave face was bringing a cup towards her. Tipping it gently so that the top of the cup obscured the lower half of her face. The cup was moved away and the face smiled.

Ava was thirsty; her throat was parched. She reached out for the cup that was left beside her bed. She'd had difficulty in estimating the distance to objects since the outbreak. A sharp pain shot up her arm as she struck the nerve on her elbow hard against the bedside cabinet.

'Goddammit!' Ava startled herself with the loudness of her own voice.

The face in the vision turned and looked over her shoulder and disappeared from view. The young face was also looking over in the same direction. The voice grew louder. Strange, she's moved away but I can hear her better. The vision looked up and the back of the figure was walking away. It was wearing a light blue outfit.

'Ava, are you ok? Let me help you.'

Ava immediately recognised it as the distant voice she'd been hearing!

'It's you', she said.

'Of course it's me Ava, everyone else is off duty.'

'No, I meant the voice I could hear.'

'I'm sorry. Nurse Barnes is off duty today, so I've been covering. I'm Nurse Amanda Holloman. I'm sorry if I was making too much noise. I was tending to young Sophia over there. Don't worry about your drink, I'll get you another. Would you like me to adjust your bed and make you more comfortable?'

'Yes please Amanda, thank you.' Ava felt the gentle hands of the nurse helping her to sit upright. The figure in the vision was leaning over somebody lying in a bed in the distance.

'There you are. Better?', Nurse Amanda asked.

The figure stepped away from the bed to reveal another figure sitting up with bandaged eyes. It was Ava. She gasped and put her hand to her mouth at the same instant the figure did the same.

'Oh my god!' Ava's heart was pounding in her chest and a sob escaped.

'Ava? Is there something wrong?', the nurse asked her.

276

'I... I'm sorry, I'm just having a moment.'

'I understand. I know it's hard now, but if Doctor Ferguson thinks you'll be ok, then I believe her.' Amanda handed her a drink. The figure on the bed took the drink, raised it to her mouth, and Ava felt the quenching liquid soothing her parched throat as she gulped it down.

'Thank you Amanda. I hope you don't mind me asking, but what's the nature of young Sophia's injuries?', Ava wanted to know.

'Catastrophic shock. Physically she's completely unharmed, but she's been more or less unresponsive since the outbreak.'

'What happened to her? Do you know?'

'Her sister told us the Monster walked right up to them. They could feel it's breath on their faces. It even touched Sophia gently on the arm', Nurse Amanda explained.

'I remember! We ran past them on the way when we were pursuing the Gorthon. They were standing holding each other, covered in blood.'

'That's them. But then Sophia's parents tried to fight off the monster and it killed them both. Quite horribly by all accounts. She hasn't said a word since. The younger sister, Jasmine has been responsive but becomes hysterical if we try to separate her from Sophia.'

'Poor babies. To lose their mom and dad like that and to witness it... It doesn't bear thinking about', Ava said sympathetically.

'Look, I'd better get back....', the nurse exclaimed; '....Nice meeting you Ava. If there's anything you need, call and I'll be over as soon as I can.' Ava felt Amanda's hand squeeze hers'

'And nice meeting you Amanda. Thank you.'

The figure in blue returned and Ava could hear the voice muffled in the distance once again. She raised her arm to be sure, as the figure sitting up in bed responded. For the first time since the outbreak, the cloud of despair and loneliness she inhabited relented. The world had not abandoned her. There was something to hang on to. The visions felt different though. Not vague and dreamlike as before, but clear and vivid like a live broadcast. Before she could think, her first reflex was to call out.

'Sophia.' Nothing, just Amanda pottering around the bed. 'Sophia please. Can you hear me?' Her vision went away from the nurse to the figure alone on the bed with the bandaged eyes. Ava raised her arm. 'Yes Sophia that's me. My name's Ava. I've been blinded. I can only see through you.'

A distant sucking sound was approaching. SCCCCHHPPPPPP! Then Ava's vision was blank. Nothing.

'Sophia! Please!' Ava couldn't tell if she'd actually shouted it or thought it. 'Please don't leave me. I'm not going to hurt you. Pleeeeeease!' She could feel herself reaching out in despair. Ava cursed herself. Idiot! How could I be so stupid! I probably freaked her out. Young girl in shock and some idiot is speaking crazy stuff to her, although she persisted in her attempt to attract the girl. 'Sophia, if you can hear me. I'm sorry, I didn't mean to scare you. Please don't abandon me.'

'Are you real?' A young girl's hesitant voice, quietly spoken, but deafening, boomed through Ava's mind.

'Yes, yes, yes! I'm in the bed opposite. With the bandages on my eyes. Please look Sophia.'

'I see you', the girl's voice echoed again.

'Don't be frightened.' Ava realised it was the phrase she first used to Billy the Gargoyle. You're not talking to a Mag Ava. Get a grip, she told herself

'I am frightened. Where is the creature? Is it gone?'

'Yes it's gone Sophia.'

'There's more, many many more. They're looking for me. Searching. I can feel them.'

'Can you see them Sophia?'

'The small one. He's scared as well.'

'Who? Who's scared?'

'Where's mummy and daddy?' Ava was shocked. Surely she must know. What do I say? 'Jasmine tells me they're dead. Is it true?', Sophia asked.

'I... I don't know.'

'You do. They're dead aren't they?'

'...I'm sorry.' Ava waited for a response, but there was only a void. An ache of sickening guilt filled her. She wouldn't come back now. Poor baby. For the first time in her life Ava felt the love of a mother towards a child. She'd always put her career first and marriage or children seemed a remote prospect. But now, more than anything, she wanted to hold Sophia tight. To be her mother. To be there for her and have that closeness that could only exist between parent and child.

'Ava.' The instantly recognisable voice of Eleanor shook her out of her train of thought. The pain of rejecting her true friend washed over Ava, as she reached toward the voice and invited.

'Come here.' Eleanor threw her arms around Ava. Their sobs mixed and became one. 'I'm sorry Eleanor. I owe you my life and I rejected you. Please forgive me.', Ava said, almost in a whisper.

Eleanor stood back but still held Ava's hand. 'There's nothing to forgive, I'd do it again if I had to.', she said, her voice choked with emotion.

'I heard you were quite the hero, jumping on the Gorthon's back.'

'You were the real hero. An unarmed civilian drawing the Gorthon towards her. Placing herself in its way. Facing down a walking nightmare. I'm trained for combat. You're not', Eleanor replied.

'So you are trained. I knew there was something about you.' Ava heard the hiss of irritation escape Eleanor's mouth and asked; 'Why are you on here, and why are you the damn cleaner? What is going on here? On a secret mission to devise advanced cleaning techniques?'

'It's a mistake. All a big fuck up on my part. Driven and twisted with the desire for revenge at all costs. But look where's it got me. Five hundred light years from home on a planet full of monsters.'

'What happened? Tell me.'

Eleanor recounted the events at the academy. The approach by Bruno. The failure, the trial, Naomi and the rape. How she worked her way onto the ship, snapping up the position of lab janitor in Pangea base. But then what to do about Bruno and Naomi. Her dilemma. Her realisation that, like Ava's, nothing could undo the past that had been set for eternity. She could kill Bruno a thousand times a day for the rest of time, but that wouldn't wipe the slate clean or make her feel any better.

'Bruno. What a sonofabitch. But Naomi sounds a real piece of work. Surely, she must have known what he was like?', Ava said.

'I don't think she really does. No woman could knowingly be with someone like that. But what can I do?'

'Don't let him get away with it, that's for sure. We'll find him and make him pay. You say he's with the SPC?'

'Yes.'

'Well we'll start there....', Ava suggested; '....Don't worry Eleanor Wells. I'll save you from yourself! Remember, justice is more important than vengeance. Focus on that. But first we have to get ourselves out of here.'

'I'm already out. I got discharged a few minutes ago', Eleanor informed her.

'Do you know something Eleanor? It takes losing something to gain something more precious.'

'How's that?'

'I'm bitching about my eyes, and poor Sophia over there lost everything. Her whole world....'. Ava spoke with regret; '....While I've been laying here wallowing in self-pity she saw her parents ripped to shreds before her very eyes, by something *I* helped to create. It doesn't matter if I warned them about the aggression, that counts for nothing. I was complicit, nothing can change that. No matter how many Mag's we kill, those people aren't coming back. Sophia's parents aren't coming back. Even though we helped to stop even more carnage happening, I am part of the cause.'

'Don't be too hard on yourself Ava. You couldn't have foreseen what would happened', Eleanor advised.

The weight of responsibility pressed down on Ava, crushing her underneath. 'How can I go through the rest of my life with this on my shoulders, it's too much of a burden, too great a load. Nothing will make it go away, so I've got a choice to make. Lie down and die, or rise up and fight. That is the question. What's happened has happened. The past is beyond recovery, but you can change the future. Rejecting the world is not an option. There's no choice, the situation has changed and we're living in a new reality now. Nobody is going to accept them inside the base, on the planet, or anywhere else. They're right to be terrified. I am, and I know them better than anyone. But how? How do we destroy the indestructible?'

Then it hit her. Like a blow in the solar plexus. The pure voice calling when the Hyperthon emerged. The pure signal on the graph they'd spotted the day after. It had to be. It was coming from the Civilian areas. It had to be Sophia, it's the only possibility. But what about the other signal? At the top. The 5:3 resonance directing the Hyperthon. That wasn't her. She used her mind to search out in the mindscape, but only emptiness lay before her.

Eleanor spoke, 'What about the Mags? Surely they won't be starting production after the outbreak. If those things are created in numbers they'll kill everyone here. Nothing will survive. The Mag's have to go.'

'Ok we have to devise a plan of action....', Ava opined; '....We both know about the Mag's. At the next meeting, we have to let everyone know the danger is only just beginning and they have to be destroyed.'

I heard from Montano that the remaining lab staff have been isolated from the rest of the base. Held under armed guard. The only one allowed out is Walker, because he does as he's told. Anything to move up the ladder. You know the type?', Eleanor said.

'Oh yes I'm fully aware of Leighton's attributes. He'll sell his own family up the river for another few inches up the greasy pole. I don't understand, Liz insisting on defending him. It's obvious to anybody with half a brain the guy's a sleezbag, but she seems somehow.....in awe of him', Ava supposed.

'There's some things I'll never understand. At the end of the day it's her choice'. There was a moments silence. Ava could sense Eleanor's hesitation. Her physical senses seemed to be on a razors edge since losing her sight. Eleanor's breathing, although almost indiscernible, grew louder in her heightened state. Here it comes...

'I know more about the Mags than I've let on', she told Ava. Ava wasn't entirely surprised by Eleanor's admission, especially considering her new found background. 'I know there are different types other than the Gorthon. I saw one after the Harry Felton incident. It was only little, about the size of a dog. It was looking at me from behind a cover in the labs. The thing I remember more than anything, was the sadness in its eyes. Like an abandoned child. There was an almost human quality about it', Eleanor said.

'It was a Gargoyle. The most dangerous type in my view. A Gorthon or a Hyperthon are huge and terrifying, but they only have one mouth and two claws. Gargoyles aren't as powerful on their own, but you saw what one did on its own. Imagine what twenty, or a hundred could do. Teeth and claws coming from every direction. They frighten me more than any of the others', Ava explained.

'What are the others?'

Ava recounted the Hyperthon emerging from the vat.

'God, that sounds even scarier than the Gorthon', Eleanor exclaimed.

'Gorthon, Schmorthon! Nothing to a big girl like you. You can kick their ass with your eyes closed.'

Eleanor gasped at the bravado of Ava and replied; 'I'm not looking forward to a rematch.'

'I didn't have much to do with the Bornix, but I know they can fly... The Hyperthon is dangerous physically but its main purpose is to exert overall control of the Mags which makes it very, very dangerous. But also the weak point. That's' where we'll need to concentrate if it comes down to it. But first we have to stop them getting to that stage, Ava suggested.

'I'm glad we're ok Ava.'

Ava felt relief at Eleanor's forgiveness, but from now on she had resolved to be strong. 'The time to sit on my butt, feeling sorry for myself is over. I have to right the wrongs and self-pity is not going to happen on my watch', she vowed.

'I know Ava. I'm going back to my quarters. We can talk tomorrow', Eleanor said, then leant forward to embrace Ava. She whispered in Ava's ear. 'No matter what happens, nothing comes between us. Nothing. Understand', she repeated.

The love Ava wanted to show to Sophia was channelled into Eleanor as she hugged her tighter than anyone else in her life. I want to be your mother as well Eleanor Wells, whoever you really are...

38

The footsteps of the figure echoed in the cavernous chamber as he walked across to greet Celina, who was looking up at the rows of vats moving slowly along, stretching into the distance. She held her hand out. 'Doctor Vaikar. It's good to see you.'

'And you Miss Novak. Let me show you around our facility.'

Celina watched the technicians as they moved along the row of vats, checking the readings on each and comparing them to the schedule on their pads. Each row contained its own size and there were four different levels. One for each Mag type. All contained the murky red brown liquid swirling lazily in its container. Occasionally a shape would push up against the side and its outline could be seen. The largest were at the bottom while the smallest occupied the top rows. It was the first time she'd seen the facility since production commenced.

'Very impressive, I must say',

'Thank you Miss Novak. As you can see, we are now working at full capacity and optimum efficiency. We have bought the average turnaround from initial mixing down to four days', Vaikar explained, as they continued to walk alongside the rows, he added, 'As per your request we have kept our team isolated from the rest of the base.'

'Yes that would be appropriate in the circumstances.' Celina's voice gave nothing of the tension she felt. The gut churning events of the past few days had taken their toll. The staff and civilians were on a knife edge of hysteria, one small spark could result in anarchy.

'I heard rumours of a.... malfunction, Miss Novak.' Doctor Vaikar's tone was inquisitive yet respectful. His eyebrows raised.

'It was contained Doctor. You need not concern yourself unduly.' The lie came easily. The tone dismissive.

He spread his hands and put his fingertips together, leaning forward slightly. 'I also heard reports of casualties...'

Celina concealed her irritation at the line of questioning. 'Yes. Unfortunately, there were some....' she admitted; '....Staff not following the procedures paid with their lives. A mistake I'm sure you, or your team won't repeat.' The implicit threat seemed to strike home. 'I'd be interested to see the emergence area Doctor Vaikar, if I may.'

They carried on walking past the rows of vats, towering above them. The pervasive humming broken by the occasional hiss or whirr. Celina shook her head in amazement and awe and thought; The things we humans build never ceases to amaze me. Little squidgy monkeys constructing ships to the stars, and building a monster factory on another world. We truly have become gods.

At the far end, the vats disappeared into an opening in the wall. Vaikar placed his hand on the scanner and a door slid silently open. What lurked inside took Celina's breath away. Metal clamps reaching inside a vat, drawing out an inert pink grey creature, streams of the steaming red liquid running back into the vat below. Lifting it almost lovingly into metal restraints, that supported its huge bulk and constrained its powerful limbs. A silver helmet was lowered and attached itself to the head. Vaikar turned to Celina and said; 'This is where the Neuroware is uploaded, as you can see this is a Gorthon. Product 010231A. Each of the species are processed in separate sealed units.'

A shudder of fear and revulsion passed over Celina as the pulsating creature came to life. The suddenness of its movements grated on Celina's tattered nerves, causing her to flinch. Vaikar's sidelong stare, left her feeling naked and exposed. She composed herself then asked;

'How long does the process take from upload to placing the creature in containment?' It took a huge effort to keep the fear from her voice.

'After upload, the creature is taken to conditioning. The whole process takes about three hours. We have an average turnover of one every four hours, we aim to...'

A blasting roar came from the Gorthon that caused Celina to let out a scream. The creature seemed to immediately sense her fear and the glistening black eyes bore into her. Wilting under its gaze, she swayed unsteadily on her feet. A grey mist fell over her vision although she tried to remain resolute. Oh no Celina. Please don't faint. Not now. The look of droll amusement on Vaikar's face made her want to dig her nails into his smirking cheeks. Taking a deep breath, she looked around the processing area, observing the seemingly unconcerned, almost bored faces of the staff.

'Are you ok Miss Novak? Would you like to sit down? Maybe I can fetch you some water?', Vaikar offered.

Celina noticed her knees were knocking. 'I'm ok Doctor. It just startled me that's all', she tried to reassure the doctor.

'Please accept my apologies. It's quite a common occurrence here.' The hint of a smirk remained on Vaikar's face.

'I quite understand. Please continue', Celina replied brusquely.

'As I was saying before we were rudely interrupted, we aim to have the Mag in containment within three hours after emergence.'

There was another roar from the Gorthon. The percussive quality made Celina feel like she'd been punched in the side of the head. This time apart from a small twitch, she didn't react.

'I must say Miss Novak, that Doctor Khan has surpassed every expectation. They really are magnificent creatures. Please offer him and his team my warmest congratulations', the doctor requested.

Even though the outbreak was only a few days ago, it felt strange to hear of Khan still being spoken of in the present tense.

Celina affected a smile and replied; 'I'll do that Doctor Vaikar. I'm sure he'll be very pleased to hear your kind words. What are the production figures?'

'Our current total output is...' He consulted his pad. 'A hundred and thirty-seven Gargoyles, thirteen Gorthons, ten Hyperthons and only nineteen Bornix I'm afraid, but we're looking to up production in the next day or so.'

'Very impressive Doctor. Ahead of most targets. I have every confidence that the Bornix will soon match the splendid figures of the other Mag's. Now I would be interested in viewing the containment areas, if you please'.

'Of course Miss Novak. Once the conditioning phase has completed the Mag is automatically transferred up to the containment area. Here's one we prepared earlier.' Vaikar gave a nod to one of the assistants and a Gorthon, held in an identical harness to the one that had just startled Celina, emerged. 'This is product ID 100899W.', Vaikar said.

Apart from a slightly bemused look, the Gorthon passively accepted what was happening as if it was a mundane daily occurrence. Its ominous bulk gently acquiescing to manipulation. The bulging thighs momentarily flexing before relaxing once again, giving those in its presence a flash of their true abilities.

'As you are aware, the instabilities have been completely eradicated. The product is calm and every precaution is taken to ensure it is in pristine condition upon delivery', Vaikar explained.

Delivery! They aren't pizzas you idiot. Celina kept her thoughts to herself, before speaking to the doctor; 'That's most reassuring Doctor Vaikar.' She watched as the harness smoothly lifted the Gorthon, seamlessly popping it into the opening provided.

'Now if you will accompany me, I will take you to the containment level where we view our product being installed into his allocated unit.' Vaikar invited Celina.

A short barking growl came from 100899W. Celina jumped, but Vaikar pretended not to notice as he motioned for her to follow him toward the waiting lift. Celina nodded, but had to stop herself from running out of the conditioning area. There was the inescapable feeling that Gorthon 100899W was watching her. Turning one last time, and instantly regretting it, she observed the thing quietly weighing her up as if it was marking her down for destruction. She stepped into the lift and felt a sense of relief as the doors swished shut behind her, feeling the acceleration of the lift as it sped upwards to the containment level. Even though the base hadn't been designed to accommodate families of settlers, she'd never been happy with it being on the same level as the Civilian areas, but that couldn't be changed now. A small bell dinged as they reached the level and the doors opened.

They walked down a small corridor. A door marked 'GORTHON CONTAINMENT: NO UNAUTHORISED ACCESS' awaited them. They passed through the door and into an air lock.

'The environment is maintained precisely at the optimum level to ensure the maximum comfort and safety of the Mags', Vaikar told Celina.

'It is of the utmost importance to keep the Mags calm at all times, Doctor Vaikar', she replied.

'Then you will be most reassured by the high quality of our facility Miss Novak.'

The inner door of the airlock opened. The warm fug of livestock assaulted Celina's nostrils causing her to gag momentarily. They stepped into the containment area. The silence made Celina think it was empty, as rows of containment pens stretched into the distance. The dim lighting made it hard to see into the individual pens. A low clicking sound with a rumbling undertone drifted out of the middle distance, amplified by the cavernous space. Celina peered into a pen. A small green shimmer of iridescence momentarily twinkled, like a fragment of a dream, just on the edge of vision in the background.

Something stirred, emerging out of the gloom on all fours, its presence seemed to push a bow wave of silent menace before it, as the Gorthon came face to face with Celina. The shining black marble eyes seemed too small for the huge head. Celina stared back, transfixed by the sheer presence of the creature. Even its breathing was slow and deliberate while it seemed to contemplate her and the puny weakness she embodied. As if it temporarily accepted its incarceration, while those on the outside were the real prisoners in the condemned cell, awaiting the appointed day of retribution. Its tongue slipped silently out towards Celina causing her to take an involuntary step back. It's glistening black presence reached toward her face, inviting her into the mouth from where it sprang. It seemed like a different creature that inhabited the mouth of the Gorthon, with a mind and will of its own. As quickly and smoothly it they appeared, the tongue returned into the mouth of its master. In a single smooth motion, the Gorthon raised itself up to its full height. The silence of its actions screamed the deafening insignificance Celina felt, as she looked up at the thing that towered over her. Its head seemed miles

285

away, perched atop a lofty mountain of flesh. The claws that hung at Celina's eye level seemed powerful enough to crush her head and pluck off her limbs with minimum effort.

'He likes you Miss Novak', Vaikar said.

'It's the first time I've been up close to one. I've only seen them from a distance or on video. It's terrible and beautiful at the same time', Celina admitted.

'Yes, very impressive isn't he? He's one of our more remarkable specimens. They've all got different personalities you know. They are fed and watered automatically but the staff sometimes give them a name instead of the dry numbering systems.'

'Oh. And what is this one's name may I ask?'

Vaikar looked up at the Gorthon, studied the pad, then smiled. 'Let me see...050290T... Ah yes. Tiddles.'

At the sound of its name, a small plaintive groan escaped Tiddles, then he dropped back down to all fours, before he tenderly stroked his flanks against the bars of the pen. Shades of blue and violet rushed in waves across his back. Vaikar affectionately caressed his finger along Tiddles flesh.

'Very touching Doctor Vaikar, I'll leave you and... Tiddles to enjoy each other's company. Now if you will please excuse me, I must be getting back. I have some pressing matters to attend to. I'll be sure to feed back your excellent work to the Company', Celina said.

'Thank you Miss Novak, and please pass on my greetings to Doctor Khan.'

'I'll be sure to do that.'

She made her way towards the airlock and blew out a long breath. I'll be so glad when Tiddles and the other abominations are out roaming the planet, sniffing out the Nadinium and well away from me, she thought. She'd never felt so homesick. Another two years of this. She was exhausted and she'd hardly started. The yearning for the peace and quiet of her garden back on mother earth seemed more alluring than ever, as she continued to contemplate. No time for homesickness now Celina. You have a conference tomorrow. Obstruct, stall, and if necessary declare martial law. Anything to contain the situation. The blocking of the emails had been effective, but it was only a matter of time before the suspicion of the civilians became a conviction, and the conviction became a certainty. The façade of the AI correspondents answering a select few of the emails would only hold up for a few more days. Whatever it takes to buy time and get out of here. The thought of another one of those things on the loose filled her with a sickening dread. Well surely that can't happen. If only she could rid herself of the feeling of impending doom, as she out a long sigh. Whatever happens,

happens Celina. She made her way back to the upper levels and the sanctuary of the executive area.

◆

Billy could see the delicate figure of the woman approaching through the bars, as he hovered over Tiddles. The look on her face of revolted fascination amused and troubled Billy at the same time. She turned to the man standing next to her and they exchanged a few words. Now Billy floated across to her. He could see inside her, knowing the black heart of treachery that lay within the words of the message, churning away in her subconscious.

"the situation can be exploited in terms of the power of shock and the disorientation of the civilian population..."

Billy knew their significance and what to do with them. The purple light had taught him well. The woman walked towards the lift, still Billy hovered. As she travelled up, he could feel the misgivings she had about her ability to put her plans into actions, as well as her longing to return home. He watched her arrive at her quarters and sit on the edge of her bed, head in hands quietly sobbing. Presently she washed and changed before going to bed and reading, unaware of the orange light in the mindscape silently and patiently observing.

Her eyes were heavy as she struggled to get through the final documents she was reading on the device, until sleep gently enveloped her. The device slowly slipped from her hand onto the bedsheet. Her breathing became slower and deeper as Billy decided the moment had arrived. He moved down and into the world of Celina Novak's dreams, planting the thoughts there, then moved back and waited. She rose slowly out of bed and walked to the desk, sat and touched the screen, punched in the access code and swiftly searched through the messages, before selecting the correct one, entitled 'Mag Outbreak and next actions', then pressed the forward option, closed down the session, switching the screen off before returning to bed and sleep, completely unaware of her actions in the past few moments. Billy felt relief as the first half of the task was complete. The Purple would be proud of him.

In the distance a green light shone dimly. Billy moved toward it and looked down on the sleeping figure, before swiftly dropping down into the dreamscape of Aaron. Visions of writhing naked flesh and dark wavy hair were abounding, as he implanted a different kind of seed, in the form of tasks into Aaron's subconscious, before quickly vacating the scenes of carnal lust.

Aaron rose from his slumber in the same manner as Celina had a few minutes earlier, walking past the stern picture of Marcus that stared out every waking

287

moment. He went to his personal screen and opened the message from Celina that awaited him. After pressing the 'Print' option, a page slid quickly from the bottom of the screen. Deleting the message and closing down the screen, Aaron carefully folded the printout and placed it in his trouser pocket. Billy watched him silently return to bed. The groans and whispers told him that the dreams had picked up where they had left off a few minutes earlier. Only the final task of pulling the message out of his pocket, placing it on his desk at work in the morning to be "accidentally" discovered, remained. Billy was confident it would be completed. After all what could go wrong? The fuse had been lit, and had started its steadily spluttering progress.

39

Marcus sat eating in a secluded corner of the Cafeteria. The soft tones of the smooth jazz piano mixed with the low murmur of numerous hushed conversations. A rare oasis from the responsibilities of his position. He toyed with the mixed fruit pie absent-mindedly as he considered the events of the past few days, where he had been thrust into the limelight. *What if it all collapses and they acquiesce to our demands? The sense of fear will quickly dissipate and the opportunity to exploit will have disappeared. People have short memories and dangers are quickly forgotten. If they don't, how do we destroy the Mag's? It took the combined power of the security teams to bring down a single Gorthon. How many more are there? They're not going to go quietly. But this was a vehicle for a power grab. The Mags weren't that important in themselves. Only the fear they generated and that had to be perpetuated.*

'Counsellor Marcus!'

He looked up and saw Aaron approaching frantically waving a document, followed by two others, rushing across toward him. The normal hubbub of the dining area replaced by the commotion of raised voices, dropped cutlery and the scraping of chairs.

Aaron arrived breathless at the table and slammed the document down in front of Marcus. 'This was left on my desk this morning!', he said.

Marcus looked up at the flushed face of Aaron who was breathing heavily, before turning his attention to the document's subject. "*Mag Outbreak and next actions*", He immediately realised its significance. It was addressed to Celina from company executives.

'I checked the outgoing emails on the server. It had level three encryption, so I viewed it with a utility from security for email monitoring and it matched', Aaron explained.

'Do you know who left it on your desk?', Marcus asked.

'No, it was there when I arrived this morning.'

Marcus read through the contents with increasing alarm, the roar of blood sounded in his ears, accompanied by the racing thud of his pulse as it drummed its tattoo on his nerves. There was no time for deliberation, only reaction.

'Has anyone else seen the contents?'

'Only sisters Odette and Antonina from our group, but others have read it on the way here.'

'Fool! You should have come straight to me before telling anyone. This should have been contained. Now it's out of control.'

'I thought you'd be pleased Counsellor. This is the proof we need to remove any doubts about achieving our goals', Aaron suggested.

'Keep your voice down idiot! Do not assume to speak for me! You do the doing, I think the thinking. Not the other way around! Got it?', Marcus said commandingly. Others had joined them.

'Is it true Counsellor? Read it to us!', one of them said. The small spontaneous gathering had rapidly grown within a couple of minutes.

Ok Marcus. This is it. You can't be seen to hide this. Think think think! The gentle background music was drown out by the increasing outrage of a small vocal group huddled in the corner around Marcus, the idyllic pictures, pastel shades and soft lighting of the Cafeteria, at odds with the storm of red hot anger that was rapidly racing out of control. Increasing numbers were drawn from across the Cafeteria by curiosity, then gripped by the explosive revelations. Some of the staff, incongruous in their cheery bright uniforms, left their stations with half served meals abandoned on their plates.

Ok Marcus now or never. Here goes. He took a deep breath and stood up on the chair, waving the paper above his head.

'This, brothers and sisters is the smoking gun', he said, almost shouting.

There was no need to feign the anger he genuinely felt, even so, he retained the ice cool head and foresight that separated him from mere mortals. Holding the document before him, he started to read selected passages.

"*All other considerations are secondary up to and including the staff and civilians*"

A howl of anger burst from those listening as Marcus continued.

"*All measures are authorised including the use of lethal force and the imposition of martial law.*"

"*Civilian deaths, while regrettable, have minimal bearing on the success or failure of the Mag project and are of little consequence*"

The gnashing teeth and shaking fists took Marcus by surprise but he continued;

'And this is the final nail in the coffin of their credibility.' He pointed his index finger upwards as he read the final excerpt, making sure to speak each word slowly and clearly to emphasise the sense of horror.

"*The situation can be exploited in terms of the power of shock and the disorientation of the civilian population by taking advantage in accelerating the test run of the new model of disaster society where the population are quickly frightened into accepting previously unacceptable policies and in particular the environmental and health impact of prolonged exposure to Nadinium. This could then be rolled out amongst other colonisation projects and accelerate its application on earth*".

A hand reached out and tore the paper from his grasp and passed it around the group

'So, all we are, is a bunch of lab rats', shouted a voice from the back.

No need for plants this time Marcus. 'It seems so brother', he concurred.

Exclamations of disgust and anger grew within the crowd. The document was furiously brandished above the heads of the crowd before several pairs of hands tore it apart, scattering it like confetti around them.

'Lie after lies fed to us, while they plotted our doom! Did they ever have any intention of telling us?', Marcus asked.

'Noooo!' Came the answer.

'How many more would they have let die?'

'All of us!', the crowd responded.

'Well now we know the answer to that question. Twenty eight men, women and children who came on this voyage to seek a better life. But all they found was betrayal and death', Marcus said.

'Liars! We've been taken all this way just to be experimented on!'

'I agree Brother, we are just an experiment!', Marcus concurred.

'Noooo!', the crowd shouted together, this time even louder than before.

'Well I for one won't lab rat in their abominable experiments'

'Kill the Mags!' The chant was taken up.

The sound of hysteria reverberated through the room. Screams of rage and fear added to the chorus of hate. Marcus noticed the quivering jowls of a Cafeteria worker. His little badge dotted with smiley faces, "Hi! I'm Darren. Fun Leader." The little eyes bulging from their sockets, sweat glistening against his livid complexion. His paper hat, covered with the zany cartoon characters, sitting at a jaunty angle upon his rounded head. A frail elderly woman, teeth bared back like a frantic startled skull. Her arm raised halfway up and her gnarled hand clenched in feeble defiance. Abhorrence and slaughter in their eyes. The forces of terror and treachery mixed into a manic cocktail of retribution.

Like a flock of birds, the crowd turned as one to the exit and thundered through the Cafeteria, sending anything in their path crashing aside. Marcus watched them go as he climbed down from the table, the chant fading into the distance.

'Kill the Mags, Kill the Mags, Kill the fuckin Mags!'

What have you unleashed Marcus? This is the point of no return. Even you can't control this outburst. I'd love to know who it was that placed the email on that idiot's desk. They spotted he's the weak link and wanted to take the situation out of my hands. The manipulator has been manipulated for once. A lesson in there for you to learn Marcus. You should put it to good use.

He picked up the tray that contained the remains of his unfinished pie, then walked towards the waste collection point, placing it on the carousel of half eaten meals, watching it disappear, wondering how long it would be before it was collected. Looking around the Cafeteria, chairs and tables strewn in all directions, he noticed a yellow balloon, emblazoned with the disembodied happy face of Darren, with his mouth open and eyebrows raised in surprise, bobbing gently along the floor. The relaxing piano melodies tinkled away in the background as Marcus strode out, and into a new uncertain future.

◆

They walked together through the Mall. The contrasting figures of Doctor Gough and his colleague Doctor Roe made their way towards their quarters. Not being involved with Mag program allowed them the freedom denied to those who were. The atmosphere of excitement when they arrived at Magdur had been replaced by trepidation and fear. The buzz of anticipation smothered by the blanket of dread, although the countenance of Johnathan Gough made it plain he was only interested in his work.

'It's a major breakthrough I'm telling you. The yield of parsnips is up seventeen point two percent, which in itself is remarkable, but in conjunction with the increased shelf life of turnips brings an increased ratio of...' Gough interrupted himself and turned his head. 'Did you hear that?', he asked.

Roe sighed wearily and said; 'Not again Johnathan. You really need to seek some professional help', the tired reply reflected the strain everyone was under.

'I have. It's you.' Gough removed his glasses to emphasise the point.

'I'm a physicist, not a psychiatrist....', Roe intoned and continued; '....I thought you'd be able to tell the difference by now. Maybe that's the random noises you keep hearing are your own jumbled up spellings rattling around inside your head...'

'You may sneer Doctor Roe....', Gough interrupted his colleague; 'but I seem to recall a certain noise a few weeks ago that turned out to actually be something, as we all know from recent events.'

'I still think you were under the influence of your super broccoli on that particular occasion. I distinctly remember Miss Wells suggesting...' Doctor Roe's head turned toward the same direction as Gough had been looking. A rhythmic shouting was getting closer. They looked at each other and Gough raised his eyebrows before he replaced his glasses, perching them on his long thin nose.

292

'What on earth are they shouting?', Gough asked.

'Sounds like "Kill" something or other', Roe replied.

The sound grew louder; the chanting became an incoherent roar. A large man, wearing a bright yellow shirt and a paper hat ambled around the corner, followed by a swirling threatening group comprised of various shapes and sizes. He pointed at Gough.

'He's one of 'em', as he made his way menacingly toward the startled academic.

'I'm one of what?'

The large man in the paper hat walked up to Gough, reached up and closed his hand around Gough's throat. 'Where's the fuckin Mags? We wanna know now', he demanded. Gough, in a state of shock, could only utter an unintelligible gargle.

Doctor Roe tried to cut in from the side, 'This is an outrage! He's got nothing to do with the Mags you idiot.'

Another man, reeking of booze and sporting a large beard cut in, 'Out the fuckin way lard arse.'

The large man holding Gough by the throat turned to the other man. 'Who you calling "Lard Arse"?'

'Sorry', replied the bearded man, before he turned and struck Roe with a right cross between the eyes. There was the crunch of breaking bone and a groan, before Roe didn't so much fall but slowly rolled backwards, striking his head violently on the ground, coming to rest in an unconscious heap.

All eyes turned back to Gough who was by now a gibbering wreck. The man in the paper hat released his stranglehold and said; 'I know you work in the labs. You know where they keep the beasts? You've got up to ten otherwise I'll knock it outta yer!'

Gough was frantic with fear, as he looked down at the cheery name badge the man in the hat was wearing. 'D... Darren, please, I only grow vegetables. I know nothing of the Mags. I'm as horrified as y...', he wasn't allowed to finish. The bearded man whipped a left uppercut into the twig-like ribs of Gough who promptly collapsed to his knees, clutching his side before a swinging boot snapped his head back, sending blood and teeth flying through the air.

'I'd only got to five!' exclaimed Darren.

'I never was good at maths', replied the bearded man as he aimed a second kick at the prone figure of Gough. 'Where's the fuckin Mags ya lanky streak of piss?', he demanded.

A low moan came from Gough, 'Eye doon nooo. Preese doon urt mu.' His ragged breathing rattling in his throat.

Darren leant down and dug his fingers into Gough's terrified face, his sweaty beetroot features inches from Gough. His teeth bared, spittle foaming in the corners of his mouth, eyes crazy as he spoke. 'We've had nothing but lie after fuckin lie from you bastards. One last time or I'll rip yer throat out.'

The only sound that escaped Gough's mouth was a feeble whimper. 'Preeeese..'. Tears of abject terror rolled from his eyes; 'I doon nooo. Preese.' A loop of bloody snot shot out and retracted from his nose as it danced in time with his desperate breaths. Blood mixed with broken shards of shattered tooth oozed and dribbled down his quivering chin.

Darren sighed, held Gough's gaze for a few moments, as if trying to read his thoughts, then turned to the gathering mob looming over them and rose to his feet. 'He don't know shit. Let's go.'

'Not until we had our pound of flesh', shouted the bearded man who gleefully aimed another kick at the helpless figure on the ground. This was immediately followed by a rain of kicks and punches from the mob as a high pitched scream pierced the air. The berserk thrashing increasing in viciousness and violence as a tornado of fists and boots hurtled down on Gough. It seemed to have no limit as the merciless pounding inflicted, built towards a crescendo.

A shot rang out and the onslaught stopped as quickly as it started.

'Back! Back Now!' The trample of the security team's boots sounded, guns bristling as the crowd drew back.

Nicklas Overgaard appeared from the centre of the squad, gun drawn. He looked around and asked; 'Where are the SPC patrols? Have they gone into hiding? Call for immediate backup and medics!'

Looking at the blooded bundle of rags that was Johnathan Gough, Nicklas leant down and checked him, then turned to one of his troopers. 'He's alive. Just. We need to get him to the infirmary.' He looked over at Roe who was by now sitting holding his head, staring vacantly at the scene before him. Nicklas turned to the mob and pointed his gun. 'What the fuck are you all doing? Are you mad?'

The bearded man stepped forward from the menacing mass and said; 'He knows where the Mags are! He's going to let us die! It's us or him.' The mob muttered in agreement. The air crackling with the threat of violence.

'I know this man!', Nicklas told him, adding; 'He grows genetically engineered vegetables you halfwit. He's no threat to anyone.'

The bearded man stepped forward emboldened by the horde at his back. His voice slightly slurred as he spoke; 'That's bollocks and you know it. You're as much in it as he is.' He pointed angrily at Gough and warned Nicklas; 'You're either with us or against us. Make your choice! You're gonna die along with the rest of us if those things break loose again.'

Nicklas motioned to his squad and the troopers lined up in front of Gough, guns drawn and pointed outward. 'I'm telling you now disperse quietly. We will use lethal force if we have to!', he responded.

'Yeah? We read that in the email!'

Nicklas looked incredulously back and asked; 'Email? What email?'

The bearded man moved nearer and held his hand out. 'You can't kill all of us. Lower your guns and join us', he cautioned as the mob shuffled inexorably forward.

Nicklas raised his gun, pointed it at the bearded man's head and shouted at him. 'No closer sir or I fire.'

The bearded man stopped and looked into Nicklas' eyes. A malevolent smile flickered across his face, before he turned to the crowd and announced; 'NOW!'

It was the final sound of his life, as Nicklas squeezed the trigger and a single shot turned the man's head into mush, spraying blood and brain matter over those behind him. His body tumbled to the ground, face missing. Only the blooded splendid beard remained. The crowd drew back and took a collective breath as they prepared to rush the troopers. In a few seconds it would all be over. Nicklas raised his gun and levelled it at them. The wide eyed blood spattered faces staring back as the deadly confrontation hung in the balance. A familiar voice sounded in the distance.

'Brothers! Sisters! Stop! Stop this madness in the name of Ykdar. Immediately! There will be no more blood spilt.' The crowd parted as Marcus made his way through, followed by Bruno and a few SPC soldiers. He looked down at the stream of blood running from the lifeless body and asked. 'What has happened?'

'He tried to rush us. I warned him. They nearly beat Doctor Gough to death. We arrived just in time.' Nicklas' voice was steady but he was shaken, as he approached Marcus. 'Counsellor. I need you to tell them to return to their quarters. We want no more bloodshed.' Then he looked across at Bruno. 'Where the fuck were you shithats hiding?'

'Out here clearing up your mess when you let the Gorthon escape, fishbrains!', came Bruno's riposte.

'More like hiding in the ladies shitting yourself. Needed your bunch of losers to dig you out when I kicked your fat arse! Feeling brave again are ya?', Nicklas said disdainfully. Bruno raised his gun and pointed it at Nicklas, who stared calmly back and dared his antagonist. 'You haven't got the guts. Women and small girls are about your level.'

'Wha...What you saying motherfucker?', Bruno was furious.

Nicklas laughed. 'We've all heard about your "heroic exploits" during the water wars, you murdering piece of shit. Not so brave when it comes to anyone who can fight back!', he said, scorn oozing out of his every word.

Marcus stood between them; 'Gentlemen! Please! We have more pressing matters at hand!' He turned to Nicklas. 'I summoned Sergeant Bruno as soon as I heard about the mob.'

Darren stepped forward, pointed to Marcus and declared; 'You're the one who put us up to it. Reading that email out at the top of your voice, whipping us up and then quietly stood back and admired your handy, yer crafty bastard.'

Marcus flushed, 'I certainly did not Brother....', he quickly refuted the accusation; 'You made me read the email, then ripped it from my grasp and started the rampage.' Darren's mouth opened and closed soundlessly, lost for words. Marcus turned to Bruno while pointing at his accuser; 'Guards seize that man immediately. He's the rabble-rouser that caused all this.'

Bruno stepped forward and snapped a pair of handcuffs on Darren before frogmarching him off. Marcus turned to the crowd. People were looking at each other in puzzlement at the change from Marcus's earlier demeanour.

'Brothers. Sisters. Please no more. Return to your quarters. I'm sure this can be resolved peacefully.' The calmness of Marcus's voice bought the atmosphere down a few notches. The crowd dispersed still muttering discontent. A team from the infirmary took Gough and Roe. Another team took the bearded man to the mortuary, his arm dangling lifelessly from the stretcher.

Marcus turned to Nicklas and spoke in a low tone; 'I don't know how long they can be contained brother. They're ready to burst like a dam and spew forth in righteous anger. I suggest you pass this back to your superiors. I don't know if I will be able to stop them next time. The sooner the demands to terminate the creatures are met, the better for all of us.'

Nicklas looked into the shining blue eyes of the preacher and knew they brooked no argument. The time for decisions was approaching fast.

40

'**He** definitely put them up to it. There was a spontaneous gathering in the Cafeteria, he spoke, they erupted in fury shouting "Kill the fuckin Mags" before storming out, going on a wild rampage and nearly killing poor Doctor Gough.', Jordan said.

Celina was looking at the collection of tropical fish she kept and maintained, as they swam in lazy random paths around their aquarium. The chic ambiance of her executive office projected the status and prestige of her position. The soft lighting enhanced the eerie iridescence of the Rothko painting that hung on the wall, as well as radiating a warm glow that seemed to be absorbed by the dark wood coffee table and cream leather of the low sofa they sat on. She stared across at Jordan and asked; 'What do we know about the casualty?'

Jordan carefully placed the fine china cup he had been sipping tea from back on the table and looked down at his notes.

'His name was Scott Allen, aged 32....', he began; '....No previous record of misdemeanours although he did witness the breakout at first hand and, like most people, was deeply shocked. Apparently he'd been drinking all day. He was warned by Sergeant Overgaard more than once before he tried to rush the security team and got his brains blown out for his troubles. Overgaard's a good man. I back his judgement one hundred percent. The SPC patrol were nowhere to be seen may I add.'

'And the man in detention?'

'Darren Lloyd....' Jordan explained again; '....Previously impeccable record as an under-fives play leader in the Cafeteria until that is, he was involved in an altercation with the chef. Was given a warning after several people said he was severely provoked. Another one taken to drink recently. He's adamant Burgman incited them. Blubbed like a baby ever since his arrest. ' Jordan sighed and shook his head. 'It all seems so out of character. The common factor was they were both listening to Burgman speak.'

Celina leant forward, 'And what did Burgman say to them?' She felt her blood chill as Jordan produced a stained screwed up document that had been taped back together and sealed in a clear plastic envelope. She'd heard rumours of its contents. He handed it to her, his silence making his feelings clear. Celina read through the contents she already knew by heart, before looking back at Jordan, not a hint of the shame she felt showing on her face. 'Where did this come from?', she asked him.

'I don't think that's as important as the irrefutable truth of the contents.' His voice remained calm, but the tension dripped off every word. 'Don't insult my intelligence Miss Novak. I'd have rioted if I'd been there.'

'Well, whatever you think Mister Harris we have to deal with the fallout, and part of that is that you are implicated with the contents of the email as much as I am.' She offered a smile of mock sympathy and sat back, adding; 'So whether you like it or not you have to stay on message. We tell them it's a forgery by Burgman, designed to stir up discontent.'

Jordan's knuckles cracked loudly as he clenched his fists before continuing in his calm voice. 'On that we can both agree, but there will be a reckoning Miss Novak when this is done. I promise you that.'

The threat didn't bother Celina. She'd seen off bigger boys than Jordan and he would go the same way as the others.

'I've issued an arrest warrant to be executed upon Marcus Burgman before your press conference tomorrow morning....', he told her; '...You declare a state of emergency and impose martial law. All gatherings are prohibited and a curfew after 8:00pm is to be effected. This of course is in the interests of public safety and people are urged to remain calm. Shock democracy indeed Miss Novak...'

'Couldn't have put it better myself. I expect it'll be the security team rather than the SPC who will be carrying out the order.'

'Correct.', he responded. Looking down, he pursed his lips in contemplation for a few moments before looking back up and straight into Celina's eyes. Jordan cleared his throat and said; 'I'm only arresting Burgman because he's a danger to this base with his rabblerousing. Not because I'm on your side. When I took this assignment I thought it would be the pinnacle of my career. I never considered for one moment that I'd be complicit in the disgusting sickening lies that slip so naturally from your poisonous lips. It really is a fucked up world where people like you control the levers of power. I'm glad my parents aren't alive to witness what you've turned me into. I hope my children will be able to forgive me one day.'

Celina stared back at Jordan coolly, and commented; 'Noble sentiments Mister Harris. Also completely unrealistic in the world we inhabit. It's now sink or swim time and we've all got a personal choice to make. '

The revulsion was etched on every line of Jordan's face. Each little red vein in his bloodshot eyes, a river of fury flowing from within, yet he spoke calmly; 'And we both know your choice don't we. Money and power. The company's stock price above everything else and those nice little share options waiting for you back on earth.'

Celina smiled and shook her head. 'In an ideal world, I'm all for morals along with the hearts and flowers approach as much as anyone else. But the difference between you and I Mister Harris is that *I'm* a realist and money will always win over morals. You can't raise an army on morals, you can't eat morals. Morals won't stop you from freezing to death or dying of thirst. They're just a useful tool to motivate people to do your will and maintain the powerful. Does that make you moral and me immoral? You look at the entire history of the human race and the money had always won. Kings, tyrants, religions, politicians and now the supranational corporations. Of course they will espouse the common good, but then again, those with money *would* say that, wouldn't they. That's their mantra, that, 'it's for the good of all'. That they had done the right thing and their sacrifices were worthwhile, but as soon as the crisis is over, they'll be just as screwed over as those they had defeated in the name of so-called morals.'

'Only in *your* warped, fucked up, dog eat dog world....', he affirmed; '....The rest of us are forced to live by the consequences, but your biggest fear is that they'll realise it's all just a big confidence trick, where people like you are just as fragile as everyone else, and you can be swept away down the sewer where you belong.'

'Very profound Mister Harris. But some of us are just born lucky and others come into this world to suffer and die.' Celina furrowed her eyebrows and nodded in mock agreement, pursing her lips in equally insincere sympathy. 'Thank you for sharing your thoughts and kind words with me....', she continued; '....I'll be sure to pass them on, but as I'm sure you can appreciate, I have a very busy day ahead of me tomorrow, and I have things that need attending to. Please return to your duties and I expect Marcus Burgman to be in custody by the time my conference starts at 11:00am tomorrow morning.' She noticed Jordan's tears of impotent rage as he stood to leave, but decided not to push her luck by commenting.

As he reached the door, he turned one last time to Celina and asserted; 'We reap what we sow Miss Novak. Just remember that.'

As the door shut after Jordan, Celina sat and thought about his words. Perhaps there was something prophetic in his rambling. Well the die is cast and nothing can change it now. She checked the contents of the email one more time and shook her head. 'I carried out your orders to the letter. To the fuckin letter.' She placed the document in her desk drawer and slammed it shut. How did he get hold of it? The mail systems are meant to be secure, but the expertise required to open it were restricted to a very few people. I'll have to order an enquiry about the security breach but I have bigger fish to fry at the moment. She stood and prepared to leave the office, looking around one last time. What will the morning bring? She sighed heavily as she switched off the light and made her way back to her quarters.

♦

The gaping hole where the door of the lab area had once been, was covered by a sheet of yellow plastic. The debris of the breakout had been cleared and tidied from the work tops. A small streak of blood on the white wall was the only sign that remained of the massacre that had taken place a few days earlier. The Mag pens sat empty, their occupants moved to the containment area. The smashed equipment left in the path of Titus the Gorthon had been cleared up and sent to recycling. Some of the lab apparatus and monitoring equipment was left as it had been by its now dead users.

In the corner a sign hung on the wall. 'Hyperthon Monitoring'. Below it, a series of screens sat blankly surrounded by scribbled notes and discarded pencils. Family pictures and drawings by children hung alongside official notices and charts. A calendar marked in red '5:3 Event. Wow!' at several points. A crackling of static broke the silence as one of the screens came to life. A series of traces made their way across the screen. All were flatlining, except one at the very top. A series of pulses made their way across the screen, gradually increasing in frequency until they became a continuous hum. A message blinked in red at the bottom of the screen.

'Alert 5:3 Resonance Detected'

♦

Aaron writhed on the floor in his quarters surrounded by his bed sheets as the purple light incinerated the inside of his head. No need for Billy this time, just direct access to plant the final part of his instructions. Aaron's eyes rolled back, showing only the white sclera, as the deafening whistling inside his head made it feel he was being electrocuted with scalding water. The white light blinded him and the taste of metal filled his mouth with a million filings. His desperate breaths came short and fast through his gritted teeth as his heart hammered away at an insane tempo, making it feel like it was going to tear its way out of his body at any moment, before bouncing its way out of his room and down the corridor. The white light transitioned to purple as the noise jumped up another level. His spine took on a life of its own as his back arched into an unnatural shape, throwing his head back. His fingers splayed in crooked distorted attitudes as the volume continued to increase, turning Aaron's body into a giant resonating wildly

300

fluctuating eardrum. Every muscle stretched to the limit of its intensity, holding his body in a vice like grip. He could feel his joints tearing and bones cracking as he expected them to explode any second. Then it stopped. Aaron immediately went limp, laying motionless apart from his breathing, which subsided to its normal rate after a couple of minutes.

He opened his eyes and sat up. His face was blank. He stood and silently made his way to the infonet terminal. His fingers raced across the terminal keyboard bringing up the security server. A few quickly typed commands found him facing the firewall.

'Restricted Access: Security Officer Eyes Only!', displayed across the screen. He typed the user id and one time access code into the box and the list of video files was displayed, scrolled down the page until he found what he was looking for, copied the file into an anonymous email server and attached it. He clicked on the address box and typed 'marcus.burgman@galactic_vistas.com', set the notification alarm to 'Immediate' before clicking 'send'.

Aaron closed the screens and logged off before returning to bed and immediately started snoring, completely oblivious to his actions just as he had been the previous night, after he dropped off the printout of the email on his desk.

♦

Marcus hadn't slept all night as he turned to the figure next to him. Antonina was sleeping soundly. It had been her turn to come to him that night. She was gentle but lacked the passion of Odette and the wit of Naomi. Still he liked her tenderness which the others didn't have. He looked at the clock. 04:17. He was still revelling in the power he had unleashed the previous day. The email had taken him by surprise, and he still couldn't figure out who had decided to leave it with a lowly administrator like Aaron Rogers. Too far down the food chain to matter. Someone so weak and unstable, who lacked the wit to conceal the explosive contents of the gift that had been left to him. Perhaps it was a test. Even Marcus's cynical and paranoid mind had been taken aback by the brazen nature of the email. You've a long way to go Marcus before you'll be a worthy follower of the Great Lord Ykdar. Still, I'm a fast learner.

A gentle gong sounded from the infonet terminal. 'Immediate Attention Required' blinked on the screen as the bonging persisted.

'Waaisit..' Antonina stirred.

Marcus shushed her gently. 'Nothing, just a message. Go back to sleep.'

He got up and walked to the terminal, pressing his finger on the message. No subject, only an attachment file. Strange... 'Anonymous' in the sender box.

He tapped on the attachment and a video file came up. This better not be some weird shit. He put his headphones on and pressed 'play'

Two figures were sitting at a desk facing each other. Recognising Celina Novak and Jordan Harris, Marcus listened to the conversation as Jordan handed a document to Celina. The rumbling anger of Jordan apparent as he rose from the desk and strode out of the room.

Marcus felt the burning acid of anger in his stomach, shaking his head he whispered to himself. 'Thank you Miss Novak. The Lord Ykdar has delivered you into my grateful hands.' He sat in silence for a few moments before he rose and returned to bed. His purpose was now crystal clear. He would speak to Bruno in the morning and give his instructions. In the moment of greatest danger, he'd never felt safer.

♦

While he was free in the mindscape, Billy's flesh and blood sat silently staring out of the cage at the men looking at the hand held devices. He hadn't seen Harry since the incident with Horace that seemed a lifetime ago. So much had changed and yet nothing had changed. No one bothered to look at him anymore. No voices in the head, no girl with the odd coloured eyes cleaning up and best of all no more pain or cruelty from the fat one. But then one day he'd awoken in a completely different place. No bright white lights. Only a vast cavernous space where the slightest sounds echoed and the lights were always dim. He'd tried to look up and down but as far as he could see there were no other creatures there. But he could sense them. He could see them in the mindscape. As far as the mind could reach. Waiting. Billy hadn't heard from the Purple for a couple of days, but he felt he'd been visited, somehow knowing what he had to do when the appointed hour arrived. The green light of Aaron floated before his, and it was Billy's job to protect him. He was expendable but Aaron must be looked after at all costs. But how when I'm trapped in here? The Purple would show him the way.

41

To: Michelle J. Farrington @ electron.com
From: robert.nash@galactic_vistas.com
Subject: Re: Are you ok?

Michelle
Are you ok? I haven't received any word from you for a while.
Something big is going to happen here. We can all feel it...
x

42

Marcus looked out from the viewing bay at the Magdurian landscape outside. Soon I'll be there feeling the warmth of the sun and breeze on my face once again, he thought. He didn't realise how much he missed Earth's simple pleasures, until he'd been sealed on the Arion with its conditioned machine-produced air. On the day of departure, as he arrived at the terminal ready to board the orbital transfer vehicle, he'd caught the briefest scent of freshly mown grass. At the time he didn't really register it, but now, thinking back, it was as if Earth was bidding a final sweet farewell to his nostrils. Would such things exist when they are finally free to breathe the air of Magdur or will the terraforming provide a whole new set of sensory delights? That would have to wait for another day as he watched Bruno walking off. He'd given him his instructions and when to act on his signal, and had sent out the word that there would be a meeting of the followers in the Cafeteria before they moved to the conference. Some had questioned his handling of the previous day's events, but he'd told them they had acted rashly. He'd seen what the power of a few words could have over a frightened crowd, but he'd been caught on the hop by Aaron's production of the email and had learnt from his mistake. Bruno and the SPC would be his guarantee this time.

'Did you really expect to take on armed soldiers?', he asked his followers that morning. 'They'd have mown you down. Wait until the pieces are in place and then we strike.' He turned to Aaron the fool and said; 'And that is addressed to you in particular.'

Marcus had noticed a vacancy in Aaron's demeanour that was in contrast to his usual bright eyed enthusiasm. Perhaps the death of that drunkard, Scott Allen had weighed heavily upon him. Aaron nodded blankly. 'Ok, go out and spread the word. Ten thirty in the Cafeteria.' This time they would use the SPC to break into the containment area and slaughter the Mags in their cages one by one. There's only a few and it won't take long. Once that's completed, we storm the press conference, demand the arrest of the leadership council, seize control of the base. I'll be unsurpassable after saving everyone from the threat of the Mags and in total control. I'll have the SPC to back me up and the security team will either join us or suffer the same fate as the traitors who called themselves the leadership council. We will start a new pure society on a new world.

◆

He's fuckin crazy. I must be even crazier for agreeing. How the fuck are we going to get into the Lab area? How are we going to kill those things? How are we going to arrest the council? And I've got an hour to think this up. Bruno shook his head as he walked out into the main concourse where Voronoff was waiting for him. He looked at his comrade. 'You won't believe what we've got to do this time.'

'After we just saved his ass! What is it now?'

Bruno quickly filled him in on the plan of action. Voronoff let out a long whistle and shook his head. 'We're putting our necks on the line here, but we've got no choice. It's either us or the Mags.'

'I know, but it scares the shit outta me. Gather the men. Don't let Gutierrez or Van Dee know. How many men are still loyal to them?', Bruno asked.

'Less than ten. The rest are a hundred percent behind you!', came the reply.

'Good. We'll disarm them when we strike. I'll meet you at the Cafeteria.' He placed his hand on Voronoff's shoulder and added. 'Now or never Mikey, now or never.'

Voronoff nodded and started to make his way back to the SPC quarters. Bruno called back to him. 'Mikey! One last thing.' Voronoff turned to him as Bruno spoke quietly into his ear. 'That Aaron. The one with a neck like a chicken.' Voronoff nodded as Bruno continued; 'Don't know why, but Marcus wants him…to meet a tragic but heroic end fighting the forces of tyranny as soon as the Mags are wiped out. Think you can see to that?'

'No problem Bruno. I'll make sure he lives on as a martyr in the hearts of all true believers.'

Bruno smiled, 'That's my Mikey!' They clasped hands and looked each other in the eye. 'If this all goes to shit, I'll see you in hell, otherwise in the Cafeteria!', Bruno said and ruffled his hair as Voronoff made his way off.

The numbers were increasing. Some were making their way to the Cafeteria, others going about their business. Bruno looked up and heard some shouting and cheering in the distance. Another riot? Not now, please. He ran towards the source of the disturbance.

◆

Eleanor made her way through the concourse towards the infirmary to visit Ava. She felt both strangely vulnerable and elated. The previous evening she'd had a visitor. There'd been a knock on the door, and Montano's smiling face appeared on the monitor. Her heart leapt. She'd suppressed such feelings for

305

longer then she could remember. Not getting close to, or trusting anybody. The twin spectres of 'Uncle' Steve and Bruno had cast a long deep shadow, blocking out the sunlight that should have shone on her heart and warmed it with love. The hairs breadth proximity to death she and Montano had experienced had bought a closeness that only those who had shared it would understand. His frequent visits and the hours talking had only increased it. There was also a closeness growing in other ways, especially when he'd shown her the wounds to his body after he had his dressings removed. She was suitably impressed and not only with the medical handiwork.

Stay calm Ellie, stay calm, she told herself....She took a deep breath and counted up to ten before she opened the door and greeted him. 'Raph. To what do I owe the pleasure?'

'I thought I'd inspect your preparations for your next special ops cleaning mission.'

Eleanor laughed as she invited him in. 'Did you think I'd need any help from a loser like you!', she joked.

Montano produced a bottle of wine. 'No but I thought you'd need help finishing this!', he said.

'That can wait until later...', she gently caressed his face before she leant forward and kissed him on the lips. It started gently but the desires they both felt took control. The first rays of sunshine and fires of passion started to thaw the frost of Eleanor's heart.

Smiling at the memory of a long passionate night, while walking absentmindedly through the crowd, she felt tired but happy. *Look at Ellie. First chance of a portion of cock and she's spread 'em like the fuckin little whore she is.* Good, and I loved every minute of it. *Once a Slut always a Slut.* What's the problem, you jealous? She became aware of excited voices next to her.

'HEY! It's the Super Janitor.' Eleanor was startled and turned quickly to be greeted by a smiling man offering his hand. 'I saw you kill that thing singlehandedly!, he said adding; 'Craziest damn thing I ever saw.' Other people recognised her and gathered around smiling, hugging her and clapping her on the back. Eleanor's stomach lurched and pulse raced as she put her hand to her head, realising that she had left her cap back in the room, and cursed herself for her carelessness. 'We owe you our lives', the man continued.

A lady appeared before Eleanor with tears glistening in her eyes. 'Thank you for saving us!', she said before embracing Eleanor.

Eleanor managed to mumble, 'You're very kind. I just tried to do my bit, that's all...'

'Do your bit!', the lady interrupted her. 'Jumping on the back of something that everyone else was running for their lives from is more than just a bit.'

The numbers quickly increased as Eleanor was abruptly swept off her feet by two burly young men, who proceeded to hoist her on their shoulders to receive the applause of the gathering crowd. A loud roar of acclamation accompanied by clapping and cheering broke out. A chant started 'Sup-er Jan-it-or, Sup-er Jan-it-or!'

Fuckin hell Ellie this is embarrassing. *I bet they wouldn't be cheering you now if they knew what a twisted vengeful slut you are, would they Ellie.* For once I agree. Smiling, she waved to the crowd. Looking out, Eleanor noticed a familiar bald head at the back of the crowd. Her smile momentarily faltered as she looked at Bruno's face, a rock of hate in a sea of smiles before it was lost under the waves. Eleanor's chest tightened and her flesh seemed to tingle. The memories rushed out of the dark voids that sat silently behind her mind, of his body and it's crushing weight pressing down on her, his hand across her mouth suffocating her, his voice whispering in her ear, and the pain, above all the pain. She looked down to the men holding her aloft. 'Please could you let me down, I'm still injured.', she told them.

They gently lowered her to the floor, ruffled and breathless. The commotion gradually subsiding. Eleanor was still shaking from the sight of her nemesis. Having run through the situation a thousand times in her head over the past two years, never in her wildest imaginings did she think it would happen this way.

'Eleanor.' A soft but authoritative voice sounded from behind her. Familiar but not instantly recognisable. The bright blue eyes shone out from the benignly smiling face of Counsellor Burgman, as he towered over her small frame. Although in the background the crowd was boisterous, those in his immediate proximity where more hushed and respectful. He leant forward and placed his hands on Eleanor's shoulders and kissed her gently on the cheek. A buzz of surprise sounded amongst those who saw such a rare gesture from the Counsellor. She noticed the expensive smelling aftershave as well as the hint of grey in the roots of his dark mane of hair.

'A pleasure indeed to meet you', he said. His smile radiated not just warmth and kindness but something else. Something that felt different. Something darker, Eleanor thought, as he addressed her. 'The hero who saved our bacon may I add.' He turned to those around him who laughed on cue. A couple just that bit too hard.

Eleanor was immediately on her guard. 'A pleasure to meet you as well Counsellor. I've heard you've been a great comfort to those who have lost loved ones, as well as acting as a representative on behalf of us to the leadership council', she remarked.

She had heard from Montano about the Counsellor's alleged role in both starting and ending the riot the previous evening.

'There's something malign about him Ellie. He speaks kind words that contain murder within them. Beware', Montano had warned her.

'You're too kind....', the Counsellor responded and continued; '....but sometimes a leading role in great events is foisted upon the most undeserving individuals. I never sought it. It found me...'

Approving nods, almost like a row of toy dogs, broke out in those within earshot.

'Great events? I don't understand...', she wasn't allowed to finish.

'Ahh. I mean the role of leadership that fate has decreed should rest on my shoulders, to guide the flock through these tumultuous times', he affirmed.

Eleanor listened to the honeyed words and felt a lurching sense of unease in her stomach. 'Oooh... I see. Yes indeed Counsellor. You have a great responsibility to us all', she said with some irony.

He moved closer and gently placed his arm around Eleanor's shoulders. He spoke near to her ear in a softer voice. 'My dear. You must have undergone many hardships in your life. I can see it in your eyes. The lack of recognition and rejection by those you counted on. The things you deserved snatched from under your very nose.'

Eleanor went rigid. What does he know? Turning her head, she looked straight at Marcus, 'What do you mean "Snatched"? What have people said?', she asked.

Marcus laughed his false laugh and told her; 'Ykdar sees into the hearts of all, and in you he sees greatness. If you wish to join our growing community I can offer you the recognition you so crave. I see a kindred spirit in you my dear.'

'I...I don't know. I'll have to think about it.' Eleanor's mind was racing to get out of the situation.

Marcus's face took on a more serious air. A hint of a frown played on the brow of a man who was used to getting his own way. 'Think? Think! What is there to think about? I'm offering you a privileged place at my side. I will not offer it again.'

'Then I will have to politely decline your kind offer Counsellor', she replied.

A gasp came from those around them. Expressions of shock and dismay abounded. Eleanor took a step back. Marcus's face had adopted a mask of anger and frustration before it was quickly replaced once again by the kindly face of paternal concern.

'Miss Wells, I understand your youthful indiscretions. Maybe when circumstances change you will quickly reconsider.' Eleanor sensed the change in tone as she stared silently back at Marcus. He turned to his group of followers.

'Come!', he beckoned, before striding off towards the Cafeteria followed by those who had surrounded them a few moments earlier. Eleanor watched them plough a furrow through the dispersing group.

Well you got away with that one. Circumstances change? What did he mean by that? Eleanor wondered. There was an undeniable air of charisma about Marcus but also of danger. Don't get too close to him Ellie. Some of the crowd were still around her. Smiling, she waved goodbye before continuing her journey to Ava in the infirmary. As she turned the large looming figure of Bruno blocked her path.

He smiled, clapping his hands and rubbing them together. 'Hi Ellie. Thought I recognised you back there. How's it going? Been a while.' Eleanor stood frozen to the spot. He leant forward and whispered in a less friendly voice, 'I should have broken your scrawny fuckin neck when I had the chance. I won't make the same mistake twice.'

Eleanor shuddered at the voice as much as the words. But the smell of sweat bought back the feeling of helplessness and hate from that morning in the holding cell over two years before. Don't show any fear Ellie or he'll eat you for breakfast, she warned herself. Stepping back, Eleanor smiled and looked Bruno directly in the eyes and said defiantly. 'Yeah great to see you too "Uncle" Valerio.' Noting with satisfaction the cockiness rapidly diminishing. Taking a step closer, she looked up at him and said; "Still the little man I see. Well your gonna be a lot fuckin littler when I've finished with your sorry excuse for an ass. Now get out of my way!' The last part she shouted loud enough for those around them to hear. Striding forward and shoving Bruno's hulking arm aside, she dared not look in his face. Her hand had started shaking again as she made her way to the Infirmary and Ava.

A shadowy figure in a cap watched the confrontation from the back of the crowd. Naomi noted with interest Bruno's stunned countenance as he made his way to the Cafeteria.

◆

Jordan Harris pushed his way through the crowd. He was leading the troop towards the Cafeteria to arrest Marcus. People stepped out of the way of the armed men while they headed towards their appointment with the preacher. He turned to the Sergeants accompanying him.

'Montano, I want your men to secure the entrance to the Cafeteria area and cover us when we escort the prisoner back to the detention area. Overgaard you will follow me into the Cafeteria and act as crowd control while I make the arrest. No one is going to fuck with you after yesterday.' Jordan noticed the look of annoyance on Nicklas' face.

'Sir....', said Nicklas; '....It's not something I took pleasure in.'

'I wouldn't have said it if I thought that Nicklas. I have total confidence and belief in you.'

'Thank you sir.'

Jordan turned to Montano. 'One more thing Sergeant.'

'Sir?'

'Take that stupid grin off your face. I need you focused and it's beginning to annoy me.'

'Yes sir, sorry sir.' Montano responded with a blank expression.

They could hear the sound of the gathering from a way back. They rounded the final corner before the Cafeteria. A line of SPC soldiers were blocking the way. Bruno stood at the front, gun across his chest. 'What the fuck are they doing here?' Jordan motioned for the troop to stop. He turned to the Sergeants and ordered; 'Montano come with me. Nicklas best you stay back here.' Jordan made his way toward Bruno. He noticed the nervous smile on Bruno's face. 'What's happening here Bruno?', he asked.

'Orders Sir.'

Jordan was flustered, 'Orders? From who?'

Bruno swallowed hard. 'To keep the peace Sir.'

Jordan struggled to supress his anger. It was bad enough carrying out a dangerous, morally questionable order from someone he didn't have any confidence or respect for. He just wanted to get it over and done with, but to have some smug gobshite blocking his way was enough to send him over the edge. 'I haven't the patience for fuckin games Sergeant Bruno. Now move your men aside.' He noticed Bruno blink as flecks of spittle escaped his mouth and landed on Bruno's bald head.

'Afraid I can't do that sir.' Bruno's impassive manner only fuelled Jordan's exasperation.

'Sergeant Bruno....', Jordan said with some pique; '....I'm not asking you. I'm ordering you! Out of the fuckin way or I'll have you and your men placed under arrest.' Bruno stared back unmoved. 'Where is Colonel Gutierrez? I'm going to have your balls on a plate Bruno.'

'The Colonel is currently...' Bruno paused momentarily and his smirk returned '....indisposed at the moment Sir', he replied.

A cold sensation rushed through Jordan's chest. Think Jordan, think. 'Bruno, we have critical orders to execute. Time is of the essence. If you don't move aside my men will be forced to take action.'

Bruno turned and nodded to the men behind. A group of them surrounded Jordan and Nicklas immediately as Bruno demanded. 'Sir, please hand over your weapons to my men.'

Jordan was aghast. 'Do you realise what you are doing Bruno....?', he asked and told the bald headed sergeant; '....This is mutiny! You will be court martialled! My men will not lay down their arms to your rabble!'

'Sir, if you care to look.'

Jordan turned back to his men. A squad of SPC soldiers appeared from behind them.

Montano immediately shouted. 'IT'S A TRAP!' A rifle butt flew up striking him across the jaw. He immediately collapsed to the ground and lay there unconscious.

A crack of a gunshot rang out. One of the SPC squad fell dead. Screams broke out as the firefight erupted. Jordan felt the massive hand of Bruno close around his throat. He looked to see the barrel of Bruno's pistol, inches from his face. 'Get them to surrender now or the next bullet is yours', Bruno ordered.

Jordan looked at the desperation in Bruno's face and said; 'You wouldn't fuckin dare Bruno. You're not man enough.'

Bruno pulled the gun away from Jordan's face. Relief washed over Jordan. I knew he would pull back... Jordan felt something press against his leg, and then he heard a shot. An eruption of white hot molten pain ripped through him as his knee was obliterated. He screamed in agony as Bruno pulled the gun back up.

'That was a friendly warning Mister Harris. Next one's for real.'

The roaring pain crippled Jordan as he looked up at the malicious face of Bruno standing over him. 'Go fuck yourself.' He managed to gasp between waves of agony. The din of gunfire increased as Bruno raised his gun once more and pointed it at Jordan's face.

'Your choice.' Bruno's disinterested, matter of fact tone only added to the surreal situation.

This can't be happening...., Jordan thought; .... to be killed by my own side. After all I've been through for that fuckin company. There was a shower of blood as a stream of bullets tore into the soldier standing next to Bruno, killing him instantly. Bruno flinched as he fired his gun. A burning sledgehammer smashed Jordan's head back as the bullet ripped its way through his scalp, ploughing a furrow of blood behind it. He saw Bruno move away and take cover as the blood ran into Jordan's eyes. A searing blaze of agony thundered through his head, and

311

even though his eyes were obscured, a grey coldness drew across his mind while the cacophony of gunfire gently faded into the background.

43

Robert Nash was still wondering why his sister wasn't answering his emails anymore, as he waited anxiously at the rear of the crowd in the Cafeteria. Was she ok? Had there been another nuclear exchange back on earth? Standing on a chair, he wasn't even sure why he was there. His neighbours had said that there was to be a big announcement in the Cafeteria that morning before the press conference scheduled for eleven. At the gathering in the auditorium a couple of days earlier, Counsellor Marcus had stood and spoken so eloquently of his own fears and of those around him. He had asked the people what they wanted and there was one thing above all. To destroy the creatures who had bought death and terror, poisoning the fresh hope that accompanied them from earth.

Robert howled at the obvious falsehoods and lies offered as excuses by the leadership council at the meeting the following day. The atmosphere was turning ugly before Marcus, once again, stood to calm the situation and appealed to the humanity and reason of the base's leadership to destroy the 'Mags' as they had come to be known. He was a man of peace and compassion that those within Pangea base looked to in their time of need. He had reigned back the crowd when they could have rightly torn down those who had deceived them, but he knew violence only begat violence. Last night he'd heard rumours of an email containing explosive allegations that had surfaced. Marcus had prevented further bloodshed when a drunken mob had attacked a scientist nearly killing him. One of the rioters had been shot dead after he attacked the soldiers, before Marcus had selflessly placed himself between the guns and the rioter's frenzy, exhorting calm. What a man, what a hero.

What had he got to say this morning? Had he extracted key concessions? 'Nothing is agreed, until everything is agreed. This is the will of the people. No deal is better than a bad one!' The rumours had swept the base and a flurry of speculation spread like wildfire, especially as the Infonet had been restricted to official announcements. News had spread by word of mouth.

Earlier that morning, Cunningham had to separate Heath and Preston. Heath who had always been the angriest, was exasperated by Preston's hesitancy. Even Robert had set aside his natural caution. It was a do or die situation and Preston's weakness had irritated him.

'I'm sick of you and your animal rights bullshit Preston....', Heath said and continued; '.... Fuck, they're not even animals! Just some abominations created as part of the great experiment and guess what... We're the lab rats, so don't give me

313

any more of your do-gooder bullshit or I swear I'll rip your head off.' And Heath certainly could do that. Preston's meek frame was no match for the youthful muscularity of his adversary.

But Preston stood his ground. 'And you want to get us killed, you big stupid oaf', he said. Robert noticed Heath's complexion become redder, the vein on his forehead pulsing like a thick blue pipe, pumping anger towards his clenched fists that were ready to strike, and yet he seemed paralysed. 'You nearly did it yesterday when you went on the rampage like a wild animal with rent a mob, stirred up by that Marcus....' continued Preston; '....Can't you see he's taking advantage of the situation? All that big show of calming things down. He bloody well started it in the first place! We were lucky it was only that bearded idiot who got himself killed.' Heath took a step towards Preston who dared him; 'Yeah come on big man. Knock me out. Prove how tough you are. That'll make you right won't it, and all our problems will be solved with one punch.' Robert had a grudging admiration for Preston standing his ground. The only sign of fear was the sweat that trickled off his brow and down the side of his face. His silver white hair and wire glasses perched on his long nose gave Preston a more scholarly appearance that seemed ill equipped for the situation.

Cunningham stepped between them, equally unable to stop the seething Heath if things took a turn for the worst. 'Guys, guys! Feelings are running pretty high. Let's cool it down.'

He might as well have been made of glass as Heath looked right through him at the unwavering Preston.

'You're a fuckin' pussy Preston.'

'Better than being a fuckin ignoramus like you!'

For a moment Robert thought Preston was a dead man as Heath's eyes widened and his muscles tensed, ready to rip Preston's head off his narrow shoulders, as the two adversaries were locked into each other's gaze. Then Heath paused momentarily and took a breath, as if the futile defiance of Preston had unnerved him. He spoke quietly and deliberately as he continued. 'You're the type who'll let your friends get slaughtered, saving your miserable neck, while you stand there wringing your hands. No balls to fight for your family and friends. As for Marcus. He's a thousand times the man you'll ever be...', he looked at Robert and Cunningham. 'You coming to the Cafeteria with me or staying with this piece of shit?' He turned on his heel and strode off. Robert glanced at Preston as he passed, feeling strangely guilty despite his anger towards him. Even then, he couldn't quite bring himself to look him in the eye.

314

Preston took off his glasses and wiped his face. His eyes seemed shrunken, almost rodent like in their sockets. Robert could feel his stare as he followed Heath.

'You're all going to die and get the rest of us killed as well. Hope you're pleased with yourselves', Preston told them as they walked slowly past.

The conversation lingered in Robert's mind as he looked around the Cafeteria. Heath was up the front with Cunningham. Preston was nowhere to be seen. The cacophony of hundreds of conversations rang in the air as the appointed time approached. Then a hush descended as Marcus arrived in the Cafeteria, rose from the multitude and stood on a table. Robert craned his neck to see better. Some of Marcus's closer followers sat on chairs either side of him. The scrawny blond one with the bony neck stood just next to him. There was something distant about him, a faraway look in the eyes Robert thought. Marcus had a different look. A look that Robert hadn't seen on him before. Normally Marcus exuded an air of calm authority but this time he seemed tense, angry even.

'Brothers, Sisters. The moment of decision has arrived.' Robert felt a thrill of excitement. Have they decided to agree to our demands? It seemed too much to hope. A murmur spread across those present. 'We have uncovered irrefutable evidence of the lowest treachery.....', the Counsellor said. A sharp intake of breath sounded around the Cafeteria, as he continued; 'We have been deceived by those who agreed to consider our demands!' Cries of anguish sounded. People looked at each other in disbelief. 'They are casting us to the beasts! A team has been sent to arrest me! Your voice is to be silenced! Martial law is to be declared!' A roar of anger reverberated around the room.

'Liars! Fuckin liars!' Robert shouted. The sense of betrayal and anger shook him to the core as he looked at those around him. Outrage on the faces of all, along with the tears of some. Screams and shouts rang out, as the sound of gunshots and explosions could be heard in the distance. The mood of rage quickly turned to one of fear.

Marcus raised his hands and appealed; 'Please, remain calm and stay in the Cafeteria for the moment. It's safe here!', he said before he disappeared into the crowd. A group of armed men appeared at the door. Terrified screams rang out.

'It's ok. It's the SPC guys. They're on our side.' Marcus told the crowd. He saw the large bald soldier with a beard come through the door. Robert noticed that he was splattered with blood as he spoke to Marcus, who listened carefully, nodded, then returned to stand on the table.

'We must act now....!, Marcus addressed the throng '....The group sent to arrest me have been fought off. We have the heroes of the SPC to protect us. We have to destroy the Mag's and tear down those responsible from the positions they have abused so terribly.'

A chant started amongst the crowd as they surged for the exit. 'Kill the Mags, Kill the Mags, Kill the fuckin Mags!'

Robert joined in. 'Kill 'em, kill 'em all!'

The voice of Marcus sounded above the horde. 'Make for the beasts lair, follow the soldiers. Don't take "No" for an answer. DESTROY THEM!'

Robert noticed a man being trampled then swallowed up by the mob as the rush to the door gathered momentum. The door got nearer as the grunts and cries of those around him increased. 'I can't breathe.' groaned a woman next to him, as the colour drained from her face. Robert tried to lift her from the crowd but his arms were trapped helplessly by his side, as the woman sank down and was engulfed. The vice like grip of the crush had absolute power over him as it swayed back and forth. His chest was being compressed and each breath an agony of effort. His legs had lost the power of movement as they fell victim to the mercy of the mob. A hand pressed down on his head as the cries became screams. It was getting quieter and the crowd seemed more distant, he could feel his strength failing and struggled to prevent his knees buckling from under him as darkness swamped him. Surrounded by the muffled shouts and a blur of images, he was being inexorably pushed to the floor and oblivion. His vision was slowly becoming a growing point of light. Am I staring into the eye of death, as it seeks me out? I've heard stories about the light at the end of the tunnel, he reflected. But it was the light of life as Robert popped out of the crowd's squashing grip and into the thoroughfare outside the Cafeteria. His shirt had been ripped from his back and one of his shoes had disappeared, but he was alive. He gulped in precious breaths of air. A raw scratch that stretched from his shoulder and across his chest pulsated with excruciating pain. Several others around him were picking themselves up in various states of distress. Looking to the entrance of the Cafeteria, Robert thought it resembled the business end of an industrial mincer with humans the product. A few people were unable to rise, some exhausted, some injured, others dead. The woman who'd been next to him a few minutes earlier lay still, a few feet away, like a shop window mannequin, glassy eyes wide open and staring lifelessly at him. Trickles of blood ran from her ear and nose. Just behind her, Heath was helping a quivering Cunningham up from the floor.

'Follow me!', a voice sounded. Robert looked around. It was the scrawny one waving his arm and pointing as he yelled. 'To the Mags! Kill them!' Robert got to his feet. The shouts surrounding him as he rushed through the thoroughfare and towards the containment area. They had to die. There's no way another could be allowed to escape.

316

◆

Robert could hear gunfire in the distance. The smell of smoke hung in the air as he rounded the bend. An SPC soldier lay dead in the passage, blood pooling around him. A deafening bang up ahead caused Robert to dive for cover.

Above the racket, he heard the distinctive voice of Bruno talking to Aaron. 'The Troopers are trying to cut us off from the containment area. Get everyone there while we hold them off!' A round whizzed between them, striking the wall behind, causing Aaron to cower on the floor. Bruno remained unmoved, and looked down disdainfully at the quivering Aaron, telling him. 'Get your sorry ass off the floor and move! My men are fighting and dying here, and all you can do is squirm around on the floor like a mincing fairy. Now get outta of my sight before I stick a round up your bony ass!' Bruno thrust a soldier towards Aaron. 'Mikey! Take the little weasel and get him into containment.'

Bruno's harshness had the desired effect as Aaron scrambled along like a fleeing lizard. Robert, deciding that discretion was the better part of valour, followed suit. Once they were past the gun battle, Aaron was back on his feet and leading them in the direction of the Lab area. Up ahead was a plain white door with the understated words. 'Private: No Access Permitted.' Aaron turned to Voronoff and said. 'This is it.' Aaron tried the lock but it remained firmly shut.

'What? You think they're just gonna leave their dirtiest secret open for all to see.' The contempt in Voronoff's voice obvious, before he kicked the door but still nothing. He turned to the back of the group and waved his arm. 'Breach. Here!', he ordered. A large blond soldier carrying a frighteningly large shotgun pushed past Robert, who noticed some food crumbs on the soldiers' body armour.

The soldier looked bored. 'Sir?'

Voronoff pointed, 'Janssen, get us through that door.' Without comment or any change of expression, Janssen aimed the shotgun at the door lock.

'Stand clear!' Voronoff shouted.

The gathering crowd drew back as a loud shout of encouragement started. It reminded Robert of the anticipative noise of the audience before an acrobat performed a particularly dangerous stunt. 'Woooooooooo!' Robert joined the growing noise. Janssen pulled the trigger and a thunderous boom erupted from the shotgun. A black scorch mark was the only visible result as the door remained unscathed and firmly shut. A rapidly lowering 'Ooooooooor.' was the response from the disappointed crowd.

Still Janssen's expression remained unchanged as he reached into his backpack and retrieved a small pork pie. Carefully laying the savoury to one side, he reached further in, this time producing a trio of white saucer shaped objects and proceeded to fix them to the hinges and lock. The crowd started slow clapping him.

'Hey this isn't a fuckin game. Get back. Now!' Voronoff shouted. The crowd reluctantly retreated a few steps further back. 'Further!' he shouted to no response. 'It's your funeral', Voronoff muttered with a shrug as he placed his hand over his ears crouched and turned from the door.

'Fire in the hole!' shouted Janssen as a blinding white flash and ear-splitting explosion ripped the door off its hinges. Robert felt like a giant had casually kicked him in the stomach, as the air was driven from his lungs and he was hurled to the ground. He lay stunned for a few moments, his ears ringing, a large orange blob persisting in his central vision. Everyone in the vicinity lay flat on their backs as a grey cloud of smoke billowed out of the hole were the door once stood.

Voronoff stood over them with a barely concealed smirk across his face. 'Don't say I didn't warn you!', he said, as the fallen slowly climbed to their feet. He turned to Janssen, who was quietly eating the pork pie he'd just rescued from the bag, with the considered deliberateness of a connoisseur. 'Isn't that out of date?' Voronoff inquired with the voice of one who had seen it too often.

Janssen sniffed the pie and glanced at the wrapping before casually discarding it. 'Not really....', he replied; '....Only a month. Anyway it adds to the flavour', then he gestured to the broken door lying twisted on the ground.

'It must be three inches thick and reinforced with steel. Whoever put it here wanted to be pretty sure nobody got through', Voronoff suggested.

'Or they didn't want whatever is in there to get out', Janssen replied before he popped the final morsel in his mouth in a matter of fact manner.

Aaron stepped forward and gingerly enquired. 'Is it safe to go in?'

Voronoff looked to Janssen, then at Aaron and broke into a smile. 'Of course. Please be my guest.' As he half bowed and held his hand out to the gaping hole. 'After you fine sir!', he invited.

A familiar voice sounded from just behind Robert, startling him. 'What the fuck is the hold up here?' He turned to see the forbidding bulk of Bruno pushing his way through the crowd.

Voronoff pointed to the reinforced door. 'We just got it off. Look.', he motioned to Bruno.

'They must have wanted to keep us out pretty badly. Right, let's start getting them through.' Bruno said, then pointed at Aaron and ordered. 'You first faggot face!'. He grabbed Aaron by the scruff of the neck and threw him in head first, sharing a cruel laugh with Voronoff who followed him in. Bruno then turned to the crowd. 'Walk this way to view the Mags!' A cheer went up as they rushed through the gap. 'Hurry, hurry, hurry!', he continued in an air of mock joviality.

Robert hung back, still shaken by the crush at the Cafeteria, when the deafening bangs of automatic fire came from his right. The cheers turned to groans of terror as the four people immediately in front of him slumped to the ground.

'Flank attack! Form up!' Bruno roared as he raised his gun and returned fire. He turned to the panicked crowd, 'Go through now!' Most were fleeing in the other direction, but Robert rushed for the door. It felt as if every gun was trained on his exposed side, waiting for the next bullet to strike home as he dashed through the door, crashing with a thud into the wall on the other side. Immediately another landed on top of him.

'Hey! This way.' Robert looked to see Voronoff waving for them to follow him from around a corner. He raised himself then ran, turned the corner and was met with another clanging roar. Another door was being blasted. The force of the explosion almost shook his bones from their sockets. Still staggering from the percussion of the detonation, his lungs where bursting with exertion as he approached the end of the corridor. The mangled door twisted off its hinges. 'GARGOYLE CONTAINMENT: NO UNAUTHORISED ACCESS' emblazoned across it. A brief burst of gunfire came from within the blasted doorway, before Voronoff and Janssen made their way through, followed by Aaron. Robert was still shocked by how loud the gunshots were, as he stepped through to be greeted by the sight of a man spread-eagled in death on the floor. A pistol next to his hand and a neat hole in his chest, just above his name badge. Robert leant forward and read it. 'Dr Kahoda Vaikar'. He looked up to speak to Voronoff, who was gazing up, mouth agape. Aaron and even the laconic Janssen were staring in awe at the sight before them. Rows of pens stretched above them and into the distance.

'Shit...' Voronoff said, then looked at Aaron and asked. 'Is there anything in them?'

'I don't know. I can't see anything.' Aaron answered nervously.

'Well you'd better take a look then hadn't you?' Voronoff motioned towards one of the pens.

'I ain't doing it! You're the brave one. You take a look.' The normal supplicant tone of Aaron replaced by the certainty of terror.

The group was gradually increasing as more people who had run the gauntlet made it into the containment area.

'Thousands of them...The lying bastards. I thought there'd only be a few.', Voronoff intoned.

Without looking, Robert spoke to the figure next to him. 'My god. It's like a factory.' He turned to see it was Bruno looking up with a resigned expression, shaking his head in disbelief.

319

'Well we're gonna close it for business right now. Marcus was right all along. We had no idea', he remarked. The bravado had gone to be replaced instead by astonishment. He turned to Voronoff, 'Right Mikey let's have a look inside.' They strode towards the nearest pen.

Despite his fear, Robert followed close behind. 'It's pitch black in there.', he commented, then pressed his face up close to the bars as he struggled to see inside. 'Come out, come out wherever you are.', he turned to Voronoff.... 'Can't see anything. Looks like it's emp...'. A loud hiss ripped the silence as a claw shot out from between the bars. Bruno's reflexes were razor sharp as he managed to whip his face out of the way. 'Wooah! That was close.', he said with some relief. Whatever had lashed out had disappeared back into the gloom at the rear of the pen as quickly as it had come. Voronoff was staring in wide eyed shock at Bruno. 'What? Mikey, tell me!', Bruno appealed. Hesitantly raising his hand to his face, he held it out in front of him, staring uncomprehendingly at the blood that covered it. A five inch cut had opened up on the side of his face and blood was streaming from it. The look of initial shock metamorphosed into a mask of rage and hate. He looked at Voronoff and said; 'Get your torch. Now.' Robert sensed the fear that all those around instinctively felt at Bruno's silent rage. One wrong word could cost them their lives. Voronoff held out the torch and didn't complain when Bruno snatched it, immediately shining it into the pen. The beam searched around, catching the odd glimpse of a leg or a claw of Bruno's intended quarry. Handing the torch back to Voronoff, Bruno silently unslung his gun from his shoulder. 'Put it on wide beam and shine it through the bars', he ordered, and glanced over his shoulder at Robert. The impassive calm features multiplying his menace. Robert swallowed nervously, I wouldn't want to be on the receiving end of that.

Everyone knew what was going to happen next, but that didn't make it any less chilling, as Bruno took careful aim through the bars. A defiant hiss came from within the pen. The first shot missed and was answered with the loud clang of the round striking the back of the pen, followed by more as it ricocheted. A piercing childlike scream burst out, as the sound of the trapped creatures' attempts to escape echoed around the cavernous vastness of the containment area. Bruno's expression remained unchanged, while he pulled his gun back and flipped a switch on its side, then pointed it back into the pen once again. This time he squeezed the trigger and poured the entire contents of the magazine into the pen. The flicker of the flame from the muzzle gave the scene a strobe like quality as Robert noticed the creature's increasingly desperate attempts to avoid the hail of rounds. Flashes of aqua liquid were captured in mid-air, as the rounds found their mark on the Gargoyle's body. The cries rose to a screeching cacophony.

320

They looked inside at the broken wounded creature's pathetic attempts to stand as it oozed aqua liquid, slipping and sprawling in its jagged efforts to find sanctuary from the tornado of death. It's wheezing the only sound now coming from within. Various scrabblings and whimpers from the other pens started to echo around the containment area. Bruno paused in the act of reloading, as if an idea came to him, turned and looked at the silent audience, before appearing to spot what he was looking for, then walked calmly toward it.

As Bruno moved past, blood streaming down his cheek, Robert spoke to him; 'Surely you're not going to just leave the thing to die slowly. It at least deserves a quick death.' The unnerving look from Bruno killed any thought of further words as he took a particularly vicious looking weapon from one of the SPC squad who had just arrived. It was connected to a backpack and a small pilot light guttered at the end of the barrel. Carrying the backpack in one hand and the weapon in the other to the pen, Bruno placed the pack down on the floor next to him, then raised the weapon carefully aiming it inside. He looked at Voronoff and motioned with a quick move of the head to stand back. The scrabbling and whistling breaths of the mortally wounded Gargoyle were diminishing. Bruno squeezed the trigger, releasing a squealing jet of flame that leapt from the end and into the pen. A hideous shriek emitted from the pen as Bruno released the trigger, halting the red hot stream of death. The blazing Gargoyle, writhing in its scorching death agony, thrashed wildly on the floor. The noise of suffering fading, then becoming silent as the final twitches of its brief existence played out before it finally lay motionless. Bruno considered his handiwork for a moment then turned away.

The putrid stench of burning Gargoyle flesh pervaded the air. Robert felt queasy as the stench seemed to convert the contents of his stomach into a gurgling tangy vat of potential vomit. He turned away and held his hand over his nose, feeling the salty taste and clammy embrace of nausea enveloping him. Taking a few deep breaths through his mouth, he noticed Aaron walk past him as if in a dream. Robert watched him making his way towards the rear of the containment area. Maybe the shock of the brutal reality had overwhelmed him; perhaps he was having second thoughts.

A distant screeching was rising, becoming louder by the second. It reminded Robert of an old jet plane he'd seen landing at a museum in the far off land of his childhood. The wind blowing in his hair as the faint gentle whistle grew, until all around him placed their hands over their ears, while the ancient behemoth roared across the airfield just above him. Taking his hands away, he tried to scream at his smiling parents, but the din engulfed his tiny efforts to compete.

Robert looked up at the rows of pens that towered over and stretched in front of him. Each one contained a Gargoyle straining against the bars, calling out. Shimmering waves of colour, pink and purple flashed across in a coordinated technicolour kaleidoscope. The rattling of the pen doors accompanied by the growing calls of the Gargoyles that swelled in power.

Voronoff walked up to Bruno and shouted, 'Looks like we're going to need a lot more flamer fuel!' Bruno nodded slowly, running his hand over the wound on his cheek. 'Hey come on Bruno. Cheer up. You'll be fine. We'll restore you to your former beauty. No one will even notice in a couple of weeks. I remember a guy who…', Voronoff stopped in mid-sentence, as the menacing stare of Bruno melted the necessity of any further comment.

'Get the men to gather the flamers and fuel. Looks like we've got a lot of work in front of us', Bruno said with intent. Not quite softly spoken but more of a low rumble that carried through the increasing noise. He looked around and asked; 'Where's that Aaron. Did he know about this?'

Robert piped up. 'I saw him walk away a minute ago. He looked unwell to me, like he was going to puke.'

Voronoff laughed nervously and turned back to the brooding Bruno. 'Seems like he hasn't got the stomach for the dirty work.'

Robert looked around and saw Aaron in front of a control panel about fifty yards away. Methodically working at a terminal, his face expressionless. 'There he is!' he pointed Aaron out to Voronoff and Bruno.

A puzzled frown appeared on Bruno's face. 'What the fuck is he up to…'

Aaron stood up and stared silently at the screen in front of him. A large red circle was flashing insistently on it. Aaron reached out and pressed it, before he turned to them and smiled.

The blaring of the Mags instantaneously fell silent. Those in the containment area stood still, as the frozen moment of time between life and death hung in the air. The universe paused for a moment, on the cusp of the different realities that lay before it.

A thunderous resonating boom signalled the start, as the wall of the containment area began to open. The mechanical scrape of the giant doors slowly revealed a panorama of further rows of pens stretching into the distance. Remote echoes of other gigantic doors opening to further areas and more beyond sounded. Each one towering in its size and scope. A crash of a thousand cymbals resounded around the cavernous area, startling Robert. It was echoed from the other areas that had been revealed. Looking up, he saw the empty hollow fronts of the pens. The ringing alarm bells of terror in his frazzled mind were magnified tenfold, as a Gargoyle silently appeared at each open door, staring out at the freedom before them...

44

The host of Gargoyles hesitated at the opening for a few moments as if they were awaiting further orders.

Bruno looked up, suddenly oblivious to the searing pain of his cheek, 'What are they waiting for?', he asked.

'I'm not hanging around to find out. We need to get outta here now!' The fear in Voronoff's voice gave it a strange warbling quality.

Without warning, the Gargoyles simultaneously burst out of the pens. The sudden synchronisation held a chilling fascination all of its own, as they formed up into four distinct groups, like cavalry ready to charge. Poised, coiled and ready to spring forward, the snapping claws, mouths drawn back, teeth exposed, hissing death. Each one flashing its own distinctive colour across the backs of the Mags. Red, Green, Blue and Yellow. The Red group scuttled in formation across the ceiling and down the far wall. A single Gargoyle moved forward from the group, rose on its legs, striking out with its claws in challenge, daring them to approach.

Bruno's stomach lurched sickeningly as he saw the Green and Yellow Gargoyles move either side of them. 'They're cutting us off and surrounding us.', he yelled. The sound of blood was rushing in his ears. 'We need to form a ring. SPC on the outside.'

Voronoff's face was grey with terror as he protested; 'There's only fifty of us and hundreds of them. We'll get ripped to pieces. We need to run for it. Fuck the civilians.'

Bruno looked around at the group of men they had encouraged, almost dragged to the containment area. A motley bunch, frozen in abject fear, who looked to him and the soldiers for salvation. You're here to protect them Bruno. First sign of trouble and you're running off and leaving them to die. That's why you're called The Settlement Protection Corps ... Hold on! They're not at the settlement yet and us soldiers have a greater intrinsic value than civilians... Ok It's survival of the fittest, and as I'm fit, I survive. Speaking to the soldiers, he told them; 'Men! We need to get outta here. Now! It's everyman for...'

'Heath, No!' The man who had spoken to him earlier was shouting, before a scream drowned out his voice. A pair of Gargoyles snatched a young man from the rear of the group. His legs thrashing wildly, face imploring as he was dragged into the cluster of waiting Gargoyles who were screeching in gleeful anticipation, ready to eviscerate.

'NO! NO! MAMA PLEAAAASE AAAAAAGGH MA...' The last sound rose several octaves as the creatures tore him to tatters in seconds. Another cry sounded as someone else was seized from the other side of the group. His legs kicking, as a pair of Gargoyles hauled him to his doom.

A soldier stepped forward and a white hot jet of flame engulfed the Gargoyles. They wriggled in the crazy quickstep of death, skin scorching and popping as the fires consumed them. Their intended victim rolled on the ground in a final attempt to douse the flames. A blazing mannequin that slowly rose to its feet. His features hidden by the orange inferno as he staggered back toward the group. The soldier stepped forward and aimed his pistol at the blazing man's head. A shot sounded which put him out of his misery, as he flopped to the ground in a blazing, sizzling heap. The smell of roast meat and flamer fuel filled the air.

Too late to run for it now, they had to stick together or die. Bruno shouted, 'Form a ring, head for the exit. Flamers on the outside. Hand your spare guns to the Civilians. Anything comes near, shoot it or cook it!' Moans of gibbering panic sounded as they formed into a huddle. A Gargoyle leapt through the air. The vengeful angel of death was met by a hail of bullets and flamers before dropping in a charred crispy pile.

They kept in formation, jogging toward the door. Any approaching Mag met its doom with extreme violence. Bruno blinked as the sweat ran into his eyes. The stinging heat of the flamers roasting his skin, drowning out the pain from the slash to his face. The was a hole where the door had once been, about thirty yards away. A whimpering desperate noise could be heard, before he realised it was coming from his mouth. 'Nearly there! Keep steady. Don't stop.' He tried to sound brave and convincing, but his voice was wavering on the edge of hysteria. The ground was shaking under his feet. Hardly daring, he looked over his shoulder to be greeted by the sight of three Gorthons thundering toward them. 'Faster, Faster! Don't look back!' Which is exactly what half of the group did. One tripped, causing those behind him to tumble over.

The group moved on, leaving them behind, desperately trying to clamber to their feet before they were pounced upon by ravenous Mags and stripped to the bone. Twenty yards and they were out. Bruno's legs felt like rubber as fear sucked the life out of them. They no longer obeyed the instructions his frantic brain was shrieking at them. A quick movement out of the corner of his eye caught his attention, immediately followed by a squelching crunch. A steaming yellow liquid was eating the face of the man running next to him. The relentless march of the acid, like boiling water poured on ice. No sound could be heard, while his head dissolved within seconds, before he fell from sight. Bruno looked up to see a winged shape swooping down on them in an almost vertical dive, before it released a small glowing bundle.

'It's the Bornix!' shouted one of the soldiers pointing up in dread. Another soldier carrying one of the flamers to his left, looked up, raised his hands to ward off whatever it was, before another crunching ball hit the backpack he was carrying. Glancing around at the acid eating through to the fuel inside, a resigned look passed across his face, as a millisecond later the pack exploded in a ball of fire, killing him and those next to him.

The group lost its shape and momentum as scattered bodies flew in all directions. Exposed and alone, it was each man for himself as the Gargoyles drove into the gap, herding like sheep the fleeing mass into small isolated groups as they took their pick. A thunderous blast came from the Gorthons. A focused hammer of sound that turned the innards of those caught in their maelstrom into jelly, knocking them off their feet, leaving them stunned and immobile, before being methodically obliterated to pulp. A man was carried aloft by a group of Gargoyles, before he was offered in sacrifice to a pair of waiting Gorthon, who graciously accepted the gift. Their tongues smoothly glided out from their mouths, tasting the air, as one held the writhing individual, while the other ended his struggles by neatly snipping his head off with a gigantic claw.

Bruno looked up and saw Aaron, surveying the massacre before him, relishing his handiwork. A Gargoyle sat at Aaron's side, loyally guarding him. Bruno raised his gun and took aim at the undernourished creep, ready to blow his little peanut sized head off in a final act of defiance. A blast of heat hit Bruno as another one of the flamers exploded, knocking him off his feet. A flaming yelping man leapt over him, before collapsing a few feet away. Another, running in a final attempt to make the door and temporary salvation, stumbled over the intestines that spilled from his open stomach, before a pack of Gargoyles descended, making short work of him. Bruno looked up to where Aaron stood. He was nowhere to be seen. The moment had passed.

Voronoff and half a dozen others reached the exit mere feet away, yet it might as well have been a million light years. So near. So fuckin near. Voronoff shouted; 'Bruno! Run for it!'

The troopers appeared from behind them. That they had been desperately trying to kill each other a few minutes earlier was forgotten. How things change so quickly. They had a new enemy to deal with now. One of the troopers knelt down, placing a small tube over his shoulder before taking careful aim. A rocket roared out of the tube, striking a Gorthon just below the neck. The creature looked down at the flaming hole, as it staggered sideways and crashed to the ground with a resounding thud. A large shadow loomed as the Hyperthon moved silently into view. Half as high again as the normal Gorthons it possessed a smooth elegance as it glided forward. The shimmering green on its skin flickered out and then to the Gorthons and Gargoyles next to it, as if directing their actions. They stopped whatever they were doing and turned as one towards the Troopers. The added firepower of the last surviving flamers bristled out from the hole in the wall, as the Gargoyles threw themselves in a futile attempt to cross the invisible force field of steel and flame.

A Bornix came tearing out the dim heights, ready to drop its lethal cargo on those below. Its wings spread wide, the edges fluttering as the air rushed over them in it's almost vertical dive. The mouth open in a wail adding a siren to the apparition of doom that careered down upon its hapless foes. A Trooper pointed up urgently, directing the attention of the one holding the rocket launcher, who changed his stance and locked on to the diving Mag before letting fly. The rocket leapt up towards the Bornix trailing smoke and sparks behind it. At the last moment the flying Mag flicked to one side as the rocket flew harmlessly past, before he resumed his plunge. Unbeknownst to the Mag, the rocket looped around, reacquiring its target before hurtling into the unsuspecting creature in a flash of orange and aqua. The smoking corpse landed a few yards away from Bruno with a sharp crack, as it split open. A series of glowing yellow balls slowly slipped onto the ground next to it. Time slowed to a crawl, as Bruno moved over to it and picked one of them up. It was warm to the touch and a distinct fizzling could be felt coming from within. Looking around, he appeared to be the last man standing. All the others either dead or at the opening.

From the frazzled depths of Bruno's mind, a familiar voice somehow sounded above the deafening racket. 'Daddy, daddy!' Bruno looked over at the mirage of the little girl jumping excitedly on the spot, clapping her hands with a look of glee on her face. Looking up at the Hyperthon towering over her, she tapped it on the leg. The strange creature returned the child's gaze, as she pointed at Bruno and said, 'Your turn...' before she faded back into the darkness from where she arose.

A shimmer of green reached out from the Hyperthon, lighting up on a pack of Gargoyles who were busily dissecting their latest victim. They stopped and turned their attention to Bruno. Moving, almost ambling toward their prey. The contemptuous ease with which his doom approached removed the numbing fear that had shrouded Bruno for the past few minutes. If they think my end is going to be a non-event they're in for a big surprise. He'd rarely thought of death. His big fear was more of being seen to be weak than actual physical danger. The cowardice that deep down he knew lurked within him coming to the surface; the unbearable prospect of humiliation was a fate far worse than anything else. A surge of anger and defiance spilled out of him as the blood continued to stream

327

down his cheek, a crimson target for the Gargoyles. 'Come on then you fuckers! Bring it on. See what uncle Valerio has got for ya!' They changed gear immediately, converging on him with frightening speed. Almost as a reflex action, he threw the yellow fizzling object in a final act to ward off death. The lead Gargoyle ran head on into the fizzler as it broke and emptied it contents over the pack. The first one dissolved into a bubbling puddle before the disbelieving eyes of Bruno. The other three writhed wildly in drunken agony as the acid slipped through them with the minimum of effort, turning their innards into liquid, leaving a burnt out husk. The breath Bruno expected to be his last burst back out triumphantly. 'HA! You thought you had me didn't ya! Well you were fuckin wrong.' He looked over to where the girl had been. She was no longer there.

Something grabbed his shoulder. The moment of triumph vaporised as Bruno screamed in terror. 'No, I don't wanna die! Please!' Tears welled in his eyes as he lost control of his bladder.

'Sergeant Bruno. Save me!' The blood soaked, gore smeared figure of Robert Nash trembled before him, the whiteness of his eyes standing out against the red mask of his face. The racket of gunfire and explosions were deafening them.

Blinking away the tears of shock and shame, Bruno briefly considered shooting him there and then, before he realised Robert was even more terrified than he was. 'Don't sneak up on me like that again', he told Robert. That's if there is another *again* for you Valerio, he thought, before adding, 'You nearly gave me a heart attack.'

'I'm sorry I was hiding under a pile of bodies. I thought everyone else was dead and I was alone. Don't leave me. I don't want to end up like Heath and Cunningham.', Robert pleaded.

'Who the fuck are Heath and Cunn...' Bruno started to say, before a screeching came from above, causing them to look up. A squadron of Bornix were peeling off one by one, starting their bombing run on the Troopers and SPC, who were still fighting off the onslaught of Gargoyles that were preventing them from turning their backs even for a second. Their attention was focused in front and they were unaware of the airborne threat closing in. Bruno raised his gun. Not a single shot had been fired from the new magazine, as its reassuring weight pressed into his shoulder. He shouted to Robert. 'Cover me!'

'Cover you? What with?'

'Keep a lookout for me, you idiot! If anything comes towards us throw one of the yellow balls at it, and don't squeeze it too hard.'

Bruno hissed with irritation as he took aim, releasing a burst into the leading Bornix, carving an aqua valley along its exposed underside. Its wings contracted in agony as it crashed into the middle of the Gargoyles. A cloud of yellow rose into the air, while a large hole was burnt into the attacking mass of Mags. Bruno took aim, bringing two more down, as the fourth one changed direction and headed straight for him. 'C'mon, c'mon I'm waiting for you', he yelled. The head on shape was smaller and harder to hit as he waited. A cry of fear sounded next to him, before the reassuring sound of a crunch and bubbling hiss told him Robert had done his job. Bruno squeezed the trigger. Nothing, it was empty. The certainty of death hit him as it must have done for every victim of dead man's click, while he watched the oncoming shape grow larger, knowing it wasn't going to miss. Over the din, he heard a whoosh, before a blur of movement caught his eye. A moment later the Bornix exploded as the rocket struck home. Bruno leapt to one side, knocking Robert off his feet, a second before the flaming Bornix crashed into the ground. Bruno rolled away as the yellow acid rained down.

'Bruno! For fucks sake c'mon! It was Voronoff's voice. 'We can't hold them anymore.' A ring of Gargoyles was growing around the besieged soldiers driving them back into the exit.

Bruno looked across at the Gorthons closing in. It's now or never time Valerio. Returning to the pile of fizzlers, he scooped some up, handing them to Robert, before taking the final few for himself. He grabbed Robert's arm and told him; 'We burn a hole through them, or we die trying. Got it?' Robert gritted his teeth and nodded. Bruno smiled as the clarity of the situation made him feel strangely serene, 'Good that's the spirit. Let's go.', he said.

Voronoff's squad opened up with everything they had on the Gargoyles immediately between them and Bruno. Robert let out a yell as he hurled the first fizzler into the rear of the mass of Mags. That's my boy thought Bruno, before hurling his own fizzlers. As they struck home, those not dissolved, fled their effects. Bruno's heart leapt as a space opened up, he could see a clear line of sight to Voronoff who was urging them on. They were sprinting to freedom, their final fizzler hurled. The rush of wind and the yell of Robert were the only sounds he was aware of. The gap was nearing. Robert dived through into the waiting arms of Voronoff. Just another few yards to go Bruno thought, as the huge grey pink shape of the Gorthon stepped between him and salvation. A large claw lashed out at him. Trying to duck out the way of its swipe of destruction, he lost his footing and crashed into the leg of the towering monster. Scrambling, he was on the other side, looking up at Voronoff, who was being restrained by Janssen, only a few feet away. Bruno turned to see the mass of the Gorthon standing over him, poised to strike the death blow. Its silhouette blocking out all behind it, as a jet of flame struck it full in the face, followed by a rocket gouging a hole in its stomach before exploding, sending innards gouting out like a decomposing whale. Voronoff's voice rose above the pandemonium, 'Now! Bruno. Get up.'

329

Bruno looked up at the smoking hole that a few moments earlier contained the beast's vital organs, the heart wildly hammering as it pumped the final few pints of blood into the air. The heart grew in Bruno's vision as the Gorthon's knees buckled and it toppled forward. Bruno tried to struggle to one side as the monstrous mass crashed down on him.

Several hundred feet away in the infirmary, Sophia sat bold upright in bed and opened her eyes. She looked at Jasmine and said; 'They're coming. It's happening…'

♦

'They've broken through to the Mags!' Marcus looked up at the news. He'd been wondering amongst the dead and injured near the door to the Cafeteria. The idea that he was in any way culpable for the deaths never occurred to him. He had held back his closest followers from attacking the Mag's. It was always best to let others do the dirty work, and if others could be found to do so, he wasn't going to stop them. Anyway he needed his disciples for the next stage of proceedings, where he triumphantly announced the death of the Mags and proclaimed himself the new leader. Those who had been crushed had served their purpose and fallen by the wayside. There were plenty left to replace them.

'It was the will of Ykdar. He has a greater purpose for them', he said. Those around him seemed to meekly concur. All except a lone hunched figure, crying over the dead body of his wife. Leon Jordan looked up at Marcus who had gone into mock compassionate mode and questioned;

'Greater purpose? Is that what you call it?'

There was a sharp intake of breath by those around. Marcus held out his hands to his entourage in the usual calming fashion and entreated them. 'Please, let him speak.'

'Oh how nice of you. Is that my reward for my wife's death? I may be allowed to speak in your majesties presence?' Leon queried again, his face contorted with grief as the tears streamed down his cheeks.

Marcus could feel the attention of those around fall on him as he spoke to his inquisitor; 'I am sorry for your loss brother Leon. I feel the rawness of your pain. We have all lost loved ones.' He looked around at the assenting nods of his followers and continued; 'In times of loss, it's only natural to question the Lord Ykdar's purpose.' He was addressing all those around now. 'You may ask. "Why me? Why am I suffering so when I've done nothing to deserve it?" But remember, we are all Ykdar's children, and sometimes we make our children suffer, when we take them to have a tooth removed or have an injection.'

330

A chorus of, 'Praise the Great Lord Ykdar!' rippled amongst his followers before he resumed;

'The suffering child does not know why those he trusts are inflicting such pain on his innocent untainted flesh, for he does not understand the greater purpose.'

A red haired woman threw herself at Marcus feet. Vaguely recognising her, he couldn't quite place her. Then he remembered. The face of sexual ecstasy when he preached a few days ago. The same feeling passed across the same area of his body.

'Oh counsellor, you are so wise. How lucky we are to have such a great man as our guide', she exhorted.

Leon laughed ironically and spat out disdainfully; 'What a load of shit! Are those empty platitudes meant to comfort me in some way? It's part of Lord Ykdar's great purpose is it? Nice Sky Lord you've got there!'

Another gasp and cries of outrage sounded. 'Blasphemer! Apostate!'

Leon turned to them. 'Look at you lot. A meek flock of sheep tamely following your master and the big sky fairy to the abattoir. At least you saved them some time by having your brains scraped out first!' The followers shrank back under the verbal onslaught from someone who, until a short time before, had been one of their own.

Marcus spoke calmly, 'Let him continue'

Leon's mouth was drawn back in a snarl of grief and hate, as he spewed out his disgust at Marcus. 'Yeah! I can imagine him now, up in the sky somewhere, writing in his big tome of wisdom, saying to himself, "So how do I make the universe a better place for all?" when a happy thought suddenly occurs. "I know, I'll let some completely innocent people die horribly for no reason. What a brilliant idea! Now why didn't I think of that earlier. Oh silly me...'". He slapped his hand to his forehead in mock realisation, his eyes looking upward, before continuing, 'What makes you so sure you're right, and all the other great ideas of the truth are wrong....?', he asked Marcus; '....Has civilisation been waiting for so long just for you to turn up? The universe is a difficult random place, and for you to say you have all the answers and everyone else was wrong, is the same cracked record that the human race has been listening to since the dawn of time, and you know it. The only thing you're interested in is selling bullshit in exchange for power and control. I was taken in by that crap and now my wife has paid with her life!' Leon knelt forward holding the body of his loved one in his arms and started sobbing. 'Now just go and leave us in peace. You've caused enough damage already.'

Marcus stood in silence desperately thinking what to do next. Remember it's important to appear resolute in the face of insults. A conciliatory gesture will suffice. Leaning forward, he placed a consoling hand on Leon' heaving shoulder, and was shocked as Leon leapt to his feet. Marcus felt the sharp crack from the punch that landed square on his chin. The pain resonated through Marcus's head as he staggered back into the arms of his horrified followers.

'Get your hands off! Touch me again and I'll fuckin kill you!', Leon shouted, his fists clenched in defiant readiness for the next round.

'Seize him!' shouted one of the entourage.

'Hold on. Can you hear that?', someone yelled. Everyone looked at each other as they became aware of a distant noise. A choir of screaming harpies rising in volume, accompanied by an insidious scrabbling of a thousand claws, was rapidly approaching.

45

'**You** spoke to him?', Ava asked.

'I saw him when those people lifted me up. I've never felt so exposed or embarrassed in my life. I could have died.' Eleanor recounted her journey to the Infirmary while Ava listened in amazement.

'You'll have to get used to that now you're a celebrity I'm afraid. So what did you say?'

'I told him how pleasant it was to meet up with old friends and I was looking forward to having tea and biscuits with him at the earliest opportunity.'

Ava laughed at Eleanor's bravado and said; 'I bet he can't wait, the snake.'

In truth Eleanor wasn't feeling that brave, but she was determined to put a plucky face on things and decided to change the subject. 'The doctor told me your mood has improved and you're ready to be discharged.'

'Yes, I discovered I can turn my Psychic powers off at will now. I'm exhausted and need a rest from the storm. I won't be joining you in the settlement and the Mags are going to be destroyed, so I've outlived my usefulness and it's back to earth for me when the next resupply arrives. Doctor Ferguson has told me I'll have new eyes. They're going to print the structures, then use my stem cells to grow over them, before assembling and surgically inserting them at a place called Moorfields in your home town, London. I've heard it's a great place.', Ava explained.

'The best. How's Sophia by the way?', Eleanor asked.

'Funny you should say, she was a bit agitated earlier. It's the first time she's shown any signs of life since the breakout. She started yelling, "They're coming", or something like that.'

'What's coming? How is she now?'

'They managed to calm her after a little while. Probably nightmares after what she witnessed. Poor babe...'

'Hi Ava!' Eleanor turned to see a smiling Elizabeth approaching, recognising her from the last few days, thinking how envious she felt that Elizabeth had been allowed into Ava's confidence, while she, was still persona non grata. But that had changed, and Eleanor felt comfortable speaking to her. Elizabeth walked towards Eleanor holding her hand out. 'A pleasure to meet you Eleanor, I'm Liz.' She took Eleanor's hand placed her other hand on top of it. 'We all owe you so much. I've heard so much about you Eleanor.' Her voice faltered momentarily.

Eleanor stood up and embraced Elizabeth. 'Thank you for your kind words

Liz.' Pity you never even acknowledged me around the labs when I was only the cleaner, snotty bitch. Only interested in wrapping Walker around your pretty little fingers…

Elizabeth sighed loudly, placing her hands on her hips as she turned to Ava. 'And you madam! What one of the seven dwarves am I getting today?'

'Probably, Dopey or Sleepy' cut in Eleanor.

Ava let out a laugh and clapped her hands in delight. 'I love you guys!' She held her arms out and embraced them both.

Elizabeth moved back looking slightly flustered and nodded. 'Looks like it's Happy then.'

Eleanor looked up at the screen. The conference was about to start. The sound was off as Eleanor noticed a tense looking Celina accompanied by Myra taking their places. The look between them didn't bode well, Eleanor thought as they started talking. 'The conference has started. Let's hear what they've got to say', she said and pressed the sound button.

Celina's voice came out from the screen. The rapid blink rate and clenched hands showed her agitation as she spoke. '..additionally in light of recent disturbances, for the interests of public safety, a curfew will be imposed between eight pm and eight am. All gatherings of more than four people are prohibited.' A rush of shouts rose from the conference.

Ava sat up. 'A curfew? Did I hear right?', she asked.

Eleanor looked up at the screen in shock but not surprise. 'You did. People are not going to stand for this. Are they mad?' As the friends watched the screen, Celina pressed grimly on.

'Additionally, a state of martial law has been declared and the use of lethal force is authorised.' This time it was as if a mute switch had been pressed as the audience sat in shocked silence. 'This will take…', Celina's head shot to the side as a crashing roar followed by screams sounded off camera, followed by a sound Eleanor and Ava knew only too well. Celina looked up at a figure off screen that cast an ominous shadow across her. 'Tiddles…' she managed to say before her face was obliterated by the giant claw that crashed down on her head, in an explosion of red. The huge pink grey shape moved across the screen, ripping Myra from her seat as she desperately attempted to flee. The claw closed around her waist and picked her up like a toy, leaving her violently kicking legs visible. Her shrieks were cut short with a sudden crunching rip, her legs twitched for a moment then hung limply, before dropping back down on the desk minus their upper half.

Ava didn't have to see anything to know what was going on. Leaning forward, grabbing Eleanor by the arm, she screamed and writhed wildly on the bed, knocking over the drip, holding her head. Ava was drenched in sweat as she ripped off her dressings. Her blood red mangled eyes reminded Eleanor of a meal of Italian meatballs in tomato sauce she once had, as Ava stared sightlessly out and shouted; 'The flames! They're purple!'

Elizabeth let out a scream as Eleanor grabbed Ava, trying to restrain her. 'Ava! It's Eleanor. I'm here you're gonna be ok'.

'Switch it off! Stop the visions!', Ava implored. Her muscles were a rock hard mass of terrified energy and frightening strength. Eleanor was losing control of her friend.

Amanda Holloman dropped what she was doing and came running over. 'What is it! What's happening?', she enquired.

'I don't know!' lied Eleanor. Then Ava went limp and laid face down on the bed. The only sound in the room was her breathing.

Amanda turned her over. Blood streamed from Ava's eye sockets.

'Ava, you need to calm down. You mustn't remove your dressings. It could cause all kinds of problems.' Amanda said, looking gravely at her patient and added; 'I'll fetch some fresh one's.' She turned to Eleanor and whispered. 'You need to keep her calm.' Eleanor nodded.

Eleanor felt cold, clammy and nauseous as Amanda made her way to fetch the dressings. She'd seen some terrible things in her time, but not the sight of a close friends' mutilation.

Ava turned to face Eleanor, her face glistening with beads of sweat and sobbed; 'I saw what Sophia saw.' I should have been switched on... Sophia was right. They are coming. I can see the Mags. Thousands of them!' The burning icy hand of fear gripped Eleanor's trembling heart as she heard a commotion then shouting from the corridor.

Nicklas Overgaard burst in followed by a squad of heavily armed Troopers. Eleanor noticed blood splattered across his battledress. 'Everyone!....', he shouted; '....The Mag's have broken out and are coming this way. There is a designated refuge in the storage areas. We need to evacuate now!' Everyone looked at him incredulously. A commotion of screams, crashing and roaring sounded in the distance. 'Move now if you want to live!', he snapped.

The stunned stillness was broken as everyone burst into frenzied activity. Amanda screamed, 'How can we move the intensive care patients? We can't just leave them to die!'

'Don't you understand?', Nicklas retorted; 'There is no time. We don't have the luxury.'

'Well I'm not leaving them to die alone!', tears ran down Amanda's face as she stood next to the bed of a sedated patient. Nicklas turned to three men behind him and muttered instructions to them. They drew their pistols as they moved around the room. Eleanor felt the horrifying certainty of what was going to happen next. 'What the hell are you doing?' Amanda screamed as the troopers moved to the beds of those who couldn't be moved. Nicklas pushed Amanda to one side before pointing his gun at the head of the patient. 'No! You can't.', Amanda shrieked. Nicklas pulled the trigger and the sharp crack of the pistol rang out. The patient jerked once and was still. Amanda's scream reverberated as three other shots sounded in the infirmary. She threw herself at Nicklas, arms flailing and shouting. 'Fuckin murderer!'

'It's a kindness compared to what those things will do to them. You're needed alive.' Nicklas grabbed her arm and twisted it behind her as she tried to hit him. He handed her over to another trooper and ordered; '....Fynn, make sure you get her alive to the storage area'. One of the troopers approached Ava, gun at the ready and looked at Eleanor. 'Can she walk?', he asked. Eleanor gulped and nodded, 'Right. Get her up and moving', he commanded. Another pistol shot popped at the far end of the room.

Eleanor pulled Ava off the bed and said; 'Stick with me.'

Ava was breathless and weak, hardly able to stand. Eleanor supported her and moved her quickly towards the door.

'Don't leave me behind. Shoot me if you have to.', Ava appealed.

'That's not going to happen Ava. I promise.' Eleanor assured her and looked up. Amanda the nurse pushed off Fynn and was helping Sophia along with Jasmine. Akeely was shepherding some more walking wounded along. Johnathan Gough, his head heavily bandaged, was among them. A smash and some blasts sounded from outside.

'They're here, we're cut off', a voice called to Nicklas from outside. A scrabbling could be heard as shouts and more shots rang out.

Nicklas turned to Fynn; 'Get them to the service hatch and along the tunnel. We'll hold them off, then follow on.'

Fynn and the others exited the ward into the main lobby area. A dead Gargoyle lay crumpled near the main entrance.

Nicklas pointed to the service hatch at the rear. 'You know the way to the storage bay. I'll see you there', he told Fynn. A skull rattling roar sounded from outside. He turned back to face the door just as the Gorthon exploded through it, accompanied by several Gargoyles. It lashed out at a Trooper, sending him spiralling through the air and crashing dead against a wall.

Eleanor watched almost impassively at the diabolical scene. She'd spent the past few days trying to supress the thoughts and feelings that came with half a lifetime of death and violence. The choices made through anger and betrayal that had so blighted her existence floated in her mind's eye. The new gentler Eleanor had found a measure of peace over the past few days, despite the turmoil around her. The reconciliation with Ava, facing down the black heart of Bruno and then the feelings she'd allowed herself to feel toward Montano, but then there was something else that lay below the surface. Instincts that made her run toward danger while normal people fled for their lives. Any fear she may have felt a few moments earlier melted away.

The fires of combat and warfare that burned in her heart and forged her character roared into life, as the warrior inside Eleanor took over. Handing Ava to a terrified Akeely, she said; 'Look after her and get her to the hatch.' Akeely nodded as Eleanor rushed forward grabbing the gun and some of the grenades from the dead trooper. She knew where to aim on the Gorthon, and looked to see Nicklas firing at the creature. A high pitched shriek came from behind. A pair of Gargoyles had pounced on Johnathan Gough. One, with all fours wrapped around pinned Johnathan's arms to his side, while the other raised up, claws poised to rip his throat out. Taking aim at the one on top, she emptied two rounds into it. The Gargoyle shot backwards just as the second drove its claw into the exposed windpipe of Johnathan, who slumped, dead before he hit the floor.

A flurry of gunfire from her left made her look back round to see the Gorthon closing in on Nicklas, dead Troopers either side of him. The Gargoyle that had just killed Johnathan closed in on him from behind. Eleanor moved and took aim in one movement, drilling several bullets into the exposed flank of the small but deadly creature, causing it to twist in mid-air, before it landed behind Nicklas and crashed into his legs. As Nicklas instinctively turned, the Gorthon seized its moment, striking out.

Eleanor shouted a warning but too late. Nicklas had the reflexes of a cat and turned to ride the blow but the crushing claw struck him a glancing blow on the arm, shattering it and spinning him around like a top, landing him winded on his front. Nicklas shouted in pain as he tried to raise himself, arm hanging uselessly by his side. The Gorthon was on him immediately, grabbing his backpack and raising him up. The rest of the troopers in the room were dead, or about to die. Nicklas looked across at Eleanor. 'Get to the hatch Ellie. Save yourself. Get to the hatch!', he shouted. A large spike of a claw burst out of his chest, the agony of death was on Nicklas' face as in a final movement, he raised his gun above his head, pointed it behind him and squeezed the trigger. The Gorthon uttered a trumpeting bellow of anger and pain as the claw instinctively drew back, dropping Nicklas on the floor. Nicklas raised his head, looked up at Eleanor, his mouth opened to say one last thing, but only blood passed his lips before he was engulfed by a pack of Gargoyles and disappeared into oblivion. The Gorthon's head was coursing with aqua Mag blood. One of the eyes was hanging out of the socket, dangling on a threadbare sinew. It looked at Eleanor, the last surviving obstacle before spotting his prey disappearing into the opening of the hatch at the far side of the room. *Time to die Ellie. You're toast!* Only Fynn remained outside.

Eleanor knew she only had a heartbeat before she was cut off and trapped. She started dashing to the hatch, but a Gargoyle was trying to head her off. Without thinking, she sprayed it with the remainder of the magazine. The moment's hesitation cost her, as the remainder of the Mags gained the lead in the race of doom. Even if she beat them, there was no time to climb through. *They're gonna rip your tits off Ellie and feed them to the Gorthon for a snack. Revenge for killing his long lost friend, ya crazy little whore.* Still she ran, her last hope gone. *Oh dear, looks like you've lost. All Fours against two legs, only one winner there. No prizes for second place in this game Ellie, only death.* Yeah, well remember if I die, you die too asshole! A bright flash to her left was followed a split second later by the explosion of a grenade that shredded her nearest pursuers. The sharp sting of splinters tore into her back as a Gargoyle leg struck her on the side of the head, sending her crashing into a row of chairs. Without breaking stride, Eleanor leapt up and burst clear. Fynn was a few feet away holding the hatch open, while firing at the onrushing Mags, who were driving forward once again. The furious wriggling legs of the Gargoyles were a blur of movement as they made up the ground. A final volley momentarily slowed them as Eleanor reached the tunnel, breathless from the frantic race. Up in the tunnel Akeely reached out an arm.

'Get in there now!' Fynn shouted.

'I'm not leaving you to die'

'Now!' Fynn grabbed her and hurled her up to the waiting hands of Akeely. 'Cover me as I climb in.'

Akeely showed surprising strength as she hauled Eleanor into the hatch before producing a gun. Inside the maintenance tunnel was about four feet square. Not enough to stand but enough to crawl along. Various pipes and wires lined the walls. Eleanor looked along the tunnel and was relieved to see Elizabeth helping Ava to safety, behind them she could see Sophia and Jasmine disappearing into the gloom.

'Ok she's in!', Akeely yelled, before she handed the gun to Eleanor, who turned and fired a burst into the lead Gargoyle, as it readied itself to take a desperate leap at Fynn while he turned to climb up into the hatch. The thundering mass of the Gorthon was bearing down on them relentlessly, its booming steps shaking the entire room, causing light fittings and ceiling tiles to tumble down. The fear was written large across Fynn's face as Akeely strained to drag him in. 'I can't do it...' she hissed through gritted teeth. Her strength was failing before Eleanor reached across and gripped his other arm. The feet of the Gorthon came into view as they gave one last heave and hauled Fynn through. The Hatch slammed shut with a deafening boom as the Gorthon slammed into the other side. Three more crashes dented the door in, but it held as Fynn crawled clear.

Fynn drew a couple of desperate wheezing breaths before he gasped, 'What took you so long, I thought I was Mag feed there.'

'You shouldn't be so fat', Eleanor responded as another blow hammered on the door.

Akeely cut in, 'Could you two stop arguing and let's get out of here.'

'Good point Doctor.', Fynn replied, struggling to maintain his self-control. 'After you ladies.' They turned to crawl along the tunnel, Akeely leading, followed by Eleanor then Fynn. The squeal of ripping metal rang out and the door flew from its hinges. 'Fuck! Move it.', Fynn ordered.

Eleanor looked back as a Gargoyle entered into the tunnel and pointed the gun, but Fynn was blocking her aim. 'Get down Fynn', she shouted. He instantaneously lay flat as Eleanor fired. The muzzle flash illuminated the interior of the tunnel, showing the bullets striking the head of the Gargoyle in frozen moments of an electric blue flickering light, as the creature succumbed to the hail of destruction. It shuddered, then was still.

Fynn looked up and over his shoulder and started to raise himself back to a crouch, when the huge arm of the Gorthon reached in and closed its gigantic hand around his outstretched leg. Fynn let out a cry of agony and terror as the Gorthon started dragging him back out into the open. In an instinctive action, Eleanor pulled the trigger and a couple of rounds slammed into the Gorthon's arm, but still it clung onto its hard won prize, its claws savagely tearing into the flesh of Fynn's legs. Eleanor pulled the trigger again but nothing happened. The Gorthon's face appeared in a gruesome portrait at the hatch, greed and hate glinting in its remaining eye, the other dangling uselessly. Eleanor knew what was coming, as Fynn hung on in desperation and terror to pipes that ran up the side of the tunnel. The Gorthon drew a breath before letting rip with the death roar that stunned and stupefied its victims. The air seemed to congeal and thicken in the close confines of the tunnel. Eleanor felt she was drowning in a vibrating jelly that would liquefy her internal organs. Fynn moved his hands to his ears before being dragged ever closer to the exit. For Eleanor, the world became a muffled underwater scene of horror. The only sounds were her breathing and the groan of metal. Fynn's pleadings a far off muted call.

The Gorthon's mouth opened in expectation, the back of the throat pulsating, a smaller second mouth ready to gulp down flesh and blood. In her befuddled state, Eleanor looked down and saw the last pair of grenades hanging from their belt. She felt as if she was looking down on herself from above, and reached down, took a grenade, pulled the clip before gently lobbing it toward the Gorthon. It sailed through the air in a graceful arc and into the beast's mouth before the open entrance of the throat devoured it. A look that resembled surprise passed across the Gorthon's face before a deep thud could be felt. The Gorthon regurgitated a tongue of flame, followed by various fragments of internal organs that were vomited out over Fynn's back, as the grip on his leg released and the beast sank from view. A great ship slipping silently beneath the waves. Fynn's mouth was moving, opening and closing slowly, a distant grinding noise that resembled language, grew more distinctive before Eleanor's hearing whooshed back and the full cacophony hit her traumatised brain.

'Ahhhh! My leg!' Fynn screamed and reached out to Eleanor. Taking his arm, she dragged him along the tunnel, ignoring his screams and protests. 'Please! Not so fast', he pleaded. Turning to speak, an onrushing Gargoyle scuttling up the tunnel caught her attention as it closed on them. Taking the last remaining grenade, she hurled it towards the Mag. They dived down and covered their ears as the explosion tore through the tunnel. A sheet of flame raced along the ceiling before dissipating. The tunnel was engulfed in total darkness, as silence reigned once again, broken only by the laboured breathing of those trapped within.

46

The din of the Gorthon echoed from the main concourse. The gleaming perfection of the shops and the allure of all that entailed had been supplanted by fire and blood. Gunfire offered a response but the smashing pandemonium of the Mag's approach grew relentlessly louder by the second. The panicked cries of the pursued mixed with the shrieks of the trapped and their final cries for mercy, before the brutal cut off.

'How much further sir?', Montano asked.

Jordan gritted his teeth against the pain of his shattered knee. But it was dwarfed by the thunderous beast from the wound in his head, that overwhelmed him. Montano supported him as well as he could, but the blood loss from his own leg wound, as well as the concussion he was suffering made it hard to tell who was supporting who.

'Another hundred yards and we're there.', Jordan told the sergeant.

They were making their way along one of the smaller lanes leading from the concourse, trying to reach the communications centre, but progress was unbearably slow. They had both regained consciousness to discover everyone gone, leaving only the dead for company. They had picked up some weapons and grenades from the gun battle casualties. A stray bullet had hit Montano in the leg, but no major artery had been hit. Only the gnawing pain remained, sapping his energy.

Jordan had called ahead but the Comms were down. It was the only place where the basewide infonet could be accessed and controlled. 'We've got to get everyone to the storage areas', he managed to say before another scalding wave of agony washed over him.

'And you've tried contacting them sir?'

'No luck I'm afraid sergeant.'

The sound of fleeing, stumbling footsteps approached them from behind. Jordan turned to look. The quick movement of his head caused a surge of queasiness and flashing lightning that almost made him pass out. The urge to vomit was irresistible as the running man approached, his desperate whimperings in sync with the hoarse breaths that his lungs forced from him. His torn clothing and wild hair were testament to his journey.

'You need to move; the monsters are just around the corner', the man said. His tears of desperation and fear had washed twin streaks through the grime of his face, as he kept looking anxiously over his shoulder.

'Well actually that's going to be a bit difficult, seeing we've both been shot.', Jordan replied. The man didn't seem to notice as he glanced back toward the sound of the Gorthon. 'Can you help us to get to the media centre to tell everyone to evacuate to the storage areas?' Jordan asked him.

He turned back to Jordan, 'Ok I've got to go. They're here!'

Jordan felt the powerless exasperation of trying to communicate with someone in shock and panic but persisted, 'Didn't you hear me? Help us to the media centre. We won't make it otherwise and nobody will know where to evacuate to.'

The man looked vacantly at Jordan and shook his head as if he were declining an offered leaflet to a substandard restaurant. 'Sorry I must be going', he said then turned to run off.

Montano raised his gun, pointed it at the man's head and said; 'I don't think you understand sir. We're not asking, we're telling you. Now come here and help us, asshole!'

The man turned back and shook his head. Terror carved in every crease of his features. 'I don't care, shoot me then. Rather that, than being caught by one of those!' He raised his hand and pointed with a quivering finger at the Gargoyle that had just rounded the corner at the far end of the lane.

Jordan and Montano dived into a doorway just before the Gargoyle turned and spotted the man who had started to run. They could hear the despairing sobs of the man being pursued by the scrabbling of the Gargoyle. Four legs gaining on the two as it flashed past the doorway, failing to notice Jordan and Montano.

'No, no, not me. I don't want to die. Let me go, I won't tell anyone. I promise...'; the man's pleas, as his steps faltered, rang in Jordan's ears. The reflections of the glass in the doorway showed the man stumbling drunkenly over as the paralysis of fear numbed his legs, while the Gargoyle approached him cautiously.

Montano turned to Jordan and whispered; 'That's unusual for a Gargoyle to be alone. It must be lost.' Jordan watched as Montano limped forward and peered both ways along the concourse. A loud hiss sounded, while the man's panting breaths turned to a keening whine, as the Gargoyle prepared to administer the coup de grace. Montano raised his gun to shoot.

Through the pain Jordan managed to grunt, 'Don't. They'll hear you and it'll bring them all down on us.'

The shots sounded, mixing in with the background noise as Montano pulled the trigger regardless. The squeals and thrashings of the Gargoyles death played out in the concourse for a few seconds before ceasing. Montano turned and pulled Jordan to his feet then said; 'We haven't got a choice, without him we won't make it.'

They slowly emerged out of the doorway. The man sat huddled up against the wall staring at his former nemesis, dead before him. Montano pointed his gun at the man. 'You! Up.' The man rose slowly, mouth agog and nodding, seemingly unable to comprehend he was alive. 'What's your name?'

A quizzical expression passed across his face as he seemed to be struggling to recall the name of a half forgotten friend. After a few moments the light of recognition shone in his eyes. 'Nicolas.' There was still an air of hesitation that lingered in his tone.

'Ok Nicolas, come here and help him....', Montano said, motioning towards Jordan; '....It's a hundred yards along there', he added and gestured along to the far end of the lane. Nicolas approached and put his arm around Jordan's waist, supporting his weight. Montano hobbled forward as Nicolas dragged Jordan as fast as he could towards the media centre.

Agony flowed over Jordan as the wound from his knee crunched with shattered bone against raw severed nerve. Feeling faint from the blood loss, a chill spread through him. He howled in pain but Nicolas was on a mission as he ignored Jordan's cries, dragging him remorselessly towards the glass front of the media centre. The noise of annihilation was growing behind them. Through the fog of pain, Jordan whispered, 'It's there on the right.' Nicolas dragged him to the door. They looked through the windows into the lobby of the Media Centre. It was intact and deserted as if everyone had left for the evening.

Montano pushed the door open and looked around before ushering in the others. A shuffling sounded from behind the security desk. Montano instantly whipped around, nervously pointing his gun. 'Show yourself now!', he ordered. The shuffling continued. The crash of gunshots reverberated in the smooth plush surroundings of the lobby as he fired several shots into the desk.

A scream came from behind the desk. 'Don't shoot, don't shoot.' A hand emerged, grasping onto the edge before a young, smartly dressed woman appeared. Her immaculate appearance in contrast to the filthy bloodstained figures before her.

'Why didn't you say anything?', Montano shouted at her. 'You could have got killed.'

'Because I didn't think you were a trigger happy asshole, that's why', came the terse reply. The woman's eyes flashed angrily as she added; 'I didn't even have the chance to say anything before you started blasting away.'

Montano recognised the woman. 'You're Patricia Fernandez the newsreader.'

'What? You want a fuckin signed picture? Let's get out of here', she urged.

'No, we're going in....', Jordan told her; '....We need to tell everyone to evacuate to the storage areas.'

Patricia turned to Jordan. 'Well good luck with that. Nearly everyone was at the conference and the rest have fled. I was going to join them when I heard the gunshots from outside.'

'We haven't got time for this shit.', cut in Montano, 'We have to get to the studio now. Everyone's lives depend on us, so get us there now!' Patricia flinched at the harshness of Montano's voice. She was obviously not used to being spoken to in such a manner. 'I said now lady, not next week!', Montano repeated.

Patricia let out a petulant snort, 'Follow me.'

'No, I need help. You can put your arm around me.'

A look of outrage and disgust spread across Patricia's face. 'You burst in here like a bunch of bums, shooting your guns and shouting orders. Do you realise how much this outfit cost, and you want to get your filthy, sweaty rags all over it. I don't think so. Meester!' She folded her arms and angrily pouted her lips.

The vanity and stupidity of the situation enraged Jordan. 'Ever wondered why everyone ran off and left you? You're worried about your clothes while hundreds of people are...'

'Leave it Sir....', Montano interrupted Jordan; 'I'd rather walk and suffer the pain.' He turned to Patricia. 'Lead on, quickly.'

A crashing noise came from just outside the centre. The throbbing blast of a Gorthon's roar accompanied by the screeching of its attendant Gargoyles filled the lobby.

Patricia screamed and immediately rushed to Montano, putting her arm around his waist and dragging him towards the Studio. 'Come on, let's go', she suddenly insisted, the pout and attitude gone. They were followed by Jordan and Nicolas, the smell of her expensive perfume mixed with the stench of sweat as they grunted and shuffled along the corridor and up the stairs to the studio.

The main screen in the control room was still displaying the empty conference hall. Myra's severed lower half still sprawled amongst the tangle of wires. The news desk sat empty in the studio, camera pointing and waiting. A bank of various screens showing innumerable broadcasts on multiple channels.

Montano looked to Patricia, 'Where's the news studio?'.

'Down the bottom, number 503.'

'And how do I make it show on all screens?'

Patricia looked along the rows of buttons for a moment before selecting one. All the channels changed to a large lady dressed in a white flowing robe and wearing a golden winged helmet singing Wagner. 'Not that one...'. She went through several more channels that included cookery, talent shows, reality shows, comedy shows and a football match.

Jordan looked up at the programs he despised as pointless trivial rubbish, played out. He was filled with sadness of the random craziness of humanity and all its glory, foolishness and vanity that the lost world represented. We've reached the stars and achieved wonders and horrors beyond the wildest imaginings of our ancestors, and all we've created is a real hell on the far reaches of the Milky Way galaxy, when we had all we ever needed back on Earth, he thought.

After a few more seconds, the empty chair and the news desk appeared on the screens. 'Ok we're ready to go.' Jordan was being taken towards the Studio by Nicolas.

Patricia looked up. 'Where you going?', she demanded.

'Show me to the Studio, I need to make the announcement.' Jordan was perplexed by her question.

'Not you. Look at the mess you're in', Patricia said gesturing to Jordan. 'Leave it to the professionals. Anyway you're too ugly!' While Jordan and Montano laughed and Nicolas stared blankly, she added. 'Tell me what you want me to say.'

'Tell everyone to get to the storage areas immediately. No waiting, no belongings, just go now', Jordan told her.

Patricia nodded, fixing her earpiece and pointing to the control panel she said; 'Press the record and loop button.' She left the room before appearing a few seconds later, scores of her moving in perfect unison in the control room screens. Sitting in the chair, she looked gravely at the camera. The screen was kind to her features under the studio lights. A distant smash sounded from downstairs in the studio. The Mag's had found their way in. Patricia glanced nervously across before turning back to the camera while the noise grew.

Jordan pressed the button. 'Ok go.' he shouted into the microphone.

'This is an emergency announcement read by Patricia Fernandez.'

'Who gives a fuck who's reading it? Just get on with it', Montano hissed.

'All civilians and staff are to evacuate to the storage areas immediately. Do not collect any belongings. Do not search around for anyone. I repeat, proceed immediately to the storage areas. This is an emergency. Save yourselves', she appealed.

Jordan pressed the stop button and pressed play and broadcast. Patricia's face appeared on all screens and devices throughout Pangea base. Her strident voice echoed out in every corner, repeating every few seconds.

The sound of the approaching Mag's grew louder in the control room. Montano shifted and stood up. 'Sir we need to go.'

'I'll be a burden and slow you all down. You go and take the others Montano. I'll hold them off as long as I can. I have to stop them getting to the studio, otherwise they'll destroy it and stop the announcement' The inexorable logic of the situation was obvious to a professional trooper like Montano. His face told Jordan he agreed. 'I deserve my fate sergeant....', Jordan went on; '....This was partly my doing. I don't want to live after this...', his voice wavering as he thought of his children back on earth. They would understand.

'Sir, don't be hard on yourself. We all did what we thought was the right thing. It's unlucky we were given the wrong objectives, for the wrong reasons by the wrong people', Montano said as the sound of commotion increased from the stairs.

'Get me outside. I'll hold them off for as long as I can...', Jordan was disrupted as Patricia came back into the room, her confident tone of the broadcast diminishing by the second.

'I can hear them, we gotta go now.' The door opened and she flinched as the sound of the Mags leapt up in volume as they exited the studio. Montano told Nicolas to wheel Jordan in his studio seat out through the door.

'Give me your remaining grenades Sergeant.', Jordan requested. Montano only had four left. He unhooked them and handed them to Jordan who ordered the Sergeant; 'Now take the others and use the maintenance tunnels as you were instructed to get to the storage areas.'

The roar of the Gorthon sounded from the next flight of stairs down. A Gargoyle burst out of the stairwell. Montano loosed a few rounds into the Mag, blasting it back down the stairs.

'Go now! That's an order Sergeant.', Jordan shouted.

Montano put his hand on Jordan's shoulder, then turned to Patricia and Nicolas. 'Come with me.'

Jordan turned to check they had gone. The low rumble of the Gorthon's breathing could be heard coming from the stairs. Unclipping a grenade, he gently lobbed it to the stairway. A brief scrabble of activity sounded before the explosion. A deep bellow of pain rang out mixed with the cacophony of wailing Gargoyles. He threw two more grenades and the noise stopped. The final one was held in his shaking hand. Do I save it for myself or not. He dared not move forward to see the result of his handiwork, but the silence spoke volumes. Checking his pistol, he saw there were eight rounds remaining. Seven for the Mags, the final one for him. Clipping the final magazine to the gun, he set it to automatic. The pain rhythmically crashed over him like waves on a beach. There was a buzzing sound from behind him, as if a swarm of bees were hurtling along the corridor.

As the rising screech of the Mag's approached, Jordan looked down at the pistol containing his death within, and release from pain and guilt. A movement from the direction of the staircase caught his eye, he turned to see the trio of Mag's rushing at him. He raised the gun instantaneously and sprayed the entire magazine over them, stopping them dead in their tracks. From behind them, the buzzing resonated along the corridor as the first of the Gargoyles tore around the corner, their legs a frenzy of movement. Jordan pulled the clip from the grenade, waited until they were about forty feet away and threw it. The lead Gargoyles turned into a spray of aqua as the cascade of grenade fragments shredded through them. Still they came, as Jordan raised the pistol and pulled the trigger. Seven rounds remaining. Six rounds, five, four, three, two, one round remaining. He pulled the gun back and held it to his head. Looking the lead Gargoyle in the eye, he saw in its mouth a ragged strip of trooper battledress. As it got a few feet away Jordan could read it. 'MONTANO' emblazoned in bold black letters across the name strip. Jordan closed his eyes and squeezed the trigger.

47

Naomi was trembling with fear and uncertainty. Her hand loitered nervously on the trigger of her gun. It was aimed at the backs of Gutierrez and van Dee as she escorted them down to the detention cells. Why had she been given this task. The accusing looks from Gutierrez as he glanced over his shoulder made her feel uneasy. Both were handcuffed but that didn't ease the deep vulnerability that Naomi felt. 'Don't turn around. Keep looking straight ahead sir!', she said, wincing at automatically acknowledging Gutierrez's superior rank.

'You can call me Josh now we're on informal terms Naomi.', he replied.

Naomi noticed van Dee shoulders shudder in an involuntary chuckle. A flash of anger shot through her. The trigger enticing her to squeeze it. 'I didn't ask for any smart arsed answers si... Gutierrez, and you van Dee can wipe that smile off your face', she said, noticing them look briefly at each other.

'Yes Ma'am. 'replied van Dee in a tone that reminded her of Bruno when he was trying to placate one of her more fevered outbursts. Where was he now? The only time she's ever *really* wanted him around. He'd know what to do. She knew what *he'd* do. Put a bullet in the heads of Gutierrez and van Dee, that's what. But Naomi wasn't Bruno, and never wanted to be either, as she cursed herself for even thinking like him, and longed for Marcus to have him killed, but not until he'd got her out of this mess.

Naomi thought back to a few minutes earlier in the concourse, after she'd been unceremoniously summoned from her quarters, still only wearing a vest and shorts. She had no inkling as to what was about to happen. Kept in the dark by Bruno until the right moment. The wolfish grin of gratification on Bruno's face when he'd handed the two prisoners to her still gnawed away. She outranked him! Yet he addressed her like a child sent to the corner shop on a petty errand.

'Lieutenant Mann. Escort the prisoners down to the detention area.', Bruno had said. Gutierrez had lunged at Bruno who stepped aside with ease as the handcuffed Colonel crashed into the wall behind. He shook his head and turned to face them. 'What the hell do you think you're up to sergeant! This is mutiny! I'll have you up before a firing squad!'

Bruno rolled his eyes in an expression of mock exasperation. 'Sir, it's for your own safety. Once this is all settled, Miss Novak will explain it all to you', he replied. Gutierrez looked up at them. His face red with fury. Spit flying in all directions from his outraged mouth.

'Miss Novak! What the fuck has she got to do with this? Do you think I'm stupid!' Gutierrez had seen through the casual lie immediately. He turned to Naomi. 'And You! You're in on this as well!' Her face burned with shame and embarrassment. 'I don't think Daddy is going to be pleased with his precious little princess. Her first posting and she's involved in an illegal uprising'.

Naomi's mouth opened to object before Bruno leant forward and spoke quietly in her ear. 'Ignore them....', he had advised her; '....I want you out of harm's way. The shits gonna hit the fan very hard, very quickly.' He stood back and grabbed Gutierrez by the front of the battledress, easily lifting him off the floor with a single hand. He spoke loud enough for them to hear. 'Any trouble, shoot 'em!'

'It's not too late Naomi!' Gutierrez's voice shook her out of her reflections. 'We know you're doing this under duress. We'll speak up for you. I'm sure General Mann will pull some strings to avoid any unnecessary embarrassment. This needs to end now. There's still time.'

'Just shut up! You heard what Bruno said. I'll shoot you if you try to escape.'

Gutierrez turned and faced her. His dark eyes staring into hers. 'You're not going to shoot anyone Naomi and you know it.' He held his cuffed hands out and walked towards her. 'Now take these things off me and end this sham now.'

The crash of the shot from Naomi's gun obliterated all other sounds in the close confines of the corridor, as Gutierrez slammed into the wall, not for the first time that day. She walked towards the prone figure, noting with satisfaction van Dee cowering on the floor next to him. Gutierrez's face was ashen and grimacing in pain, holding his neck where the round had sliced a furrow. Blood dripped between his fingers as he looked up at Naomi.

'I said shut the fuck up Gutierrez', she warned him.

He sighed and looked at van Dee who helped him up, before they continued on their way toward the detention area in silence. After a couple of minutes, they rounded a corner. She recognised Anderson, one of Voronoff's squad who stood at the ready. Fear writ large on his face.

'Where you been. Did you hear that shot a minute ago? All hells breaking loose up there!', Anderson said, looking around fearfully, his nervousness amplifying Naomi's.

Naomi's legs wobbled as she struggled to maintain control of her bowels. The sickness of fear rampant in her. 'What's happened?', she asked.

'They went to finish off the last remaining Mags but something happened.'

'Something! What Something?'

'I don't know but not many made it out alive', Anderson informed her.

Naomi opened her mouth to speak but a familiar voice resonated from the speakers. 'This is an emergency announcement.' They looked at the face of

Patricia Fernandez staring out from the screen. '...evacuate to the storage areas immediately...Save yourselves.' Then the announcement repeated.

Naomi suddenly became aware of a choking, gargling sound and turned to see Anderson desperately clawing at van Dee's handcuffs around his throat. His tongue protruding and eyes rolled back as his struggling legs buckled from under him.

'Wha...', too late she noticed the clenched interlocked knuckles of Gutierrez hands a few inches from her, a fraction of a second before they crashed into her exposed jaw. A blinding pure white light of pain exploded in her head, then nothing.

◆

Reece Coleman sat on the bed staring at the cell wall. He'd forgotten how long he'd been there. The only signs that time still existed was when a meal popped out of the slot in the base of the door. At first he'd banged his fist on the door, incessantly demanding to be released immediately. That came to a halt when the guard had abruptly opened the door, delivered a crushing right cross that catapulted Reece back into the opposite wall. Awaking with a head like a boulder, there was a pool of dried blood on the floor in front of him. Immediately, he leapt to the door and resumed the hammering, demanding liberty or death. The door snapped open and the guard stood there. A towering block of implacable solid muscle that stared back at him. The guard made to raise his hand, Reece started in fright, stumbling backwards, sprawling on the floor. The blow struck without a move.

The light was on all the time. At first he'd been unable to sleep, but after a while, sheer tiredness forced him to drift off. He didn't know how long he'd dozed. It could have been five minutes or ten hours. There was no way of telling. Time itself seemed to have become a sickness, sucking and dragging on his mind, turning everything into one big frozen now, where it was impossible to tell one moment from the next. Reece used hunger or the need to use the hole in the floor that passed for a toilet to tell if significant periods had passed. There'd been no contact with the outside world since he spoke to Celina Novak. Was it yesterday or last week? It seemed like it could even be years ago.

Why hadn't Ava visited him? Some friend she turned out to be. Probably turned collaborator with Khan, and his lickspittle Chiang. Reece thought about the Mags and the experiments. Had they bought the Hyperthon under control? Had production actually started? What if one escaped? He shuddered at the thought. What about the 5:3 resonance. A blizzard of questions flew through his mind in an unending torrent, but no answers were forthcoming. There was the day he woke up floating near the ceiling before crashing to the floor. The sprained wrist and lump on the head told him it wasn't a dream.

Then there were the voices. Crying, shouts then screams. The banging on the wall, more screams then silence. Other times he'd heard Ava calling out. 'Reece help me. The Mag's, they're coming...', then a young girl's voice calling for her mother. Another little Girl laughing, 'Daddy, daddy it's your turn.' Sometimes they spoke to him in his sleep, other times he was sure he'd heard them when he was awake. There were other things as well. Dark things that threatened him in the night. Different colours flickering in and out like ghosts, hovering on the edge of a dream. The echoing cave of emptiness stretching into eternity before him.

The violent rattle of the keys and the trundling of the locks crashed through Reece's fragile mind. The figure stood at the door, eyes wide, blood streaming from a searing gash in his neck. Reece sat staring at him in numbed silence. The figure looked back for a moment before disappearing, leaving the open door waiting for Reece to pass through it. Rising from the bed, he shuffled slowly towards the exit. At last someone had seen sense and realised the absurdity of locking him up, and half expected to see Ava walking in, telling him it had all been a big mistake and they had heeded his advice, then another part of him stopped him in his tracks. What if it was a trick? To lure him into attempting an escape before shooting him in the back. He could hear a woman's voice over the loudspeakers. Something about storage areas and evacuation.

Then the man stumbled in. His soiled underpants and single sock were all that covered his lower half. A ripped, bloodstained shirt clinging precariously to his quivering white flesh. A little badge still attached to the shirt like a precious memento of a faraway time. "Hi! I'm Darren" it proclaimed. "Fun Leader".

'What are you waiting for!' Reece immediately recognised the voice that had been crying.

'You're real...' was all his befuddled mind would allow him to say.

Darren's jowls wobbled momentarily in consternation. 'Of course I'm real you twat, and so are those monsters coming our way, so if you don't wanna become a tasty snack, come with us!'

Another voice sounded from outside. 'Right let's go!' Darren looked over his shoulder and turned, leaving a stunned Reece staring at the space he'd just vacated.

'Monsters? What monsters?' Reece asked then followed through the door to see Darren's foot disappearing around the corner. 'Wait for me.', he shouted, and set off in pursuit. There were two figures spread-eagled on the floor. One lifeless with his neck twisted at an unnatural angle, the other, still breathing as blood

351

streamed from her mouth. Reece's legs were wobbling after so much forced inactivity as he desperately tried to keep up with the others. Disorientated at the sudden vast, seemingly endless corridors, it felt like he was running backwards. His lungs were rasping in desperately needed air as he forced himself to keep going. Eventually he saw Darren doubled over, face bright red and woofing in big gulps of air. Two soldiers, deep in conversation, stood behind him. Both of them carrying guns.

'I couldn't just shoot her in cold blood and I wasn't going to let you either.' The one with the bloodied neck said. The other instantaneously raised his gun at Reece as he rounded the corner. 'He's ok, I just released him from his cell', the blood-stained one disclosed.

Reece collapsed at the soldier's feet, unable to move another inch. He tried to speak but wheezing was the only sound he was capable of. The one with the gun was still pointing it at him. The soldier slowly lowered it. 'van Dee' was on the name patch. He looked across at the other one. 'Gutierrez'. They muttered something to each other Reece couldn't quite make out. Gutierrez stepped forward and told Reece; 'We're making our way to the forward storage bay. If you want to come with us you'd better get up now and get moving. We're not going to be slowing down for you two.'

'Please, just another minute.' They looked over at the pleading Darren as he staggered to his feet.

Van Dee Snapped back. 'We haven't got a minute. They're coming our way and I don't wanna be around when they get here.'

Reece sat up and asked. 'Who? Who's after us. What's happening?'

The others looked at each other in astonishment. Gutierrez spoke first. 'Seriously. What Planet are you on!' he frowned momentarily before quickly adding 'Don't answer that!'

'The Mags.' said the voice quietly from behind Reece. Turning to face Darren, his remaining sock half hanging off, Reece felt as if a tsunami was raging inside his head, desperately trying to burst through his cranium and out into the open, growing louder and louder causing his vision to vibrate. The face of Darren morphed into a shimmering pink blob as the roaring increased.

Reece started to tumble forward, head over heels, stomach lurching. A red hot surge of gorge rose in his throat as he vomited out the contents of his stomach on the floor. 'No, no, no.' His voice weak and quivering with shock, tears tumbling down his cheek; 'I warned them and they carried on...' He heard a click of a gun being cocked and a hand grabbed him by the collar. He opened his eyes. The muzzle of the gun dominated his vision as the ferocious face of van Dee stared down the barrel into Reece's eyes, the grip of van Dees shaking hand tightening.

'You knew about these things? You helped create them?', van Dee asked.

Reece could see the beads of sweat almost squeezing their way out of van Dee's pores, as if his anger was trying to fight its way out of his body in liquid form.

'You were part of the lie. All those people dead because of you...Women, children, innocent people wanting a better life.... destroyed', Darren said.

The moment he heard the words pass Darren's lips, Reece knew all of that and more. 'Shoot me. I don't care. I don't want to live.'

'With pleasure.' van Dee growled as Reece prepared to meet his maker.

Reece closed his eyes and took one last breath. He felt strangely serene as he wondered if he would feel anything before the bullet obliterated his final thoughts.

'Killing him is the easy way out. Let his life be a punishment. Let every minute be a torture.' It was Darren again.

van Dee blinked a few times and tensed his shoulders ready to pull the trigger. Reece knew this was it.

'Hey what's that?' They turned to Gutierrez who was clearly concerned; 'Can you hear it? A scrabbling sound. It's coming this way!'

Echoing through the corridor, came the sound of a thousand Gargoyle feet, carrying their masters on the relentless quest for new victims. Growing louder by the second, filling the air with their purpose and their malice.

van Dee released his grip on Reece and let him drop to the floor. The thud reverberated in the confined corridor, the sound of the Gargoyles approach halted momentarily, before redoubling and heading their way. A diabolical screeching accompanied the sound of their march.

'Where's it coming from!' van Dee asked and looked across at Gutierrez.

'I can't tell. We don't want to run into them.'

Reece looked up and saw the door a few feet away. 'In there.' he managed to croak.

They looked over at the electrical cupboard. The brightly coloured warning sign on the door, of the man being struck by a gigantic bolt from the heavens seemed somehow appropriate in the circumstances. The sound of the Gargoyles was getting louder. Darren was the first to reach the door. The look of his disappointment told them everything they needed to know about the available room as he stepped in. 'Not much space left.', he told them.

Reece looked up at Gutierrez and van Dee and appealed; 'Leave me here. Give yourself a chance.'

'And alert them to our presence....?', Gutierrez responded and added; '....You're even stupider than I thought. Today isn't your day to die.' He grabbed Reece by the scruff of the neck and thrust him into the cupboard.

'Move over, you fuckin fat fuck', Gutierrez growled at Darren as he squeezed in alongside van Dee, closing the door just as the first Gargoyle rounded the corner.

♦

The face of the woman was upside down. Her mouth moved but the high pitched deafening whistle was the only sound Naomi could hear. Sitting up, she held her face. The jolt of pain from her jaw shot through her in an electric blue bolt of lightning. She tried to open her mouth but the first millimetre was as far as she got before the scraping sound inside her head and unbearable pain told her otherwise. Blood dripped from her mouth over her vest and shorts. Looking around, she saw that all the cell doors were open. There was no sign of Gutierrez, van Dee or her gun. She flinched as she saw the dead body of Anderson. His grotesquely twisted neck, bulging eyes and protruding tongue reminded her of a surprised cartoon character from early childhood. Yet this was more like one of the graphic novels she'd read as a teenager. The nightmarish imagination of the authors superseded by reality.

Unsteadily, she rose to her feet, holding onto the desk for support, looking up at the screen. The woman was still speaking, but Naomi still couldn't make out the words, despite the whistling in her head starting to recede. It was obvious they were of crucial importance as she tried to wrack her memory right up to the point where Gutierrez's knuckles appeared. A few of the woman's words came to her. 'Evacuation, storage area', emerged from the fog of her memory. Something had happened but what, she didn't know. Was there a fire? Had the walls been breached. Anderson had said something.

The maddening blankness in her mind was a wall separating her from the rest of the world. Naomi gingerly ventured toward the open cell doors to check if anyone was still in there. She thought about calling out, but her jaw gave her a sharp reminder of its predicament. Anyway, she wouldn't hear any reply so what was the point? Working her way along the row of cells, one by one, until just before the final one, she remembered. The words of Anderson calling out. "They went to finish off the last remaining Mags but something happened, not many made it out alive..."

Naomi felt the sickening certainty of the danger, she and everyone else was in, break through the wall of amnesia that had blocked her mind since she regained consciousness. They've broken out. All of them. The carnage caused by a single Mag had given her nightmares for the past few days. The thought of scores, or even hundreds of them running amok, was too awful to contemplate. Well at least

354

Bruno is probably dead, the fuck. I hope they ripped his cock off. Smiling briefly, her thoughts turned to Marcus. Did he survive? She was lost without him. Her one true purpose in life taken away. What if they're all dead and I'm the only one left alive? She couldn't believe that. There must be somebody left, but are we outnumbered by the Mags? She'd sat through the briefings after the breakout and shivered, seeing the different types and their capabilities. The Gargoyles were the scariest. The sudden movements and ferocious purpose were unnerving even on video. What would it be like to come face to face with one, or a hundred of them? They could be approaching now.

The whistling had gone and only the throbbing pain of her jaw remained. The sounds were still muffled like she was hearing the world with pillows over each ear. Then she felt the grip on her arm. Naomi leapt in the air and screamed. The loud click of her jaw and its accompanying pain shot through her. Landing on her back, eyes filled with tears, she looked up at the figure over her and kicked out at it instinctively.

'Wooah there, you're ok.'

She looked up at the face of the woman in battle fatigues, the insignia of a trooper scout on her shoulder. Two figures stood behind her. A tall blond man and a small dark skinned woman. The look of concern on their faces told Naomi they were friendly.

'You're safe', mouthed the scout, her hands downwards in a calming gesture. Naomi realised she could hear again. Not very well but enough to understand.

'I... I can hear you... just....' the scout smiled as Naomi admitted; 'I'm sorry, you took me by surprise.'

'That's ok. You're right to be jumpy. We could hear the cell doors banging a mile away. I'm surprised you never bought a pack of Gargoyles down on you', the scout posited. The confirmation of the breakout made Naomi's stomach lurch even though she was more or less certain anyway.

'What happened to you?', the scout asked while looking down at the body of Anderson.

'I was coming down to check on the prisoners....', Naomi lied. '....I was attacked from behind. I don't remember anything else. Next thing I knew I woke up, everyone had gone and he was dead.'

'We found some dead on the way here. Huddled in a passageway. It may have been them.' It was the blond man from behind her. He walked towards her and gestured towards his companions. 'This is Kalpana, AI specialist and this is Corporal Auger Security team blue, but you can call her Denise. I'm Magnus Eriksen from Robotics, and you are?', he extended his hand.

Naomi was surprised by his direct manner as she shook Magnus' hand. 'Lieutenant Naomi Mann. SPC.' She winced as she realised she wasn't wearing her fatigues. Only a bloodstained vest and shorts.

The others looked over at Denise who stared at Naomi with suspicion in her eyes, as her finger moved towards the trigger of her weapon.

'I've just returned from a firefight with SPC squads. Some of my friends were killed by them', Denise told Naomi.

'SPC! Killing troopers? Why?' Naomi's shock was genuine and heartfelt. She knew her role in detaining Gutierrez and van Dee but she never signed up for a war with the Troopers. She could feel the scout's stare boring into her. 'Look, I never knew anything about it, in fact when I think about it, it's probably the reason I ended up on the ground with a sore head.', she told them. The scout looked over at the others.

Magnus stepped forward, his clipped accented voice clear and precise. 'You need to understand Naomi that the SPC are the cause of all this. Them and that crazy preacher who whipped the civilians up into a frenzy of fear before he urged them to destroy the Mags. He used the SPC as his personal army, ambushing the Troopers before storming the Mag pens. Well, you could say they bit off a little bit more than they could chew. Nearly all of them are dead and the Mags are on the loose. Most of the base's population has been torn to rags by those things and the few survivors are heading for the storage bays. They're the only safe areas left in the base. That's where we're heading.'

The enormity of Magnus' words struck Naomi like a thunderbolt. The talks with Marcus, the endless nights of being humped by Bruno in order to lure him to Marcus, for what? For the pair of them to plunge everyone into this nightmare. Sinking to her knees, she placed her face in her hands, the sobs coming thick and fast. 'I never realised. I was so stupid. So fuckin stupid!', she confessed.

'You never realised what, exactly?', Naomi looked up and saw Denise standing over her.

In spite of her desolation, the slick liar that Marcus had taught her to be took over. 'They sent me down here to get me out of the way. My Dad's a General. They knew I'd never agree.' Her words stuck in her throat, the shame of her role in the disaster trampling on her conscience, smashing it to smithereens. She noticed with relief Denise nodding slowly to the others.

'Ok, get up. You can come with us for now, but if I even have a sniff you've been lying I'll cut your throat. Understand?', Denise warned her.

Naomi looked down at Denise's hunting knife hanging in its scabbard, and didn't doubt for a moment that the trooper would carry out her threat, with the utmost severity if she discovered the truth. She swallowed hard, nodded and said;

'I swear it's the truth.' I just hope we don't run into Gutierrez or van Dee. Please let them be the bodies in the passageway, she mused.

Magnus stepped forward. 'Ok everyone. This way to the storage area.' They started to move out. Naomi looked up at the screen where the announcement had been read out. It was blank.

♦

'The batteries are running low. I can hardly see a thing.' Eleanor had been handed the little pen torch by Amanda and had been using it to navigate through the tunnels. The fear in Eleanor's voice made Ava's breath catch in her throat.

From the first moment the purple flames had leapt out of the mindscape at her, Ava's seared mind had struggled to comprehend the world around her into a coherent whole. The screams and gunshots, the debilitating panic and the bellowing roar of the Gorthon, a sonic earthquake that reverberated through her, served as an instant reminder of the agony and terror of a few days earlier. The explosions, shouts and the noise of Mags entering the tunnel in the distance as Elizabeth dragged her, stumbling along the tunnel gave a manic strength to Ava's weakened wobbling legs, that were only fit for an occasional short trip to the bathroom. She could feel the quivering of Elizabeth's hand as she tried to control her fear. The shuffling, heavy breathing and whimpering of those around her told their own story of the frantic flight along the tunnels to the sanctuary of the storage areas. And now they were lost in the darkness, not that it made the slightest difference to Ava in the world of permanent night that she inhabited.

'Are you sure we're heading in the right direction Ava?', Eleanor asked.

'I...I think so. It's hard to say.', Ava was unsure. All she could sense was a dull swirling menagerie of colours that throbbed in and out of focus in the distance. She thought it was the combined glow of a multitude, each one weak but their sum calling like a thousand whispers, shifting and wafting aimlessly, making it almost impossible to feel exactly where they originated. Then there were other shapes, visions and emotions vying for her attention. The sparkling diamond that swept ahead in the distance, diminishing to a point of light, before returning. She'd seen it before when hunting Horace in the cooling plant. Now they were the prey as she looked back at the assembly of dull orange points of the Gargoyles that seemed to surround them, drawing closer. Some in packs, others alone. Below them, a group scrabbled along one of the main corridors accompanied by a rumbling blood red that drove them on, inexorably pursuing a single spot of light, before surrounding it as the lone light flicked for a few moments before winking out. Above them, another group passed, the thrum of their steps resonating on the

357

roof of the tunnel. Then there was the vision from someone or something rushing along the tunnel. Ava felt its source rapidly drawing closer.

'There's something approaching', Ava voiced. There was a sharp intake of breath from those around her.

'Where's it coming from Ava?' Again the urgency in Eleanor's voice betrayed her trepidation, but also an implacable determination that this time comforted Ava.

'Up ahead on the right. It's getting stronger. I think it can see us...'

'I can hear something...I'm not sure if...What the fu...', Eleanor interrupted her friend, but she too wasn't allowed to finish as a scream resonated through the tunnel that was rapidly echoed by everyone else.

A man's voice sounded. 'Whoa whoa, hold it!'

'Shit! You nearly gave me heart failure. Who the hell are you?' Eleanor asked and laughed. The sighs of relief sounded around Ava.

'Martin, Martin Preston. I managed to escape the madness and climb into a hatch. There's no way back out. The base is swamped with those things...I was about to...'

The vision in Ava's mind grew stronger, she could see Eleanor's face weakly illuminated by the failing torch and the back of someone that grew larger with each second, bearing down on Eleanor. Overwhelming fear grabbed Ava by the throat, strangling the life out of her, nearly paralysing the words that finally leapt out.

'There's something else there...'. The squealing hiss of a Gargoyle sounded as Ava saw it leap over the back of Preston, recognising the face that filled its sight as it flew through the tunnel towards Elizabeth. Ava's mouth open in frozen horror, her face filling the Gargoyle's field of view as the front claws drove towards Elizabeth's chest. She felt Elizabeth's hand ripped from her arm as the Gargoyle reached her. The start of a scream from Elizabeth was immediately transformed into a gurgling groan. Her eye filled Ava's vision as the Gargoyle ripped into her face with its slashing teeth. Ava lashed out to where she thought the Gargoyle was, instead striking the wall of the tunnel, sending an agonising bolt of pain up her arm, before she crashed to the floor.

A primal howl sounded above her as the Gargoyle turned from the limp figure of Elizabeth towards the banshee face of Akeely, teeth drawn back and eyes bulging, rushed forwards. A claw lashed out as Akeely raised her arm, taking the full force, but she still hurtled forward, raining blows down. Ava sensed the confusion and fear washing over the Gargoyle, as the dervish thrashed blow upon blow down on its head. An arm from behind flashed across, before it closed around the Gargoyles throat, squeezing the life, aqua tinting the gloom of the

358

Mags view.

In a blur of movement, Eleanor's face appeared, teeth gritted and arms thrashing wildly as the claw raised itself, ready to drive deep into her exposed throat. Ava tried to raise herself to save her friend, to place herself between the point and Eleanor's flesh, but she knew it was too late. 'Ellie!' Her desperate scream cut through the air, as she saw Eleanor turn her head to look over, before turning back to the Mag and through it into the eye of Ava's mind, almost welcoming death. The claw was poised ready. What's it waiting for? To draw out the final agony, before she realised the hold that had enveloped the Mag and looked up to see the beautiful, glittering diamond hovering above, reaching its light down into the Gargoyle, holding it in place as a flash of metal appeared from the side, and into the eye of the Mag. Fynn's guttural roar ended with a squelch, immediately followed by a crunch as Eleanor's face disappeared and the vision turned a pure white, which drew slowly into the distance growing smaller and smaller, emptying the whole of the mindscape until it faded to black.

The sound of laboured breathing and groans filled the tunnel as Eleanor broke the spell. 'You took your time! What were you waiting for? Christmas? she said to Fynn'

'I couldn't see anything after you dropped the light. Or would you rather I stabbed you in the head?', the trooper responded testily.

'Get this thing off me will you. It stinks', Eleanor insisted.

A wheezing sound could be heard amongst the whimpering. A hand grabbed Ava's arm. A weak voice barely audible sounded, 'Ava...Help me...'

'Liz is that you?' Ava reached up to Elizabeth face. The metallic smell of blood filled Ava's nostrils as her fingers slipped on its wetness. A bubbling wheezing was escaping through a gash in Elizabeth's throat.

'I'm cold Ava...' Her voice was fading fast.

'Hold on Liz.' Despair filled Ava as she heard her friend's breathing quicken.

'Tell Leighton...' Elizabeth's hand squeezed Ava's arm tight as she struggled to breathe, every word an effort.

'Tell him what Liz?' Ava asked. Elizabeth grip was rapidly weakening.

'I forgive him...He was a good father to me...Tell him I always loved him...', Elizabeth's voice was hardly audible.

Ava was stunned into speechlessness as Elizabeth's hold waned, and her hand slipped lifelessly to the floor, as her last breath gently whistled to a stop. Walker was Liz's father and I was too stupid to see it all along.

The shock and grief made Ava feel like a huge stone had appeared in her chest, weighing down on her heart and lungs, growing into her throat, stifling the cry of pain that was trying to fight its way out of her...

48

Attilio's high pitched scream filled the Cafeteria as the first Gargoyle entered. Paralysed with terror, his legs buckled from under him and he collapsed to the floor. Even Marcus's calm exterior faltered at his first sight of a live Mag. The implacable purpose, the unrestrained viciousness, the undiluted violence it embodied vaporised any pretence of control as he tried to maintain a façade of authority.

The first group of Gargoyles spewed through the door of the Cafeteria, tearing into the dead and dying left by the crush. Leon Jordan looked apathetically at the onrushing mass, making no attempt to escape, almost embracing death, as the Gargoyles set about him. He died without a sound, unlike the others who ran for their lives but on the whole, failed immediately.

A tidal wave of gnashing teeth and slashing claws moved with inescapable speed, hunting down all in their sight. What in the name of the gods have you set loose Marcus? He had seen off the rats but nothing could be done against such uninhibited ferocity. All the guns in the world couldn't hold them back. Is this my punishment for my overblown self-importance? For daring to claim that I speak for the Great Sky Lord Ykdar, who has sent a reaping retribution down upon my head. You have failed utterly Marcus. All you've worked and hoped for has come to naught. Only dismemberment and damnation await you. A tear trickled from his eye as the slaughter unfolded before him. To survive the rats, the cult, the unforgiving streets, his mother, and find his doom within the goal he had relentlessly sought, was the bitterest irony of all.

A lone Gargoyle looked up from its victim's mangled corpse and its stare fell upon Marcus. It weighed him up for a few moments as it moved slowly and purposefully forward, with an inevitability that only magnified the certainty that an unstoppable killer had him marked as its next quarry. A fire blazed ferociously in Marcus's heart. Without looking, he instinctively reached out to the table, grasping the first object he found to protect him and delay death's imminent approach. Hardly daring to tear his eyes away from the Mag, he looked at the plastic fork that represented his last hope of survival. Only the litter of scattered bodies, and parts that once belonged to them, lay between Marcus and the Gargoyle, that was picking its way through them toward him. A few feet away, the body of a woman lay facing down, matted red hair strewn across her features. Marcus noticed a hint of movement on the body. Her eye stared out at him through the hair, as she started to tremble. He recognised the woman who, a few minutes earlier, had thrown herself at his feet in adulation. At that moment, the Gargoyle hesitated, considering the strange shaking object. Gingerly it reached out a leg and prodded it. A squeak escaped the trembling woman's mouth, causing the Gargoyle to momentarily recoil. Marcus watched in mute repulsion.

The survival instinct indelibly ingrained into every atom of his being screamed for him to run, to leave her to her fate. Everyone else was expendable, enablers or shields that could be cast aside after use, but her pleading eye held him in its gaze. Her life was entirely dependent on what he did in the next few moments. The slightest wrong move would result in instant ripping death, but she had given him a lifeline, a way out of the hell he had created. A strange sense of obligation towards her flickered in the cold empty cavern of Marcus's heart. She had given him a precious few extra seconds of life. Some fleeting moments to save himself, and if possible her. The Gargoyle's attention was now focused solely on the woman. It reached out once again, this time with more force, digging into her back. She recoiled and sat up, looking into the face of the creature, her breaths short and desperate. Without thinking, Marcus picked up a chair, placing it in front of him like a shield, and charged the Gargoyle. Marcus this is certain death. What are you doing? At the last moment the Gargoyles attention switched back to the white square object with legs, just as it crashed into him. Marcus was momentarily surprised at the lack of resistance from the creature, as he sent it skittering and thrashing back across the floor. A stray claw slashed him across the calf as he drove the Gargoyle back, leaving it to waste a few seconds in a struggle with the chair.

Marcus looked around the Cafeteria at the huddled groups of Mags busily involved in dispatching their chosen quarry. The one that had attacked him and the woman was the sole loner. The woman was still sitting and staring at the Gargoyle thrashing wildly in its struggle with the chair. Marcus searched around for a means of escape. Behind the food counter was the silver grey door that led to the kitchen, the only sanctuary in sight. A few survivors were moving slowly around the bundles of Gargoyles trying not to be noticed, they all seemed to look at the white robed figure of Marcus as he lent over the woman, then dragged her to her feet.

'The Kitchen. Quickly!' the invective of his words galvanised the woman into action as she shook off the torpor of terror. The other survivors saw where he was going and started heading the same way.

On the giant screen at the end of the Cafeteria, Marcus noticed a bizarre series of random images appearing, until it finally settled on a shot of the base's news reader. A voice sounded above the screaming of the victims and the screeching of the Mag's. All activity in the room stopped. Even the Mags hesitated from the task of tearing limbs from bodies and flesh from bone, to look up at the familiar face staring out from the giant screen. The woman gave a small nod of acknowledgement to someone off camera before facing back.

'This is an emergency announcement read by Patricia Fernandez.' Her voice, authoritatively resonated as she continued. 'All civilians and staff are to evacuate to the storage areas immediately. Do not collect any belongings. Do not search around for anyone. I repeat, proceed immediately to the storage areas. This is an emergency. Save yourselves.' The screen then flicked back to the start. A brief acknowledgment, followed by the statement. 'This is an emergency announcement ...'. A Gargoyle moved toward the giant screen looking up at the huge figure that was oblivious to its approach. It drew back and raised itself on its hind legs, emitted a venomous hiss, then launched itself at the face on the screen. It bounced off the smooth surface, looking up as the woman continued unperturbed. As one, the massed Gargoyles launched themselves at the face on the screen. A smashing writhing mass of limbs, claws and teeth tearing at the indestructible image towering over them.

The surviving settlers looked at the open door into the main concourse to make their escape and ran toward it. As they reached it, a man came rushing through from outside pursued by a pack of Gargoyles. As he stumbled, they were on him in a flash blocking the exit, his final sounds cut brutally short. The escapees looked desperately around. Marcus shouted to them. 'The Kitchen! It's our only hope!'

Attilio emerged from under a mass of bodies. His shock of white hair smeared in blood, as his legs discovered their true purpose and he propelled himself in huge, almost hopping strides towards the sanctuary of the kitchen, the black greatcoat flapping behind him like a giant bat.

From outside, the crackling sound of a Gorthon boomed its way into the Cafeteria, followed a moment later by the doorway exploding in a blizzard of fragments as the implacable mass of the giant Mag crashed through, its presence overshadowing everything else in the room. The final survivors rushed toward Marcus as he reached the Kitchen door. It felt reassuringly solid even though there was a small round porthole in the middle looking out. Holding the door open, he frantically waved them through. 'Now, now, now! Come on!' Marcus urged as he saw the last couple running from the far side.

The Gorthon opened its mouth to its full extent before it let rip a bone shattering roar, the air shimmering before it as a giant claw smashed into the face of Patricia, the screen exploding in a shower of sparks and shards. The disembodied voice continued, 'I repeat, proceed immediately to the Storage areas....' The Gorthon looked down at the mass of Gargoyles and made a low guttural sound as if admonishing them for their wasted efforts, before directing them towards the kitchen.

Marcus watched from afar, slamming the door shut then locking it as the final couple of fleeing survivors hurled themselves through. Closing his eyes, he leant back against the door. The cool metal felt good against his burning skin as he let out a long breath. His legs were shaking as he heard the ragged breathing and moans of the others trapped in the kitchen with him. Opening his eyes, he saw a collection of slumped and broken individuals. Attilio lay in a star shape, staring at the ceiling. The red headed woman on her knees hardly daring to believe she was still in one piece. Moving her hair from across her face, she looked up at Marcus, her breathing heavy, eyes red, tears streaming down, nose running and mouth agape.

'You...' another breath, 'You saved me. You attacked the creature and fought it off to save me...', she gasped.

Marcus was struck dumb. The shock and violence of the last couple of minutes, too much for his frazzled brain to process.

Another voice sounded, 'He saved us all.' It was Attilio as he slowly climbed from the floor.

The red haired woman rose to her feet and moved to Marcus, putting her arms around him. He could feel her racing heart as she embraced him, the feel of her breath on his neck as she whispered softly in his ear. 'I owe you my life...I owe you everything... I owe...'. She stopped in mid-sentence and he felt her body suddenly stiffen, as her deafening scream blasted down on Marcus ear drum, causing a high pitched whistle of pain to shoot through his head and land on the nerves of his teeth. Drawing back, she looked in shock and astonishment over Marcus's right shoulder. Instinctively, he moved away from the door and turned to see the probing malicious eye of the Gorthon staring through the porthole. Its shining blackness embodying the implacable sense of evil and violence that it represented, peering into the very centre of those it beheld, projecting an overwhelming feeling of hatred and fear into their hearts.

Marcus's trembling throat constricted as he tried to control his breathing through the rapidly diminishing, wheezing hole of his windpipe. The eye disappeared and a heartbeat later, the door shook violently as the smashing claw of the Gorthon struck the first blow. The glass of the porthole shattered, spraying glass over those inside as they cried in terror and despair. The door held fast but immediately, the head of a Gargoyle thrust its way through the open porthole which was just big enough to allow the body of the creature through, shaking side to side as it wriggled inch by inch into the kitchen, its claws gaining purchase and pushing the rest of it out. A yell of fury rang out as one of the survivors leapt forward brandishing a meat cleaver, hacking it down on the exposed neck of the Gargoyle with all his strength. A squeal of pain split the air as the Gargoyle's struggles were now concentrated on escaping back through the porthole. Its arms held out in a pathetically vain attempt to stem the torrent of blows raining down upon its head and body. The cleaver sliced effortlessly through the arms, sending the twitching deadly claws to the floor. The eyes of hate had transformed into a stare of terror. A loop of slime drooped lazily down from the open mouth as a childlike scream of mindless terror escaped the Gargoyle.

The man furiously hewed away, the creature's blood spraying in all directions. His teeth gritted, while he grunted repeatedly. 'Die! Die! Fuckin Die!' The Gargoyle's struggles weakened as the cleaver bit deeper into his exposed flesh with every furious blow, until he hung limp and lifeless through the porthole. The last threads of tissue holding the Gargoyles head to its body were sliced through by the final blow of the cleaver. The body slipping back, disappearing through the porthole while the severed head landed with a squelch on the tiled floor. A final flicker of defiance playing across its dead features.

The man turned to the group and told them; 'Get whatever you can from there. As long as the door holds we can fight them off. The knives are back in the...'

The claw of the Gorthon shot through the porthole and the huge claw closed around the man. The suddenness and shock caused the cleaver to drop from his grasp, clattering on the floor next to his feet. He tried desperately to reach down but the giant arm ripped him back through the porthole, bending him double and tearing off his arm from the shoulder, before he finally vanished from view, his severed arm and bloodstains of his violent exit the only sign he had ever existed. A moment later, the tongue of the Gorthon gracefully snaked through the porthole, searching around before entwining silently around the still twitching arm. The laboured breathing of the survivors as they watched in petrified disbelief was the only sound in the room. With a suddenness that was almost too fast to see, the tongue whipped the disembodied limb back through the porthole.

Another crash sounded as the Gorthon struck another blow on the door. The silvered reflections on its surface of those inside, were distorted by the fault line where the door had buckled under the onslaught. Marcus's mind was racing as he spoke; 'There must be a fire exit somewhere. Go and check. This door isn't going to hold for much longer. Everyone grab a knife, anything as long as it's sharp. If this is the end I'm not dying without a fight.'

The close proximity of death had emboldened him. The certainty of them or us gave him a new energy and the blanket of fear was cast away. Mags or Rats, it didn't matter anymore. The urge to fight greater than the fear of death, as his mind was reduced to a shining bright point of blinding clarity. No restraints, no holding back. Just the simple question of live or die.

Another blow struck the door, still it held. The red headed woman placed a huge shiny carving knife into Marcus's hand. The solidity of the grip and the unyielding sharpness of the blade imbuing him with a sense of invincibility. The head of a Gargoyle appeared at the porthole. Marcus strode forward and looked into the vicious eyes of the creature a few inches from his face. The stench of its breath struck him like a blow and he steadily raised the knife before striking down onto the head of the Gargoyle. A crunch of bone gave a moment of resistance as the blade sank into the soft tissue of the brain. From his side, another blow was struck by the red headed woman into the eye of the already dead creature. She in turn was joined by several others and they silently rained down a torrent of sharpened steel into the head. Each blow bringing new courage as the Gargoyle withered under the onslaught.

Another blow fell on the groaning door. At the top, a gap had opened as a claw from outside peeled it back like a tin of sardines. Marcus leapt up and sank the blade of the knife into the claw. A howl of pain and fury vented through the open gap. Several more smashing blows bent back the top of the door opening a Gargoyle sized gap. Yet another head forced its way in through the porthole to be met yet again by a rain of blades. A hiss sounded as Marcus saw the first of the Gargoyles emerge from the gap above. He leapt up again and slashed wildly but this time the Gargoyle climbed up the wall and across the ceiling. Several more climbed through, forming up alongside the first one.

A call came from the rear of the Kitchen, 'We've found the exit!'

Marcus turned to the others, 'Go, now, to the back', he ordered. Looking up, he saw the first of the Gargoyles pounced down from above, straight towards him. Instinctively lashing out, he deflected the creature towards a fryer full of superheated fat. The screeches of the Mag and the bubbling popping of its skin being cooked, resonated about the kitchen. The crackling creature recoiled from the vat of fat, crashing into an overhead pipe, breaking it open. Water spurted from the open gap and into the fryer. A blinding white sheet of flame leapt up engulfing the Gargoyle and spreading rapidly through the kitchen. Marcus saw through the wall of flame that all the others had escaped, leaving him on the same side as the Gargoyles. One by one they dropped down in front of him.

He could feel the heat and heard the cry from behind. 'The monsters are in the Fire Escape!' He turned to see the shimmering shapes through the haze of the Mags setting on the figures. The sound of gunshots could be heard in the distance.

He turned to face the Gargoyles who were closing in on him. He felt no fear as his grip tightened on the handle of the knife…

365

49

The giant doors sat open, showing the towering rows of the pens that stood open and empty, stretching into the distance and up to the darkness of the heights above. Stillness dominated the containment area. Small flickering fires played out, hungrily licking their way along the limbs of the dead. The odd twitch here and there, steam rising from the yellow puddles that dotted the scene were the only movements. A mangled mass of death formed a rough semi-circle around the exit. Half devoured human remains merged with the husks of Gargoyles and Bornix. A few feet away, the solid mass of a Gorthon, a mountain of flesh and malice taller than a man, that even in death, conveyed a sense of menace even the fiercest creatures couldn't match in life. The glistening blackness of the eyes that stared sightlessly out, the mouth containing the rows of razor sharp teeth hung slackly open, steadily dripping aqua into a lazy trail, forming one of the countless tributaries leading to the river that mingled the blood of men and Mags.

A stifled sound broke the silence; a movement of the Gorthon disturbed the stillness. The flank of the Gorthon began to rise, animated with life in contrast to the creatures' dead limbs. An arm emerged from where the Gorthon met the floor. The gap widening as the shoulder then the bald head smeared in aqua, slid out. The upper body followed and stifled grunts of effort sounded as Bruno finally freed himself from under the creature's clinging sucking mass. He lay for a few moments, the only motion was the rise and fall of the chest as his lungs tried to draw in desperately needed air.

He'd waited, cocooned inside the carcass of the Gorthon, the muffled sound of explosions and gunfire gradually fading away. Groaning and gurgling gases that still existed in the dead Gorthon's digestive system were the only remaining sounds. At first he mistook them for the roars of the other Mags but the sounds eventually ceased, leaving only the fetid air that was gradually suffocating him. The steady relaxation of the body sinking into decay shrank the space inside, crushing down on Bruno.

He slowly and carefully wiped away the gloop that obscured his eyes then looked around. First of all, moving just his eyes, then his head and finally sitting up and observing his surroundings. Rolling over onto all fours, he crawled close to the flank of the Gorthon using it as cover. Moving cautiously up the side, he peered over the edge, the only living thing in the vast cavernous space. No sound, no movement, no life. Only Bruno, cast adrift in a sea of death and stillness.

'Fuck, fuck, fuck…' The visceral fear and terror of their flight was blazing bright in his mind. The Gargoyles, the Bornix, the Fizzlers. The gash on his cheek, the face of the soldier just before he was consumed by the fireball, the dissolving man, the intestines, Aaron looking down on them, his pet Gargoyle at his side. All played in the crazed, jumbled phantasmagoria of his memory.

A mechanical whirr sounded, its volume magnified by the vast emptiness of the area. A hiss of a door opening sounded at the front of a pen. Then the familiar scrabbling of a Gargoyle as it emerged. Over the top of the Gorthon, Bruno watched as it observed its surroundings for a few moments, sniffing the air and finding its sense of direction. Then with a frightening suddenness unique to Gargoyles, it scuttled off toward the exit in search of its brethren, the sound of its movements fading into the distance until silence was once again restored. From another containment area, the blood chilling sound of a freshly minted Gorthon's primal roar, resonated and rang throughout the empty space. How the hell? They must still be producing somehow. Are they the leftovers from before the breakout or is someone still in control? Time to get out of here Bruno. Looking around, he searched for something to protect himself. Alongside the dead hand of a trooper, he saw what he was looking for. An automatic rifle lay where it had fell at the moment of its previous owner's death. He walked over, still checking his surroundings. A Gargoyle lay across the body of the trooper, frozen in their death struggle before they joined each other in eternity. Bruno reached out with his foot and pushed the Gargoyle off the trooper. It rolled off and laid on its back, limbs stiffly pointed at jagged angles. A look of pain and horror remained on the trooper's face, the glassy eyes, a stark reminder of his final moments before the ragged gash that had opened up from his throat to his chest had been inflicted by his nemesis.

Bruno shook his head sadly, picked up the weapon and checked the ammo. Just over twenty rounds, not much against such a horde. Even the reassurance of such a powerful weapon gave him no great sense of comfort. One shot would bring the whole Mag army down on his ass. If only they'd told us what lurked within, we wouldn't have come within a hundred miles of this hellhole. The forces released were unstoppable and unsurvivable. What was that weasel Aaron doing? Was he behind the whole thing? Why? Why would he unleash such a force upon his fellow humans? Surely they would turn on him. How did he know the release process?

Then there was the industrial scale of the operation. Pangea base was just a massive Mag factory. What did they expect to do with so many of them? There was enough to match every man woman and child inside Pangea. The questions whirled around Bruno's head, but no answers were forthcoming. Those who knew were probably dead. Then a thought occurred to Bruno that froze his blood. Am I the only survivor? The only human left alive inside a base full of killing creatures? I need to find someone, anyone.

He searched around for some more ammunition, picking up some scattered magazines. All the flamers were gone, along with the rockets and their launchers. The split and mangled body of a Bornix, lay glistening where it had fell. It looked almost shrunken in death. Only about the same size as a Gargoyle. The spread of its wings in flight had multiplied its menace. Then Bruno realised the answer was before him. The fizzlers, you fuckin stupid fuck. Cursing himself for his stupidity, he leant over the body of the Bornix and prized apart the opening in its belly. The dull yellow glow of the fizzlers flickered just out of reach in the darkness of the Bornix innards. Returning to the dead trooper, he saw the combat knife still in its scabbard. Bruno drew it out and admired the big shiny blade that despite its obsolescence, had always held a macabre fascination for him. The precision cutting edge and terrifying curved point, large enough to peel a fully grown Gorthon like a potato, had a simplicity and beauty that belied its diabolical purpose. Why didn't we get issued with these? Such ease and lethality rolled into one. Returning to the Bornix, the blade sliced through the tough outer skin with a pleasing exactness, cutting back the flesh until the six fizzlers were exposed. There was a backpack a few feet away. He emptied the contents and returned to the fizzlers placing them carefully inside, each one warm to the touch. Working his way around the dead Bornix, he collected nearly thirty more, filling two backpacks, the first he wore while the other was carried.

Feeling a bit safer, Bruno made his way to the hole in the wall that had once been the exit, turning for one last look at the vision of annihilation and ruin. Casting his eyes across the twisted mass of bodies and carcasses, thinking only an hour or so earlier, all those dead had been as alive as he was now.

The hiss from the opening of another pen sounded. The distant shape of a Gargoyle appeared at the opening, just as Bruno ducked out into the passage leading back to the main concourse. A flickering light was the only illumination. Nothing stirred, only more bodies entangled in death. The sound of the Gargoyle's scuttling approach was the only sound Bruno was aware of. Placing the backpacks on the ground and leaning the rifle against them, he pulled out a fizzler then stood poised at the doorway. His focus concentrated on watching for the shadow of the Gargoyle as the sound of its footsteps grew. A loud snarling hiss rang out from behind. Bruno let out a cry as he spun around to see a pair of Gargoyles that were heading back from the concourse facing him, red patterns shimmering across their back. Without thinking, Bruno rushed forward and hurled the fizzler straight at the pair. It missed the first Gargoyle, splashing its contents over the second, leaving it screeching in agony, thrashing and squirming as the acid dissolved him

368

through numerous entry points, each one of them spewing smoke that had been exchanged by the acid for flesh. Bruno was transfixed by the din. It had an almost musical quality as it filled the passageway, a fusion of pipes and choirs in a discordant harmony of clashing sounds that rose and fell in time with the progress of the lethal liquid, until the climax of the crescendo, and the final note fading. The first Gargoyle watched with Bruno in silence.

Bruno stood lost in morbid captivation, watching the final moments of the Gargoyle play out. A cold dread tingled over him, the instinct of knowing you're being surveyed by malign eyes. Turning slowly, he knew what it was and that his luck had finally run out. The Gargoyle from the containment area had come through the exit and stood on all fours silently observing him, as curious about him as he was repulsed by it. He looked beyond the creature in vain at the two backpacks behind it, fizzlers bubbling merrily away inside and beyond reach, his gun leaning at a jaunty angle against them. Looking down at the knife in its scabbard, he slowly reached down to unsheathe it. A vicious hiss came from the Gargoyle at the first hint of movement. It slowly moved forward, each step clacking as the points of its claws met the floor, beating a jagged uneven drumbeat. The dark eyes took on a strange incandescence, another kind of shimmering black that somehow stood out in the darkness. Flickers of green and blue flitted across its back. Why isn't it attacking me? What's it waiting for? Is it scared of me? He'd seen the strike of lone Gargoyles earlier. The drawing out of the moment, relishing the anticipation then without warning or pity striking as quick as lightning. All pretence of deception had gone, as Bruno reached down, drew the knife and held it out in challenge. He'd faced death too many times in the past couple of hours to feel any fear, only a cold assessment of the odds stacked against him. The single knife against the two sets of claws and glistening teeth. One in front and the other from behind. His soft skin against the toughened hides. His honed reflexes to the Gargoyle's instantaneous lethality. His only hope, a strike to the head and a race to the backpack before the second Gargoyle could run him down. A race between his blade and signals from the Gargoyles black eyes travelling into the brain, being computed and the correct decision being converted into actions. Perhaps he won't even have that as unconscious impulses bypassed the process and the decisive response ripped into his belly. A hiss from the second Gargoyle behind him made Bruno's mind up, time to strike or die.

Bruno could feel the blood of the Gorthon running down his arm, before he strode purposefully towards the Gargoyle. It remained impassive, almost acquiescent as he approached. Subtle shades of green and blue shimmered in waves across it's back, as if a stone had been tossed into a pond and landed with a gentle plop. Next to it, wisps of vapour entwining each other as they swirled

369

casually up from the still dissolving companion. A light flickered in the enclosed space of the corridor as Bruno raised the knife above his head. Speed and aggression, that's what he'd been told during training and that was the policy that defined his life. Still the Gargoyle didn't move. What's it waiting for? Is it injured? Can't it see me? Is it a trick? All this was academic as he bought the blade of the knife down on the head of the Gargoyle, driving it deep into the creature's skull, squelching through the brain and obliterating any consciousness that dwelt there. The legs splayed out, the giant invisible boot of immediate death stamping down on it. Bruno quickly withdrew the knife that was dripping with aqua blood, along with parts of the brain that had until a few moments earlier, been contemplating the humans' approach, trying to decide if the strange shiny object it was holding constituted a threat. Why did it just meekly accept its fate? The stupid brute. Not even an attempt to save itself. Oh well, you snooze, you lose. There were no more time for any other thoughts as he whirled around to face the Gargoyle that had come from the Containment area. It stood in the same fashion as the one he'd just slaughtered. He looked at the rucksack containing the fizzlers as well as the gun behind it, thought about pushing his luck one more time and started to move towards his intended victim with the same purpose in mind. In the doorway behind it, a shadow appeared followed by the familiar clack of footfalls as another newly released Gargoyle rounded the corner and entered the corridor. It looked at Bruno and raised itself on its legs, jabbing out it's claws in defiance, emitting a vicious squealing hiss, teeth bared, ready to sink into any human flesh they came into contact with. It dropped back on to all fours and quickly joined its companion in arms.

Bruno's nerve broke, as he turned and ran towards the door at the far end of the corridor, leading to the concourse that Janssen had forced open in a very different universe to one he now endured. As he leapt over the remains of his last victim, his foot landed on a hard object, causing him to roll his ankle. The scalding pain and sound of ripping tendons exploded up his leg as he crashed into the brutal unyielding solidity of the wall at full speed. Through the warped mirror of his vision, he could see the exit in the distance. He dragged himself off the floor, forcing himself to continue, pumping his legs, gritting his teeth in a vain attempt to fight off the pain. Not daring to look back at his pursuers, he stumbled towards the light of the concourse, expecting any moment the sting of a Gargoyle's claw to bring him down and join the long list of Mag victims. The cooler air of the opening caressed his face as he drew near, hardly daring to believe he'd made it as he emerged reborn out into the light. He risked a glance back down the corridor.

A familiar voice echoed from the far end. 'Daddy...'

The pair of Gargoyles were ambling towards him as if they were on a morning stroll without a care in the world. Looking at the scene around the entrance, Bruno saw the bodies of SPC soldiers, civilians and troopers, intermingled with various types of Mags, but no weapons were visible. Only an empty pie wrapper and some crumbs in their place. The rhythm of the Gargoyles' footsteps approaching from the corridor could be heard behind him, as he started to hobble away.

Bruno's heart leapt as he heard voices from just around the corner. 'There's none left here, let's make our way back now.'

'Hey! Hey! Hey! Over here!', he shouted. Two troopers appeared and moved towards him.

'Ok we've got you!' one of them said as they moved towards him. They were within touching distance as Bruno tried to run, but the pain from his ankle shot up his leg causing him to stumble forward. A familiar scrabbling came from behind as he hit the floor. The running feet of the troopers stopped as the shadows of the Gargoyles flew along the ground in front of Bruno, seizing upon their prey. The sickening suck of ripping flesh sounded before either of their victims could cry out, as the innards started to fly in all directions. Bruno rose to his feet and witnessed the feeding frenzy, as one of the Gargoyles turned towards him. The cold cruel eyes glinting in triumph before returning to feast once again. The legs of the dead troopers protruding from the bloodbath. This time Bruno didn't look back as he stumbled away as fast as his excruciating ankle would allow, into the abandoned emptiness that was once the Arion.

50

Eleanor peered into the darkness ahead but couldn't see a thing. Looking back over her shoulder, she whispered, 'Can you still sense it Ava?'

'Yes, it's not far ahead now.' Ava's voice was weak as she was led along the service tunnel by Akeely. 'Another twenty or thirty yards.' Further back she could hear the groaning of Fynn mixing with the sobs of Sophia.

'What is it Ava? Can you tell?', Eleanor asked. She hated the blindness and vulnerability of the pitch black. Something, anything could be inches from her face and she wouldn't know it. They had been stumbling around in the dark for the past few hours trying to find their way towards the forward storage bay. They had heard the screeching of Gargoyles hunting for them in the distance. Ava's psychic senses had helped to avoid them and keep a safe distance, but they were getting closer. Eleanor was pretty sure they were going around in circles. On a couple of occasions, they had come across another hatch. The thin sliver of light showing the outline. Eleanor had carefully inched it open, but the wall of Mag flesh flowing like a river along the corridor had made her snap it shut again before she was spotted.

'I don't think it's a MAG', Ava ventured.

'You don't *think* it's a Mag.' The irritation evident in Eleanor's voice. 'That's not much comfort to me Ava. Perhaps I should ask it first!'

'I'm doing my best...' The hurt in Ava's voice caused Eleanor to immediately regret her sharp tone. *Biting the hand that feeds you Ellie. Genius move.*

'Ok Ava, Sorry. I trust you....' Eleanor was contrite. '....We could die of old age in these tunnels, we can't get out and we're lost. It isn't a Mag so it can only be human. There's nothing else for it, I'm going to call out.' There was a murmur of trepidation from the others but it died down after a few moments. They knew they were rapidly running out of options. You'd better be right Ava, or we're in the shit.

'It's getting closer.' Ava's voice reflected the shredded nerves of the group.

Eleanor could hear it now. Her blood froze as a scuttling noise in the distance sounded. So much for "I don't think it's a MAG". *It's gonna leap outta the dark and rip your face off before you even realise it Ellie. Don't you ever give up? Not while there's fun to be had at your expense. No way outta this one.* Holding her hand out in front of her, she groped into the blackness. *Fat lot that'll do ya!* The mocking cynicism of the voice grated on her nerves, but Eleanor wasn't going to give it the satisfaction of knowing. It's not a Mag, I trust Ava. *I thought you'd have learnt to trust nobody by now. Still, once a sucker, always a sucker I suppose.*

That's why you're so popular with the guys. Hyuk hyuk hyuk... Well I'd certainly be a sucker to take any notice of your bullshit wouldn't I! *Don't worry Ellie, you won't have to take any notice of me for much longer.* The noise was getting closer. The struggles of its source increasing. She took a breath, and was about to call when a clatter and a grunt sounded from just ahead. A shaft of light shot across the tunnel as muffled curses could be made out.

'Hey!' The sound of her own voice after the silence startled Eleanor. 'Who is it?' The noise stopped. 'Don't worry we're not Mags!', she announced. A laugh rang out, echoing along the stark passageway.

'I should think not! There aren't any Mags with a London accent like that!' The figure poked his head around the corner and shone his torch into Eleanor's face, blinding her with the dazzling light, as she held her hand up. 'It's Ryan Baxter. I was sent out from the storage areas to search for survivors.', he explained.

Eleanor looked back along at the group following her. They were all shielding their eyes, all except Ava who was smiling.

'See, I told you it wasn't a Mag.' Ava said. The laughs of relief rippled among the group. Eleanor moved towards Ryan.

'Well well, if it isn't Super Janitor herself!', he quipped.

Even though it was the first time they'd met, she embraced him like a long lost brother. 'Thank you, thank you Ryan.', she replied. He rubbed her on the back and despite the pain of her injuries, she smiled.

'You're welcome my dear girl', he laughed. 'How many are there of you?'

'About twenty I think. Half are walking wounded. We escaped from the infirmary when the Mags broke in. We just about made it. Some Gargoyles broke into the tunnels and we've been hearing them in the distance. One broke through and attacked us earlier. We lost someone, before we killed it. How far is it to the storage area?'

'Not far. About ten minutes from here. We've got over a hundred already and more are coming in every few minutes.', Ryan told her. For the first time Eleanor felt safe. At least for the moment.

There was a gasp of fear from behind. It was Ava, 'The Mags! They're right behind us and approaching fast.' The fear in her voice told them the Gargoyles were nearby.

The familiar scrabbling could be heard. Cries of despair broke out amongst the survivors.

Eleanor looked up at Ryan and urged him. 'You get them to the storage Bay. I'll draw them off in the other direction.'

373

Ryan nodded. 'You'll need these', he said, thrusting the spare hand torch into Eleanor's hand and his gun into the other.

She spoke to the group. 'Follow Ryan, he'll lead you to the storage area. It's not far. I'll divert the Mags to follow me and I'll catch you up there. GO! NOW!'

The survivors shuffled past her crouching in the gloom, whimpering in fear. Fynn was stumbling along at the rear, his grey pallor told Eleanor he hardly had anything left. He smiled and offered; 'Give me the gun. I'll finish a few off before they get me. Save yourself.'

'What? And all that fun saving you goes to waste. I don't think so matey. Go now before I shoot you in your fat ass!', Eleanor told him.

Akeely rushed out of the darkness and grabbed Fynn by the arm. 'You two still arguing!', she hissed before dragging him protesting along the tunnel.

Eleanor listened as the shuffling and scraping of the group faded into the distance. *Hope you've got enough ammo Ellie.* From the other direction, the sound of the Gargoyles' approach grew louder by the second.

Eleanor heard the group of Gargoyles as they rounded the bend and set off in pursuit of the civilians. She crouched in the darkness, letting the first few pass before she opened up on them with Ryan's gun. The flash of the muzzle and the squeals of the Gargoyles told her she had struck home. The second group were approaching as she switched on the torch and swiftly made her way along the tunnel that was at right angles to the way the others had gone. Pointing the beam back from where she'd come from, open hungry mouths and white teeth of a rabid mob were illuminated in the harsh glare as they hurtled towards her. Their sole intent, to kill.

'C'mon you fuckers. Bring it on!' She raised the gun and popped a shot into the leader. It struck his neck, the impact hurling him backwards into the others, instantly creating an angry ball of thrashing legs and snapping teeth as they strove to reach Eleanor. She fired another couple of rounds into the group before turning and half crouching, ran along the tunnel. *Can't be much ammo left now Ellie. Not enough for all of them. It'll only take one to finish you off.* Sometimes I think it'll be a price worth paying to shut you up once and for all.

The noise of pursuit was growing behind Eleanor. It was easier for the Gargoyles to move along the confined space. Even standing on all four legs, they still had a few inches between their head and the roof of the tunnel, as they started to gain on her. Once again she shone the torch back at the group. Only a few remained. Instinctively turning into a side tunnel, she made sure they followed by waving the torch at them. 'Hey! This way!', she called. The mouths, claws and eyes seemed as a single entity closing on her. Taking careful aim, she fired two more rounds. Only three left to deal with. Again the fallen Gargoyles hindered the pursuers, as Eleanor illuminated the way ahead. Except there wasn't a way ahead, as the blank wall of the dead end reflected the light back at her. 'Shit!' There was no time to think as she turned once again and took aim. The crash of the round resounded as it found its mark between the eyes of its victim. From behind, the first one leapt over the still twitching corpse, meeting the same fate as Eleanor's next round sliced a path through the jugular that continued to pump its contents in an arc for a few seconds before the flow stopped. The final pursuer poked its head carefully over the bodies of the dead leaders, before ducking back behind them. Eleanor's heart pounded in her temples as sweat ran into her eyes, temporarily blurring her vision. The Gargoyle seemed to sense her momentary vulnerability and bounded over the bodies. Eleanor raised the gun and fired. The round struck the roof of the tunnel before ricocheting down, striking the Gargoyle a glancing blow on the shoulder. It recoiled and screeched in defiance as Eleanor raised the gun to deliver the kill shot. She squeezed the trigger. Click. *Oops, that didn't go well did it.* The chill of horror spread out from her heart, up into her throat and along her limbs as the Gargoyle instinctively knew the end had arrived. It moved forward, teeth drawn back in full display. What a stupid way to die Eleanor. Trapped in a dead end tunnel.

Eleanor inched backwards as the Gargoyle slowly moved towards her. The cold black eyes reflected the torch's light back at Eleanor. The unyielding hardness of the tunnel floor suddenly gave way to cold metal that dipped down slightly. Her weight bore down, making the creak of salvation that she'd craved. Moving past, the beam shone down on it. The words 'Service Hatch' stencilled in bold red above the round handle. Lifting the torch, demented eyes and razor teeth hurtled toward her, as she reached down, turned the handle and lifted the hatch. A moment later the Gargoyle crashed into the other side of the upright metal with a loud bong, driving it back into Eleanor's face and sending the gun clattering along the remainder of the tunnel and into the wall. Her nose crunched and the taste of blood immediately filled her mouth. Her arms shook as the strength of the Gargoyle took her completely by surprise. In a strange way its small size gave its strength a more frightening feel than Titus the Gorthon. Eleanor Looked down at the corridor below her feet. Whatever's down there couldn't be as bad as what's up here, she thought, before dropping down, slamming the hatch behind her and turning the handle, locking it shut. *Lucky bitch!* Ha! Sorry to disappoint you. She smiled triumphantly to herself.

Eleanor looked along the empty corridor. She held her hand to her face and looked down at the blood. The throbbing pain from her nose pulsed in a steady rhythm. Out of the corner of her eye, she caught a movement. A shadow of something or someone was approaching. Wanting to call out, the growling and

375

unsteady thumping footsteps made it impossible to tell if it was man or beast. The shadow grew as the thing approached the corner. Eleanor ducked into a side passage. Another dead end! There was a security door at the end. Rushing toward it, she frantically tried to open it, but it was locked and nothing short of a key or explosives was going to budge it. The sound of the thudding steps grew louder as she gripped the handle in despair. The shuffling steps came to a halt at the entrance of the passage.

'Well look who it is...' The familiar voice sent a freezing tidal wave of fear through Eleanor as she turned to see Bruno waiting at the other end, dripping with aqua slime, holding a huge shiny knife in his hand. 'I seem to remember we've got some unfinished business.', he said. A smile spread across his face as his gleaming white teeth shone out against the strange gunge that caked his face.

The years of thinking back to that morning in the cell and the outrage committed on her mind and body, the rampant injustice and suffering she had endured blazed with the fire of a supernova within Eleanor, melting the fear she felt, replacing it with a towering rage that could only be slaked with Bruno's blood.

'Yes, here we are little man. Let's see if you're big enough to finish the job properly.', she scoffed at him. The sneer of hate and fear spread across Bruno's face as he started to move forward, his knuckles white as he gripped the knife. Noticing the limp he was carrying, she quickly calculated how to take advantage of it, when the shadow appeared at the end of the passage. The light from behind darkened as Bruno turned to face the vast muscular bulk of the Gorthon that stood over him. The slow clicking that rolled out of its throat ended in a bark that sounded like a small bomb. Eleanor's legs turned to jelly before they collapsed under her, as the Gorthon's tongue snaked out and delicately caressed Bruno's quivering face.

'No..No, please no.' His plaintive voice ringing in Eleanor's ears as another voice sounded inside her head.

Failed again. Nice knowing you Ellie...

51

The rows of vats stood silent and motionless along the production line as Aaron looked up at the spectacle. The bodies of the technicians lay sprawled and scattered around the facility in various states of mutilation. Next to him, Billy, Aaron's pet Gargoyle stood guard over his master. Caressing the Gargoyles head absentmindedly, he studied the screen.

'Full Automation: Press to Proceed.' The words displayed in bold white on the red background. He reached out to the screen hesitating momentarily. The vats would be fuelled by the vast tanks contained in the bowels of the base with the potential to produce millions of Mags. A whole planet full. The mixture for each one measured to perfection, the billions of Nano machines set in motion, assembling each creature atom by atom, molecule by molecule until it was drawn from the VAT, the Neuroware automatically uploaded before transportation to containment, if it could be called that, as no containing took place, only release. All at the press of a button. His finger travelled the final few inches and pressed the screen. The hum of machinery sounded as the vats resumed their journey along the production line. Aaron smiled with satisfaction, his function complete, and looked down at Billy, the Gargoyle looking back up in adoration, nuzzling his head affectionately into Aaron's leg, letting out a gentle mewing sound. Billy took a couple of steps away, raised himself on his legs, then without warning, slashed his claw across Aaron's throat, nearly severing his head. A spray of blood splashed across the screen partially obscuring the words. 'Full Automation Initiated: Press to Stop.' The Mags were in control.

Billy looked down at the lifeless body of Aaron. He thought back to the cage, the orange light of Horace and the cruel face that had inflicted so much suffering on him, remembering the betrayal of Ava, the gift of power and control over his own destiny the Purple had given him. What he would do with that power he hadn't decided yet, but there was one thing he was sure of. His implacable hatred of humans and all they represented. Even though they were his creators, he would be their doom. Raising himself up once more, Billy stretched out his arms and threw his head back, letting out a screech of triumph as his eyes, wide open blazed with a purple fire.

◆

The magnetic forces had been building for days. The twisted loops of roiling incandescent plasma strained against the stars mass, as yet another titanic struggle on the surface of Ereus headed towards its conclusion. The great arc above the churning surface of the star could take no more, as it snapped, hurling billions of tons of charged particles, moving at thousands of miles a minute out into space, towards Magdur.

****

If you have enjoyed reading Nadinium Sky, please consider leaving an honest review on Amazon.

You can follow RAGeorge on:

https://www.facebook.com/rageorge.author.5

https://twitter.com/RaAuthor

Or Email me: rageorgeauthor@gmail.com

Printed in Poland
by Amazon Fulfillment
Poland Sp. z o.o., Wrocław

50989656R00230